This book is dedicated to the memory
of Constable Michael Sweet,

Morituri...

and to his friend Constable John Latto
of the Metropolitan Toronto Police.

Other books by Carsten Stroud

Acknowledgements

My sources for this book were legion, and few can be thanked publicly for fear of judicial retribution.

I wish to express my gratitude to:
Linda Mair
Kirsten Hanson
Inspector Don Keith, CO VPD Drug Squad (Ret.)
William Marshall, Chief, Metro Toronto Police
Inspector Jim McIlvenna, "E" Division RCMP
CST. Joseph Fitzpatrick, D Watch, Burnaby RCMP
The members of D Watch, Burnaby RCMP
Detective Rick Crook, VPD Major Crimes
Detective Al Cattley, VPD Major Crimes
Sergeant R.M. Gruzuk, OPP
Constable David Hobson, OPP
Douglas Payne, RCMP Ret., Western Pacific Group
Detective Ken Kilpatrick, VPD Major Crimes
Leon Bourque, VPD Major Crimes (Ret.)
Sergeant Grant MacDonald, VPD Major Crimes
Staff Sergeant Fred Biddlecombe, CO VPD Major Crimes
Staff Sergeant Chuck Conkel, Metro Toronto PD
Doctor Laurel Gray and Carm Zenone
Marlys Edwardh and Clayton Ruby
Edward Greenspan
George Jonas
The staff of the John Jay Institute, NYC
The staff of the BSU, FBI Quantico, Virginia
The staff of the *Vancouver Sun*
The staff of the *Toronto Star*
The staff of the Canadian Press
The staff of the *Vancouver Province*
and crime reporters across the country

Contents

Waste no more time
arguing what a good man should be.
Be one.
—Marcus Aurelius, *Meditations*

CONTEMPT
OF COURT

A Word of Advice

I've worked as a crime writer for close to twenty years, and I don't like what I've been seeing.

Our judges don't see, and to my mind, don't care, how their legal games affect the street; the shrinks are still going around and around in ever-diminishing circles; the corrections people are out of control; social workers are all over the justice system like a plague of missionaries; the Young Offenders Act is still creating gang violence and feeding new talent into the criminal mainstream. Lawyers are playing asinine games with the Charter. And our rulers, soft and well-insulated from the street, are entertaining themselves with delusive constitutional games because that's so much more fun than attending to the real problems in this country.

As for the rest of us, we have been sheep. We have given up our streets, we're nervous in the parks and we're making cocoons of our houses. We are getting used to being afraid.

That's not good enough for me, it's not good enough for my children and it shouldn't be good enough for you.

This book is a picture of our streets and our courts and our justice system, drawn from my own experiences. Everything in it is true. I describe nothing I haven't seen myself or that is not completely documented, a matter of public record. You won't like it, but if I get it right, you may get mad enough to DO something about it. At least, I hope so. Because if you don't, you'd better get used to staying home Friday nights.

ONE

Something Vile

June 3, 1985—Wilseyville, California

Red ants were everywhere, thousands of them in the scrub grass and all around the garden. The sergeant watched them flowing over the yard like pink Chablis or something worse and he thought, "What the hell are they living on?"

He looked up at the house, scratchboard and cheap paint far up on the hillside, the Sierras in the distance like a tidal wave of blue rock, the snowline showing in the fading sunset light like foam on the crest of it, and then he looked back down towards the house and the blackness beyond the patched screen door.

The rest of the guys were watching him carefully. It was his call. They'd do whatever he asked them to do. Cicadas burred in the treeline and a wet steamy heat lay on everything like a fever dream. He looked down at the red ants in their millions, and under them the hardpan clay and the black earth.

And then he knew, and the chill took him and shook him hard.

Five years later he'd wake up and remember this moment. But by then he'd be out of Calaveras County.

He brought his boot down hard on a platoon of ants and pulled himself into shape. He climbed up the creaking wooden stairs and walked across the porch. The screen door waited for him, blank and black and full of threat, like the lid on a coffin. The air was as thick and hot as lava, but he could feel the chill in his lungs. He reached for the handle and was pleased to see that his hand was steady. The metal was hot to the touch.

Edmonton Journal, 16 July 1989

CANADIAN EXTRADITION LAWS INVITE CRIMINALS, CRITICS SAY

By Tom Barrett and Greg Owens

EDMONTON, Alberta

Startling new evidence about alleged mass-murderer Charles Ng appears to support claims that Canada's extradition laws are an open invitation to US killers.

Ng decided Canada was a safe haven with soft extradition laws even before his alleged California murder spree, a former prison associate of his has told the Royal Canadian Mounted Police.

The 28-year-old Hong Kong native carefully researched Canadian law, compared it to that law in other countries, and made formal preparations to escape here, the witness says.

The ex-convict claims he and Ng did the legal research in the library of Leavenworth Prison in Kansas, where Ng served two years for an offense committed while he was a US Marine.

The unidentified man apparently claims Ng tried to recruit him for a macabre survivalist brotherhood that planned to acquire female sex slaves. He is expected to be a key witness at Ng's trial in California, if and when it is held.

The witness says Ng examined laws and extradition procedures in Mexico, Brazil, and Hong Kong before choosing Canada.

Another consideration was the fact that Ng had a sister living in Calgary, although Ng also believed the Canadian border was easy to cross and he thought he could blend in easily with its large Asian population, the former prisoner says.

When the US police started closing in, Ng used his long-planned escape route through Chicago, crossing the border at Windsor, Ontario, and making his way west to Calgary.

Alberta RCMP Sergeant Ray Munro, Canada's chief investigator in the Ng case, says he stumbled across the information about Ng's research on Canada during an interview with the American prisoner in May 1988.

He says a Court Order prohibits him from naming the witness, whose evidence is apparently crucial to the case against Ng.

The evidence is also powerful ammunition for critics of Canada's lengthy extradition procedures. They have complained loud and long about Ng's lingering presence in Canada since his arrest in Calgary on July 6, 1985.

"This validates what I have been saying in the House of Commons about our country becoming a haven for killers," says Bill Domm, Tory member of Parliament for Peterborough, Ontario.

Domm has been trying to radically shorten the extradition appeal process, which may drag on for years in Ng's case.

American officials say the evidence illustrates that American criminals are finding Canada an increasingly attractive escape site.

"You don't have to look into a crystal ball to realise that there are more guys coming," says San Francisco District Attorney Paul Cummins.

"This is just one example of the knowledge US killers have of the extradition laws and the problems they have created for the American investigators in trying to get them back."

The word is out that Canada is a safe haven for killers, he says.

Cummins believes the heart of the problem is a Canada-US Treaty clause that enables Canada to deny extradition in any particular case unless American authorities agree to waive the death penalty.

Cummins, who will be one of the prosecutors in the Ng trial, says two key witnesses have died and others have moved or are becoming confused about facts because of the time that has passed.

"Let's put it this way, our case certainly isn't getting any stronger."

American authorities allege Ng formed a brotherhood with Leonard Lake to kidnap people and turn them into sex slaves or murder them to obtain weapons and other assets.

Investigators who examined the site where most of the killings are alleged to have occurred discovered widely scattered human remains and homemade videotapes of women being threatened and sexually abused.

Lake committed suicide in police custody shortly after his arrest in 1985.

Alberta courts have ruled there is enough evidence to extradite Ng to California, where he faces 20 charges, including 13 for murder. But Ng is appealing that decision to the Supreme Court of Canada.

The case could drag on for years even if the high court refuses to hear the appeal and the federal justice minister orders him extradited without seeking a waiver.

You could see the river from the guard posts or the upper windows of C Block, see the broad, brown water riffled by the winds, throw your heart all the way into Missouri. Or you could walk across the roof, if they didn't shoot you first, and look west across the hazy blue infinity of Kansas, see the sun go down into China under a bruised and shaded sky.

Some days the clouds would roll up into amber and green and blue-black thunderstorms, a slate-grey rain would hammer the windows and walls and a volley of cracking booms would shake the cells. At night, if the block was quiet, you might hear the trucks winding out on the highways, hear the Northstars and the Kenworths growling and chuffing up the long slopes into the Great Plains, and the names would flicker in your head like highway signs in the grey tunnel of your headlights.

Topeka, a hundred miles away, and south to Wichita, and Dodge City far beyond that under the big black night. Or north to the Nebraska border, where the combines slice through an ocean of rust-colored wheat and the yellow dirt hides the bones of Red Indians and fleet little ponies, and the interstate runs like a lava river into the Territories, to Little Big Horn and Billings and Bozeman in Montana.

If you could get over the razor-wire you could get to Topeka, and a man in Topeka could shift his shape and sideburns and catch a rig to Wichita on "eye three-five, the sundown road," and a man could shape-shift again in Wichita, clear the airport video and fly away to Butte, or Bozeman, or all the way to Cheyenne in Wyoming and up into the foothills to Coeur d'Alene, get himself into California and back to Leonard's place in Philo...

No—they'd look for him in Philo.

Maybe he should think about Canada some more.

His sister was up in Calgary, Alberta, in the middle of whatever the Canadians called Chinatown, and in Chinatown nobody talked and one slope was pretty much like another.

Jesus...Leavenworth. It was hard to say your life was under control when you were only twenty-two years old and you were looking at a Dishonorable Discharge out of the Marine Corps and you had two years to serve in Leavenworth Prison.

This was hard-time too, hard-time in The Crotch's worst brig, the rockpile at Fort Leavenworth, Kansas, where they ran your ass by the numbers and everybody did everything at the double and they could beat your ass into burger-bits for a sideways smile.

And yet they had a weight room and a gym—and a big yard, and the pogues even had a *law library*—that was like giving the wolves the keys to the nursery. A smart man, a man with ambition and plans for himself, could learn a lot in the Leavenworth law library.

Take this extradition thing, for example.

Cops hated a man on jackrabbit parole to make it across any border. For one thing, getting another country's cops to pay attention to your problems was hard, and if the runner made it to someplace like Mexico or Brazil or back to Hong Kong, then he could get lost in the back-alleys of the Third World, where any cop that can't be bought can be rented.

So it made sense for the educated man thinking about taking jackrabbit parole to give due consideration to destinations, and the law library had a lot of good advice in this area.

Canada, now…Canada was showing real promise for a man in his situation. It had a lot of Asians, and damn few Asian cops, damn few cops at all who could speak Mandarin or Hakka or Vietnamese or any Asian dialect. And in any decent Chinatown, it'd be a silly man indeed who couldn't find some way to make himself useful to a Tong or to the Vietnamese, especially a man with two years in the United States Marine Corps and a brown belt in the arts and a firsthand understanding of weapons.

You could see why countries with shared borders needed to come up with legal agreements about fugitives. In 1976, the United States and Canada had signed something called the Canada-US Extradition Treaty. It was supposed to make extradition automatic and easy between the two countries.

When the treaty was being negotiated, quite a few American states had laws forbidding capital punishment, and in most of the courts there seemed to be a strong prejudice against the whole idea of executing criminals. At the same time, the big buzzword was "rehabilitation," as if a criminal was just a sick kid who needed some chicken soup and a day in bed watching *I Love Lucy* reruns. But the "rehabilitation" concept wasn't as strong in Canada at that time. The Canadians looked as if they were about to pass legislation to make capital punishment legal again.

So the representatives on the American side of the negotiating committee lobbied for, and received, a codicil, a clause in the treaty which basically said that extradition "may be refused"— and that was a big word, "may"—if the state or the nation seeking the extradition of a fugitive had a legal death penalty on the books.

In other words, if a man being pursued on a charge of murder that *might* result in the death penalty made it to a place where the death penalty was illegal, then his lawyers could make certain that the clause got invoked, and the chances were good that the runner might never get sent back to answer that charge.

The funny thing was, after the treaty got signed, the world turned, as it usually did.

The liberal wave hit Canada a couple of years late, as usual, and the idea of capital punishment was rejected out of hand by the politicians and corrections professionals in the country.

In the meantime, through the early 1980s, the wind had been changing in the United States. Now the American people were pushing for executions and the government of Canada was against it. The clause had been turned around.

Now it meant that a man on the run for murder in a state with capital punishment might be able to avoid the death penalty, avoid even being returned to face trial, if he could get into Canada and make enough noise.

And even better, Legal Aid in Canada was absolutely free, and the books were full of cases where Canadian lawyers with civil rights fixations had taken case after case all the way to their Supreme Court to have the issues decided.

That took time. Years. And time was the one thing prosecutors hated. No matter what the crime, no matter how pissed-off the cops and the District Attorney, enough time goes by and witnesses die or lose interest, memories get hazy, cops retire, new DAs come along with new attitudes, the victim's family gets to be a nuisance around the courthouse and nobody can remember what the victim looked like. The press guys are into something else. People forget.

Interesting clause.

Now, Mexico was a problem. Not a lot of Asians. And they didn't have any strong objections to driving some killer on the run up to the border, shoving him into a US sheriff's car and the extradition rules be damned. They'd even been known to take troublesome prisoners out into the hills and give them the *ley fuga*, the law of flight. Out of the car and told to run, and a bullet in the back at about twenty yards. Ten if they were drunk or bitchy or just bad shots.

Jesus...the possibilities. It could make a man dizzy, like standing on the edge of a cliff, to think too much about that kind of thing. Lying in his cell, listening to the trucks on the interstate and the men coughing and the ship-engine rumble of the block, the cans flushing, the sound of boots on the iron catwalks and the low talk of the guards, thinking about the distances, about Canada or Mexico or Hong Kong or just being *outside*, on a map of the possible. It was a kind of vertigo.

A long way to come from the stunted, twisty streets of Hong Kong, from the smells and the noise and the crush of ten million people, the tuk-tuks and the trucks and the press of the buildings all around, and the mountains like a stone wall, the air reeking of sweat and rotted fruit and diesel smoke...people making money and a hell of a lot more people working for pennies a day, and all the time you had China on your back-porch and the clock running on that lease.

Well, he'd seen a lot of the world since Hong Kong, thanks to Mom and Dad and the United States Marine Corps.

Now the court-martial...that was a time.

Those self-satisfied officers with their tan faces and their round eyes and the fruit salad on their chests. The slatted room in Kaneohe, the Marine Air Station in Hawaii, with the sun coming in through the blinds, the stripes already on him.

Punitive Articles of the Uniform Code of Military Justice...a general court-martial with the base Commanding General behind the desk, the droning voice of the clerk, standing there at Parade Rest, listening to the rat-fucks talking about him like he was already in Kansas doing military push-ups in a six-by-eight cell.

Article 121. Larceny and wrongful appropriation. Any Marine who wrongfully takes, obtains, or withholds (by any means) any money, personal property, or article of value of any kind...

How about two M-60 machine guns, three M-79 grenade-launchers, four M-16 assault rifles, seven .45-calibre semi-autos and three of those outstanding Starlite Scopes at 20K a pop?

Jarheads couldn't even hold him in the brig. The FBI finally caught up to him in Philo, California, and that wouldn't have happened if he hadn't been stupid enough to leave that ad Leonard put in *Soldier of Fortune* lying around in his footlocker...

At the court-martial the brass, in that down-the-nose-we-know-you're-a-piece-of-chink-shit way they had, gave him a chance to make his point, tell them why he had broken his oaths and his undertakings as a member of the Corps.

He could see the look they had, like how could a pogue like him get past The Island, get through Boot and the DIs and the songs and the stories about Ira Hayes and the flag on Suribachi, and Danny Daly at Belleau Wood, Guadalcanal, the halls of Montezuma...

So he explained it all, in little words so they could understand—how goddamned bored he was, after all the talk about warriors and let's not forget IGMS Zero One Zero Niner, the Laws of War, all nine points...so he thought, well let's pick up the pace a little around Kona, stealing C-4 to blow up a truck. The bit about putting cyanide in the mess hall salt-shakers took the starch down a bit. He told them he'd sold small arms, killed a bunch of cattle, even dropped heat tabs into barrack storehouses, started other fires around the base.

They didn't believe any of it. They thought it was big talk from a little slope who wouldn't get with the program.

They sent him down the hall to be evaluated by an army shrink. He had to sit and listen to all that shit about his childhood...about old Dad the traveling salesman, his cases stuffed with cameras and tape-decks, drag-assing around the South China Sea, ass-kissing the Japs...and his mother, that bitch, getting on him all the time about fighting, about stealing, about his gun catalogues...he even knew about Bentham School in England, now there was a hell-hole for discipline, made the Corps look like McDonald's...and then the private school in California. If he had even half the money his parents had pissed away trying to make a man out of little Charlie Ng.

He had a good time with the pogue, talking him up and down, reading him as a do-good dipshit who couldn't find his face with a flashlight. You could tell the guy anything...

But he didn't tell him much about Leonard Lake, and about Leonard Lake's...plans.

Well, maybe he conned the shrink and maybe he didn't, because when it came down to the general court-martial...

The brass sat up in the hardback chairs at Kaneohe Marine Air Station and offered him two years in Leavenworth and a Dishonorable Discharge if he'd plead guilty to the theft of military weapons.

And his hand-picked courtroom buddies—he'd used his rights under the Uniform Code of Military Justice to have one-third of the court made up of enlisted men—his compadres sat in a row with their faces paved over and stared at a spot about three degrees to the right of his head, and in two days he was in leg-irons on a bus with iron windows and his next stop was Fort Leavenworth Military Prison in Kansas.

IGMS Zero One Zero Niner—the Marine Corps Laws of War.

Marines fight only enemy combatants.

Marines do not harm enemies who surrender. They must disarm them and turn them over to their superior.

Marines do not kill or torture prisoners.

Marines collect and care for the wounded, whether friend or foe.

Marines do not attack medical personnel, facilities or equipment.

Marines destroy no more than the mission requires.

Marines treat all civilians humanely.

Marines do not steal. Marines respect private property and possessions.

Marines do their best to prevent violations of the Laws of War.

He'd think about those laws when he was sitting in the prison library, putting his time in, waiting for two years to go by.

No wonder the United States couldn't make it in a real war. It was too bad he'd been too young for Vietnam. That was a true test of the killer, a way to separate the men from the pogues. How the hell do you expect to win a war when you don't have the will to do what's necessary? The Cong had it, had the spirit of the warrior. Bushido. The Ninja way.

He'd talk about this to some of the other jarheads in Leavenworth, try to get them to understand how it was going to happen, how the West was rotten and dying and weak, and when the war, the last big war, came, as it must, it would be the true warriors who would survive. The only kind of earth the meek would inherit would be the first shovelful that hit their dumb dead faces.

Endless nights in the cellblock, they'd go round and round it in whispers, or sit up under the bleachers against the east wall, where the men smoked roll-your-owns and worked on their tans, and talk about the towelheads and push-starters in Iran and Libya and what the country ought to do about them—black-glass the whole sector and turn it into a skateboard bowl. There was talk about the tripwire vets from Vietnam, guys who had come back with the war in their hip pockets and gone up into the hills to get ready for judgement.

And about women...about the way women had changed America. What it would take to straighten them out. How you should go about it. How to get their attention, and what to do with it when you had it.

Maybe this was his time of testing. His Vietnam. In this place, you became strong or you went under. Maybe it was the same— a year in Vietnam or two years in Leavenworth. If a man took it the right way, as a lesson, a test, and he learned the lessons that were in front of him, then he would be ready.

He and Leonard would be ready.

Leonard was ready now. Leonard was already into it.

Alone in his bunk at night, alone with the smell of sweat and semen, the trucks making the long, low grade under the black bowl of the midwestern night, the sounds of toilets flushing and boots on the catwalks, with metal all around him and a stone on his chest and his hands busy under the blankets, his mind outside under the sky, whatever he was in the process of becoming, the world was still turning and the sun was somewhere in the east over the South China Sea, it was morning in Hong Kong and in a few hours it would be morning in Kansas. No one could stop that...

So, in the spring of 1983, the day came when they called him out and gave him fifty dollars and bus fare and quick-marched him to the gate and threw his duffel out into the roadway.

Adios, they said. We'll be looking for you.

Charles Ng was *outside*. Back on the map of the possible.

June 2, 1985—South City Lumber, San Francisco

Jesus, what's this? thought the clerk, watching the compact little Chinese guy going down the aisles in the building supply store in South City.

He might as well be wearing a sign saying SHOPLIFTER AT WORK. The guy walks right in out of the sunshine and dicks around for a while, looking over his shoulder, picking up this and putting that down, avoiding eye-contact like he was going to be invisible if he didn't look at you.

And then he picks up a forty-pound bench vise, with a price tag of $64.99 and strolls—just like that, he strolls, a strong little son of a bitch—out past the cash registers, carrying the bench vise like it was a souvenir of the South City Lumber and Supply Company. It was kind of scary, as if the guy didn't give a damn if you tried to stop him, as if he had already thought about that and he was ready for it.

Instead of doing the usual, going over to the man himself, the clerk decided to call in the police, and for once the cops were right on the scene.

The Chinese guy was halfway across the parking lot on his way to a Honda Prelude when the cops rolled up and the clerk met them at the doorway.

The cop rolled his eyes, got out of the cruiser and followed the Chinese guy over to the Honda, catching up to him just as he opens up the trunk and puts the vise down into it.

The Chinese guy looks up and see the cop walking towards him, and the cop thinks, Now this is wrong. I've seen this on the threat-scenario videos. There's something weird here, because the Chinese guy makes eye-contact and doesn't look even a little bit worried. What else is in that trunk?

The cop puts a hand on his .357 and starts to react.

The drive-side door of the blue Honda pops open. This guy— a big, beefy, bear-looking white guy with a balding head and a heavy wrap-around beard—this guy has his hands up in front of him, palms out, smiling and talking fast and loud.

"Hey, ahh, officer, is there a problem?" The Chinese guy is standing a little away from the car now, nothing in his hands.

The cop relaxes a bit and looks back at the white guy, who is still smiling and talking fast through his scruffy brown beard, and his eyes are going this way and that.

"Hey, don't tell me my friend didn't *pay* for it? Man, I don't believe that! Listen, the guy's new in the country. Helping me out with some renovations, you know? I don't think he's got a real good grip on how things work here. I asked him to go in and pick us up a vise but seeing you I think maybe he forgot to *pay* for it. I got the money right here, officer!"

Now the beefy guy starts digging into his jeans and the officer has to watch his hands, thinking something is wrong here but not sure exactly what it is. This guy looks hinkier than the Chinese guy, and when the cop looks over to see what the Chinese kid is doing, there's nobody there.

Goddamnit! God-*damn*-it!

Immediately, the big beefy white guy is on his face on the hood of the Honda, and the cop is on the radio getting some more units into the area, putting a description of the Chinese kid out on the air. People are stopping to watch and this guy is *still* trying to get some money out and turn around off the hood, so the cop makes his point right then and there.

"Sir, please shut the fuck up, sir, and put your hands back on the car, sir."

Something seems to run out of the man as the cuffs snap on

his wrists. "Okay, okay…man. Take it easy. I didn't mean nothing. I can explain this."

"What's your friend's name, Mr.…" The cop has the guy's ID out now, a California licence. "Mr. Lake?"

Lake, pulled around now and facing the cop, starts to shake and his eyes are jerking everywhere. Fear starts to rise off him. What *is* this guy's story? All the cop's instincts are telling him that this is no ordinary shoplifting bust.

"Ah, I think his name is—" and he says a name that sounds to the officer like Chucking.

"Chucking? What is that? How do you spell it?"

Lake can't answer now. He is shaking, and it seems to the officer that Lake is about to faint. This is very bizarre here, even for a dumb shoplifting bust; this man is much too worried.

"You have ownership for this car, Mr. Lake?"

"Well…it's borrowed, and I don't know, maybe in the glove compartment…"

"Who's it borrowed from, Mr. Lake?" the officer asks as other cars pull up and a sergeant arrives. In the background, other cops are telling the bystanders to move along.

"Aahh…well…a guy gave it to me, officer."

"A guy *gave* it to you? What was his name?"

Lake blinks and trembles, losing it as the cop watches him.

The cop rolled his eyes again and they took him to the cruiser and shoved him into the back. They had an MDT, a Mobile Display Terminal, in the cruiser. They entered the details of Leonard Lake's identification and waited a few seconds for the machine to process it. While they were waiting, the sergeant got the plate numbers and the vehicle registration numbers off the plaque under the front windshield and they put those into the machine as well.

Leonard Lake seemed to be getting smaller and smaller in the back seat, a massive, almost tidal silence was coming over him.

A shout from the cops over at the Honda. A group of them were looking into the trunk. They were looking at a brown paper bag. Inside the brown paper bag, they'd found a .22-calibre Ruger semi-automatic pistol, fitted with a silencer. And the trunk was stained with some kind of black-brown liquid substance, and of course, in the mind of every cop, every brown stain is a blood stain.

The sergeant was trying to keep everybody from doing stupid things, like picking up the Ruger barehanded or screwing up whatever forensic evidence might be in or around the car.

He still had no idea *why* they ought to be worried about lab work on the car. But a runaway Asian and a Ruger with a silencer was a good place to start.

The MDT started running out a row of numbers on the screen.

Leonard Lake was an ex-Marine with a history of confinement for mental instability, assaults, weapons offences, sexual assaults, possession of stolen property. No current warrants on him. General discharge from the service, which meant not honorable but not criminal either. Vietnam service in a rear-echelon capacity. No combat record. Never in the bush. Under investigation once as a peddler of "snuff films" and other sadomasochistic pornography.

In the backseat, Lake was slumped against the side door, cuffed and silent, staring out at the parking lot of the shopping mall and the sun-baked streets beyond it.

Cars involved in the widening search for the Chinese male were calling in to Communications from the surrounding blocks. Coming up empty. The cops can feel him slipping away. If they didn't get a line on him in the next few minutes, the odds of picking him up got very long.

"Keep them at it," said the sergeant. "And notify Oakland and San Jose as well."

The MDT came back again. The car was registered to a man named Paul Cosner, a car salesman showing an address over in Marin County. No wants. No warrants. But a tag notation from the detective division of the SFPD: *Please call if stopped.*

"Call the division, see what they want this Cosner guy for."

Over at the car, the other uniform cops were gingerly picking their way through the Honda. There were holes in the upholstery and holes in the car body. Perhaps they were bullet holes.

Okay, thought the sergeant. A Ruger, bullet holes, maybe some blood. And a guy with a major sheet driving somebody else's car.

"You have anything to tell us, Leonard?"

Lake shook his head, looked up at him, looked away.

"Okay," said the sergeant, turning to the arresting officer who had answered the original shoplifting call from the store clerk. "He's yours. Take him back to the station and we'll see what he's got to say for himself."

They were halfway back to the division house on Baxter when the call came through from the detective bureau.

Paul Cosner had been listed as missing by his sister, Sharon Selitto, of San Francisco. Cosner had never returned from a meeting with a prospective buyer.

His sister had filed the Missing Persons report in January of 1984, seventeen months ago.

No one had seen or heard from the man since.

In the station-house, waiting for the detectives to arrive, Lake sat for a long time in silence, cuffed to a chair in the duty room. The officers had Mirandized him and offered him a coffee and a phone call. Lake said he had no one to call.

They asked him if he wanted to have someone call his ex-wife, or a family friend, or a lawyer. Lake refused them all, politely and quietly.

They asked him who the Chinese male had been. What was his name?

Lake seemed to think for a while.

"His name is Ng. Charles Ng. Enn Gee. He used to be a Marine. He was in it with me."

"In what, Mr. Lake?"

More silence.

Finally, he told one of the officers he'd be prepared to make a complete statement and sign it.

They uncuffed him and took him into an interrogation room.

Lake asked for a yellow pad and a pencil and started to write, stopping once to ask for something to drink.

A uniformed officer brought him a Coke.

He thanked her, and slipped something into his mouth as he reached for the Coke.

"What was that?" said the officer as Lake drank the Coke.

Lake just swallowed again and stared at the Coke can in his hands. In thirty seconds, he doubled up and hit the floor.

He was in a coma in three minutes and dead in four days.

The San Francisco detectives went to work on Lake and Charles Ng.

A Charles Ng, date of birth December 24, 1960, in the Crown Colony of Hong Kong, came up on the system, showing a conviction for Felony Theft in Hawaii and a two-year prison term in Leavenworth. Ng's address was listed as a small apartment in the Mission district downtown.

Two detectives were sent to check out Ng's address.

A check with Pacific Power showed Lake as paying utility bills on a hunting cabin near someplace called Wilseyville, in the Calaveras County area of the Sierra Nevada, a hundred miles east of San Francisco. A cop who knew the place said Wilseyville was a supply junction for campers and vacationers from the city, supposed to be a bunch of tripwire vets and hunters out there, a few leftover hippies.

Ng wasn't at his apartment.

The police then applied for warrants to search Ng's flat and to get the Calaveras County cops out to Leonard Lake's cabin in the Sierras. Norm Vereen and two other Calaveras detectives drove out to Wilseyville the next day.

Lake's house on the Blue Mountain Road was a shabby yellow wood-frame on three acres of land in a stand of trees and scrub brush. A cinder-block shack stood beside the house. A collection of abandoned cars and a truck moldered in the driveway. The ragged lawn was running to weeds and choked with bits of machinery and car parts.

It was a brutally hot day; the yard was thick with the red ants and the hazy air alive with flies and bees and wasps. The house itself had a long veranda, sagging with dry-rot, the paint blistered and flaking off. Norm Vereen was the sergeant in charge of the detail. He stood in the yard for a time, wondering about the ants.

Then he led the officers up the steps and opened the screen door and stepped inside. It took a while for their eyes to get used to the room. It smelled of dry wood and dust and smoke.

After a while, they could make out a large and ragged easy-chair pushed up against a wall, under a painting of a mountain lake. The easy-chair, sweat-stained and bursting, had been rigged with leg-irons and handcuffs.

Near the stuffed chair was a lot army cot covered with a grey sheet and towels. A twisted piece of lace was lying on the floor next to the cot. One of the men picked it up with a pencil. It was a bra, torn, or cut with scissors.

A video camera stood on a tripod facing the chair, next to a pair of strong arc lights. To the right of the chair was a large Sony television and a Panasonic VCR. Next to the television was a battered carton full of VHS videotapes.

"Oh, man," said one of the detectives. "I don't like this."

"Okay," said Vereen, a career detective-sergeant with two kids of his own. "Get me one of those tapes. See if the power's on. Some of you guys toss the yard. See what's in that shack out at the side."

He pushed a videotape into the VCR. The set flickered and fluttered.

"Let's see what these assholes have been up to."

TWO
Looking Away

Let's not. At least, not right now.

Let's not do this for a couple of reasons.

First of all, because what Ng and Lake did is at once terrible and terribly ordinary; they replicated in dreary and relentless detail the brutalities and degradations of every other serial killer in the history of the planet, from Haroun al Raschid to Ted Bundy. I've seen it all before, enough to sicken my heart and take some years off my life.

In a book called *Close Pursuit*, I described such a killing in a painfully accurate passage, telling myself as I did so that although the killing was shatteringly vile, perhaps to face it, and force my readers to face it, would help to end such things.

Clearly, I was wrong. Nothing has changed since I wrote *Close Pursuit*; violence accelerates, vile things bloom overnight, and nothing I have said or done in the last twenty years has slowed or deflected the trajectory of evil in the slightest. My hope that I could contribute, in a small way, to the process of change turned out to be nothing but arrogance and self-delusion.

Many women have come to me over the last twenty years to tell me that to use my skills as a writer to bring such things to vivid life was to contribute to the problem. I used to dismiss my criticism as feminist fascism. Now I'm not so sure. And if I'm no longer sure, I think I have a responsibility to comply until I can prove that there's no connection between writing about sadistic crimes and contributing to the violence.

I said in the beginning of this book that I have been writing about crime for close to twenty years. But, like you, I've been living with it as long as I've been on this planet. Forty-six years, by the time you read this. I've seen it in various places around the world, from Mexico to Southeast Asia. While I was in New York, working at the Four Eight Detective Area Task Force in the South Bronx—I was driving a squad car and carrying around a gun and a radio for the boss of the South Bronx Homicide Squad—our four-precinct area was averaging roughly one and a half killings every twenty-four hours, most of which I drove to and looked at while Vernon and his buddies tried to sort out who did what to whom with what.

I wasn't operational. I was just another observer, a JAFO, as they called it in the army. I didn't really have a lot to do. I wore a blue pinstripe and held the radio. I kept my mouth shut and my feelings to myself. I felt the weight of sadness in the room, the weight of the death in my chest. Behind me, the uniforms would keep the public on the far side of the yellow ribbon. There'd be the usual rough talk and muttered curses, the grim jokes that cops use to keep the pain at a distance.

All around me the evidence techs would bag and brush and wipe. The cameras would flash like sheet lightning, freezing the corpse in the glare, a stroboscopic image of blood and torn flesh, naked limbs in a tangle like a doll thrown against a wall. I'd look at the face—if there was one—and try not to see what was there: the remnants of the last moment, caught and carried into eternity by the muscles and the skin, while the spirit blew away into the night. And all I could think about was…*what* could do this?

Quite often the killer would still be there, sitting in a corner of the kitchen with drying blood on his wrists, drying blood ground into his pores like red earth, and a couple of detectives would be talking to him in a casual, conversational manner, like people at a desk trying to close a deal. The air was always one of negotiation and polite inquiry.

I'd stand in a corner out of the way and watch the killer work his side of the street, knowing that the cops wanted him dead, knowing that even the uniformed guys who brought him a coffee and a couple of bagels wanted him dead, but still everybody was civil and soft-spoken and calm. Something ugly was on the floor in the next room, but now all we had to do was clean up a bit, work out our positions, come to a consensus.

And the worst thing about it was always having to listen to the guy's voice, to pay attention to what he was saying. That was when I'd feel the .45 pressing into my ribs and it would be hard to breathe and the heat of the place would become oppressive and dense, as if something were coming off the killer, something vile, something of basements and ditches.

Yet the guy would go on, making his points, looking for understanding, looking for advantage, and it was always the same story.

START TAPE

"So, you understand—you've been Mirandized?"

"Yeah."

"So, you still want to talk about—here or at the station—and you can have a lawyer with you—but, you know, if—"

"No, I got something to—it wasn't my fault, you—"

"It was someone else did her?"

"No—I mean, I was *here*, but—"

"Was anyone else here?"

"When?"

"During the evening here, when it happened?"

"Ah, no—not that I remember. I been cranking and she was cranking with me and like we just—somebody coulda been here, but we wouldn't—we was really cranking it and so—"

"How long since you had some?"

"Me? Oh, man, you don't—*long* time, man."

"So you were clean when this happened?"

"Clean, no…not clean. We was into it good."

"So just tell us in your own words what happened."

"Well…she's big-time into the crank, hah? And we just got our check so we had—we got some—and when I come home with it I seen her—she had already done up, hah? Like she was into it, and I asked her where she got *that* from, because, like, we didn't have any shit. And she says she ain't done no shit and I says well, you got some in your arm and she says no, she ain't. So I know she's lying, hah, and then I think, well, she didn't have no money, so she musta done the guy for it—"

"Done the guy?"

"Hugo, who we buy from, he was over and I figure she give him something for his—you know, she turned over for him, and like that's WRONG, man! She's my old lady, right? So I'm doing my thing, you know, out there, getting the shit, like I'm supposed to, takin' care of business, and all the time, here she is back here tricking with Hugo. And then she LIES to me about it, my old lady, she's all wired up and she's telling me, hey, she didn't DO it when all along I know she's got no shit to trade, and I guess I sorta lost it."

"How did you lose it?"

"I just wanted to teach her, you know, not to fuck around with me, not to turn no trick without I tell her, and she says, hey, fuck me, like I never done nothing for *her*, so then I come over and we get into it and…I guess I went a little too far there, but it was like the crank was taking over inside me, eh? Like I was watching me but I wasn't at the wheel. I just kept at her, and after a while she wasn't moving or nothing and I figured hey, wow, this is some heavy shit here and it's all Hugo's fault."

"The dealer?"

"Yeah. Hugo, he knows this is my lady here."

"So where's Hugo?"

"Well, he's not around."

A moment of quiet contemplation here…

"You do Hugo too?"

Another long silence. Cups clatter on hardwood. Somebody in the background coughs. Clothing rustles. My tape-recorder is picking up a steady, muted drumbeat here. It took me a while to recognize it as my heart. Finally…

"Yeah, I did. He's out in the back. Fucked him up good."

"So you did them both?"

"Her I did under the influence of my criminal mind. On account of I couldn't help it because of the crank controlling my brain, eh? But Hugo, that was self-defence, him or me."

STOP TAPE

A few minutes later, we have found Hugo. Hugo shows every sign of having been dead for at least twenty-four hours.

RUN TAPE

"So, we found Hugo."

"Yeah."

"So, we got a problem here."

"Yeah?"

"Yeah. Hugo's been dead since yesterday anyway."

"Yeah? So?"

"So you said you did Hugo tonight."

"Did I say that? No, I meant, I did him for doing her."

"Hugo killed her?"

"No, Hugo was popping her, and that's wrong, so I took him out and when he was pissing I did him good. Then I did her."

"You did Hugo yesterday?"

"Yeah, I been TELLING you!"

"Then why kill her today? Why not kill her yesterday?"

"Yesterday I didn't know she was holding out on me."

"So you didn't kill her because she was unfaithful, because of her sleeping with Hugo?"

"Huh?"

"You said you killed her because you found her playing around with Hugo."

"Well, okay, that too. But mainly—"

"Mainly because she was holding out on you, on the crank?"

"Yeah, I mean I KILLED a guy for that crank!"

Another long pause...

"Who'd you kill for it?"

The guy looks at us for a minute, clearly annoyed.

"I TOLD you! I popped Hugo for it."

"You told us you killed Hugo for screwing around with your old lady. Now you're saying you killed him for drugs."

"Hey, he OWED me, man. I let him screw my old lady, didn't I?"

"You said you didn't know she was sleeping with Hugo until this evening."

"Yeah?"

"And you admit to killing Hugo yesterday?"

"Yeah."

"So why'd you kill *her* tonight?"

A long pause...

"Tonight was when she held out on me. Anyway, it wasn't ME that killed her, it was the crank that killed her. The crank Hugo give me—"

"The crank you took from Hugo after you killed him?"

"Yeah, but if he hadn't had the crank I wouldn't have killed him for it and I wouldna had it to fuck me up with and she'd still be alive."

"So what you're saying is—"

"Yeah! Hugo killed her, man. Hugo as good as done it himself."

A long silence here, and background noises, someone out in the hall coughs, in the street I hear kids running and talking and police radios hissing with cross-talk and static. Cars going by on Vyse Street.

Finally a cop whose name I have forgotten says: "Man, you're a piece of work."

STOP TAPE

Anyone who has raised—or tried to raise—children will recognize the substructure of this conversation: the egocentrism, the slippery evasions, the twisted logic and, underneath it all, like a seam in the earth, a complete absence of anything resembling sadness or true remorse. Children, and criminals, will often cry when they're confronted with some evidence of a wrong committed, but the tears are for themselves.

Children, given the right kind of compassionate and consistent care, will grow up eventually and take on the pleasures and burdens of the adult world—fall in love, hold jobs, be true to one another.

True criminals never will.

In their book *The Criminal Personality*,* Samuel Yochelson and Stanton E. Samenow undertook an exhaustive empirical study of the criminal mind at work. Beginning with the classic Freudian-Jungian psychoanalytic assumptions, the doctors soon found that the criminal mind-set bore little or no relation to classic psychoanalytic theory and was actually immune to such standard therapeutic approaches.

* Samuel Yochelson and Stanton E. Samenow, *The Criminal Personality: Volume One, A Profile for Change* (New York: Jason Aronson, 1976).

One of their insights touched upon the question of "semantic variance"; in other words, what a criminal means by a word or phrase is almost always very different from what you or I might mean. The authors provide a list of examples taken from several years of careful observations of convicted felons in a therapeutic environment. Trusting that we agree on the meaning of the following words, I'll simply give you the criminal version of the meaning:

BORROW: receive something that belongs to someone else with no sustained intention to return it.

CAN'T: synonymous with won't; a refusal to cooperate.

CLEVER: an opinion contrary to the criminal belief system; foreign to his views.

CLOSENESS: a person who does everything the criminal wants is "close" to him.

CONFIDENCE: super-optimism with fear cut off and no humility; a shallow, cocky state of certainty.

LONELY: without someone to control, mainly a sex partner.

MANHOOD: refers to conquering, outwitting, overpowering—usually with respect to sex or fighting.

ORDINARY: a "slave," a "sucker," "weak"—in short, "a zero."

PARANOID: refers to suspicion based on something that warrants suspicion; not a reference to an abnormal mental state.

PLEASURE: high-voltage excitement, usually through doing something forbidden.

POLICE: anyone who checks up on the criminal and holds him accountable.

PRIDE: notion of being better than others. Refusing to yield to another person. The idea that if one does not maintain his superior position, he is nothing.

PROBLEM: a jam in which the criminal has been apprehended and held accountable or a situation in which he is barred from a criminal objective.

RIGHT AND WRONG: "right" for the criminal at the time. What serves his ends.

SQUARE: refers to the stupidity of living responsibly.

TRUST: refers to whomever the criminal can control. He trusts who he can control, someone who will not snitch or inform. (*Social workers please note!*)

TRUTH: telling enough of what happened to satisfy the questioner while leaving a lot unsaid.

TO BE VIOLATED: to have one's criminal way of life interfered with.

WEAK: "sissy," "lame"—lacking the guts to do the forbidden.

You're aware that denying the shared meaning of words and the spirit that informs language is to deny tacit knowing. It's a tactic used by people whose agenda is not understanding and communication but rather deception, concealment and control.

Now if someone will just clue in the justice system…

THREE
Crossing the Bar

An intriguing illustration of the denial of tacit knowing was provided by a couple of members of Canada's Supreme Court when, after a long fight paid for entirely by the Canadian taxpayers, Charles Ng got his day in court.

After about a million dollars of taxpayer-funded Legal Aid and federal expenditures, after years of delay, after unimaginable emotional trauma to the families of the victims and after a lot of lawyers were well paid for their time, the question finally landed in front of the bench.

The question was framed in the most complex legal language possible, but what it boiled down to was this:

Shall we send this obvious slimeball to well-deserved judgement back in California, or might it be that our scruples about capital punishment are more important than the rights of several people who died deaths more horrible than most of us can imagine?

(I might add at this point that while I am unwilling to go into nauseating detail about what Charles Ng and Leonard Lake got up to—and I know more about it than I ever wanted to—the depressing fact is they videotaped themselves doing it. There is no doubt whatsoever in the minds of anyone connected with the case that Ng and Lake physically performed the tortures and the violations that the videotapes record. I imagine that even the Learned Judges of our Supreme Court knew that.)

Here is evil. What are you gonna do with it?

Here's what they did...

IN THE MATTER OF SECTION 53 OF THE
SUPREME COURT ACT, R.S.C. 1985, C. S-26.
IN THE MATTER OF A REFERENCE BY THE
GOVERNOR IN COUNCIL CONCERNING THE
SURRENDER BY CANADA OF THE EXTRADITION
FUGITIVE CHARLES CHITAT NG TO THE UNITED

STATES OF AMERICA, AS SET OUT IN ORDER IN
COUNCIL P.C. 1990-1082, DATED THE 7TH DAY
OF JUNE, 1990.

CORAM:
The Rt. Hon. Antonio Lamer, PC
The Hon. Mr. Justice La Forest
The Hon. Mme Justice L'Heureux-Dubé
The Hon. Mr. Justice Sopinka
The Hon. Mr. Justice Gonthier
The Hon. Mr. Justice Cory
The Hon. Mme Justice McLachlin
Appeal heard: February 21, 1991.
Judgement rendered: September 26, 1991.
Reasons for Judgement by:
  The Hon. Mr. Justice La Forest
Concurred in by:
  The Hon. Mme Justice L'Heureux-Dubé
  The Hon. Mr. Justice Gonthier
Reasons for Judgement by:
  The Hon. Mme Justice McLachlin
Concurred in by:
  The Hon. Mme Justice L'Heureux-Dubé
  The Hon. Mr. Justice Gonthier
Dissenting Reasons by:
  The Hon. Mr. Justice Sopinka
Concurred in by:
  The Rt. Hon. Antonio Lamer, PC
Dissenting Reasons by:
  The Hon. Mr. Justice Cory
Concurred in by:
  The Rt. Hon. Antonio Lamer, PC
Counsel at hearing:
For the fugitive Charles Chitat Ng:
  Don W. MacLeod
For the Attorney General of Canada:
  Douglas Rutherford, QC
  Graham Garton, QC

For the interveners:
For Amnesty International:
  David Matas
  Emilio S. Binavince
For the State of California:
  Brian A. Crane, QC
File Number 21990

...Ng was charged in the State of California with several offences, including twelve counts of murder. If found guilty, he could receive the death penalty. Before trial, Ng escaped from prison [sic] and fled to Canada where he was arrested. The extradition judge allowed the US's application for his extradition and committed him to custody. The Minister of Justice of Canada then ordered his extradition to Canada pursuant to s.25 of the EXTRADITION ACT without seeking assurances from the US, under Article 6 of the Extradition Treaty between the two countries that the death penalty would not be imposed or if imposed not carried out. The Governor General in Council, in accordance with s.53 of the Supreme Court Act, later referred two questions to this court. These questions raised the same issues considered in KINDLER v. CANADA (Minister of Justice) SCC no. 21321 September 26, 1991.

Notice that the court was faced with *two* cases of flight from the United States to avoid death in the same year. Kindler was found guilty in Pennsylvania of Murder One, Kidnapping and Conspiracy. The jury recommended death.

Kindler was a very nasty person, but he managed to reach Canada after escaping prison. Amnesty International and various civil liberty groups got involved and the case came before the Supreme Court at the same time as the Ng hearing. The issues were identical. One of the things this situation makes clear is that the killers in the United States are reading their case law very carefully.

The questions and this Court's answers are:

QUESTION 1:
Would the surrender by Canada of an Extradition fugitive to the United States of America, to stand trial for wilful and deliberate murder for which the penalty upon conviction may be death constitute a breach of the fugitive's rights guaranteed under the CANADIAN CHARTER OF RIGHTS AND FREEDOMS?

ANSWER:
NO. [LAMER CJ and SOPINKA and CORY JJ dissenting would answer YES.]

QUESTION 2:
Did the Minister of Justice, in deciding pursuant to Article 6 of the EXTRADITION TREATY BETWEEN CANADA AND THE UNITED STATES OF AMERICA to surrender the fugitive CHARLES CHITAT NG without seeking assurances from the UNITED STATES that the death penalty would not be imposed on the said CHARLES CHITAT NG or, if imposed, would not be executed, commit any of the errors of law and jurisdiction alleged in the Statement of the Claim filed in the Federal Court of Canada (Trial Division) by the said CHARLES CHITAT NG on October 30, 1989, having regard to the said Statement of Claim, the reasons given by the Minister of Justice for the said decision...

Now this is why we are all here today. Ng's lawyer, acting on his client's request, appealed the Justice minister's decision to get Ng the hell out of Canada as quickly as possible. The Justice minister did so after Madame Justice Marguerite Trussler of the Alberta Queen's Bench ruled that Ng should be returned to California. She ruled that enough evidence existed to bring him to trial on twelve murder charges, and that he be held in prison to await his surrender to US sheriffs.

Ng smiled.

His lawyer, Don MacLeod, paid for by Legal Aid, said he would appeal the case through every avenue, something he predicted would take five years. No doubt MacLeod, as a skilled trial lawyer, knew that such a major delay in Ng's criminal trial would seriously impair the prosecution's case, perhaps to the extent that Ng, an obvious psychopath, would walk. And, in all probability, kill again.

Like all good lawyers who are confident of getting paid, MacLeod saw only The Higher Purpose and was prepared to pursue it to the last dollar of taxpayers' money.

...and to any other material which the Court in its discretion may receive and consider?

ANSWER:
NO. [LAMER CJ and SOPINKA and CORY JJ, dissenting, would answer YES.]

All the lawyers and the Honorable Justice Sopinka referred mainly to the *Kindler* case, while Cory, who was also dissenting from the decision to extradite Ng, cited a European Court case called *Soering and Eain v. Wilkes*.

Now, for the purposes of this discussion, the most illuminating portion of these various weighty arguments was provided by the Honorable Mr. Justice Cory, who felt that he had a good case for keeping Charles Ng here until the United States promised not to execute him. And it was on this single issue that the emotional subtext of the court hearing was played out.

It's clear from the various rulings delivered by the justices that each one of them had strong—although divergent—feelings about the death penalty. However, it was a generally accepted principle that, all in all, the death penalty was a very bad idea, that sending Ng off to California to face it was a heavy responsibility and that nobody was going to do that without taking a look over his or her shoulder to see if the Charter was against it.

This supports a couple of my contentions about the justice system in general. First of all, I intend to prove that many judges very quickly arrive at a gut feeling about the correct disposition of a case, and then spend the rest of the trial looking for an iron-clad justification (rather an apt word, don't you think?) on legal grounds for this felt inclination.

That is, in its very essence, the nature of the justice system, and that's why we, as citizens concerned with ethics and justice, should pay close attention to the kind of people we are allowing to be appointed to our courts.

If you feel completely outside that loop—and most of us are—then you are not truly free, because you have abdicated your influence in the matter of justice, and you are now in the position of being judged—and ruled—by people who have no ethical, moral, emotional or political kinship with you.

Second, the case raises the issue of Wittgenstein's Paradox on Rules (upon which more in a moment), because no one who framed the Charter imagined that a mouth-breathing bottom-crawler like Charles Ng would be slithering under it for protection.

You can never know, when you first drop a legal stone into the pool of the law, just what ripples will result. Nor can you tell what vile thing may be sleeping at the bottom of the pool, and what will happen now that you have awakened it.

Anyway…back to the Court…

In order to understand the Supreme Court's take on the Ng case, we need first to browse a bit through their views in the matter of *Kindler*.

…the unconditional surrender of the appellant seriously affects his right to liberty and security of the person. The issue is whether the surrender violates the principles of fundamental justice in the circumstances of this case…the Court has held that extradition must be refused if the circumstances facing the accused on surrender are such as to "shock the conscience." There are situations where the punishment imposed following surrender—torture, for example—would be so outrageous as to shock the conscience of Canadians, but that is not so of the death penalty in all cases. While there is strong ground that, barring exceptional cases, the death penalty could not be justified in Canada having regard to the limited extent to which it advances any penological objectives and its serious invasion of human dignity…

There you have the bias. I believe it was Trudeau who said, upon refusing to allow a national referendum on the capital punishment issue, that "it was too important an issue to be left to the citizens."

This is what comes of allowing yourself to be ruled by "your betters." What you may be feeling in the back of your neck right now may not be a boot, but it's certainly a very pricey Florsheim Eagle.

> ...that is not the issue in this case. The issue is whether the extradition to the US of a person who may face the death penalty there shocks the conscience...

Exactly whose conscience the Court is concerned with is a little foggy. The context suggests that it is the conscience of the people of Canada. But, as we have seen in the Trudeau quote, rulers and judges hold very different views on such things from the rest of us (read *rabble*) and since, as we look around, we see only judges and lawyers in the room, I think we may safely deduce that the Court is primarily concerned with what might offend its own conscience.

> ...The Government has a right and duty to keep criminals out of Canada and to expel them by deportation...otherwise Canada could become a haven for criminals.

[*Too late!*]

> The issue has arisen in several recent cases in relation to persons facing the death penalty for murder. Similar policy concerns apply to extradition. It would be strange if Canada could keep out lesser offenders...

[...which we don't]

> ...but be obliged to give sanctuary to those accused or convicted of the worst types of crimes.
> In summary, the extradition of an individual who has been

accused of the worst form of murder in the US, which has a system of justice similar to our own, could not be said to shock the conscience of Canadians...

[Thank you]

...or to violate any international norm. The extradition did not go beyond what was necessary to serve the legitimate and compelling social purpose of preventing Canada from becoming an attractive haven for fugitives. The Minister determined, in the interests of protecting the security of Canadians, that he should not, in this case, seek assurances regarding the penalty to be imposed. On the evidence before the Court, the Minister's determination was not unreasonable and this court should not interfere with his decision to extradite without restrictions.

So far so good, right?

Wrong.

If what has just been recorded here sounds like simple common sense, it did not strike the dissenting justices that way.

As I observed before, this is all about our alleged national aversion to the death penalty.

Perhaps.

Or mayhap it is just about the aversion some members of the Supreme Court have to the death penalty. The dissenting opinions from Cory and Sopinka are given over to establishing legal justification for something concerning which they clearly hold an emotional and spiritual conviction.

From Cory:

In the Case of MILLER v. THE QUEEN (1977) 2 SCR 680, this court considered the validity of legislation which provided for capital punishment of persons who were convicted of the murder of police officers or prison guards acting in the course of their duties...

About the only practical defence a prison guard or a cop

might have had when facing a man who knew he was bound for a life in prison.

> ...the Majority of the Court upheld the death penalty provision of the legislation on the ground that JUDICIAL DEFERENCE SHOULD BE PAID TO THE EXPRESSED WILL OF PARLIAMENT [emphasis added]. I would observe at the outset that this reasoning is inconsistent with the approach which has been taken since the passage of the CHARTER. Unswerving judicial deference to the perceived intent of Parliament is no longer a determinative factor...

What Cory is saying here is that he regards the Charter as placing a duty upon him to ignore the wishes and intentions of Parliament—and by extension the people of Canada—if he believes that whatever has been legislated runs contrary to his interpretations of the Charter as it may apply to a particular case.

In other words, he's the boss here, and nothing the people say counts for diddly if he can use the Charter to back him up. You can see how the Charter has profoundly altered the nature of this country, and in ways not foreseen by the politicians who helped to impose it on us all.

Then Cory refers to the capital punishment debate in 1976 and 1987:

> In free votes in both 1976 and 1987, a majority of the members of the House of Commons supported the abolition of the death penalty. These votes, held after extensive and thorough debate...

From which all members of the public and all delegations holding briefs were arbitrarily EXCLUDED. Remember Trudeau's contention that it was too important an issue to be left to the people of Canada.

> ...demonstrate that the elected representatives of the Canadian people found the death penalty for civil crimes to be an affront to human dignity which cannot be tolerated in

Canadian society. These votes are a clear indication that
capital punishment is considered…

[by Cory and Sopinka and the rest of our masters]

…to be contrary to basic Canadian values.
The rejection of the death penalty by the majority of the
 members of the House of Commons on two occasions…

Cory is careful not to say "by the people of Canada." Nor
does he think it relevant to note that the actual vote tally in 1976
was 148 to 127. Hardly a telling majority.

…can be taken as reflecting a basic abhorrence of the infliction
 of capital punishment either directly, within Canada, or
 through Canadian complicity in the actions of a foreign state.

I find it grimly amusing to watch a Supreme Court judge take
two contradictory positions at the same time. In one portion of
his ruling, he makes it clear that he does not consider himself
bound at all by what Parliament—and the people—might legis-
late, provided he can find a Charter justification, and on the
other hand he proceeds to wrap himself in the flag and align
himself—quite ringingly, I thought—with the very same noble
polity he has only a few pages before so imperiously dismissed.
  He reminds me a bit of the Queen of Hearts in *Through the
Looking-glass*. Like most lawyers, Cory has no trouble believing
in impossible things, and can probably believe as many as three
or four different impossible things before breakfast.
  Anyway, Cory concludes by taking the high ground:

…the preservation of Canada's integrity and reputation in the
 international community…

[Or, at least, the reputation of the Supreme Court]

…require that extradition be refused unless an undertaking is
 obtained pursuant to Article Six. To take this position does

not constitute an absolute refusal to extradite. It simply…

Simply! What he's about to propose is politically *explosive*. Justice Cory chooses not to consider that the Ng case is a very nasty one, that most of the people of California want Ng to die, and that District Attorneys in the United States are elected officials. I spoke to officials in the US court system while I was covering the Ng story, and they knew damn well that any kind of deal made with Canada that implied some measure of leniency for Ng would be political suicide. Cory is a man of great political sophistication—he made it to the Supreme Court, didn't he?—and he knows damn well what he is asking for.

> …requires the requesting state to undertake that it will substitute a penalty of life imprisonment for the execution of the prisoner if that prisoner is found to be guilty of the crime.

However, at the end of the day more thoughtful heads prevailed and Charles Chitat Ng was promptly bundled off whence he came, ultimately to face a jury of—well, one would hope not a jury of his *peers*—but a jury of solid citizens with solid judgement. With any luck at all—after about five *more* years of legal intervention and assorted appeals at $1 million per year in legal fees to a gaggle of American lawyers—Ng will walk down a long hallway towards a condign conclusion that he has richly deserved.

Aside from the fact that Ng has provided work and cash-flow for quite a few lawyers, what can we infer from this sorry spectacle?

Well, several things, I suppose.

One, justice, while perhaps blind, is not without prejudices.

Two, Supreme Court justices are no freer from these prejudices than the rest of us, but they have much more power to enforce them.

Three, lawyers will argue anything.

But the central inference from this case, and from all the cases I am about to present in this arguably depressing inquiry, is this one:

Our judges constitute an exclusive and highly influential

cadre of men and women who consider themselves empowered by the Charter of Rights and Freedoms to dispense justice according to their lights and completely unencumbered by the wishes of either the people of Canada—to whom they are procedurally deaf—or the operations of Canada's Parliament.

When one considers how little influence any of us has on the selection and appointment of judges in this country, one begins to discern the outlines of a kind of judicial tyranny. A polite tyranny, a *thoughtful* tyranny, supported by a kind of internal logic, operating in accordance with its own rules and precedents of course, but, ultimately, unrestrained by anything outside itself.

The operations of power are inevitably corrupting, and judges are in no way inoculated against hubris, arrogance and isolation from the sensibilities of their countrymen.

We are in a time when most of the citizens of this country, of this continent, feel excluded and unrepresented by their elected officials. How should we regard this other, and even more untouchable, elite?

Make no mistake, this elite has no experience of real violence; it knows nothing of the dangers and frustrations and sorrows of the cities and towns in our time. Further, it is constitutionally (in all senses of that word) incapable of understanding and reacting to the gathering anarchy of our age. They are in all ways above it, content to flatter themselves with the brilliance of their interpretations, the consistency of their case law and the prestige of their positions, while the rest of the country confronts the loss of almost everything that makes civilized life possible: safety for our children, security for our property, respect for our lives and our futures, the freedoms of the parks and walks, the sanctity of our hopes.

We are, supposedly, guaranteed these freedoms as a fundamental principle, part of the fabric of Canadian life.

Part One, paragraph 1, subsection (a) of The Canadian Bill of Rights describes this particular right:

The right of the individual to life, liberty, security of the person and enjoyment of property, and the right not to be deprived thereof except by due process of law.

In conducting themselves as they do, many justices create consequences that act to the detriment of these basic rights as defined by this act. In fact, some justices seem to operate with a clear, persistent and pervasive disregard for the protection of these basic rights, in effect using the Charter of Rights and Freedoms to overrule and erode the fundamental freedoms guaranteed to all citizens by the Bill of Rights. As a consequence, these particular justices, who have been shown by their record and their rulings to be contributing to this violation of the Bill of Rights, may be said to be operating in willful defiance of the Act. A legal description of it might be contained in the phrase "contributory negligence."

If it can be established by an impartial panel that the individual records of these justices demonstrate a consistent and long-standing inclination towards rulings that are inimical to the protection of society, then there are processes available to Parliament to set these judges down.

I'd be intrigued to hear a detailed explanation of why this could not be done.

Anyone?

So…why couldn't we find a speedy and intelligent way to deal with something as obviously vile and degraded as Charles Chitat Ng? Why is justice not so much blind as ethically astigmatic? In short, what's wrong with our justice system?

Let's start at the beginning.

FOUR

Monday Morning

It's a cold and rainy day in January. We're in courtroom number 305 of the Provincial Courthouse on Main Street in Vancouver, British Columbia, just down the street from police headquarters. Presiding today is Judge E. Cronin, and the matter before him is a discussion of the merits of a warrant that had been issued to members of the RCMP Drug Squad. The warrant resulted in the arrest of one Daniel Neuenschwander and some others after a kick-in at a residence in Kitsilano, namely 2211 Yew Street.

Representing the Crown is Gerald Straith, young, quick, blond, with an athletic build and a wry sense of humor. Straith is an ad hoc prosecutor, a lawyer who has a private practice and who is, from time to time, hired by the Crown to prosecute a certain offence. Ad hoc lawyers represent a growing trend in the Canadian justice system since there don't seem to be enough full-time Crowns to deal with the massive caseloads currently weighing upon our courts.

The defendant, Neuenschwander, is a wiry young man in casual clothes, with longish black hair that lies in a tangle over the collar of his shirt. He leans back in his chair, at ease, and talks from time to time with his lawyer, a man named Kenneth Young.

Young is the Hollywood ideal of a defence lawyer—tanned, hair in a long version of a 1970s razor-cut, well-turned-out in expensive grey tweed and grey flannel trousers. His voice projects well and has a pleasing baritone rumble.

At the raised bench, Judge Cronin presents a stern picture; a pale-pink balding man in his middle years, with shiny skin and pale eyes, he projects a kind of cranky punctiliousness and is quite formal in his speech. An air of generalized impatience and a slight disdain for the process seem to arise from him in a kind of aura that settles over and dominates the nearly empty courtroom. The judge sits with his right side turned away from the room. A small man, only his head and shoulders are visible to the room as he studies the documents before him. His right arm is seriously deformed and he writes with difficulty and seems unwilling to be observed at this task. Now and then he sits forward to say something to the clerk.

Straith has reached the point of the hearing where he is narrating the events that led up to the arrest of Mr. Neuenschwander. Judge Cronin is leaning back in his chair, his face closed and immobile as he attends carefully to the ad hoc prosecutor. What follows is a factually accurate but abridged version of their conversation. I think you'll find it illuminating:

Straith: Well, Your Honor, quantities of cocaine were found in that residence, and I—

Cronin: That's not the—I'm curious as to what it was that Corporal Bruce observed that persuaded him that there was Reasonable and Probable Grounds for a warrant.

Straith: Corporal Bruce and other members of the Drug Squad were engaged in their usual work—

Cronin: Cruising the downtown area looking for activity that suggested drug-trafficking?

Straith: Yes, Your Honor, and they observed—I think the records—Corporal Bruce testified at some length about this— that they had observed a man who was a known drug-trafficker—

Cronin: How did they know this?

Straith: The man was known to them, Your Honor, as a man they had previously arrested for drug-trafficking, for NIP and PPT many times, so they decided—

Cronin: They just decided to follow this man?

Straith: That's how it works, yes. And they observed him for some time—a matter of hours—they saw him approach another man who was also known to them as a dealer, and they saw an exchange take place.

Cronin: They were in a position to see this?

Straith: According to Corporal Bruce, they had them both in sight and they saw—

Cronin: And this person who they were first observing, he allegedly was then followed to 2211 Yew Street, I understand that, and he was under the personal observation of Corporal Bruce all that time?

Straith: Corporal Bruce or other members of the squad who were in radio communication, there was a Constable Weeving and a Constable Janes—

Cronin: So Bruce did not have the individual under his personal observation at all times?

Straith: No, Your Honor, I think his statement to the magistrate—

Cronin: Seems to suggest that he did, to me.

Straith: Well, he or a member—

Cronin: It seems unclear…if it was Janes or Weeving, then there should have been something to that effect in the request for the warrant and that doesn't seem to have happened.

Straith: Well, there was a great deal of activity at 2211 Yew Street that was observed by the officers and that began as soon as the individual returned to the duplex.

Cronin: This would be Carzones or Munoz or Marino?

Straith: (looking at notes) Carzones, I think…

Cronin: And what kind of activity was observed by Weeving and Janes and Bruce?

Straith: Cars would pull up to the address and a person would go up to the door—

Cronin: 2211 Yew Street?

Straith: Yes, Your Honor, and there would be a conversation at the door or—

Cronin: With the occupant?

Straith: Yes, Your Honor, and with Munoz or one of the others, and there'd be some kind of exchange—

Cronin: Now I'm going to stop you there. Just what was it that the officers saw? This exchange?

Straith: A man stands at the door, or sometimes they would meet at the car, or inside it, and they would turn towards each other—

Cronin: That's it? Just turn to face each other? I mean, it seems to me that…it's normal for two people sitting in a car to turn to face each other, wouldn't you say that?

Straith: Yes, Your Honor, but in this case, the actions suggested to—they seemed to fit the profile of drug-trafficking, and that persuaded the—

Cronin: I'm uncomfortable with that phrase, "fit the profile," and I'm asking exactly what did the officers actually *see?*

Straith: Well they saw several people arriving at various times and each time there would be a meeting at the door—

Cronin: Never inside?

Straith: Sometimes there would be that, but usually it was a meeting and then there would be an exchange, in that something would be handed to the defendant and then something would be handed back, and this fit the profile of drug-trafficking as the drug squad officers have experienced it—a known trafficker and a lot of people who were users—

Cronin: Bruce knew they were users?

Straith: Some of the people were known to the officers as people who were drug users, and so therefore the conclusion was drawn that there was Reasonable and Probable Grounds that drug-trafficking was going on at the address, and so Corporal Bruce decided to go and apply for the warrant.

Cronin: On that basis only?

Straith: Well, you have an individual known to the courts, who has made many many appearances in front of the court as a defendant charged with NIP and PPT, who has been convicted many, many times of being a trafficker and who is now engaging in the classic kind of behavior that has always indicated that he is trafficking, and he is being watched by experienced Drug Squad officers—

Cronin: What's he actually doing—I get the idea—the officers see this man, he comes out of his house a few times to talk to people—

Straith: That fits the profile—

Cronin: I mean, suppose I am in my house and I decide to go out to the back garden six or seven times, well, it seems to me that these Drug Squad officers would look at me and they'd say I was engaged in behavior that fit the profile of a drug-trafficker.

Straith: Your Honor, these are people who are known to be drug—to be in that culture—and the officers have a lot of experience—Corporal Bruce is a very experienced member of the squad with many, many years observing this kind of thing, and he had every reason to believe that what he was looking at was—

Cronin: Supposing I only go into my garden twice? Is that— does that fit your profile?

Straith: No…I mean, it was in the judgement of experienced officers—

Cronin: I'm not persuaded that the relevant section of the Charter is intended to apply to police officers.

Straith: It's a protection against unreasonable search or seizure, and under *Debot*—

Cronin: I'm quite familiar with *Debot,* but I think the Charter is intended to convey that the definition of Reasonable and Probable Grounds be Reasonable and Probable to any citizen, not to police officers in particular, and—

Straith: Section 10 refers to the peace officer and on his belief about Reasonable Grounds.

Cronin: The grounds must be reasonable to the person who is assessing the situation.

Straith: That would be the police—the peace officer—

Cronin: I'm not persuaded that Reasonable in this section necessarily refers to the officer but to a private uninterested bystander. If you have the test be reasonable to a police officer, I think you weaken the Charter defence against unreasonable search and seizure because all a police officer would have to say is, well, it was reasonable to me, and that would be—

Straith: With respect, Your Honor, drugs *were* found in the duplex—

Cronin: That's after the fact of the warrant.

Straith: Of course, Your Honor, but it does suggest that the judgement of the police—of Corporal Bruce was accurate—

Cronin: The question is, did he have Reasonable and Probable grounds *before* the warrant, and from what I've heard—well, it seems that any citizen who goes out to his garden too often is going to attract the attention of the Drug Squad, and I think that would be very—that would be—this is in violation of the Charter protection and sets a dangerous precedent.

Straith: Your Honor, the Drug Squad is presumed to have special knowledge—

Cronin: It has to be reasonable to anyone, it would have to be drug-trafficking so obvious that anyone who saw it would know it was drug-trafficking.

Straith: But drug-dealers try to make their actions appear ordinary, to avoid that sort of thing, so it seems to me that—

Cronin: Well, I have a lot of trouble with this, and I don't think—it seems to me that there's a real danger here, when you have Drug Squad officers just going ahead and arresting on that kind of evidence.

Straith: But that's always the kind of evidence they get, Your Honor, and we have to—

Cronin: Well, it's getting late here, we'll break and I'll give the matter some thought.

Straith and Young and the defendant stand. Cronin sweeps out on black wings. Portents swirl in his wake.

Straith: (to Young and his client) Well, I guess your client will be out golfing next week.

Young: (laughing) I'd say so.

What's disturbing about this exchange is the interpretation that Judge Cronin was putting on the Charter protection against unreasonable search and seizure. If his contention holds, then it makes the police effort against drug-trafficking very, very difficult.

It was, at one time, quite accepted that a policeman was on an equal footing with the lawyers and the rest of the officials of the court. He was "an officer of the court," a member of the priesthood, and it was a given that his judgements were entitled to the same kind of respect, the same assumption of honesty, the same impress of professionalism as were the statements of the Crown, or the defence, or the judge himself. The usual description of this forensic concept is "acting in good faith," and, historically, it carried with it a kind of imprimatur. Certainly, lawyers and judges have not surrendered their title to this assumption of basic honesty and honorable intent. They seem, however, to have decided to deny the same privilege to the police.

Clearly, times have changed in Canada.

Ordinary citizens will have trouble with His Honor's contention that the fact that drugs were seized at 2211 Yew Street has nothing to do with the justification for the warrant. The ordinary citizen might think that the possession of drugs was a vindication of the officer's judgement, and anyway, aren't we trying to crush the drug trade? And isn't truth and justice the whole point of the justice system?

The answer to all these questions is no.

We are most definitely *not* trying to crush the drug trade in Canada. As a matter of fact, the courts are doing everything they can to *encourage* the drug trade.

An eminent jurist has observed that "Judges do no administer Justice; they are present to administer the Law." A pivotal distinction.

Truth, the literal record of the event and the consequences of it, has no place in the justice system as it is currently constituted. In fact, it has no legal meaning.

Once you grasp that, you begin to understand how we have become what we have become, and since Canada follows the United States by a distance of about ten years, we need to understand how both systems came to be what they are.

And what are they?

Legal dictatorships operating in a moral vacuum.

FIVE

Ozymandias

Justice Oliver Wendell Holmes, in a commentary on *Olmstead v. the United States,* said, "I think it is a lesser evil that some criminals should escape than that the government should play an ignoble part." Justice Holmes was speaking from the promontory of a great continent of moral thought, a continent dedicated to the supremacy of the rights of the individual.

From this rarefied height, Holmes pontificated, secure in his belief that the state somehow embodied the best that was in all men, and was therefore worthy of the blood of innocents that might be spilled by guilty men loosed in the world.

Clearly, in this view of the affairs of men and the state, the law has a higher calling than the mere deliverance of individual retribution. The law has in it something of…the divine. It shares in and draws its power from an alignment with the "eternal verities."

Holmes's words strike a dismal echo today in the stony canyons of modern experience. But in the beginning of history, where, it may be suggested, Holmes has left his heart, this view of man as a part of a larger harmony was everywhere held and everywhere celebrated.

The dream-myth of Periclean Athens (which survives today in neo-Dionysian belief systems like militant environmentalism and some New Age cults) saw man as a citizen in a serene stasis where the opposing forces of creation and decay were held in perfect balance by the wisdom of divinely guided rulers.

The Sophists, the Western world's first empirical scientists, suggested that the outrageous variety of human urges and actions was clearly inconsistent with any divine order. Law and morality had no claim to absolute value, had nothing in them of cosmic inevitability. Justice was a product of reasoning men, as were the values upon which justice was constructed.

Plato attempted to secure and reinforce the power of human justice by connecting it to something higher and more perfect than the city-state. According to Plato, human realities were only the imperfect shadows of cosmic archetypes. In *The*

Republic, Plato described a moral Utopia where justice prevailed when the city and its government conformed to ideal archetypes. Not surprisingly, these archetypes would be discerned for the masses by the philosopher-kings who ruled Utopia. In this city, there would be no need for a code of human law since the guidance of these clear-seeing kings would be all that was necessary for harmony and peace.

The Stoics interpolated this Platonic code around the end of the fourth century before Christ, suggesting a kind of *jus naturale,* a natural law, which was the worldly incarnation of the *lex aeterna.* The existence of inborn and inherited reason in man was a proof of the cosmic order (an idea later employed by G.K. Chesterton as proof of God's existence), and therefore all men were—or bloody well ought to be—subject to a universally valid moral law.

The Romans adopted these Stoic principles, while sensibly rejecting the noble but ill-fated attempts of the Greeks to keep the power of law in the hands of all citizens. The Romans established the first class of legal specialists, jurisconsults and praetors, which foreshadowed our own lawyers and magistrates.

Cicero's *De Res Publica* provided a system for the translation of general Stoic principles of the *lex aeterna* into straightforward precepts for everyday legal decisions. Again, the Romans quite naturally believed that this *jus gentium* was a law that applied to all people, Roman or barbarian. It also provided the Romans with a neat rationale for global imperialism, which they called the *Pax Romana,* a nice scruple that never troubled Alexander the Great or Tiglath-Pileser I of Middle Assyria.

In the Middle Ages, Thomas Aquinas, like Saint Augustine before him, in the ongoing attempt to reconcile the Dionysian volatility of early Christianity with the requirements of a powerful and politically aggressive Church, developed a kind of compromise.

Human law, which had its origins in divine inspiration, was still a creation of human reason for the benefit of everyday society, but its power reached only to the edge of the eternal law, that innate sense of good and evil that flows directly from the divine. According to Aquinas, the enforcement powers of human law stopped when they came into conflict with God's law. By extension, any human law that found itself in conflict with divine law was not good law, but law that had somehow strayed from the true path, and was therefore not binding on men.

This was a principle that depended upon the will and the enforcement mechanisms of the Holy Roman Church, and it's not surprising that secular law has grown ever more powerful as the power of the churches has declined.

The first clear sign of the rise of the mercantile powers and the decline of the Church came in the writings of Niccolo Machiavelli. Machiavelli saw the power of the state to rule as an end in itself, entirely separate from the law of God or any kind of divine inspiration. Order was preferable to chaos. Therefore, whatever tended to preserve order (in this case, the rule of princes over the masses) was by definition a good thing. A simple way to restate the complexities of Machiavelli's advice, and it hardly does the man justice, is to say that if the end is to preserve order over chaos, then that end justifies any means.

While this is not a particularly persuasive argument in the twentieth century (an era that has seen more than its share of blood spilled in the name of order), it's still possible to discern in Machiavelli early forms of the current *literalness* of the justice system. Once free of transient, God-inspired moral values, the law becomes a system for preserving the ruling classes in the name of peace, not a means of educating the common man in matters of moral action and Godly behavior.

We might be more sympathetic to this principle if we were actually forced to live in the medieval world, a world Matthew Arnold might forgive us for describing as "a vast and darkling plain, swept by confused alarums of struggle and flight, where ignorant armies clash by night."

(Actually, Arnold would most definitely NOT like to see Dover Beach used as a prop for Machiavellian pragmatism, since his poem was an expression of his pain at seeing the tide of faith withdrawing from the shores of human experience.)

Well, the fact remains that when any kind of status quo was better than blooded blades glittering in the fires of burning villages, a point Hobbes made even more forcefully in *Leviathan*.

For Hobbes, the state was civilized man's only defence against other men, men who, in a state of nature, were driven by only three needs: desire, fear and the urge to get children.

In Hobbes you can see the bitter fruit of Machiavellian ethology; what a change this is from the early Greek vision of man as fundamentally good, as part of a harmonious cosmic balance, as necessary to *what is* as the clouds or the rivers or the deer in the forests. In Machiavelli and Hobbes you can hear the ancient voice of Apollo, of cold reason over spiritual epiphanies.

Now, with Hobbes, there is no safety in this life, no defence against the natural bestiality of the human animal, other than the immersion of self, the complete submission of man to the State, the Leviathan. It can be argued that Hobbes and Machiavelli were the first to teach us to fear ourselves. It is certain that they taught us that our only safety lies in submission to the great Leviathan of the law.

After Hobbes, the course of the law has run in two roughly parallel streams. In one, the struggle of what is natural in man to balance what is natural to the state burst up from the earth in the United States—and in Canada, in a rather diluted form—where it was held to be self-evident that natural man had inalienable rights to life, liberty and the pursuit of happiness. It was therefore the only business of the Republic to secure these rights, for all men in the name of all men.

(Strangely, this development coincided in the United States with immersion in a revolutionary war against a like-minded society, England, the birthplace of common law. True, the wellsprings of American law run as much from the French Enlightenment as they do from English Common Law, but the tribal connection is there. Few Americans will like this reading, but a case can be made that the Revolutionary War was not so much a rebellion of the common man against Hobbes's Leviathan as a kind of leveraged bail-out with a gunpowder clause, in support of the economical aspirations of a rising merchant class.)

The other stream, antithetical to the idea of natural law for natural man, became a kind of forensic Darwinism under the teachings of the French philosopher Montesquieu and the sociologist

Auguste Comte. To these men, abstractions such as natural harmony and inalienable essential rights were outmoded, archaic survivals of a Greco-Roman idealism. Change and adaptation of the law, rather than consistency and solidity, were the keys to modern legal principles. The Napoleonic Code is therefore almost incomprehensible to the North American mind, steeped as it is in concepts of individual rights. A system where a man must prove himself innocent to the satisfaction of the State or suffer the consequences is anathema to the West, perhaps rightly so. Auguste Comte would tell us that is purely our social preference.

The American justice system, although founded on the principles developed in English Common Law since the Magna Carta (AD 1215), has drawn from several wells to create a unique and turbulent pool of experiential law. The principle of the inalienable right of the individual to certain pursuits, to a basic freedom of life and choice, drawn from early Grecian archetypes of man as semi-divine and naturally good, has led to the evolution of an adversarial system rather than an inquisitorial one.

In France, and elsewhere in Europe, it is the purpose and privilege of the State (Hobbes's Leviathan) to discover, by rigorous questioning of all parties, just where the crime lies and who must pay. In America and in Canada (another curious hybrid of French and English legal traditions), the State stands in *loco parentis* to the accused, in accordance with the emphasis on individual rights, and acts only as an arbiter of two opposing forces: the prosecution and the defence. The State does not concern itself with an epistemology of truth, but only with technical calculations of something called Due Process.

As Holmes made clear in his injunction, any State holding this view has a higher obligation; it is not enough simply to ferret out the evil-doer. A State so dedicated must act to preserve the rights of the common man, who is considered innocent until the prosecution can provide overwhelming proof of his guilt. All principles of criminal law, especially those that tend to assist the accused and drive policemen and ordinary citizens wild, have their origins in this elegant and noble enterprise.

A shining road. Paved with the best intentions.

Canada, something of a fledgling country currently involved in an ugly squabble between nestlings, brought a constitution back home from England under Prime Minister Pierre Trudeau and shortly after that developed its own version of the United States Bill of Rights. Called the Charter of Rights and Freedoms, it was proclaimed in force on April 17, 1982. Articles 7 to 14 describe the basic legal rights of Canadian citizens:

7. Everyone has the right to life, liberty, and security of the person and the right not to be deprived thereof except in accordance with the principles of fundamental justice.

8. Everyone has the right to be secure against unreasonable search or seizure.

9. Everyone has the right not to be arbitrarily detained or imprisoned.

10. Everyone has the right on arrest or detention:
a. to be informed promptly of the reasons therefor;
b. to retain and instruct counsel without delay and to be informed of that right;
c. to have the validity of the detention determined by way of habeas corpus and to be released if the detention is not lawful.

11. Any person charged with an offence has the right:
a. to be informed without unreasonable delay of the specific offence;
b. to be tried within a reasonable time;
c. not to be compelled to be a witness in proceedings against that person in respect of the offence;
d. to be presumed innocent until proven guilty according to law in a fair and public hearing by an independent and impartial tribunal;
e. not to be denied bail without just cause;
f. except in the case of an offence under military law tried before a military tribunal, to the benefit of trial by jury where the maximum punishment for the offence is imprisonment for five years or a more severe punishment;
g. not to be found guilty on account of any act or omission unless, at the time of the act or omission, it constituted an offence under Canadian or international law or was criminal

according to the general principles of law recognized by the community of nations;

h. if finally acquitted of the offence, not to be tried for it again and, if finally found guilty and punished for the offence, not to be tried and punished for it again; and

i. if found guilty of the offence and if the punishment for the offence has been varied between the time of commission and the time of sentencing, to the benefit of the lesser punishment.

12. Everyone has the right not to be subjected to any cruel and unusual treatment or punishment.

13. A witness who testifies in any proceedings has the right not to have any incriminating evidence so given used to incriminate that witness in any other proceedings, except in a prosecution for perjury or for the giving of contradictory evidence.

14. A party or witness in any proceedings who does not understand or speak the language in which the proceedings are conducted or who is deaf has the right to the assistance of an interpreter.

Any American will recognize the similarity of these clauses to the basic legal guarantees developed in the American Constitution and from various Supreme Court rulings over the past twenty years. The fundamental clauses are worth remembering, because they are the source of much of our current unhappiness with the justice system:

THE SECOND AMENDMENT:
A well-regulated militia, being necessary to the security of a free State, the right of the people to keep and bear arms shall not be infringed.

THE FOURTH AMENDMENT:
The right of the people to be secure in their persons, houses, papers, and effects, against unreasonable searches and seizures, shall not be violated, and no warrants shall issue but upon probable cause, supported by an oath or affirmation, and particularly describing the place to be searched, and the persons or things to be seized.

THE FIFTH AMENDMENT:

No person shall be held to answer for a capital, or otherwise infamous crime, unless on a presentment or indictment of a grand jury, except in cases arising in the land or naval forces, or in the militia, when in actual service in time of war or public danger; nor shall any person be subject for the same offense to be twice put in jeopardy of life and limb; nor shall be compelled in any criminal case to be a witness against himself, nor be deprived of life, liberty, or property, without due process of law; nor shall private property be taken for public use without just compensation.

THE SIXTH AMENDMENT:

In all criminal prosecutions, the accused shall enjoy the right to a speedy and public trial, by an impartial jury of the State and district wherein the crime shall have been committed, which district shall have been previously ascertained by law, and to be informed of the nature and cause of the accusation; to be confronted with the witnesses against him; to have compulsory process for obtaining witnesses in his favor, and to have the assistance of counsel for his defense.

THE EIGHTH AMENDMENT:

Excessive bail shall not be required, nor excessive fines imposed, nor cruel and unusual punishments inflicted.

THE THIRTEENTH AMENDMENT: (December 18, 1865)

Section One: Neither slavery nor involuntary servitude, except as a punishment for a crime whereof the party shall have been duly convicted, shall exist within the United States or any place subject to their jurisdiction.

Section Two: Congress shall have power to enforce this article by appropriate legislation.

THE FOURTEENTH AMENDMENT: (July 28, 1868)

Section One: All persons born or naturalized in the United States, and subject to the jurisdiction thereof, are citizens of the United States and of the State wherein they reside. No State shall make or enforce any law which shall abridge the privileges or immunities of citizens of the United States; nor shall any State deprive any person of life, liberty, or property, without due process of law; nor deny to any person within its jurisdiction the equal protection of the laws.

Wonderful writing, actually, at least in the earlier amendments. Elegant, clear, resonant, as cadenced and classical as a Palladian façade or a Beethoven sonata. In these fine, cursive engravings we can see the grace of reason—vital, supple, informed and numinous in the heart of the New World. In F. Scott Fitzgerald's poetic phrasing:

> These are my fathers. I knew them all, with their hearts of
> new earth in the forest-heavy darkness of the Seventeenth
> Century.

For those of you at all interested in the differences between Canada and the United States, you need look no further than the second paragraph of the Unanimous Declaration of the Thirteen United States of America and compare it with Article Seven of the Canadian Bill of Rights. In the Canadian version, the ringing American phrase "…that they are endowed by their Creator with certain unalienable Rights, that among these are Life, Liberty, and the pursuit of Happiness" has been changed to read "Everyone has the right to life, liberty, and security of the person."

What a fall is this! Anyone who imagines that minor amendments in language have no real significance in the greater world has a serious case of cosmic astigmatism. This is a truth that lawyers have understood for centuries.

And, as it happens, the lawyers did get at those first elegant amendments to the Constitution, as anyone with a love of language will be able to tell by comparing the elegance of the earlier amendments with the more clumsy and forensically prolix phrasings of the Thirteenth and Fourteenth Amendments.

One of the first warning signs of the growing power of lawyers over the law is an increase in words such as "therein" and "whereof." These words appear nowhere in the first amendments, but they show up like the first symptoms of the Pox in the Thirteenth and Fourteenth. They are the first indicators of the decline in clarity of thought that has brought the justice system to its sorry state today.

The collapse of language and forensic elegance assures the primacy of lawyers as certainly as the invention of a lock for the Gates of Heaven has kept priests and ayatollahs off the dole for ten thousand years.

This is worth looking at a little more closely.

You will have noticed the regular reoccurrence of certain words in legal statutes designed to govern the affairs of men, and particularly in statutes addressing moral or "right" behavior. It's an inherent element of semantics that there are some attitudes, actions, value judgements, methods of human interaction that cannot, by their very nature, be precisely described.

Words such as "unreasonable," as in the Fourth Amendment:

> The right of the people to be secure in their persons, houses, papers, and effects, against *unreasonable* searches and seizures...

Or "obscene," as in Section 163 of the Canadian Criminal Code:

> 1. Everyone commits an offence who:
> a. makes, prints, publishes, distributes, circulates, or has in his possession...any *obscene* written matter, picture, model, phonograph record or other thing whatever...

Or "knowingly," as it later appears in the same statute:

> 2. Every one commits an offence who *knowingly*, without lawful justification or excuse...

Or "reasonable cause to believe," as it appears in Section 70, 10/2 of the New York State Criminal Procedure Law:

> *Reasonable cause to believe* exists when evidence or information which appears reliable discloses facts or circumstances which are collectively of such weight and persuasiveness as to convince a person of ordinary intelligence, judgment and experience that it is reasonably likely that the

offense was committed and that the person involved...

Or practically all the adjectives and adverbs contained in this formal jury instruction given by Washington D.C. judges to all juries when they are about to retire to consider their verdict:

> *Reasonable doubt,* as the name implies, is a doubt for which you can give a reason. It is such a doubt as would cause a juror, after *careful* and *candid* and *impartial consideration* of all the evidence, to be so undecided that he cannot say he has an *abiding conviction* of the defendant's guilt. It is such a doubt as would cause a *reasonable person* to hesitate or pause in the *graver* and more *important* transactions of life. However, it is not a *fanciful doubt* nor a *whimsical doubt* nor a doubt based on *conjecture.* It is a doubt which is based on *reason.* The government is not required to establish guilt beyond all doubt or to a *mathematical certainty* or a *scientific certainty.* Its burden is to establish guilt beyond a *reasonable doubt.*

And in this example of legal writing concerning insanity, from Section 16 of the Canadian Criminal Code:

> 16.1 No person shall be convicted of an offence in respect of an act or omission on his part while that person was *insane.*
> 2. For the purposes of this section a person is *insane* when the person is in a state of *natural inbecility* or has a *disease of the mind* to an extent that renders the person incapable of *appreciating the nature and quality* of an act or omission or of *knowing that* an act or omission is *wrong.*
> 3. A person who has *specific delusions* but is *in other respects sane* shall not be acquitted on the ground of insanity unless the delusions caused that person to *believe in a state of things* that, if it existed, would have *justified or excused* the act or omission of that person...

Reading through these passages, one fact emerges again and again. For any of these legal admonitions, instructions or definitions to work well (that is, to work as the writer or the speaker has intended them to work), there must be a common ground of understanding concerning the values and actions described.

"Reasonable," "obscene," "knowingly" and the others must, in the mind of the receiver, call up a set of characteristics, a flavor of intent, or a limit on behavior, that is *nearly identical* to the archetype in the writer's mind. In other words, what we hear or read must be what was spoken or written, it must have the same meaning and weight for all of us as it has for the speaker or the writer, and we must all agree to be governed by that shared sense of meaning. To deny that shared sense of meaning, that semantic kinship, is to make many kinds of civilized interaction nearly impossible.

We've already seen the effect it had in Judge Cronin's court. The power to rule on these kinds of semantic distinctions in legal writing is the essential power of judges, and the source of most of their idiosyncratic influences. A jurist such as Judge Cronin, whose record in these matters suggests an agenda regarding drug prosecutions rather at variance to the assumptions and expressed wishes of the people of Canada, can quite literally stand the meaning of a law on its head.

Yet the fact is that each of those concepts will have profoundly varying meanings for each individual. What is "reasonable" to me may seem deranged to you, or self-destructive, or immoral (whatever *that* means). The degree to which I know violence may differ from that kind of *knowing* of violence you may possess. You may be a victim of a rape or a mugging or a criminal assault. While I have been involved in several physical confrontations in connection with my work, I have so far managed to avoid serious injury. So my understanding of injury is limited to a combination of my objective observations and my ability to extrapolate from my personal experiences.

But for the victim of something like rape, that kind of *knowing* will be searing, devastating, profound, complete and lifelong. That is an entirely different level of *knowing*.

Again, the matter of obscenity. Were Mapplethorpe's pictures of "deviant love" obscene, or were they daringly and brilliantly expanding? One man's obscenity is another man's recreation.

On the other hand, we all share many identical concepts of obscenity, don't we?

Let's test that.

The riots in Los Angeles and in Toronto?
The Rodney King beating?
Taping the Rodney King beating?
Jane Fonda ratting out American POWs in Hanoi?
Jane Fonda in an exercise video?
Jimmy Swaggart in a cheap motel?
Jimmy Swaggart on television later, seeking forgiveness?
Charles Keating Jr. and Lincoln Savings and Loan?
The Satanic Verses?
Dudley Laws?
The Gulf War?
The Reverend Al Sharpton?
Lifestyles of the Rich and Famous?
Sam Kinnison?
Jeffrey Dahmer?
Payments to Clifford Olsen?
Abortions?
Unwanted pregnancies?
State-controlled abortion panels?
Clarence Thomas?
Necklacing in South Africa?
Winnie Mandela?
The Delta of Venus?
The Kids in the Hall?
Crack-addicted babies?
Drive-by shootings?
Jesus of Montreal?
Mark Lépine of Montreal?
Francophone teenaged sign-police?
Black kids looting downtown Halifax?
White cops trying to arrest black kids in Halifax?
A crucifix in a jar of urine?
A photograph of a crucifix in a jar of urine?

The point of this exercise is to illustrate how far apart we can all be on any subject, and yet how vital it is to agree. And how crucial to our agreement, to our ability to live together, is a sense of semantic kinship, and beyond that, a willingness to share semantic kinship.

The truth of it is that we do share in a deep and broad sense of familial connectedness. It's a wonderful enigma that most of us do have a pretty good idea of what is meant by "reasonable" or "probable" or "knowingly." The mistake many of us make is in confusing our difficulty in describing these intellectual sensations with the sensations themselves.

A man may see a person walking a block ahead of him in the street, walking away, and somehow know instantly who the person is—by something indefinable in the walk or the carriage. But if you ask this man to tell you the process, the internal cognitive and perceptual calculations made, he will not be able to describe them. One of the hardest things for humans to do is to think about thinking; if we consider our thoughts carefully, we know only that somehow we have come to know.

Someone who can surf will have a hell of a time explaining *how* he surfs—how the board feels, how he *knows* that rising and rushing away—how he *knows* how to cut back and ride out and hit the rails—but he will know he knows, and anyone watching will know that he knows.

This kind of knowing, this sense of semantic and experienced kinship, has been called, by the philosopher Michael Polanyi, "tacit knowledge." Tacit Knowledge is one of the fundamental dynamics of the practice of law.

The more a legislator attempts to tighten a definition of a crime or an omission or a rule, the greater danger there is that he will destroy or severely limit the tacit knowledge we all share about law.

William of Ockham once said that "entities should not be multiplied without reason." The maxim, which has come to be known as Ockham's Razor, is perhaps more colloquially reflected in the phrase "Keep It Simple Stupid." Or…"If it ain't broke, don't fix it."

The more we attempt to define something, the greater the

possibility of confusion. The more complex a mechanism for defining something, the greater the possibility of a breakdown.

Judges I have spoken with have said, not for attribution, that they quite frequently *know* very early in a trial what is the right, the just, disposition in a case. They do not know how they know, but they know that they know. They spend the rest of the trial trying to find a legal justification for what their intuition is telling them to do. (A damned good argument for making bloody well certain that we choose our judges very carefully!)

Jurors have said the same, as have lawyers for the defence and for the prosecution. And cops.

This intuitive sense of what is the right course arises from a shared body of experience and a shared worldview of right and wrong behavior. At least, one hopes that it does.

One of the fundaments of intuition is "tacit knowing," that kind of knowing that escapes a detailed explanation or analysis—in fact, quite frequently dissipates into smoke and incoherence if an explanation is attempted. The drafters of legislation who are wise will trust this intuitive, tacit knowing. Fools and scoundrels—and certain types of lawyers—use this suppleness of the law to confound it. They pretend—for the sake of the argument at hand—not to share this tacit knowing. This is a kind of rhetorical aikido. They use the power and weight of their opponent to overthrow the argument.

Lawyers who do this willingly and frequently ought to be aware that Dante has reserved a special circle of Hell for those who deliberately degrade language. (Politicians and ad writers ought to note this as well.)

Although there may be a transitory advantage gained by the tactic (a case won or stolen, a man in jail or set free), the cumulative effect of the denial of tacit knowing is to force the men and women who draft laws into an escalating cycle of semantic complexity.

This phenomenon of legal prolixity (which creates an ever-tightening coil of rules, definitions, subclauses, defining clauses, exceptions, inclusions), this Laocoön of involuted logic and opaque syntax, has been addressed by Wittgenstein in his Paradox On Rules.

Wittgenstein held that any attempt at "unearthly or superhuman precision" was doomed to failure, that without a recognition of the subtlety of knowing and the difficulty of defining what is known, no rules were possible at all.

You will have an intuitive—a tacit—understanding of this at once. The more detailed your attempt to describe this internal sensation, however, the more obscure your insight will seem. This elusive dynamic is a consequence of brain-wiring, of the instantaneous Gestalt that is thought. It seems we can't catch ourselves in the act of thinking, but only in recognizing that we have thought and that, by some quite marvelous necromancy, we have been presented with a perception. Integrating these perceptions into a coherent whole—an opinion or a judgement—is a process that is extremely vulnerable to experience and the coloration of personality. In order to carry on business with our neighbors and friends and lovers, we learn to accept the loss of precision and the subtle alterations of meaning that are the subtext of any communication. We accept the compromise in clarity in order to reach an approximate agreement regarding the essence of the communication.

You can see this happening in a conversation between married couples or in long-term friendships: a thought begun by one and finished by another, nonverbal cues, a quality of look and posture, shorthand historical references, brevity but complete understanding. What they actually say is only an element in their nearly perfect communication. They share a semantic and experientail kinship that sustains their relationship. That may actually *be* their relationship.

A sure sign of incipient trouble between friends and partners is the phrase "That's not what I meant" or "You're not listening." Of course the partner is listening, if we're talking about the biomechanical function of hearing. What has been withdrawn is their tacit agreement to accept the subtext, to share in the process of understanding. Maybe that's why everybody hates lawyers, because they withhold that kind of agreement for a living. That is in itself a demonstration of Wittgenstein's Paradox.

Wittgenstein's Paradox is what you inevitably run up against if you violate the principle of Ockham's Razor, and nowhere is this limitation more evident, and more destructive, than in the law.

Essentially, Wittgenstein's point is that rules alone, analyzed as logical constructs compelling or forbidding certain types of thought or behavior, can never mean anything. (In this, I suppose, he had an intuition of Deconstruction.) Without the element of tacit knowing, all rules are empty, because all language can be said to be empty unless we agree to infer the same meaning from the visual code of letters.

And the more complex and prolix laws become, the less they can compel, until finally the law becomes something like a Piranesi drawing, an intricate and shadow-laden antiquity full of cul-de-sacs and oubliettes where nothing lives and no one moves and no light ever comes. (Sort of like Revenue Canada.)

Language, without our agreement to understand it, is just sound and fury. Laws drafted in an attempt to pin down precisely the evanescence of human nature are doomed to strangle. This is what is meant by the conflict between the *spirit* of the law and the *letter* of the law.

In the modern age, much evil is done by men and women who deny tacit knowing and extract every inch of advantage from the letter of the law. We have all heard politicians say, "Well, I did nothing *illegal,* or "I made a *mistake.*" This kind of argument is a deliberate denial of tacit knowing and does great damage, not to the law alone, but to the membrane of shared sensibilities that binds us all together and makes things such as marriages, friendships and civilized societies possible.

To deliberately degrade or manipulate this unspoken agreement for a transitory advantage is to be truly criminal. Children and teenagers do it all the time, which is why we limit their responsibilities and powers. Yet this kind of manipulation, this intentional distortion of the spirit of the law, is what lawyers do, and is, in fact, what our system of justice compels them to do. It's quite literally their job to fail to understand what the framers of any law actually meant.

So you can see how important it is to have some kind of legislative control over the judicial system, over the activities of lawyers and judges.

Well, we don't.

Our two justice systems have created a cadre of men and women who operate outside the democratic principles upon which our nations are based. It was not always thus, but it's thus in spades right now. For example, in the drug courts, judges are doing pretty much whatever the hell they please, in spite of the fact that we spend billions a year fighting what we laughably call "The Drug War."

But that's another story. I'll get to it in a while. First I think we have to look at the courts themselves, in order to fully appreciate how isolated they have become.

SIX

Askov

Before we set out on this journey, there are a couple of things you need to get ready for. The first is that you're going to have to wade through a lot of legal transcripts, and the reason you're going to have to do that is because I don't want to be sued into penury by a pissed-off judge or a cranky defence counsel, and the only way I can avoid that is to make sure that you have a clear idea of the precise elements of any legal decision that I am ripping up and throwing across the room.

Why?

Because of Fleming on Torts.

Fleming said this about fair comment:

> Fair comment on matters of public interest is deemed of such surpassing social importance in a democratic community as to outweigh the competing claim to unqualified protection of individual reputation... [But]...for the defence to be available...the opinion stated is based on facts actually presented, or in fact present to the mind of the readers or listeners, so that they may be in a position to judge whether it is such that might fairly be formed on the facts. The sting of the allegation is, of course, largely minimized if the reader is given an opportunity to form his own judgement on whether the suggested inference is supported by the facts proferred...

Well, you get the idea. Fleming goes on at some length, but the essence of the matter is that unless I place the exact words of the judge in front of you at the same time that I make my comments, some lawyer is certain to argue that I have libeled his auntie and waved my privates at his reputation and then set himself about the task of driving my family naked into the blizzard and hauling me off to Newgate wrapped in heavy chains.

The second reason I have quoted many of these documents at length is that otherwise you'd never believe what passes for logical thought and honest discourse in our nation's courtrooms.

So I'll try to make it as interesting as I can.

As we go down this tunnel, I want everybody to hold hands and hang on to these two principles: Polanyi's theory of tacit knowing and Wittgenstein's Paradox on Rules.

Let's see how much trouble we can all get into if we decide to screw around with just one word in just one subsection of the Charter. Let's pick the word "reasonable," as we find it in Paragraph 11, Subsection (b) of the Charter of Rights and Freedoms. You'll recall that Paragraph 11 deals with the rights of a person charged with an offence. Subsection (b) reads: "to be tried within a reasonable time."

Sounds fair, right?

Forming that clause must have given the lawmakers a warm, cuddly feeling. It's such a Mom-and-apple-pie issue, isn't it? I mean, we don't want people languishing in the oubliettes or pining for justice swift and condign, do we?

Of course not. Just ask Elijah Anton Askov and his buddies, Ralph Hussey, Sam Gugliotta and Eddie Melo.

Once upon a time, in a land far away, there lived a businessman by the name of Peter Belmont. He was a very nice businessman who wanted everyone to be happy. One of the ways he made people happy was by giving them nice things to look at. The nice things that Mr. Belmont wanted people to be happy looking at were lots and lots of female naughty-bits.

Up close and personal, as it were.

Mr. Belmont was in the business of supplying strippers and table-dancers to various peeler bars in Quebec. He was making a nice living at it and he decided, in the fullness of time and the fatness of his wallet, to expand his service into Ontario.

Now there lived in this province, in the magical Kingdom of Brampton-on-Peel, a young man by the name of Eddie Melo, who was also a very nice man who wanted to make people happy by giving them lots of naughty girls to look at from real close up while quaffing watered-down beer and torquing huge amounts of their paychecks in sleazoid suburban bars.

When Mr. Eddie Melo heard that a foreign princeling from a faraway land was trying to bring his own young ladies into town, Mr. Eddie became unhappy.

Mr. Eddie went to his friends Elijah Askov and Ralph Hussey and Sammie Gugliotta and asked them what they thought he should do about this stranger in their midst. They all thought very hard about it until drops of blood appeared on their foreheads and they had to go lie down.

After a few hours of rest, they decided, well, shucks, why don't we just go to see Mr. Belmont? We'll tell him that he has made us unhappy and that he can make us happy again by agreeing to share the money he will make by bringing in pretty young girls with neat naughty-bits to Ontario for guys to look at very closely while sipping tankards of watery beer.

And that is what they did.

But Mr. Belmont did not play fair. Mr. Belmont went to the evil Sheriff of Toronto, who said, Hey, that's not right, and the evil Sheriff gave Mr. Belmont a bodyguard disguised as a chauffeur who was *really* a police officer.

That was not very nice.

It was not nice because one night when Mr. Belmont and his bodyguard were visiting a tavern in Concord, Ontario, they were followed by Mr. Eddie and his friends. When Mr. Belmont and his driver left the bar and drove away, Mr. Eddie and Mr. Askov and Mr. Hussey were worried that something might happen to them on the way home, so they drove alongside Mr. Belmont's car and forced it to the side of the road. Then they got out and walked over to the car to show Mr. Belmont and his driver the shiny new knives and sawed-off guns they had purchased from a local wizard.

But the evil Sheriff had the place surrounded, and lots and lots of the evil Sheriff's men came out of the bushes and refused to listen to reason and took away the shiny new guns and knives and placed heavy chains and various restraints on Mr. Eddie and his friends and thusly bundled them off unto the local dungeon, wherein they languished many weeks, since the evil Sheriff persuaded the evil Judge to refuse them bail, and all because they had some petty rules about the public wavings-about of shotguns and knives and suchlike items of the wizardly craft.

Now you may be wondering how these trivial matters came to

the attention of the Nine Wise Guys who dwelt in the Castle of
the Supreme Court in the far-off and fabled land of OTTA-
WAH, which was many leagues distant from the Kingdom of
Brampton-on-Peel, where these events had unfolded.

Bestir thee not, and cease to mutter, especially you in the
back there. All shall be revealed.

I have obtained, through investigative necromancy beyond the
ken of mere civilians, a copy of the judgement rendered by the
Nine Wise Guys from the land of OTTA-WAH.

I'll let *them* explain it to you.

THE SUPREME COURT OF CANADA
ELIJAH ANTON ASKOV, RALPH HUSSEY, SAMUEL
  GUGLIOTTA and EDWARD MELO
v.
HER MAJESTY THE QUEEN

CORAM:
The Rt. Hon. Brian Dickson, PC
The Rt. Hon. Antonio Lamer, PC
The Hon. Mme Justice Wilson
The Hon. Mr. Justice La Forest
The Hon. Mme Justice L'Heureux-Dubé
The Hon. Mr. Justice Sopinka
The Hon. Mr. Justice Gonthier
The Hon. Mr. Justice Cory
The Hon. Mme Justice McLachlin
Appeal heard: March 23, 1990
Judgement rendered: October 18, 1990
Reasons for Judgement by:
  The Hon. Mr. Justice Cory

Now I'm not going to type out the whole damned thing, but
I'll cite the relevant passages. You'll get the idea. Herewith,
from Cory:

It is necessary to set out the proceedings following the arrest in
  some detail. The appellants Melo, Askov and Hussey, were

initially denied bail. They were detained in custody for almost six months. On May 7, 1984, they were each ordered to be released on a recognizance of $50,000. Gugliotta was released on December 2, 1983, shortly after his arrest on a recognizance of $20,000. The terms of the release for all the appellants involved reporting to the police and abstention from communication with their co-accused. These conditions were varied from time to time to permit more freedom of movement for the appellants. All the applications which were made for more lenient bail conditions were granted. Nonetheless, the appellants remained under considerable restraint.

[Sounds like a good idea to me...]

Askov was re-arrested on an unrelated charge on October 1, 1984.

[naughty naughty...]

With three of the accused in custody, the Crown, in a commendable manner, was prepared as soon as December 1983 to set an early date for the preliminary hearing.

This is important. The *Askov* decision is all about *unreasonable* delay of trial...

However, *at the request of the appellants* [emphasis added] the matter was put over to February 14, 1984...

Delaying a trial is a standard defence tactic. Witnesses die, files get lost, memories fade, the blood dries, the media get bored...

...when all counsel agreed on a date in the first week of July for the preliminary hearing to be held. *At this time it was specifically indicated that an earlier date could be arranged if a request was made by the appellants* [emphasis added], but none was forthcoming.

When the preliminary hearing commenced on July 4, 1984, it
could not be completed because another preliminary had been
set for a later day in the same week. As a result, the
preliminary hearing could not be completed until September
21, 1984, some ten months after the arrests.

On October 1, 1984, the appellants appeared before Judge
Keenan presiding in the assignment court. A trial date was set
for the first available date, which was October 15, 1985, more
than a year away and nearly two years from the date of the
initial arrests.

A few things to point out here: defence *always* demands a
trial even if they intend to plead guilty, because sometimes the
witnesses don't appear on the trial date and defence can then
demand a trial knowing Crown cannot make the case without
witnesses. And most defence lawyers routinely double- or triple-
book clients on a given day so that when a case is called forward
it has to be postponed because defence is somewhere else in the
building. When they are called before the judge, they explain
that they were detained in another court, failing to mention that
they knew damned well it would happen. Another delay. Only
innocent people truly want a speedy trial and a fair hearing.

Despite what seems far too lengthy a delay, an earlier date
could not be set due to other cases which had priority…

[Other cases involving the accused…]

…because the accused was in custody or because the offence
date was earlier than that of the case at bar.

[The various accused were busy being criminals and were
complicating the picture with other legal delaying tactics…]

On October 25, 1985, when it was apparent that the case
simply could not be heard during that session, counsel for the
appellants and the Crown appeared and the case was put over
for trial to September 2, 1986.

Now this is the crux. While defence claims to want a fair and speedy trial, they have just passed by their second opportunity to insist on an earlier date. Both times, they held their tongues and agreed to another delay. Why? Read on.

When the trial finally began on that date, counsel for the appellants moved to stay the proceedings on the grounds that the trial had been unreasonably delayed.

[In violation of Para 11, subs. (b) of the Charter…]

Fast forward here…it went from there to an Appeal court. The Stay Petition was denied by the Appeal Court, which noted as follows:

The Court of Appeal found that perhaps the most important factor in reaching its decision that there had been no breach of the Charter was the conduct of the appellants when the final adjournment was granted and the last trial date set. At that time, although some of the appellants announced that they were ready to proceed on the first scheduled date, not any of them objected to the one-year adjournment and no allegation that any prejudice had been suffered as a result of the delay was advanced. In the opinion of the Court of Appeal the appellants should have objected to this delay, even if they thought such an objection was futile.

And we have not been shown that it would have been futile. As a matter of process, cases *can* be shuffled to suit defence if the defence squeals loud enough.

It was found that the silence seemed to be a deliberate move aimed at concealing the intentions of the appellants to seek the Charter-based remedy of a stay later in the proceedings.

Sounds reasonable, right? Not to the Supreme Court it didn't…Cory went on to make these points:

Although the primary aim of s. 11 (b) (THE CHARTER) is the protection of the individual's rights…there is a community or societal interest…a collective interest in ensuring that those who transgress the law are brought to trial and dealt with…there are as well important practical benefits which flow from a quick resolution of the charges. There can be no doubt that memories fade with time. Witnesses are likely to be more reliable testifying to events in the immediate past…it can never be forgotten that the victims may be devastated by criminal acts. They have a special interest and good reason to expect that criminal trials take place within a reasonable time…all members of the community are thus entitled to see that justice works fairly, efficiently, and with reasonable…

[There's that word again…]

…dispatch…the trial not only resolves the guilt or innocence of the individual, but acts as a reassurance to the community that serious crimes are investigated and that those implicated are brought to trial and dealt with according to the law.

[So far so good. Every word a jewel of reason…]

…Further, implicit support for the concept that there is a societal aspect to s. 11 (b) can be derived from the observation that the last thing that some wish for is a speedy trial.

[Even Cory recognizes this…]

…This factor was noted by T.G. Zuber in his REPORT of the ONTARIO COURTS INQUIRY (1987) at page 73:
"It is however the observation of this inquiry that those accused of crime and their counsel are often disinterested in trial within a reasonable time…"

[Cory also cites Doherty on this…]

"…It hardly enhances the reputation of the administration of
justice when an accused escapes a trial on the merits NOT
because he was wronged in any real sense, but rather because
he successfully played the waiting game."

Cory states this clearly, and then goes on to render a judgement that makes it possible for thousands of criminals to do precisely that. He does so by arguing that silence is not a waiver of
rights, and that the Peel regional courts are the most badly back-
logged in the nation, which is true.

In a sense, his decision to uphold the Charter defence here
seems intended as a rebuke to a court region he perceives as
inefficient. If that was his intent, the consequences were rather
more widespread.

…I am well aware that as a consequence of this decision, a
stay of proceedings must be directed. This is, to say the least,
most unfortunate and regrettable. It is obvious that the
charges against the appellants are serious. Extortion and
threatened armed violence tears at the basic fabric of society.
The community has good reason to be alarmed by the
commission of serious crimes.

Some people more than others. I don't think there's much
chance that members of the Ontario Supreme Court would try to
muscle in on the Supreme Court of Canada's territory, and if
they did, I doubt they'd use a sawed-off shotgun as part of the
attempt. Cory can afford to take the long view here, since his
butt is very well protected. Unlike yours and mine.

There can be no doubt that it would be in the best interest of
society to proceed with the trial of those who are charged with
posing such serious threat to the community.

[Speaking of well-protected butts, here comes that *but* we
were waiting for…well, actually, it's a *yet*.]

Yet, that trial can only be undertaken if the CHARTER right to trial within a reasonable time has not been infringed. In this case, it has been grievously infringed and the sad result is that a stay of proceedings must be entered. To conclude otherwise would render meaningless a right enshrined in the CHARTER as the supreme law of the land...

Cory goes on to dismiss the idea that defence was maneuvering for a Stay by Charter ruling...

...The appellants certainly neither took nor were responsible for any direct action...

[Other than the normal defence tactics previously cited...]

...that caused the subsequent two-year delay which is in itself unacceptable. Therefore, the question of delay as a consequence of direct acts of the appellants need not be considered...The complete transcript also reveals that there was no evidence to even support a finding that the appellants had a concealed plan to wait until the delay was unreasonable before complaining or bringing a motion...the onus always rests with the Crown to establish that a delay was occasioned by direct actions of the accused as in CONWAY or that the actions of the accused manifested a deliberate or calculated tactic undertaken to delay the trial.

An interesting statement. Cory knows full well that all defence lawyers routinely employ delaying tactics before coming to trial, but he seems confident that these delays were not specifically intended to create the grounds for a Charter Stay. How he accomplished this telepathic feat he does not say. He is right, however, in his contention that it is up to the Crown to bring forward such an allegation and to prove it beyond a reasonable doubt—a practical impossibility, since it requires the defence counsel to assist in their own prosecution.

Cory ends with this comforting prediction:

The foregoing review indicates that there is no basis upon

which this delay can be justified and, as a result, a stay of proceedings must be directed. Courts may frequently be requested to take such a step.

[No shit, Your Honor—just watch!]

Fortunately, Professor Baar's work…

Carl Baar, a professor at Brock University, had filed a paper stating that the delays at Peel Region were not typical of the rest of the nation, so Cory felt safe in establishing a precedent that he felt no one could manipulate to his advantage. He was dead wrong.

…indicates that most regions of this country are operating within reasonable and acceptable…

[Those words again. Remember your Polanyi and your Wittgenstein.]

…time limits with the result that such relief will be infrequently granted…

[*Hah!*]

However, in situations such as this where the delay is extensive and beyond justification there is no alternative but to direct a stay of proceedings.

Thus spake Cory and the rest of the Nine Wise Guys, with variations on the theme. Essentially their position was that the Charter guarantees a speedy trial, and that the ultimate authority on the degree of speed that is reasonable is the Supreme Court of Canada. This is interesting, since the framers of the law are, one assumes, legislators, yet the final arbiters of what the legislators actually meant are the nine members of the Supreme Court of Canada—none of whom are elected, all of whom serve until they go ga-ga and none of whom live in your neighborhood.

Is it just me, or are any of you finding it hard to breath?

Well, was Cory right? Or did there follow hard upon his coat-tails a flurry of Charter Stay Pleas under *Askov?*

Well, that depends on how you define the word "flurry."

How does the figure 75,000 strike you? In the months immediately following the *Askov* decision, there were at least 75,000 cases before the nation's criminal courts that were either Stayed under *Askov* or voluntarily withdrawn by nervous Crowns because the accumulated delays were approaching the rather vague deadline defined imperfectly as unreasonable. These cases included charges of rape, aggravated assault, drug-trafficking, theft, extortion, armed robbery—you name it, they Stayed it.

Is that a flurry? Or a blizzard?

Whatever you call it, it involved a lot of legal snow and a hell of a lot of shoveling. Obviously, somebody goofed *big time.*

Was it Cory and the rest of the Nine Wise Guys from Ottawa? They don't think so.

As far as the Supreme Court is concerned, "they seen their duty and they done it." If as a consequence a whole boatload of wharf-rats and cockroaches saw daylight and scrambled out of the bag, that's just the price we all pay for having a jim-dandy new piece of legislation like the Charter and a Supreme Court as vigilant and rigorous in defence of…

…in defence of…

…well, surely not Askov et al., at least not directly.

No, let's say vigilant in defence of *freedom!*

Yeah, that's the ticket! Freedom, and Due Process and all that neat stuff that people say they want until something goes haywire and they end up in front of a judge and suddenly what they want is anything but Due Process and a speedy trial.

Well, that's not their problem, is it?

If you don't like the Charter, you can write your Member of Parliament and she'll say, Well by neddy-jingo, looky what we have here! A letter from one of my constituents who thinks the Supreme Court has its head stuffed up its pantleg, and he'd like me to go back to the House and *get something done about it!*

And the MP will see to it that the constituent gets a black-

and-white glossy—personally autographed—and a snappy form-letter on real nice bond—and an orange and a Christmas card later—but not much else will happen because the MP is up to her garters in *more important business*.

I have obtained from a highly placed police source—who shall remain nameless because he's bigger than me—a *confidential report*—God, how I love saying things like that—that details just some of the consequences of the *Askov* decision. It is not meant for your eyes—not much is meant for your eyes in this country— but I think you'll find it diverting.

Let me read you the best bits...

AN ESTIMATE OF OUR COSTS FOR PREPARING CASES THAT MAY NOW BE AT RISK FOR WITHDRAWAL OR HAVE ALREADY BEEN LOST

On the face of it this question is most easily answered by determining the number of cases on the books beyond a certain age since the method commonly accepted for determining if a case is in danger of being lost is the length of time required to bring the matter to trial. This in itself creates a problem however as there has been no definitive interpretation of the time frame implied by the ASKOV decision. The parameters used vary not only from region to region and court to court, but from Judge to Judge.

The commonly accepted date has been widely held to be in the vicinity of eight months and this is the time often quoted in the popular press. But there are examples on a weekly basis of cases which have been within the system for in excess of two years that Judges at the General Court have refused to stay.

Even if an arbitrary date is assigned the above question is difficult to answer in a specific concrete fashion owing to the manner by which cases are tracked in the [CENSORED] region—

The [CENSORED] computer system considers the inception of a case to be the date that an Information is sworn. As a result the computer does not give a proper representation of the

status of a case in the spirit of the ASKOV decision…
because the date an Information is sworn often has no relation
to its status before the court. For instance, if a police officer,
in the course of an investigation, decides that it is appropriate
to obtain a warrant in the first instance, the officer must swear
the Information prior to obtaining the warrant…

[Which starts the *Askov* clock…]

…in spite of the fact that it may take literally months or years
to execute the warrant…

Most criminals dislike warrants and tend to bug out fast if a
cop shows up at the front door with a warrant in his hand. That's
why we have cops—to catch guys who don't want to be arrested
on a warrant.

…but the case will be shown by the computer to have dragged
on since the date the Information was sworn…The following
statistics have been supplied by the Attorney General
regarding cases dated from the swearing of an Information to
the projected trial date in the [CENSORED] region:

Under 8 months	over 8	total
34,704	19,024	53,728

The Crown's office at the General level states that there are
virtually no cases now in danger of being lost under ASKOV,
[but] even taking into account the possibility that the Attorney
General's statistics may be somewhat inaccurate…

[Being stats, they usually are…]

…it would be a safe and conservative estimate that, as of
March 1, 1991, there are in excess of ten thousand cases in
danger of being lost under ASKOV.
Once again, it must be underlined that there is no safe
defensible length of time required by officers to complete

cases. However it is not implausible to state that each case will take a minimum of three man hours to complete. This takes into account typing, statement taking, and the general organization of the required reports.

Detectives in the [CENSORED] police force are paid at the rate of approximately $26.00 per hour. There is an equal or greater number of Detective Constables preparing cases for trial. They are paid at the rate of approximately $24.00 per hour.

Therefore it is a safe presumption to state that the ABSOLUTE MINIMUM cost to the Force for preparing cases in danger of being lost (under ASKOV) is ($25 x 3 hours x 10,000 cases): $750,000.

Using the same rule of thumb the approximate cost to the Force…

[A large municipal force…]

…for preparing cases which have already been lost between 22 October 1990…

[Four days after *Askov* came down]

…and 15 February 1991 is (approximately 4,500 stayed criminal cases x 3 hours x $25) is: $337,500, for a total cost to this Force alone of: $1,870,000
as a result of the ASKOV decision.

CHART TWO:
CATEGORIES OF OFFENCES WITHDRAWN—ALL COURTS WITHIN THE FORCE'S AREA OF OPERATION FROM 22 OCTOBER 1990 TO FEBRUARY 15, 1991:

Type of Offence	Number Stayed
Administration of Law	195
Breach of Court	318
Driving Offences	130
Impaired	1,368
Assault	611

Extensive Assault	164
Sexual Assault	41
Sexual Offences	79
Theft Under $1,000	562
Theft Over $1,000	204
Fraud	353
Nuisance/Mischief	321
Conspiracy	2
Break and Enter	198
Firearms Offences	142
Drug Possession	71
Trafficking	50
Prostitution	24
Forcible Confinement	3
Other Criminal Offences	174

Approximate number of officers affected by ASKOV: 10,180 officers.

An additional consumer of court time is the common defence tactic of demanding a trial even when they have the intention of pleading guilty. On the trial date they (defence) wait to see if all the required witnesses appear. If all the witnesses turn up a guilty plea is entered. If some witnesses do not appear, defence demands a trial, knowing that the Crown is not in a position to prove the charge...

The recent ASKOV decision appears to have removed much of the motivation that ever was present for the defence to come to an early resolution of the matter. All parties are now aware that if a trial can be delayed beyond a certain...

[And entirely arbitrary]

...point, the case will be stayed under ASKOV.

Contributing to this is a sense of uncertainty many people feel in the court system about what the specific application of the ASKOV decision is. There seems to be no clear-cut definitive interpretation among Provincial Court Judges about what the implications of the decision are, or even if it applies to their courts. This sense of uncertainty carries over to Crown and defence. There is no delineation between what will be continued and what will be stayed, so all but the most flagrant cases are being argued in court.

Another cause of delays has been the lack of dependable interpreters for some of the less common languages that have turned up in [CENSORED] in the recent past. An accused person has the right to a trial with an interpreter. Unfortunately, there have been instances where an accused has assured the arresting officers that he is comfortable in English, but the trial Judge has not been satisfied and the case has been delayed until a suitable interpreter could be found.

There are some languages spoken...for which there are virtually no authorized interpreters or the ones that are recognized are undependable and do not appear in court on the appointed date.

There have also been instances where persons quite capable of speaking English have suddenly demanded interpreters. As already mentioned they have a constitutional right to do so, and the case is delayed again.

A prominent local jurist has also directed that the cases heard in her court which are not resolved on the trial date will be brought back on a day to day basis instead of the weeks or months that were common practice in the past. This may dissuade the defence tactic of delaying cases in an attempt to trigger an ASKOV argument...Another of her directives is that henceforth prisoners will not be brought into bail court until their defence counsel is present...this means that the time-consuming practices of the past, where accused persons were brought from the cells when no counsel was present, will end.

The Attorney General directed each Crown to review all outstanding charges to identify appropriate cases for withdrawal. The guidelines list a series of less serious criminal offences and two tests that must be given.

What's happening here is that Cory's *Askov* decision has had the effect of a de facto decriminalization of the following offences, something he did not foresee:

FAILURE TO COMPLY

BREACH OF PROBATION

  Kind of undermines the power of a probation order...

CAUSE A DISTURBANCE

FALSE PRETENSES

  So start writing those rubber checks...

FRAUD ACCOMMODATION

MISCHIEF UNDER $1,000

  Calling all vandals!

THEFT UNDER $1,000

  Calling all petty thieves!

JOYRIDING

  Calling all car thieves!

POSSESSION OF NARCOTICS UNDER $1,000

  Attention Drug-Dealers!

FRAUD UNDER $1,000

SOME SIMPLE ASSAULTS

These charges are being de-emphasized as a direct consequence of *Askov*. Too many cases equal delays and delays can lead to an *Askov* plea, so Crowns have to cut their caseload, and this is where they start.

Where they'll finish, no one knows.

Certainly not Justice Cory et al.

What this all boils down to is that our Supreme Court took a legal decision that had far-reaching and entirely unforeseen consequences. Thousands of rapists and drug-dealers and car-thieves and check-bouncers and window-smashers and back-alley muggers and vandals and myriad varieties of criminal scumsacks walked into hundreds of courtrooms across the nation and grinned hugely as their counsels asked for and got the charges thrown out entirely, and it also means that at least an equal number of victims, people who had been raped or assaulted or whose car had been wrecked or who had been thumped senseless in an alleyway, had the unique privilege of sitting at the back of the courtroom and watching the guy who did it walk away on what must have seemed like a trivial technicality.

The victims were then, one supposes, left alone in the court-room to ponder the value of their citizenship and the esteem—or lack of it—in which they are held by the highest courts of the land.

And since we're counting, we have seen that the *Askov* decision cost at least one large Canadian police department over one million dollars in wasted payroll, and it took up the time and brought down the morale of at least ten thousand police officers and detectives in that department alone.

Now, how many departments are there across Canada?

I think it's safe to say that Justice Cory's little miscalculation in the matter of *Askov* has cost Canada one hell of a lot more money than he could earn in the rest of his lifetime.

By the way, why is it that nobody seems to think that damaging the morale of a police officer is a bad thing to do? I mean, think about it. The next time you wake up in the middle of the night because you've heard someone slamming around downstairs and you go down to look and there's a whacked-out, drugged-up hardcase ripping your VCR out of the wall-unit, who are you going to call for some help?

Not Justice Cory and the rest of his crowd.

And probably not a civil liberties lawyer.

You're gonna call a cop, right?

And when you do call him, you'll want him to come along pretty briskly, and to be enthusiastic and energetic on your behalf when he gets there.

Well, maybe we should stop working so hard convincing our cops that *they* are the bad guys, the ones who've got to be watched.

More on this later.

So *Askov* went sour and a hell of a lot of cases went belly-up and our sense of personal worth took another drop. None of which, I suspect, would have kept the Honorable Mr. Justice Cory and his cronies awake for longer than a few minutes. Because they were about a *higher business* than the protection of any individual victim. Victims are peripheral to their delibera-tions, not solely because the chances that one of them will be a victim are roughly equal to the chances that the French will repay their war debt, that the *Titanic* will sail into New York Harbor and that Joe Clark's testicles will ever descend.

No, it's more important than that.

They are defending the Charter.

And the Charter defends us all.

Well, at least, it defends those of us who get cranky and threatening over our right to earn money by making it possible for blue-collar wage-slaves to quaff watery beer and ogle the naughty-bits of women young enough to be their daughters.

So one can presume that there came a day not long ago in that far-off kingdom of Brampton-on-Peel that the word came from the fabled land of OTTA-WAH that the Nine Wise Guys had delivered themselves of a verdict.

Then was there much rejoicing deep in the dungeons of the Evil Sheriff of Toronto, and Mr. Eddie and his friends grew very big smiles and slapped each other on the back and went home to their little ones and the tumultuous applause of all the pretty young girls they owned.

And off they all skipped to their sleazoid bar to quaff watered-down beer, to munch on tasty snackies, to put their feet up on the tables and call for their jolly minstrels to strum and blat into their lutes and sackbuts, and they belched, and they farted, and they all settled down happily ever after to ogle the naughty-bits of a whole regiment of young ladies.

And the bad prince from faraway Montreal?

I guess he went back to Montreal and told all his friends that they'd better not fool around with Mr. Eddie and associates, no sirree!

And why not?

Because Mr. Eddie and his boys have friends in very high places indeed.

SEVEN

Rush to Judgements

Some of the more intuitive members of this expedition may have sensed by now that I bear just the *teensiest* bit of anger when it comes to these matters.

You're absolutely right.

Maybe this is a good time to provide you with one of my clip-out reference cards to keep with you until the next time you feel the boot on the back of your neck or find yourself bearing a fardel for a proud man. It's from an oath of allegiance sworn between the states of Aragon and Catalonia sometime around the twelfth century:

> We, who are as good as you,
> swear to you,
> who are no better than us,
> to accept you as our king and sovereign,
> provided you observe all our liberties
> and laws—
> but, if not,
> not.

I'd like to see this up in neon letters at the back of every courtroom in the world, where the judges and the lawyers could get a clear look at it as they went about their duties. Perhaps under a picture of Mussolini and Clara Petacci hanging from a lamppost.

So what have we seen?

We have seen that the Charter has placed judges above the wishes of the electorate.

Now, a simple question for all of us: How the hell did we get here?

It happened quite slowly and with inexorable legality, beginning with the *Marbury* decision of the United States Supreme Court. Justice theory, like acid rain, respects no borders. What flowers in the US will soon be causing allergic reactions in

Canada. The two systems are in a constant state of philosophical interaction. Looking at the United States is like looking at Canada ten years in the future.

So let's do that.

Since many of our judges in Canada are taking their cues about rights and Charter interpretations from the American Supreme Court, it's important to understand how the US and Canadian Supreme Courts achieved such an ascendancy over their legislatures, so much so that, in fact, these courts now sit in judgement upon all legislation and have become the Ultimate arena for the settlement of philosophical disputes about justice and freedom.

One of the reasons this ought to upset you will emerge as soon as you ask yourself, when was the last time *you* voted for a judge, or felt that you had *any* control at all over the appointment of a justice to the Supreme Court of Canada?

In the past twenty years, the power of legal language to alter the moral landscape of the United States (and, by a kind of cultural symbiosis, Canada) has been completely usurped by lawyers and consolidated at One First Street North East, Washington, DC. 20543, the current address of the United States Supreme Court—a body composed, by no coincidence whatsoever, of former lawyers. (For anyone who feels like calling them up and kicking around a few ideas for judicial reform, the number is 202-479-3000.)

Created by the Judiciary Act of September 24, 1789, under the auspices of Article Three, Section One of the Constitution, the United States Supreme Court is the ultimate court of appeal. Cases both criminal and civil are heard by this court *only* after every other legal venue has been exhausted. In general, the Supreme Court will agree to hear only cases that raise "substantial federal questions," or matters of law that require a learned interpretation of case law as it may be affected by one or more of the amendments to the Constitution. The Supreme Court justices stand *in loco parentis* to the people of America, incarnating the authority of the Founding Fathers of the country, and their interpretations of the correct applications of the amendments have a profound and frequently eternal effect on the lives of every citizen.

These men and women are the Cardinals of the Law. Theoretically, the People are the Pope.

Theoretically.

Intense political and factional combat inevitably arises over the appointment of Supreme Court justices (as anyone who was paying attention during the Clarence Thomas hearings will recall) because it is through the Supreme Court that a president leaves his mark on the nation. Interpretations of the law are just that: interpretations, matters of judgement and intuition, informed by study and experience, of course, but nevertheless fallible human judgements subject to all manner of outside pressures and influences.

Each justice has his or her body of private experience, a private sense of the *Zeitgeist* of the nation, that will color a response to a variety of forensic stimuli. The current US Court is said to be right-wing and authoritarian. Our own Court runs towards a kind of limousine-liberalism. Earlier Courts have made decisions that showed a concern for individual rights over the rights of the State, rather in harmony with Justice Holmes's maxim that the State should not play an ignoble part. Some of those decisions are worth knowing by heart if you want to understand why it seems to be so hard to get bad people into prisons for a long enough time to make an impression on them.

I'm concentrating on the US Supreme Court here for a couple of reasons: our Court follows the American Court by a ten-year lag, so looking south is like looking into a crystal-ball; and, our Court commands some respect in comparison because it shows—with the exception of some decisions around the Winnipeg Strike and the Japanese-Canadian population in 1941—some restraint and level-headedness. That's not to say they couldn't run wild; they just haven't yet.

The point of this exercise is to de-sanctify the court. Most of the reasons that ordinary people have such a deep and pervading respect for the Court have to do with a kind of collective amnesia about its decisions. Taking the long view, a sensible citizen will have no more respect for our courts than for our Houses of Parliament, especially since we have precisely the same kind of people running both: ex-lawyers.

So let's see what our best legal minds can get up to if you don't keep them on a tight leash.

First, the pivotal decision that started it all:

Marbury v. Madison (1803)

Referring to the Judiciary Act of 1789, Chief Justice John Marshall established the first precedent giving the US Supreme Court the power to overrule an Act of Congress. In a sense, *Marbury* took the power to "say what the law is" away from electoral representatives and delivered it into the hands of appointed lawyers.

In the intervening years, lawyers and judges have built upon this foundation to the extent that the modern edifice of the law now looks suspiciously like a fortress, where the brandy-snifting priests of law debate esoteric niceties in an atmosphere serenely and seraphically free from unruly intrusions on the part of the rabble.

Dred Scott v. Sanford (1857)

In a less-than-shining decision, the US Supreme Court upheld the right of an owner to own his slave even if he travels with him into a state declared "free" by an Act of Congress. The Supreme Court denied Dred Scott's appeal for freedom by ruling that the Missouri Compromise of 1820, which prohibited slavery in sections of the Louisiana Purchase, violated the Fifth Amendment rights of owners to their property, in this case the slave, Dred Scott. Scott was not allowed to sue because the Court held him to be property and not a citizen. The Fourteenth Amendment was Lincoln's response to this Supreme Court ruling, and one of the reasons for fighting the Civil War.

Dred Scott is presented here as a cautionary illustration for those people whose respect for the Supreme Court rests upon an imperfectly developed sense of history. Clearly, the Supreme Court of 1857 was, politically, a horse of a much different color, and ridden by some rather unsavory people.

Civil Rights Cases of 1883

This US Supreme Court decision ruled against the Civil Rights Act of 1875, allowing private individuals (club owners, hoteliers, head-waiters) to segregate their commercial and private holdings in defiance of the Fourteenth Amendment. The Court held that this Amendment applied only to state action and delivered no power to enforce integration in private transactions.

Segregation of various public sectors (courthouses, train-stations, public washrooms, buses, in particular segregated railroad cars in Louisiana) was given Supreme Court approval in *Plessy v. Ferguson* in 1896, a ruling that put the phrase "separate but equal" into the language. This decision by the Supreme Court effectively postponed racial equality for decades, until it was overturned in *Brown v. Board of Education* in 1954.

Schenk v. The United States (1919)

A draft-resister distributing pamphlets that suggested that the First World War was not a particularly good idea attracted the attention of the federal authorities. His attempt to use his constitutional protections under the First Amendment right to freedom of speech was set aside by the US Supreme Court, which ruled that the pamphlets represented "a clear and present danger" to the welfare and security of the United States. The Chief Justice in this case was Oliver Wendell Holmes. (In this instance, Holmes did not think it at all ignoble that someone's feeble attempt to propose alternate interpretations of an insanely murderous foreign adventure should be forcibly suppressed by the powers of the State.) Holmes added to this ruling in later decisions by suggesting that a simple "bad tendency" of certain writings or speeches to cause "a clear and present danger" was an adequate ground for censorship. The Supreme Court, of course, was the final arbiter of what constituted "a clear and present danger." It still is.

Korematsu v. The United States (1944)

Once again the Supreme Court came to the rescue of repressive powers by upholding Franklin Roosevelt's Executive Order Number 9066, which enforced the evacuation and internment of 120,000 Japanese-Americans (known as *Nisei*), on the grounds of "military necessity." In its defence, it ought to be pointed out that the Court did issue a ruling called *ex parte endo,* in which it suggested that persons who could prove their loyalty to the nation should not be interned. The Court reserved for itself the final right to decide who was loyal and who was not. Canada treated its Japanese-Canadians the same way, with much the same reaction from the Supreme Court.

Dennis v. The United States (1951)

In keeping with its historical role as "ballast for the ship of state," the US Supreme Court upheld the conviction of eleven American Communist Party members for belonging to an organization that proposed the "violent overthrow of the government." This ruling was mildly in conflict with *Schenk v. The United States* in that the American Communist Party of 1951 had about as much chance of violently overthrowing the government as a gaggle of rabid ducks, and therefore seemed hardly to constitute "a clear and present danger." This troublesome detail was handily finessed by the Court when it held that one could discount the actual probability of the overthrow and simply address the "gravity of the evil" proposed. This decision provided a quasi-legal basis for Senator Joe McCarthy's brief but memorable impersonation of Cotton Mather a few years later.

With *Brown v. Board of Education* in 1954, Chief Justice Earl Warren took the US Supreme Court in a new direction, using the powers of the Court to act as the protector of individual liberties, seen at the time as at jeopardy in many parts of the nation. Certainly, he was right in many decisions made in this era, and it is now possible to look at the Court without having one's appetite affected.

It *is* hard, rereading this brief history of a selection of US Supreme Court decisions, to say the words "The Majesty of the Law" without getting a near-fatal lip curl.

However, good intentions do not necessarily make good law, and many of the decisions of the Warren Court had far-reaching and, in some cases, disastrous repercussions in the nation's courts. Not, arguably, because the decisions were ill-founded or poorly taken.

Given some of the outrageous abuses during the mid-1960s in matters of race and religion, it was obvious that something had to be done. But, in accordance with the operations of Wittgenstein's Paradox, it was at this point that certain rulings began to come down that created opportunities for certain kinds of lawyers to block justice and impede sensible criminal prosecutions. (And, by the way, to bill whacking great hours of chargeable time.) The most problematic decisions were:

Gideon v. Wainwright (1963)

In this matter, the Court held that the Sixth Amendment guaranteed access to a lawyer and that this access should be swift and speedy since it was a right deemed to be fundamental to a fair trial. After *Gideon,* all the states were required to provide, free-of-charge, Public Defenders to any defendant who could not afford to retain an attorney. This provision was limited to felony cases, but in a later decision, *Argersinger v. Hamlin* (1972), the ruling was interpreted as extending to *any* case that *might* result in a term of imprisonment. This ruling was a good one, and few reasonable men or women would wish to see it curtailed. Especially in light of some of the Supreme Court's own rulings in the past. And, true to form, Canada soon followed this lead.

Escobedo v. Illinois (1964)

This ruling extended the right to counsel to apply to that time immediately after arrest when a prisoner is in the control of the arresting officers. *Escobedo* forced the police to allow lawyers to counsel their clients as soon as they came into the station-house. Any unreasonable delay was grounds for dismissal of the case—a tough rule, and subject to many abuses in the lower courts. But a nice tool for the defence. Again, Canada has in effect provided the same rights, after dithering on the issue for a few years.

Miranda v. Arizona (1966)

Rights under *Gideon* and *Escobedo* were greatly enhanced by this famous decision. Under *Miranda,* a case of rape, the Supreme Court ruled that Miranda's confession to kidnapping and rape was wrongfully obtained, in that the prisoner was not provided with a lawyer in the station-house, and not advised of his rights to remain silent (under the Fifth Amendment). The Supreme Court decided that Miranda's confession was therefore inadmissible as evidence, since it was, in a way, the "fruit of a poisoned tree." Apparently the Court could not eat of it without harm, and declined to hear it. Miranda's case made it obligatory for the police to give the now-classic Miranda Warning to all charged suspects. Again, Canada has followed this lead with its Charter Warnings and Cautions. The Miranda Warning, given to all charged suspects in the United States, reads as follows:

You have the right to remain silent. You have the right to an attorney. You do not have to answer questions. If you do decide to talk, anything you say can and will be taken down as evidence and used against you in a court of law. Do you understand these rights as I have explained them to you? Having heard and understood these rights, are you prepared to answer questions?

Miranda was a watershed decision, loosing a deluge of subsequent decisions that emphasized the supremacy of the rights of an accused person over every other consideration.

For example, the fact of Miranda's actions—the kidnapping and rape of a young woman—was clearly subordinated to the greater good of constitutional protections. For the first time in America, the rights of a victim to equal protection under the law were, by inference, somehow less important than the theoretical harm the State might suffer if it allowed a technically flawed confession to enter the court record as evidence. The effects of this decision on Miranda were obviously in his favor. The record does not note the effects of the decision on Miranda's victim.

We have now arrived in a *terra incognita,* the land of Wittgenstein, and we have reached it by way of Holmes's Olympian pronouncement that it is better that a criminal should escape than that the state should play an ignoble part.

Miranda was a momentous decision, not because the decision was a bad one, but because it is a quirk of human constructions that every moral act has many consequences in the web of society, and the end of every tremor in the web is not easily seen when at the first entanglement. Nor can we see who or what creatures in the web will react to our arrival.

In this case, the step taken was the moral judgement that Miranda's rights to a fair trial were more important than his victim's right to personal safety or, failing that, a sense of her own value as a human being and a cherished citizen of the United States. Not that Justice Warren would have seen it that way. No judge ever does. It is the burden and privilege of the Cardinals of Law to serve a Higher Good, the Rule of Law. Miranda's victim perhaps will take some comfort from her role as a kind of martyr, a sacrifice on the sacred altar of the justice system.

This is the linking element of all these Supreme Court decisions—in Canada as much as in the United States—that the fate of any single victim is not really the issue. The issue is that certain inalienable rights be protected at all costs. This position is made rather more palatable by the way in which the Supreme Court phrases its decisions.

This was *Miranda v. The State of Arizona,* not *Miranda v. Some Poor Fool Who Got in His Way.* Miranda's crime was not against a single woman. It was against the State. Therefore, it is up to the State to pursue its grievance against Miranda in a legal and proper manner, in accordance with the highest traditions of the justice system. It would not be fitting for the State to sink to Miranda's level.

This interpretation of crime, and in particular of Miranda's act of rape, of course much easier for the members of the Supreme

Court than it was for the victim. After all, it wasn't the members of the Supreme Court who were dragged into an alley and fucked up the ass. So *easy* to be impartial and fair and attend to Due Process when you're not on your face in the mud praying that this monster doesn't kill you or—more likely—wishing that he would because what he was actually doing was worse than death. Given the choice, most victims would change places with a judge any day of the week; citizens can be forgiven for wishing that could happen now and then, just to keep these guys in touch with reality.

In Canada, our version of *Miranda* is what the cops call "Chartering," and it runs this way:

> I am arresting you for ————. It is my duty to inform you that you have the right to retain and instruct counsel without delay. You have the right to telephone any lawyer you wish. You also have the right to free advice from a Legal Aid lawyer. If you are charged with an offence you may apply to Legal Aid for assistance. Do you understand? Do you wish to call a lawyer now?

And the Caution…

> You are charged with (or will be charged with) ————. Do you wish to say anything in answer to the charge? You are not obliged to say anything unless you wish to do so, but whatever you say may be given as evidence.

And the Caution Supplementary…

> If you have spoken to any police officer or to anyone with authority or if any such person has spoken to you in connection with this case, I want it clearly understood that I do not want it to influence you in making any statement.

And the Caution to a young person…

> You are (will be) charged with ————. Do you understand this

charge? It is my duty to tell you that you do not have to say anything about this charge unless you want to. Do you understand this? It is also my duty to tell you that whatever you do say will be taken down in writing and may be given in evidence at proceedings against you. Do you understand?

In the case of the juvenile, the Caution can't even be given unless the person has a guardian—usually a lawyer—present, and it has to be given in a language the kid can understand, and the lawyer will tell the kid to say nothing, and the case probably won't get to an actual trial anyway, because of all the liberal construings that have to take place, and all in all you can see why cops *hate* the Young Offenders Act and will usually drive around the block just to *avoid* a teenager.

Subsequent US rulings are generally taught as a kind of cop haiku that runs:

Weeks Mapp Gideon Massiah
Miranda Escobedo Mallory Elstad
and the New York Court of Appeals...

These are the rules that now define the limits of police behavior and the kinds of information a US court will hear. The Canadian Charter of Rights and Freedoms has created essentially the same dynamic in Canada.

Weeks and *Mapp* were federal and state decisions on tainted evidence. Tainted evidence is any fact or material item relevant to a prosecution that *might* have been obtained in an improper manner. That is, a manner not in accordance with the Supreme Court view on how evidence *ought* to be obtained. if, in the opinion of the trial court, any evidentiary material has been "tainted" in this manner, it will refuse to allow it to be brought forward (see Judge Cronin). Recent Court decisions such as *Stone v. Powell* and *Coolidge v. New Hampshire* have altered— critics will say eroded—*Mapp* so that, under some circumstances, evidence obtained under a technical violation *may* be entered if the results of exclusion might tend to bring the administration of justice into disrepute.

Gideon means that the suspect gets his call to a Public Defender no matter what. *Massiah* means the suspect has a right to retain and instruct counsel after being indicted. *Escobedo* means that the suspect can't be interrogated in the station-house unless he's seen a lawyer or unless he's waived his right to see a lawyer. If he wants to see a lawyer, and the lawyer tells him either not to answer questions, or not to answer *that* question, or to SHUT THE HELL UP, there's not a thing the cops can do.

Mallory was another Supreme Court decision, which forbade what it called "prolonged interrogation" in the station-house. In other words, a suspect who agreed to answer questions could not be required to answer questions for too long, or answer them in an atmosphere of veiled threat or disapproval, or in an uncomfortable chair, or be prevented from leaving without good cause, or be subjected to tricky and deceptive tactics.

And *Elstad,* the classic "fruit of the poisoned tree" case, means that any evidence obtained without a warrant, or accidentally discovered, or blurted out by a suspect who has not been properly Mirandized and given every opportunity to SHUT THE HELL UP or to sit around with his lawyer and say, "Nope nope ain't gonna say nothin'," is fatally tainted, a violation of Fourth Amendment or Fifth Amendment rights (in Canada it's Section 8 of the Charter) and no court in the land will let it enter the room.

The New York Court of Appeals added to the complications when it ruled that a man being stopped in the street for questioning, but who had not been charged yet, could light out for the Territories and no cop could legally pursue him.

In Canada, some of the more recent decisions that are driving the cops insane—such as *Askov*—clearly show that the Canadian Supreme Court sees itself as the staunch defender of individual liberty, which sounds damn fine and ringing, until we ask ourselves, against whom are they defending this theoretical individual?

Against the rest of us?

Damn right.

In decisions such as *Duarte,* which severely limits police surveillance of drug-traffickers, and *Wong,* which attacks the police use of video surveillance, and in *Stinchcombe,* which mandates that the defence counsel shall be the final arbiter of what constitutes a full and complete disclosure of the case for the prosecution, and in every other case where the Charter has come up against the rights of the collective, the Supreme Court has come down hard against the rights of all of us to be protected against some of us.

In Canada, our Supreme Court makes its judgements out of the inherited tradition of English Common Law and the more recent developments of the Charter and the Bill of Rights, but the interpretation—the mind-set—is fundamentally the same. Here's a shorthand list you can memorize for the next time you hear about some outrageous court decision. I hope it helps.

The Law is not about truth; it's about what you can prove.
It's better for the guilty to go free than for the law to take part in an ignoble act.
Evidence wrongfully obtained will taint the whole case.
Judges are the last arbiters of the law in all matters, no matter what juries may think.
The law stands between the individual and the power of the State. It also stands between the criminal and the vengeance of an aggrieved public.
A criminal offends against the State, not against an individual. It follows that the victim is merely a part of the State's evidentiary calculation, and has no other place in the justice system. (Hard to convince a raped woman of this, but frankly the system doesn't care.)
Technical adherence to the mechanics of the law is more important than any peripheral harm or grief that may descend upon victims or their families as a result of a dismissal.
Justice is not only blind itself, but may blind the public whenever it feels that the trial ought to proceed in camera or under a press ban.
The court is a place where the criminal comes for judgement.
The court is obliged to consider the rehabilitation of the criminal above victim rights or other considerations.
Victims are emotional and create messy scenes.

What was in the criminal's *mind* is more important than what he actually *did*.

Judges are impartial and attend only to the argument, in an environment seraphically free from the taint of personality or emotionalism. Which is why the reality of the street and the collisions thereof, and the blood, and the smells, have no place in the court. A judge cannot allow his judgement to be impaired by reality. Reality is messy too. Just like victims.

Juries are twelve good citizens and true, but it's okay to try to pack your own with as many brain-dead hermits as possible to avoid the *possibility* that one of them might actually have an *opinion* about the matter at hand.

Lawyers are respected officers of the court, and may be considered part of the club. The *fear* that motivates all lawyers is first created in them in law school, where the only mortal sin is to be caught without a persuasive rebuttal. Law professors eat lambs like that for brunch. So the driving fixation in any lawyer's mind is not whether he or she may be in the right or in the wrong; what keeps him or her awake at night is being defeated in an argument. (If you question this, you might attend, as I have, any number of moot courts and third-year seminars. My uncle, Wishart Spence, was a justice of the Supreme Court of Canada, so I was able to get some firsthand experience in this dynamic.)

The law's a game, with winners and losers (lawyers both) who know each other pretty well, who drink with the judges and play tennis with the clerks and who will meet after your trial to down some single-malt and ride each other about how clever they were.

Cops stink of the street, and have to be watched carefully.

The general public are, finally, a suspect laity, a laity not consecrated with the blessed oils and waters of a degree in the law, and distinguished from cops only in that cops are far more likely to have guns and most often wear easily recognizable uniforms.

Needless to say, the rise of the Supreme Court as a social force has made the lives of working cops a hell of a lot harder. That's not necessarily a bad thing. And the decisions were made with the best intentions, in a climate of severe racial repression. At the time, they were perhaps even necessary to the greater good of the nation. But, like all laws, they last a lot longer than the troubles that brought them into being. And like all laws, they are only as good as the men and women who use them. And there are many trial lawyers out there, not only in criminal practice, who are gleefully prepared to violate every principle of tacit knowing and shared semantic kinship to use these laws any way they can. A final quote from Lord Brougham, a famous British barrister:

> An advocate, in discharge of his duty, knows but one person in all the world, and that person is his client. To save that client by all means and expedients, and at all hazards and costs to other persons, and amongst them, to himself, is his first and only duty; and in performing this duty he must not regard the alarm, the torments, the destruction which he may bring upon others.

In the interest of honesty, Lord Brougham might have added, "...for a price."

It follows, therefore, that a law used by a bad man, or a bad man's lawyer, is a very dangerous thing, a small entanglement in evil from which many larger evils might spring, and to know the right path through this moral thicket is not an easy thing.

But we do know that whoever controls judgements of this nature has what amounts to the power of veto over anything the electorate—or the rabble—might propose.

This is not democracy.

EIGHT

Quislings

Well, that's one hell of a contention. I seem to have just said that the Canadian Supreme Court has become an enemy of the Canadian democracy. Perhaps I ought to try to prove it.

Let's take our alleged "War on Drugs."

Many, many years ago, when we were young and there were wolves in Wales, a lot of us were thrashing about the house in love with some dimly perceived confusion of Marxist dialectic, stoned out of our gourds on sinsemilla, trashing our rooms, burning our bras, racing up and down our parents' sensibilities with all the charm of a runaway cheese-grater, bitching about our creature-comforts and ruining our chromosomes.

Then we all grew up, had children and came to the horrified realization that the guy who was driving little Cody and little Melissa off to French Immersion *might be stoned!*

So we all decided that drugs were BAD, and we sent our cops off to DO SOMETHING ABOUT IT.

So far so good, right?

Wrong.

We forgot to tell our judges.

Once again it gives me great delight to announce that I have obtained—through means too covert, dangerous and downright brilliant to be described here—even more highly secret and confidential documents from SECRET SOURCES, and these documents contain the details of our progress against drugs.

Basically, our War on Drugs is being NIBBLED TO DEATH BY DUCKS.

And the ducks are wearing long black robes.

Here's what I mean...

VANCOUVER POLICE DEPARTMENT
INVESTIGATION/CONFIDENTIAL/89/12/29
TO SUPT. ZIOLA Cmdg Investigation Division
Subject: Drug Court—Judge Cronin

Three more drug court cases have been brought to my attention where Judge Cronin has, in my opinion, misapplied the law.

1. Ronald Wallace FERRIS—DOB 24 Nov 60 FPS#380109B Convicted in 1980 of NIP [Narcotics in Possession] Cocaine and NIP Hash and given a Conditional Discharge.

Charged on 89/07/20 with PPT [Possession for the Purpose of Trafficking] Cocaine.

Charged on 89/12/06 with PPT Cocaine.

In the latter case, FERRIS stated to an undercover member that he sold drugs for a living and wouldn't rip him off. On 89/12/07 FERRIS pled guilty to both charges and was sentenced to 30 days by Judge Cronin. At that time the judge allegedly asked FERRIS how he wanted to serve his time. After some dialogue between the accused and the judge, the judge decided he could serve his sentence on Mondays and Tuesdays.

It is my opinion that a 30 day sentence for two trafficking convictions is totally out of line taking into consideration the problems that cocaine causes our society. In allowing this individual to serve his 30 days on Mondays and Tuesdays, only makes it appear as if the judge is doing his best not to upset this man who has admitted he sells drugs for a living. I recommend we pursue having this sentence appealed.

2. In the case of R vs JORGE-OLVERA, JORGE-OLVERA was charged with PPT Cocaine. Cst 33103 Littlejohn, RCMP, who had been called to give expert evidence, was in the witness box being questioned by the Crown. The Crown was attempting to have Cst. Littlejohn give evidence as to how the amount of cocaine found in the possession of the accused would be consistent with possession for the purpose of trafficking. Judge Cronin advised Crown Counsel it was not a proper question and would not allow Cst. Littlejohn to give evidence on the point. The judge explained that the amount of drugs a person had in their possession had no bearing on whether it was for the purpose of trafficking or personal use. He further stated that a person could have three ounces on his person and it could still be for his own use. He compared this scenario with that of a person having ten bottles of whiskey in

his house; it didn't mean he was selling it—it could be for his own personal use.

Judge Cronin concluded by stating it was up to the court to decide whether a person has drugs for the purpose of trafficking or for his own use.

The judge's last statement is certainly correct. However, shouldn't the court hear the evidence of experienced drug investigators who have considerable knowledge in this area before making that decision?

In my opinion, expert evidence to explain how traffickers operate is essential to every possession for the purpose of trafficking case. First, individual drug abusers who are not trafficking usually would not buy more than they could use in a short period of time.

They simply do not want to take the risk of either being caught with it in their possession or being ripped off by other users. Secondly, the way drugs are packaged is often a clear indicator that the person in possession of the drug has it for resale. It just doesn't make sense that a user would package a gram of cocaine into four decks unless he or she was actively trafficking that cocaine.

3. The case of R vs JACKSON. JACKSON was charged with NIP Cocaine. The case appeared in court for trial on 89/12/21. In this case, Det 650 Carr had given evidence of his observations that would supply the information required to give the police reasonable grounds to search the accused. During the cross-examination, defense counsel S. Goldberg questioned Detective Carr on the size and location of the Observation Point (OP). Det. Carr refused to answer those questions citing public interest and the fact that to reveal that information may hinder future investigations.

Det. Carr had on two occasions stated he had a clear view of the incident. When Carr refused to answer those questions directed at him, that he would identify his observation point, defense counsel stated he had no more questions and sat down.

At this point, Judge Cronin asked Mr. Goldberg if he wished him to order Det. Carr to answer those questions. Goldberg quickly stood up and made that request to the judge. Judge Cronin then ordered Det. Carr to answer. Carr objected but the judge persisted. Carr then answered the initial question, which concerned the diameter of the hole he was looking out of, 3", and reiterated that he had a clear and unobstructed view.

Mr. Goldberg continued to ask questions which if answered would lead to the easy identification of Det. Carr's observation point. Carr again refused to answer stating that to do so could hinder further investigations in that particular bar. Judge Cronin ordered him to answer. Carr continued to object on the grounds that to answer could hinder further investigations. Judge Cronin then stated it was more important to answer the questions to help defense's case than to protect the location of the observation point (even if it would) hinder further investigations. Det. Carr stated that if this line of questioning continued, it was the same as drawing a diagram of the OP for everyone to see. The Judge then said that Carr may indeed have to draw a diagram to please the court on this matter and it was up to the court to decide what was in the public interest. At that point, Det. Carr requested an adjournment to seek independent legal advice. Judge Cronin granted the adjournment.

The advice of senior Crown Counsel was sought and the decision was made to stay the charge. The charge was stayed (Stay Of Proceedings, or an SOP).

Divulging the location of a police observation point is opposed for two good reasons:

(1) The building may be damaged or the owners/operators may be singled out for threats or violent attacks by suspects.

(2) The fact that if the location of the OP is known to the suspects, the OP loses much of its value to possible further investigations.

I believe it was inappropriate for Judge Cronin to order Det. Carr to answer those questions that would tend to identify the location of the OP. The only good reason for the defense to seek this type of information is because they question that the police witness can see what he described from that point. In this case, Det. Carr, on at least three occasions, stated that he had a clear and unobstructed view of the events he described and barring evidence to the contrary, should be believed.

I also believe this charge should not have been stayed for this reason and recommend consideration may be given to relaying this charge.

If these types of decisions go unchallenged, they will certainly occur more frequently in court.

Forwarded for you information and any action you deem appropriate.

D.W. Keith, Inspector 211.

And...

VANCOUVER POLICE DEPARTMENT
INVESTIGATION/CONFIDENTIAL
ASSISTANT INSPECTOR DOERN I/C VICE SECTION
90/01/03
SUBJECT: JUDGE E. CRONIN

1989 has been a year in which we witnessed a dramatic and unprecedented increase in the use and trafficking of narcotics of all types, and in particular of cocaine.

Decisions and sentencing of the courts display no realization that the drug problem has reached epidemic proportions.

Judge E.J. Cronin has consistently displayed a wanton and reckless disregard towards the general public he was appointed to protect and serve. His entire attitude towards drug users and traffickers brings the administration of justice into disrepute as never before seen. Judge Cronin has set himself up as public enemy number one of law enforcement and the general law-abiding public. The following are a few examples of Judge Cronin's outrageous disregard for protection of the public:

On 89/12/14, I was present in Judge Cronin's court when an accused by the name of PETERS pled guilty in front of him for NIP [Narcotics in Possession] and FTA [Failure to

Appear]. The accused admitted to a record for NIP in 1984 for which he was sentenced to 30 days and a record for NIP in 1986 for which he received 10 days. The accused admitted that he was aware he was supposed to appear in court regarding his present charge but he felt he should remain in Ontario rather than come back to BC to face the charge. The accused's lawyer informed Judge Cronin that the accused had also been in custody recently for 7 months on an "unrelated matter."

Judge Cronin stated, "I'll take the fact that he was in custody for seven months into consideration and suspend the passing of sentence on these matters." The decision can only be considered as incorrect as Cronin had no authority to apply an unrelated matter to sentencing in present charges. I might add that he did so without even checking to verify the accused's story.

On 89/12/14, I appeared in Judge Cronin's court in the matter of RONALD FERRIS...

[Note the reoccurrence of our Ronald here, even though he had just received a dispensation from the same judge to serve his thirty-day sentence on Mondays and Tuesdays.]

...Case #89-101588. The accused was charged with PPT Cocaine in an incident that occurred on 89/07/20. While he was on bail for this charge, he trafficked an "8 Ball" of cocaine to a Drug Squad undercover operator on 89/12/13. The accused pled guilty to both offences before Judge Cronin on 89/12/14.

The Crown asked for a term of incarceration on both offences since the accused had a previous record and had committed the second offence of trafficking while he was on bail for the first charge. Crown made a very good representation to sentence. Judge Cronin disregarded Crown's submissions and embarked on one of his usual inappropriate dissertations on cocaine use and trafficking:

QUOTE: "Cocaine is not attractive because it is cocaine. It is attractive because it is illegal."

The accused was sentenced to 30 days concurrent on both
  charges and the judge went on to suggest that the accused
  could serve intermittent time.

On 89/12/22, I appeared in Judge Cronin's court on the case of
  MARION TRIFF, case #89-102127. The facts of the case are
  as follows:

On 89/09/27, I received information from a reliable informant
  that Marion TRIFF was in Room 215 of the Patricia Hotel and
  was in possession of a quantity of cocaine which she intended
  to traffic and use.

I confirmed the room in question was rented by TRIFF and
  Drug Squad members went to Room 215 to determine how
  many persons were in the room and to secure the room when
  the opportunity presented itself.

The fact that this hotel is frequented by known drug users and
  it would have taken a minimum of one hour to obtain a search
  warrant made it impractical to obtain a search warrant before
  entering the room. I ordered an entry under Section 495,
  CCC…

Note: Section 495 of the Canadian Criminal Code, Arrest
Without Warrant by Peace Officer, allows a police officer to
make a warrantless entry if he has reasonable and probable
grounds to believe a person is committing or is about to commit
an indictable offence AND (d)(ii) he needs to "secure or preserve evidence of or relating to the offence." Seems pretty clear
in the case of Triff, right? Let's see…

…to secure the room and to preserve evidence. There was
  no intention to search the room before obtaining a search
  warrant. The situation on entering the room was such that a
  search warrant was not required as the narcotics were in plain
  view. I made all of the aforementioned very clear in my
  evidence in chief and also the fact that TRIFF was well-
  known to me as a cocaine trafficker and user and I had been
  present in court when she was convicted of PPT Cocaine.

The prosecutor who presented the case was Mr. John Cliffe.
  Mr. Cliffe made a presentation that can only be considered as

"excellent." All facts were well presented along with some case law in support of Crown's submissions. Judge Cronin then went into a senseless and rambling dissertation of pure nonsense with regard to the fact that we should have had a search warrant before entering. He stated that "it only takes a few minutes to obtain a search warrant. If it takes longer, there must be something wrong with the system. You can come to me or any other judge, come to my house or phone me anytime of the day or night."

He went on to say that not getting search warrants before entering dwelling houses could lead to innocent people having their doors kicked in because someone told police they had drugs. He at no time acknowledged that I knew TRIFF was a trafficker nor did he acknowledge the fact that the entry was made to secure the room and persons in it before obtaining a search warrant; the entry was NOT made for the purpose of searching upon entry.

The end result was the Judge Cronin disallowed the evidence and dismissed the charges. There are several errors in his decision and Mr. Cliffe is in agreement that the decision is inappropriate and not based on fact and existing high-court case law.

Judge Cronin's decision was no doubt based on his own personal feelings which border on the bizarre on numerous occasions. I am requesting a transcript of the case and that it be appealed.

I am also formally requesting telephone numbers and addresses of sitting provincial court judges in Vancouver be made available to drug squad members, as suggested by Judge Cronin.

I've withheld this officer's name because to publish it would be to expose a serving officer to the malice and vengeance of the justice system.

In case I'm giving you the idea that Judge Cronin is the only judge creating curious precedents and sending messages of boundless forgiveness to drug dealers, I offer for your amusement...

VANCOUVER POLICE DEPARTMENT
90/04/09   CONFIDENTIAL
MISTER JOHN LOO
CROWN COUNSEL
DEPARTMENT OF JUSTICE
1055 WEST GEORGIA STREET
VANCOUVER BC
V6E 3P1

Dear John:
RE: DAVID LIM—FPS #330543C

As per our telephone conversation, the following is a list of
Crown Counsel Reports in which LIM is the accused. All
these reports were submitted from this office to the
Department of Justice for charge approval. The first list was
either stayed or not proceeded with. The second list of cases
has gone to court and the results are recorded.
I am requesting that you review the first list and supply this
office with the reasons the Justice Department has not
proceeded to court on these files.

Case No.	Charge	Date	Disposition
87-91141	NIP Cocaine	87/05/17	Not Proceed
88-101594	PPT Cocaine	88/08/17	SOP
88-102302	PPT Cocaine	88/11/29	SOP
89-100204	PPT Cocaine	89/01/26	Not Proceed
89-101724	PPT Cocaine	89/08/09	SOP
88-101784	PPT Cocaine	89/08/18	Not Proceed
90-8850	PPT/NIP Coc.	90/01/30	Pled NIP 10
90-13072	NIP Cocaine	90/02/13	SOP

List Two

Case No.	Charge	Date	Disposition
88-102324	PPT Cocaine	89/11/30	NIP @ $400
89-100384	NIP Cocaine	89/02/14	Dismissed
89-100420	PPT Cocaine	89/02/24	NIP - 1 Day $500 Fine

89-100956	PPT Cocaine	89/04/28	Guilty Suspended 2 Yrs Prob.
89-102209	PPT Cocaine	89/10/10	NIP - 1 Day
90-14131	PPT/NIP Coc.	90/02/16	NIP - 1 Day
90-24542	PPT Cocaine	90/03/22	Chg Reduced

It appears that we, in the Criminal Justice System, have failed
society in our dealings with this individual and I believe a
review is in order.

Thanks for your co-operation.

Yours truly,

D.W. Keith, Insp 211

i/c Vice Section.

The foregoing is of interest because our Mr. Lim becam
embroiled in yet another drug-related morass, which, in the full
ness of time, came to the attention of another esteemed jurist, thi
time the Honorable Mr. Justice H.A.D. Oliver, of the Suprem
Court of British Columbia. Mr. Justice Oliver was asked to rul
on the legality of the warrant executed against one of the defen
dants. The forum for this inquiry was a legal procedure known a
a *voir dire*. *Voir dire* inquiries are at the cutting edge of Charte
challenges because they take place without the messy intrusion
of the commoners—there's no jury—and are conducted by th
Learned Judge in rather the same way that European judges ru
open court hearings; he can ask any questions regarding the wa
evidence was acquired, or any other matter that may attract hi
interest, and, more important, his rulings are rarely reporte
Look for more and more *voir dire* hearings; the judges lov
them because they have all the power.

So, in this *voir dire,* Mr. Lim's name comes up a few time:
and the judge's reasons for ruling as he did are representative c
attitudes across Canada. I think you need to know how peopl
are thinking…

NUMBER 901149
VANCOUVER REGISTRY

IN THE SUPREME COURT OF BRITISH COLUMBIA

HER MAJESTY THE QUEEN
  AGAINST
ALEXANDER JOSEPH CAYER
RULING OF THE HONORABLE MR. JUSTICE H.A.D.
  OLIVER
MRS. J. JORDAN   APPEARING FOR THE CROWN
BRIAN COLEMAN ESQ APPEARING FOR THE
                             DEFENCE

THE COURT:

At 7:00 pm on the 9th day of August, 1989, Constable
  Littlejohn, RCMP, on duty with Detective Smith of the
  Vancouver Police Department saw David LIM, known to him
  as a small-time cocaine and heroin trafficker. LIM was in or
  near his green pick-up truck in the parking area of the Shell
  Service station at the northwest corner of Burrard and Davie
  Street. The officers established surveillance and radioed for
  police assistance.

At 7:35, Littlejohn observed accused (ALEXANDER JOSEPH
  CAYER) using a pay telephone.

At 7:43 LIM was approached by the accused who was
  unknown to Littlejohn, Smith or any of the other police
  officers involved in this investigation. LIM and the accused
  conversed briefly and then crossed the parking lot of the Shell
  service station and small shopping complex. Littlejohn says
  that he then formed the opinion that LIM was engaged in a
  drug deal with the accused and sent out a radio transmission
  to the other officers, who rushed in. There is some conflict in
  the evidence of where it was that LIM and the accused were
  next seen but I find as a fact that they were observed standing
  in the entrance of an open ground-level parking area
  underneath an apartment building built on stilts over the
  parking area in question. The parking area was open all
  around.

[Remember that point; it's pivotal!]

It was a sunny day, described as bright sunlight. There is
  no suggestion that the two men were endeavouring to hide

III

behind any vehicle nor that they were surreptitious in their movements.

I find that the description by a distant observer of the conversation in the Shell parking area between LIM and the accused as "guarded" is an opinion so lacking in particularity that I am not prepared to give it any weight.

Constable Rae, RCMP, on duty in a police vehicle with Constable Hiller of the same force, received a radio transmission at 7:30 pm of the sighting of LIM.

[Oliver has forgotten about Littlejohn.]

He parked his police vehicle at 7:38 pm in the Esso service station across Davie Street from the Shell Station where he saw LIM, who was known to him also.

At 7:43 he saw the accused approach and speak to LIM. Neither he nor any officer involved could say from where or how the accused had appeared, whether by car or on foot, whether from one of the stores forming part of the small shopping complex belonging to the Shell service station area or from outside that area. Rae saw LIM and the accused walk through the parking lot toward a covered breezeway and, with Hiller, ran in pursuit. Rae arrested the accused and told him: "You are under arrest for possession of a narcotic."

After the arrest, Rae searched the accused and found a package containing white powder, a needle and a syringe as well as a bunch of keys, which keys he handed to Corporal Hildebrand, RCMP. The arrest was a warrantless one. Constable Rae, the arresting officer, testified: "I felt I had reasonable and probable grounds to arrest the accused because," and then he gave the following reasons:

"One, I knew LIM to be a very active coke user and trafficker—

[So do we…his record precedes him…]

Two, LIM appeared to be waiting for someone;

Three, LIM and the accused immediately went to a concealed area;

Four, I felt they were about to engage in a drug transaction."
To justify a warrantless search by a peace officer the Crown
must satisfy the requirements of Section 495 of the Criminal
Code of Canada. It is not sufficient that the officer honestly
believed he had reasonable grounds. The test is...

[*Pay attention now*—here's the key.*]

...whether a reasonable person in the place of the officer
would also have believed he had grounds to make an arrest.
The Crown suggests that the fact that LIM had made a
telephone call some ten minutes before the accused was first
observed is an additional ground for the warrantless arrest.
There is no evidence to satisfy me that the fact that such a call
was made had been communicated to the arresting officer, nor
does the arresting officer include that fact in the grounds
which he lists for forming his belief. In any event, there is no
evidence as to the person to whom that call was made or that
LIM reached the number he was dialing. There are
innumerable persons to whom the call could have been made,
not excluding the police. It will be borne in mind that LIM,
though a well-known drug trafficker who was found in
possession of several packages of drugs on this occasion, was
never charged.

[No, he wasn't; he had not yet accepted the package. Oliver
eems to have a poor head for minutiae.]

To conclude that LIM's call was to the police would be mere
idle speculation, as it would be to conclude that it was the
accused who LIM was calling.

Here Mr. Justice Oliver might be tipping his hand a bit; he
might believe that Lim was helping the police, was in fact an
informant, and Oliver was therefore reluctant to be part of that
process, and he might in fact see Cayer as a victim of entrap-
ment. The fact that even he admits there's no evidence for this—
and we in fact can see that the Vancouver Police Department has

made Herculean efforts to bust Lim—does not stop him from raising the rumor in his ruling, something he has no business doing. This might suggest a bias against police procedures and against police officers in general, in spite of his professional oaths to remain impartial.

Maybe now's the time to let you know that David Lim is a notorious drug-trafficker in Vancouver—as his record suggests—and to imagine for a second that Lim is acting as a police informant is to show a degree of naiveté that would be embarrassing to a newt let alone an experienced trial lawyer (defence) who is now a Supreme Court justice.

> In considering grounds three and four of the grounds listed by
> the arresting officer, I find it is incorrect to say that they
> immediately went to a concealed area. They did not go
> immediately and when they did it was not to a concealed area
> but to a place readily visible to or observable by any passerby.

Wrong! Littlejohn has said it was out of the way and not easily observed, and in fact was so hidden that Littlejohn lost sight of the two men, and it was up to Rae to pick them up after being warned by Littlejohn. That's how drug busts go…it's always a matter of a cop's judgement, something Oliver knows very well.

By the way, I *did* go to the location and walk through the scenario as it has been recorded, and the parking area is quite separate from the street, an ideal place for a quick exchange of drugs. Further, over the past few months, I have witnessed several unmistakable drug transactions taking place in this precise location.

> It will be remembered that LIM was the individual known to
> the police both as a trafficker and as a user of narcotics.
> Nothing was known about the accused.

This contention is cloudy; Cayer had previous hits for NIP and PPT, but it may be that Cayer was not known to these particular Drug Squad members. This is an area that Crown should have examined more fully, because as it stands it has given Oliver the room for a misunderstanding.

There was no physical contact between LIM and the accused.

Wait a minute...I thought that Lim and Cayer had slipped out of the sight of the officers. So how can Mr. Justice Oliver make this claim? All he can say is that he was not persuaded by the testimony, but he cannot, by a kind of juristic necromancy, deduce that no contact took place.

There were no motions indicative of anything being handed by one to the other [!!!!]. No money was seen to pass [!!!!]. Leaving aside Constable Rae's gut feeling that LIM and the accused were about to engage in a drug transaction, we are left with nothing but a strong suspicion of LIM and a weaker suspicion of the accused for being seen to talk to and walk with a known user and trafficker.

Having distorted the narrative to his liking, Mr. Justice Oliver will now proceed to cite case law in support of the altered narrative...let's watch.

In R. v. Storrey, 1990, Vol. 1, SCC, Reports, p. 241, it was held that:
"The police need not demonstrate anything more than reasonable and probable grounds..."
It was implicit in that ruling that anything less would not suffice. There must be rational grounds for the officer's belief that he has reasonable and probable grounds. Guilt by association will not by itself suffice. Mere suspicion cannot serve as a substitute for the belief required by the statute.
I find that the police did not have reasonable grounds to arrest the accused and that the warrantless arrest of the accused was in the circumstances unlawful. I have carefully considered the judgement of my Brother Drost in the case of R. v. Tunney, June 1990, unreported Number CC900159, which I distinguish upon its facts.
In considering the legality of the search of the accused at the scene of and following his arrest, I have had my attention drawn to the fact that a quantity of cocaine was in fact found

on the accused person as a result of the search. The existence
of that substance in the pocket of the accused prior to its
discovery was a factor unknown to the searching officer prior
to its discovery...

[What about Section 495 of the CCC? What about R. v.
Collins, NCA Sec. 11?]

...and cannot now be retroactively applied to bolster those
grounds of which the officer was previously aware.
In the words of Hart, J.A., in the case of R. v. Stevens, Nova
Scotia Court of Appeal, 1983, 35 C.R., 3rd Series, at P.11:
"In my opinion no police officer has the right to search any
person based upon suspicion alone. He must have reasonable
and probable grounds...

Obviously not to him, but to some mythical and totally inexperi-
enced bystander; someone just out of a ten-year coma ought to
do nicely, or maybe a Supreme Court justice, at least until he
became too experienced at sensing drug exchanges and had to
disqualify himself.

You see the problem here? If experience renders you ineligi-
ble for the job, since you see what an ordinary man might not,
how can any cop do his job and keep his standing in the court?
Wittgenstein tried to warn us about this kind of thing, but we
didn't listen, did we?

...for believing that the suspect is committing or has
committed an offence and must seek his justification under
the Criminal Code provisions relating to lawful arrest or some
other special statutory authorization. If the police officer
searches on suspicion alone he has committed an illegal act,
and one that, in my view, would be within the meaning of
'unreasonable' in Section 8 of the Charter."
I respectfully adopt those words in ruling the search of the
accused person in this case to have been unreasonable.
Having concluded that there was an infringement of Section 8
of the Charter, I must now consider the appropriate remedy.

The onus is on the accused to establish that the admission of the evidence improperly obtained in the proceedings would bring the administration of justice into disrepute. There will always be public criticism of the rejection by the Courts of evidence clearly indicative of the commission by an accused person of a criminal offence for what members of the public...

[He means us; the unwashed rabble...]

...may perceive as the breach of a technical rule.
In the present case the course adopted in the arrest and search of the accused appears to have been a shortcut employed by the officers...

This is a knuckle-rap; Oliver thinks the cops have been naughty and is taking away their accused as a punishment. This may be the emotional reason for a decision for which Oliver is now trying to find a legal justification. Don't look at me like that. It happens all the time!

...to avoid the need for a longer and more thorough surveillance. Had the officers been willing...

[Those lazy cops...always out to dodge their professional responsibilities! What can you expect from people who aren't even college grads, let alone lawyers!!]

...to continue their observation they might very well have secured in fairly short order the reasonable grounds needed both for a lawful arrest and for a lawful search.
On the other hand, it might well be that nothing further would have occurred and that LIM and the accused might have gone their respective ways...

[Maybe to bingo, or croquet, or maybe a mugging and a little B and E for extra cash... we'll never know, will we?]

…without anything happening to justify further police action.
In all of the circumstances it seems to me that we are not
   dealing here with the breach of some minor technical rule.
   The only evidence of the existence of the drug and of its
   possession by the accused…

[At least, the only evidence Oliver wants to consider…]

…was obtained by his unlawful arrest and the violation of his
   right to privacy.
In balancing the competing interests I must also have regard to
   the interests of the citizens as a whole in protecting the rights
   and freedoms guaranteed to them by the Charter.

[This is called Taking The High Ground—the elitist hubris
that makes judging so much fun.]

To allow investigating officers to adopt shortcuts by making
   arrests and searches based on suspicion, even strong
   suspicion, rather than reasonable and probable grounds,
   would tend to lead to a lowering of the investigatory
   standards required by law…

Once again, is this the bias speaking? Does he see himself as
a bulwark against a police state? In spite of the fact that Drug
Squad officers are highly professional and energetic and take
real pride in a good solid bust and view sloppiness and shortcuts
as a breach of ethics? Yes, cops do have ethics, and they're just
as strong as those of lawyers and judges. I know some cops will
take offence at that last statement, but I'm trying to be fair.

…and of a resultant erosion of our liberties which in the final
   analysis would be seen by thoughtful members of the
   community…

[He doubts there are any, but it's polite to say this…he's
probably thinking of other judges, and maybe his golfing buddies. Trust me, he doesn't mean *you*.]

...as more shocking than the rejection by the Court of the evidence unlawfully obtained in the present case. It is therefore my ruling that pursuant to Section 24, Subsection 2, of the Canadian Charter of Rights and Freedoms, the admission of the evidence resulting from the search of the accused person would bring the administration of justice into disrepute...

[A key phrase; watch for it...]

...having regard to all of the circumstances, and it is accordingly excluded.
In conclusion I feel compelled to add...

[Okay, now we find out what he was really pissed-off about...]

...that in a case where I have already found that there has been an unlawful arrest and an unreasonable search, I find it disturbing that a corporal of the RCMP, in company with several detectives of the Vancouver Police Department, knowing that a search warrant was being applied for by a constable, and knowing that it had not yet been granted, should have proceeded anyway to enter the accused's dwelling...

Oliver hates Section 495 of the CCC, we can assume, since it gives police the right to make Charter decisions about entering and preserving evidence that judges can't control. In this case, the detectives had an accused in possession who had offered his keys. A search of an addict's residence is standard procedure, as Oliver well knows, since he made one hell of a nice living defending this sort of person for many years before he arose, like Christ Ascendant, from the Vale of Tears unto the Mount and the Perquisites Thereon, one of which is the sheer nasty fun of torturing all the cops he had to fight with when he was back down there in the snake-pit with the rest of us.

What he's doing here is another knuckle-rap. What this is all about is turf; Oliver's marking out his by pissing all over the drug cops and freeing their prisoner. *He* rules here, boyos, and you'd better not forget it!)

…by the use of keys seized from the accused and to arrest a young woman found there on a purported or ostensible charge of possession of cocaine for the purpose of trafficking, without any apparent basis for such a trespass or entry…

[What about Section 495 of the CCC?]

…or for such an arrest, and to detain her there in police custody for as long as it suited the purpose of the arresting officers. Once a search warrant had been granted and that fact had been communicated by radio to the RCMP Corporal in charge of the search, the young woman was evidently turned loose without any further action.

It's standard procedure to keep a resident of the dwelling present so that the resident can see, and may be called on to testify, that no search was carried out until the warrant was obtained, and, further, to protect the officers from being charged with theft or willful destruction of property by the accused, a routine defence maneuver. Once the warrant was obtained, they let her go, which was actually a kindness and may have been prompted by compassion.

This is clearly not Oliver's opinion, and it reveals his animosity for the cops, whom he regards as untrustworthy. It is clear that he does not consider them officers of the court, which, in point of law, they are. More elitist contempt for the blue-collar cops.

The imperative of enforcing the law is respect for the law. The Court must start and end on the premise that police must behave lawfully. Zeal in enforcing the criminal law must be balanced by public recognition of the inviolable rights of the person…

Actually, it's the inviolable rights of an accused person, since it's clear from the way the justice system treats them that victims,

nce victimized, become part of the evidentiary packet and are
ot considered inviolate. In practice, this concept of inviolability
f rights serves only the criminal, which is all well and good, but
t least let's say so out loud and not wrap our rhetoric in the
lag…

   …and any departure from that standard by the officers to
   whom the public are entitled to look as models of lawful
   behavior…

   [Not only unwashed rabble, but gullible…]

   …is likely to damage the reputation of the force to which the
   officers belong and to lower the public respect for the
   administration of justice.

   [So there…]

That is the end of my ruling in this matter.

   Reacting quickly, the cops persuaded Peter MacNeil, of Ray
Connell and his associates, to attempt an appeal. The VPD were
concerned about the precedent Oliver was setting, and perhaps a
little angry as well.
   Here's how it went…

VANCOUVER POLICE DEPARTMENT 91/11/25
Mr. David Frankel, QC
Senior General Counsel,
Department of Justice,
1055 West Georgia Street,
VANCOUVER, BC

Dear Mr. Frankel:
RE: R v. ALEXANDER CAYER

Mr. CAYER was charged with Possession for the Purpose of .
   Trafficking in Cocaine on August 9th, 1989.

On 91/03/04, upon completion of his trial in the Supreme Court of British Columbia, Mister Justice H.A.D. OLIVER dismissed the charge. Very succinctly, the reasons were given that the search was unlawful and that to admit the real evidence showing that CAYER was found in possession of approximately two ounces of cocaine would bring the administration of justice into disrepute.

It was our opinion that the case had been properly investigated and that ample grounds had been established to make a legal search and lawful arrest.

Over and above this submission, we believe the exclusion of this type of evidence does more to bring the administration of justice into disrepute than its acceptance even if the search had been technically unlawful. The key issue here, we suggest, should be that the police were acting in good faith.

It is our contention that decisions to exclude real evidence often causes the public to come to the wrongful conclusion that everything is not on the up and up. It is important that the administration of justice from the initial arrest through to the conclusion of all appeals is not only fair and just but appears to be fair and just and in the best interests of society as a whole.

The case was reviewed thoroughly with the investigators and we concluded that the evidence had been properly obtained and presented fully in court.

At that point, I telephoned Mister Peter MacNeil who was the Ad Hoc prosecutor on this case. We discussed the investigation, the evidence at trial, and the possibility of applying to have the case appealed. Subsequently, Mister MacNeil advised me that he had written the Department of Justice Appeals Committee on this matter and had recommended the case be appealed. A short time later, I received notice that the case was being appealed and the appeal papers were served on CAYER by our detectives.

I have now been informed the appeal has been abandoned. Would you please supply this office with the reasons this appeal was not proceeded with.

CAYER is a mid-level trafficker who has a previous

conviction for this type of offence and as a result is of great interest to us.

Yours truly,
D.W. Keith, Insp. 211,
i/c Vice Section.

And in due course, Inspector Keith got this fax…

RAY CONNELL
BARRISTERS AND SOLICITORS

NOVEMBER 22, 1991.
VIA FACSIMILE

ATTENTION: INSPECTOR DON KEITH
VANCOUVER POLICE DEPARTMENT
312 MAIN STREET
VANCOUVER BC
V6A 2T2

Dear Sir:
RE: R. v. ALEXANDER CAYER

Please find attached a copy of our letter to the Appeals Committee of the Department of Justice with respect to the above noted matter. If we can be of any further assistance, please do not hesitate in contacting the writer.

Yours very truly,
Ray Connell,
per Peter M MacNeil

And the letter itself…

RAY CONNELL
BARRISTERS AND SOLICITORS

PETER MACNEIL

MARCH 19 1991.
DEPARTMENT OF JUSTICE
2800-1055 WEST GEORGIA STREET
VANCOUVER BC
V6E 3P9
ATTENTION: Ms. Joy Gardiner
 Criminal Appeals Clerk

Dear Ms. Jackson:
RE: Regina v. ALEXANDER CAYER
 our file no 0142/03565
 Suggested Crown Appeal against Acquittal
 Justice File No: VC-96081

Please place this letter before the Appeals Committee for their
 consideration of a Crown Appeal against acquittal to the
 Court of Appeal. The details are as follows:
Full name of accused and aliases, if any:
Alexander Joseph CAYER
Aliases: Michael Karl Beckman, Mario Joseph
 Roberge
DOB: December 14, 1958
FPS Number   977199A
Date of Off: August 9, 1989
Court: Supreme Court of British Columbia
 The Honourable Mister Justice Oliver
 Offences of which defendant acquitted:
 Possession of Cocaine for Purpose of Trafficking
Defence: Brian Coleman
Plea: Not Guilty
Jury?   Judge Alone

Note: This is a *voir dire,* and, as I mentioned before, the
judge runs a *voir dire* because it is assumed that the matter
involves legal calculations that are beyond the ken and powers
of the rabble.

You remember the rabble, don't you? If you've forgotten, put the book down and go into the bathroom and look into the mirror. Unless you're Dracula, there's a face staring back at you and that face is one of the rabble. You may not like this, but you'll never doubt it if you've spent even one day in any court on this continent.

Okay…now come back…bring a beer…and we'll sit down together and watch the rest of this sit-com…

Length of Trial—two day Voir Dire
Date Acquitted—March 4, 1991
The suggested grounds for appeal are:
1. That the learned trial judge erred in finding that Cst. Rae of the RCMP lacked reasonable and probable grounds to arrest Mister CAYER.
2. That the learned trial Judge erred in that determining whether reasonable and probable grounds to arrest existed; he assessed the grounds held by the arresting officer (Cst. Rae) instead of the officer who directed that the accused be arrested (Cst. Littlejohn).
3. That the learned trial judge erred in that he excluded the real evidence obtained as a result of the search of Mister CAYER incidental to his arrest without applying the 3 stage analysis outlined in R. v. Collins…

Collins v. The Queen is described in Section 11 of the Narcotics Control Act; it details some of the grounds on which an officer may search a suspect. It gives some leeway in the matter and has been upheld by other courts, so Oliver's decision is not unchallenged by precedent.

…and other Supreme Court decisions. In particular the learned trial judge failed to consider that the evidence was "real evidence" and that the police officers were acting in good faith.
4. Upon such other grounds as counsel may advise.
The trial of this matter commenced on February 28, 1991. A voir dire was held to determine whether these were reasonable

and probable grounds to arrest CAYER, and whether the "real" evidence found on CAYER should be excluded pursuant to Section 24 (2) of the Charter.

My notes indicate that the following evidence was heard on the voir dire.

The circumstances are as follows:

1. The Crown called five witnesses on the voir dire. There were no defence witnesses called.

2. On August 9, 1989, Cst. Littlejohn of the RCMP and Det. Smith of the Vancouver Police Department were driving southbound on Davie Street at Burrard. They observed a person known to them as David LIM at the Shell gas station located at the northwest corner of Davie and Burrard. David LIM was well-known to Cst. Littlejohn as a small-level Cocaine and Heroin dealer. Cst. Littlejohn had arrested David LIM on a number of previous occasions for a number of narcotics offenses.

3. Cst. Littlejohn and Det. Smith decided to conduct surveillance on LIM. They set up a surveillance position on the northeast corner of Burrard Street, about 150-200 feet from LIM's position. Cst. Littlejohn used binoculars to assist his vision. LIM was in a vehicle which was parked in a mini-mall parking lot which formed part of the Shell station.

4. At 7:33 pm LIM exited the vehicle and went to a pay phone where he made one call. The call lasted approximately one minute after which LIM returned to the vehicle.

5. At 7:38 pm, LIM exited the vehicle and walked around the parking lot. He appeared to be looking around and to be waiting for someone.

6. At 7:43 pm, as LIM was standing by the vehicle a male approached LIM from the north. This male was Alexander CAYER. CAYER was not known to Cst. Littlejohn or Det. Smith.

7. During their surveillance, Cst. Littlejohn contacted other members of street crew and requested their assistance in the surveillance of LIM. These members arrived at various times during the surveillance.

8. LIM and CAYER had a brief conversation after which they

walked away together through the mini-mall towards the north lane of Burrard.

9. Constable Littlejohn testified that he felt he had reasonable and probable grounds to arrest CAYER and LIM. He testified that he had observed over 1,000 drug deals take place and that he had made approximately 150 purchases in the capacity of an undercover operator. He testified that the activity which he observed had all of the earmarks of a street level drug transaction. In particular, he mentioned that LIM was well-known to the street crew as a street-level trafficker; LIM had made a phone call from the pay phone and then waited for someone to arrive; CAYER arrived within a short period of time: LIM and CAYER had a brief conversation and then walked away together towards the laneway; as LIM and CAYER walked away they were looking over their shoulders and around the parking lot: LIM and CAYER were observed standing in an unlit area in a covered parking lot with no one else around them.

10. Cst. Littlejohn formed the opinion that a drug deal was taking place…

[Christ! Mother Teresa would have formed *that* opinion! We've all seen enough on TV to know what this kind of action was all about!]

…between LIM and CAYER. As LIM and CAYER went out of Cst. Littlejohn's sight, he radioed to other members of street crew to move in and arrest LIM and CAYER.

11. When Cst. Littlejohn got to the north lane of Burrard he observed LIM and CAYER standing together in an enclosed parking lot. There were no other people in the parkade. LIM and CAYER were not standing near any automobiles. Cst. Hiller and Cst. Rae rushed up to LIM and CAYER and placed CAYER under arrest. Cst. Hiller and Cst. Rae located two one ounce bundles of cocaine on Mr. CAYER. Each bundle of cocaine was packaged in a plastic baby-bottle liner wrapped with black electrical tape. The two bundles were 81% and 83% pure respectively. In addition, $1,300 in Canadian Funds

was located on CAYER. There were no drugs or money located on LIM. Both LIM and CAYER were arrested, Chartered and Warned without incident. There were no statements of value taken from CAYER or LIM.

12. A search warrant was eventually obtained for CAYER's apartment. The search located no further cocaine; however, a box of baby-bottle liners and numerous rolls of black electrical tape were found.

What does this tell us?

THE HONOURABLE MISTER JUSTICE OLIVER'S DECISION

The Honourable Mr. Justice Oliver rendered his decision on the voir dire on March 4, 1991. I was not able to attend at this time and my review of his decision is based on notes taken by Jennifer Jordan of our office. Oliver, J. commenced his decision by reviewing the evidence heard on the voir dire. He found that Cst. Littlejohn had formed the opinion that LIM was involved in a drug deal with CAYER…

Selling…or buying? Since most small-level street dealers buy on consignment, the fact that no drugs were found on Lim could mean that Lim had not yet accepted his consignment.

…and that Littlejohn sent out a radio transmission to the other members of the Drug Squad who rushed in. Oliver, J. found that Hiller and Rae grabbed CAYER and that Rae formally placed CAYER under arrest. Oliver, J. then reviewed Rae's grounds for arresting CAYER. Oliver, J. found that Rae's reasonable and probable grounds were the following:

1. LIM's reputation.
2. LIM appeared to be waiting for someone.
3. LIM and CAYER meet and immediately go to a concealed area.
4. Rae felt that LIM and CAYER were about to engage in a drug transaction.

Oliver, J. also considered the Crown's submission that LIM's use of the pay phone be considered as reasonable and probable grounds for his arrest. Oliver, J. found there was no evidence to show that Rae was aware of LIM's use of the telephone. RAE did make comments to this effect in cross-examination...

Drug Squad members have radios so they can tell each other that the suspect is doing when he is out of sight of some of the crew. Littlejohn would have let every member know about all Lim's movements; it's standard procedure.

Oliver, J. found that even if Rae had been aware of LIM's use of the telephone, there was no evidence to show who LIM was calling and therefore it was of no assistance in establishing reasonable and probable grounds to arrest LIM and CAYER.

Oliver, J. found that the parkade in which LIM and CAYER were arrested was not concealed as it was an area which was visible. This is contrary to the evidence of each of the police officers who testified that the parkade was covered and that there were no people in the area.

Did Oliver, J. go and look for himself, as I did? Since it became such an issue, why didn't Crown ask for a video or a photograph of the exact location so that the Learned Judge could see for himself?

Oliver, J. found that Rae had nothing more than a suspicion...

What about Littlejohn's observations? And you have to start asking yourself just what kind of actions Lim and Cayer could have performed that *would* meet Oliver, J.'s rather astigmatic standards for a drug transaction. What if Lim set up something like a lemonade stand with a big COCAINE sign on it? Or perhaps Cayer could wander through the neighborhoods pushing a wooden wheelbarrow—through streets broad and narrow—crying "Cocaine and hashish, alive-alive-oh"?

…and concluded that CAYER's Charter of Rights had been infringed. He found that the breach was not a minor or a technical breach. He found that the evidence was obtained by an unlawful arrest and the violation of CAYER's rights to privacy. He found that he had to balance the conflicting interests between protecting the public and protecting freedoms guaranteed by the Charter. He concluded that the admission of the evidence obtained would bring the administration of justice into disrepute and therefore excluded it pursuant to Section 24 (2) of the Charter.

Please advise me if the Appeals Committee decides to recommend that this sentence be appealed.

Yours truly,
RAY CONNELL
Per Peter M. MacNeil.

And the answer…?

DEPARTMENT OF JUSTICE
PO BOX 11118
2800-1055 WEST GEORGIA ST.
VANCOUVER BC V6E 3P9

DECEMBER 20, 1991

VANCOUVER POLICE DEPARTMENT
312 MAIN STREET
VANCOUVER BC V6A 2T2
ATTENTION: INSPECTOR D.W. KEITH
 IN CHARGE OF VICE SECTION

Dear Sirs:
RE: R. v. Alexander CAYER
 Our File No. VC-96081 (A)

Thank you for your letter of November 29, 1991, which I understand to be an inquiry as to why the appeal by the Crown has been abandoned.

The reasons for Judgement disclose findings of fact made by the Trial Judge upon which he was free to conclude that there had been a breach of Section 8 of The Charter. He so concluded and he ruled that the search was not reasonable.

While others may be of different views, it remains the function of the Judge to find facts based on the evidence and to apply the Law. The Learned Trial Judge in this case did so in manner which is unassailable and it is for that reason that the Appeal has been abandoned.

A copy of the Reasons for Judgement of Mister Justice Oliver are enclosed for your ready reference.

Yours truly,
T.A. Dohm, Q.C.

A curt dismissal, that one. Go away, copper, and trouble the counsels of the Wise and Great no more; busy yourself in the gutter and tug not upon our robes nor plague us with entreaties as we go about the burden of rule.

This kind of tone is generally described as "the Insolence of Office." Canada has more than its share of this kind of thing. And most of it is coming from our esteemed judges, who don't seem to be getting the message that *we don't want our kids to use drugs* and that this is the *general will of the people*.

And, unless I'm sorely mistaken, isn't that another way of saying *democracy?*

NINE

Coyotes and Sheep

I suppose I should say that Judge Cronin and Judge Oliver do not necessarily reflect the opinions of the management, or even of the majority of judges.

I should say that, but I'm not going to.

Because I don't believe it.

And the fact that our judges hold the fashionable view that drugs are not a criminal matter but rather a *social* problem, an illness, forces us all to pay a terrible price—a price extracted from us by a ruling cadre who have no experience of life on the streets of our cities and towns.

This just in:

The Vancouver Sun, 1 April 1992
OTTAWA PLEDGES ANOTHER $270 MILLION
IN WAR ON DRUGS
By Gordon Hamilton

> After five years and a cost of $210 million, Canada's so-called war on drugs has been called both a success and just another bad trip at taxpayers' expense.
>
> Despite mixed responses to the drug strategy, Health and Welfare Minister Benoit Bouchard announced Tuesday another $270 million for a second five-year term. Bouchard said the program, called Canada's Drug Strategy, has had many successes.
>
> But a 1991 report on the strategy shows Canada is little closer to defining this country's drug strategy than when the initiative was launched five years ago.
>
> "Needs less talk and more action," states the report, the result of two months of consultation.
>
> Jan Skirrow, former director of the Canadian Centre on Substance Abuse, who helped prepare the report, also said the drug strategy has had little impact on lowering drug use in Canada. "I would defy anybody to find any effect."

In BC, Health ministry officials said the drug strategy has paid for preventive programs for community groups but that co-ordination between Ottawa and Victoria has been a problem. Insp. Vince Casey, head of the Vancouver RCMP drug section, cited use of the military for drug interdiction as one program success.

Bouchard credited the anti-drug program for a decrease in the number of heavy drinkers, a reduction in deaths among 16- to 25-year-olds from impaired driving and a 50-percent cut in the use of stimulants...

...They took $210 million in government money and spent it without knowing where it came from or what they were trying to accomplish: That damning condemnation of federal drug strategy comes from an internal government report...

...the $210 million committed in 1987 was spread over five years and in six different components; treatment, which received 38 percent of these funds; education, 32 percent; enforcement, 20 percent; research, 20 percent; international co-operation, three percent; and national focus, one percent.

Drug enforcement concentrated on anti-drug profiteering, the use of Armed Forces—including its CF18's—in interdiction, co-operation between Canadian authorities and those in source countries, and enhanced intelligence through new computers...

Hello?

Is the Supreme Court listening?

Is *anybody* listening?

Nothing in the budget about enhancing the intelligence of our judges. Well...maybe the *next* $270 million will go for that. By the way, if it's hitting you that a lot of people seem to be making a very good living from the drug trade, and that not all of them are dealers and importers, then you have begun to see the hidden factor in all of this. Things won't change until we all get tired of paying for talk about change and study about change and things such as "national focus," which have God knows what to do with change. In the meantime, the consultants and the rest of the people who make their living ear-deep in the federal trough look like they're going to have another great year.

We've looked at these matters in very fine detail, and I appreciate that you're probably wondering—as the guy said in the elevator—why I've called this meeting.

We've paid a lot of attention to the judges here, and to the evidentiary dynamic, to the interplay of personalities and tensions in a court of law. It's fascinating stuff—I hope—and it is pretty representative of everything I've observed in the last twenty years of my life.

The Canadian justice system has gotten itself in quite a tangle with this new Charter, rather like a litter of kittens in the knitting basket, and most of the people in that basket are pretty well persuaded that what they're doing is not only fun but *damned important* as well. There is a sense around the Halls of Justice that the priesthood is engaged in nation-building, that they are constructing an alabaster temple of thought and case law that will guide and succor the weary jurist, provide illumination for the professors, amaze the law students and generally confound the yokels for years to come.

And perhaps they are. It resonates with the same celestial music that arose from the US Supreme Court a few years back, which we've already discussed in great detail. As I said, Canada follows the States by about a ten-year delay.

And you can certainly see active, supple and occasionally brilliant minds at work in the courts, especially in the higher courts. These are truly men and women of substance and gravity, true believers with their hearts and minds fully enlisted in what they obviously consider to be a civilizing and vital work.

I've given lawyers and judges a hard time over the years—except for the times I've needed one—and I've certainly been cutting, even flippant, about them in the preceding chapter.

This is harsh, I admit.

I do not doubt for a moment the sincerity and honesty of most judges, especially in Canada. And I admit as well that lawyers for the defence—rather like coyotes and hyenas—are only doing what they have been bred and raised to do, however unattractive their efforts may seem to those who find themselves in opposition to them.

So…?

So remember that film with Rod Taylor, back in the early 1960s? *The Time Machine?* Based on an H.G. Wells story, it describes a society at the end of history—remember *that* phrase?—composed of the languid and extremely white people known as "the Eloi" (from the Hebrew word for father, I think). They lived in a kind of hallucinatory version of Periclean Athens as interpreted by Maxfield Parrish. They beguiled the tedious hours sipping nectar and well-water and taking up artful positions against the architecture, dressed in soft robes made of natural fibres, eating delicately from the Four Holistic Food Groups (fruit, bran flakes, Nanaimo Bars and marmalade), discussing philosophy and the arts and the meaning of life while some pre-Raphaelite anorectic dressed up in a Liona Boyd outfit plucked on a lute. (Reminds you of Ottawa, right?)

And set against them, were "the Morloch," hairy troglodytes given to lurching about the territory smelling bad and pursuing disagreeable culinary fixations. They lived in caves and preyed upon the Eloi, who were too busy studying their reflections in the pool to notice that a hell of a lot of them were ending up down in the catacombs as rack-of-Eloi in a shallot sauce.

A heavy-handed allegory, I know, and like all allegories an oversimplified view of a complex issue. But like the guy said when he hit the bull between the eyes with a two-by-four, first you have to get their attention. Because our version of the Eloi—the judges and the criminologists and the civil libertarians and the rest of the insulated purists who constitute the priesthood of the justice system—are in real danger of becoming something even they never imagined: totally irrelevant.

Our version of a good society is attractive and persuasive, and so far it's worked pretty well, all in all. But it is only a version, and like all versions, it can be edited by reality. We are currently obsessed with rights and freedoms. We are the crankiest and most litigious society in history. The whining drone of victims' groups provides a kind of adenoidal threnody over which the brittle criticisms of the self-righteous rise to form a very narcissistic concerto. We're all jostling for a place in the orchestra. Christ, even middle-aged white males are pushing their way to the front of the music hall, bellowing about their fathers and banging away on drums. We're choking ourselves on self-esteem and civil rights and affirmative action. We're getting to be exceedingly tiresome. Seen from a distance, we must look like sheep bleating about the fodder.

While the Learned Trial Judge in the previous chapter was playing silly-bugger with the vice cops, something far more important and elemental was going on: David Lim was getting away with it again.

In an outstanding article in the March 1992 edition of *Vancouver* magazine, writer Terry Gould quotes David Lim on the subject of his career as one of Vancouver's worst drug offenders:

> Anybody that deals drugs in Vancouver doesn't worry too much about the courts...the gang guys, the independents — they all get away with lots. My lawyer used to win my cases with constitutional stuff that said the police violated my rights when they searched me...we plea bargained quite a bit. Meanwhile I'd keep putting down 25,000 cash for a pound of coke every week, deal it in ounces for 40 grand all over town, bang or freebase the profit, then go buy more...to tell the truth, they should have gotten their act together and stopped me sooner...my opinion now is that when you arrest a guy for dealing, he should do the time and, if he wants it, treatment. If you're going to do a war on drugs, do it right...

I'd be curious to hear how the Honorable H.A.D. Oliver reacted when he read that quote, if he read it at all. Lim is—was—may be again—a dangerous drug-dealer. He carried weapons and sold drugs to anybody with the cash and he was—and has the potential to be—a truly criminal asshole with the typical criminal mind-set. (Something Oliver knew very well at the time he rendered his decision on *Cayer*.) And pay attention here...Lim has the outrageous *gall* to blame the system for letting him get away with it. There speaks the true predator.

Well, by now you're probably saying to yourself, okay, okay, there's a great deal of smoke-and-mirrors in the justice system,

specially when it comes to drug-dealers, but that's just one little
spect of the national crime problem, so why all the attention?
Vhy should we care if a couple of judges go all soft and senti-
mental when they see some low-life druggie slouching into court?
Most of us don't have contact with the drug world anyway.

Well, first of all, that's a pretty callous dismissal of the terri-
le damage that drugs cause in the tenements and ghettos of the
United States and Canada. It isn't the poor people who fly or
oat this shit in; it's wealthy drug-importers with houses in
Westmount and Shaughnessy and Forest Hill who reap the ulti-
ate profit, while the poor sons-of-bitches on the street kill
emselves and each other with metronomic regularity. We dis-
gard their destinies at a tremendous cost to our own safety, not
o mention our pretensions to morality. You don't see gunshops
nd drug-dealers on the streets in the moneyed neighborhoods.

My point is, nothing happens in isolation. What hurts the
poor hurts us all. When a jurist such as Judge Cronin compli-
ates a fairly straightforward drug prosecution with ever more
subtle twistings of the Charter, he makes the prosecution of all
rug cases more difficult, because the justice system runs on
recedents.

By the way, Judge Cronin has come in for some fairly specific
riticism here, but I do not mean to suggest that he is in any way
a anomaly. You're hearing about him right here because his
ecisions are referred to in a lot of the police files I have obtained,
nd I wanted you to see what happens when cops take the trouble
 complain about the judgements of judges. (Not much.)

There are many other judges doing pretty much the same
ing with nauseating persistence. For example, Vancouver was
cently stunned by the kidnapping and rape of two young
omen by a Toronto fugitive, David Alexander Snow.

Snow, known as "the Cottage Killer" back in Ontario, was
anted in connection with several attacks and murders commit-
d in the Kawarthas. He made it out to British Columbia (fol-
wing the course of far too many of Canada's criminals) and set
mself up in a strip of forest by the Trans-Canada in North
ancouver. Then he proceeded to abduct a young girl, whom he
eld for ten days. Then he kidnapped another, and was in the

process of trying to kill both of them when an RCMP officer found his forest camp.

He ran, leading the RCMP on a mountain chase that ended at the Bridge House Restaurant, where a security guard managed to overpower him while Snow was busy trying to kill yet another woman, this time a fifty-three-year-old survivor of Auschwitz.

When Snow was caught, he had the woman down on the ground, after a twenty-minute struggle; he had wrapped a plastic bag around her head and was tightening a coat-hanger around her neck.

The matter came before Judge Jerome Paradis, who had this to say about whether Snow was actually guilty of Attempted Murder:

> I cannot conclude that the placing of the wire around the neck
> of the victim and the placing of the plastic over her head are
> sufficient to establish a specific intent to kill.

I could cite examples of this kind of witless misjudgement right across the country, but I think the point is made. Cronin and Paradis are symptomatic of a general malaise that affects most of our judges: a profound misunderstanding of the nature and the consequences of their behavior.

Right now, I've stressed the ways judges use the Charter to overpower our efforts at drug law enforcement for two reasons.

First, as I have been tediously repeating, this used to be a democracy and now it isn't, and one of the reasons it isn't is that our judges have seized upon the Charter of Rights and Freedoms to squirm out from under parliamentary control.

Once again, here's what Justice Cory had to say about the issue, in his dissenting ruling on the extradition of Charles Ng:

> In the case of MILLER v. THE QUEEN [1977] 2 SCR 680,
> this Court considered the validity of legislation which
> provided for capital punishment of persons who were
> convicted of the murder of police officers or prison guards
> acting in the course of their duties. The majority of the Court
> upheld the death penalty provision on the ground that judicial

deference should be paid to the expressed will of Parliament. I would observe at the outset that this reasoning is inconsistent with the approach which has been taken since the passage of the Charter. Unswerving judicial deference to the perceived intent of Parliament is no longer a determinative factor....

Cory reminds us—not that we need it—that the Charter has freed the courts from democratic restraints as the *Marbury* decision freed the US Supreme Court.

This is *not* a minor alteration in legal definitions.

We have lost the power to influence our courts.

Which brings me to the second reason that we need to be able to influence our legal system. The judges have decided that drugs are a societal problem, not a legal one.

They are very, very wrong.

The drug trade in Canada drives almost all the other crimes that bedevil and affront us all, and the courts don't seem to understand the "ecosystem" into which they are pouring the undiluted effluent of their intellectual diversions.

Or they don't give a damn.

I'm not sure which.

TEN

The Sheep Look Up

Maalox, anyone?

I begin to understand why I'm doing so much drinking lately. It's not that this kind of thing hasn't been going on for thousands of years. I mean, nobody is suggesting that Hammurabi got it right the first time.

But isn't it time we managed just a few inferences from the evidence before us.

I'm using the variance between our so-called official attitude towards the drug trade and the attitudes demonstrated by our courts as an example of the ways in which a democratic consensus about an important issue can be derailed by our judges.

It's not the only example, not by a long shot. But it's certainly a powerful one. I would have thought that our judges, being the puissant and ratiocinative little dickenses they are, would have detected some kind of causal relationship between their decisions about drug cases and the general crime rate. This is not readily observable.

We are left with two possible deductions.

One, our judges don't see the connection between their actions and the drug trade, in which case they're more than a little dim.

Or two, they don't care.

Personally, I'm going for the second choice.

And it's too bad they don't care, because it just so happens that the drug trade drives a lot of other crime, so when they blow a chance to crush a dealer, they're blowing a chance to greatly decrease a wide variety of collateral crime, which even they would have to admit is something the people of Canada can get behind in a big way.

Too many people—including judges—think that criminals are like doctors, that each one has a specialty, an area of expertise. There are neurosurgeons and proctologists, and no one expects a neurosurgeon to call in a proctologist to assist him in a surgical procedure (unless the patient is Joe Clark or Brian Mulroney).

But criminals aren't crime specialists; to push the analogy, they're general practitioners. They'll try anything if there's a buck in it.

Can you hold still for a few illustrations from my files? I think you'll find them persuasive, even if our judges don't.

INVESTIGATION DIVISION:
SUBJECT: Murray Gordon WATSON,
   DOB 63/02/11
   FPS#3991147B

This party is a lock-pick expert. Intelligence indicates he has been responsible for hundreds of B&E's throughout the lower mainland since 1983. He is a known heroin addict and has sold and used a variety of other illegal drugs. He is a career criminal.

WATSON became a Strike Force target because a large number of B&E's were occurring, particularly in the Team Seven Area, that fitted WATSON'S MO to a Tee. Also because he was found in possession of a police scanner, lock-picks, and miscellaneous expensive jewellery which he could not account for.

Surveillance showed that he continually drives erratically and very fast, up to 80 KPH on side-streets, and is often high on drugs while driving. He is a constant danger to all who use our streets. To surveil this individual properly is a dangerous undertaking.

Strike Force followed this party the best part of three days. This surveillance culminated in the arrest of WATSON on charges of B&E x 5 and possession of break-in instruments (lock-picks).

WATSON was kept in custody for a show-cause hearing which took place on 90/06/05. At that time the prosecutor informed the judge of the above and that he was also currently before the courts on the following charges:

NIP times three
FTA [Failure to Appear] times three
Drive While Prohibited

Defence stated that he, WATSON, wished to get off drugs and

be in a drug-free house. The Judge stated that he could see no reason to keep WATSON in custody and released him to re-appear on 90/06/12.

WATSON has the following record:

Date/Location	Convictions	Disposition
81/10/03 Vanc.	Trafficking	Susp. Sentence and Probation/3 years
81/11/10 Vanc.	NIP	$50 fine/one day
84/01/05 Vanc.	B&E/Theft	Susp. Sentence and Probation/one year
84/09/06 Edmon.	Possess Stolen Prop x 3	Nine Months on Each Charge (concurrent)
85/09/16 Vanc.	Drunk Driving	$350 fine/14 days
85/11/18 Edmon.	Theft Under	$75 fine/14 days
87/02/16 Vanc.	Assault GBH Stolen Prop Stolen Prop Over $1,000	9 Months and Prohib from Poss. Firearm Ammo, Explosives for five years/ release and 1 year on each/ conc/probation 2 years.
89/01/09 Vanc.	Theft Under	$250 fine/five days
89/07/21 Vanc.	Drunk Driving	$500 fine/five days
89/08/17 Vanc.	Theft Under	$75 fine/five days.

NOTE: This subject admitted to our investigator he has been responsible for at least fifteen thousand B&E's in Vancouver. Submitted for your information.

Now anyone out there with a functioning gag-reflex has to be asking himself why the hell this busy little creep isn't sitting on his butt on a cold metal bench watching a patch of blue sky through a chicken-wire grid. Well, the answer is—once all the legalisms are stripped away—that over the years whole series of judges didn't take the guy very seriously, and they didn't take him seriously because when they looked at him, they saw a drug addict, and the current fashion in this victim-obsessed age is to see a drug addict as someone with a sickness, a disease, not unlike postnasal drip.

Why this doesn't infuriate people who are suffering from *real* diseases—such as cancer—which they in no way wished for or worked on acquiring, escapes me entirely. Our little buddy Watson here showed the kind of dedication to his habit that would make a wolverine's eyes mist up with speechless admiration.

Now this document…

VANCOUVER POLICE DEPARTMENT
INVESTIGATION:
FINANCIAL INSTITUTION ROBBERY
SUSPECTS—DRUG RELATIONSHIP:
Per our previous conversations on this subject, the Robbery
  Squad recently researched the backgrounds of each person
  charged with a financial institution robbery in Vancouver
  from May 1, 1989 to May 1, 1990.
NUMBER ARRESTED: 56
NUMBER DRUG-DRIVEN   43
PERCENTAGE DRUG-DRIVEN   75%
It is difficult, due to multiple drug use, to precisely determine
  which drug was being used by a suspect at time of arrest but
  the Robbery Squad estimates that cocaine is the drug of
  choice for 70 to 75% of the drug-driven suspects.
R. Law, A/Inspector
i/c Major Crime Section

And this…

VPD—FRAUD SUSPECTS—DRUG INVOLVEMENT:
  92/01/25
1. Detective Shakespeare has charged Scott Galloway, 20
   years, with numerous counts of false pretences and forgery.
   Monies obtained were approximately $15,000. Used the
   money to support cocaine habit.
2. Detective Todd has charged Mark Barber, 30 years, with
   false pretences, where he obtained goods which he sold to
   support drug habit. Obtained in excess of $12,000.
3. Detective Mancell charged Carl Joe, 22 years, with credit
   card fraud. Accused stole friend's card from the mail and

received cash advances and ATM withdrawals for a total of $1,200 used to purchase drugs.

4. Detective Joyce has charged Brian Gerald Mortimer-Lamb with 2 counts of uttering a forgery by the encashment of two cheques for $700. The accused has alcohol/drug related problems.

5. Detective Esakin has laid 43 charges of obtaining goods by false pretences against Lily Bronowski, 38 years. She obtained approximately $4,000 in merchandise that she would sell for cash. Friends and witnesses state that she is a prescription drug abuser.

6. Detective Preddy charged Lisa Marie Walsh, 26 years, with 3 counts of credit card fraud where she obtained approximately $3,500 to keep herself and her boyfriend in drugs.

7. Detective Mitchell charged Rhonda Gaynor, 25 years, with two counts of theft and 11 counts of credit card fraud. Accused stole ID and credit cards from hospital patients and obtained $4,916.00 in cash and merchandise. She used funds to support her soft drug habit.

8. Detective Preddy has charged Michael Marinakis, 37 years, with numerous counts of credit card fraud. (See Lisa Marie Walsh above.) Marinakis obtains cash advances and uses funds to support himself and his girlfriend (Lisa Marie Walsh) with drugs. He has obtained in excess of $10,000 and continues with the same MO as soon as he is released from custody.

9. Detective Misewich has charged Harold Ekstram, 25 years, with 5 counts of uttering a forged document. Accused obtained $2,700 in cash. Money was apparently used to purchase drugs for himself and his friends.

10. Detective Mancell has charged Heather Ann Williams, 39 years, with fraud and forgery. The accused, in her position of book-keeper, defrauded the YMCA of over $205,000 over a two-year period. When arrested the accused stated that she got tied up with a group of cocaine users. She used the money to support her cocaine habit and to buy drugs for her friends.

11. Detective Carriere has charged Antonio Aresta, 32 years, with 10 counts of obtaining money by false pretences. He obtained $12,733 which he was spending on his drug habit.

He is presently being investigated for theft of his parents' vehicle and also for forgery of his parents' signature to get funds from their bank account.

12. Detective Price has charged Doug Rankin, 32 years, with 5 counts of forgery. Accused is dependent on drugs and alcohol. He obtained $1,205 to support his habit.

13. Detective Esakin has charged Mary LeCouffe, 39 years, with 5 counts of obtaining money by false pretences. Accused admitted to being an alcohol and soft drug abuser. Accused is presently entered into an alcohol treatment program.

14. Detective Price charged Laura Lynn Halldorson, 24 years, with 12 counts of forgery. She obtained $1,350 from her mother's bank account by forging her mother's signature. The funds were used to pay off an outstanding drug debt.

15. Detective Esakin has charged Anthony Pereira, 21 years, with 8 counts of obtaining goods by false pretences. The accused purchased in excess of $6,000 in merchandise. He converted the merchandise to cash. Although the accused made no admissions it was apparent that he is a casual soft-drug user.

Bear with me…you need to see this stuff…

VANCOUVER POLICE DEPARTMENT—
INVESTIGATION
90/06/07

TRAFFICKERS/BREACH OF UNDERTAKING

On 90/05/30 the RCMP and the VPD Drug Squad commenced the round-up of sixty-nine accused, who were wanted for trafficking in either heroin or cocaine. To date, forty have been arrested. The Crown took a position and argued to keep all of these accused in custody. They were successful in keeping five. The remainder were released and were given "No Go" to the area of 100 East Hastings.

The conditions for release were, on their own recognizance, a small cash bail or with one surety. In each instance, a "No Go" order was issued for the area encompassed by Main on the east, Pender on the south, Cambie on the west, and

Cordova on the north.

As of this date, the following accused have been re-arrested for Breach of this undertaking:

ECHEVARRIA, Fred
GREEN, Mark
HO, Trong Son
LE, Dai Hung
NGUYEN, Thai Van
CHAU, Van Thang

The document goes on to list the personal and criminal histories of these six men. Each has been a persistent drug offender and criminal for many years, most are or were on welfare, each has been tried, convicted and given a variety of minor sentences for crimes such as:

> Theft Under $1,000
> FTA times Two
> Personation with Intent
> Breach of Probation
> Armed Robbery
> Possession Stolen Property Over $200
> Narcotics in Possession
> B and E and Theft
> Deal in a Forgery
> Impaired Driving
> Violation of Mandatory Supervision
> Use of Stolen Credit Card
> Mischief
> Escape Lawful Custody
> Assault
> Uttering a Forged Document

The longest sentence handed down in one of these charges was two years, for a couple of B and Es, and the next highest was one year, for Armed Robbery. On the average, they received sentences varying from Suspended, or Time Saved, to Probation. In the judgement of the detectives involved, each man is at high risk for repeated offences in all of these areas.

Naturally, each of these men managed to go right on doing whatever they felt like, much to the distress of any honest citizen who happened to get in the way.

Why is this okay with you?

Why aren't we on our way to Ottawa with torches and feather pillows and pre-heated barrels of roofing tar?

Beats me.

Well, in the fullness of time, the cops got angry…

VANCOUVER POLICE DEPARTMENT   90/04/20

Meeting with MICHAEL DANBROT—Department of Justice

On 90/04/12, Staff Sergeant Smith of our Narcotic Squad and I met with Mr. Brian Purdy, the Department of Justice BC head. The purpose of this meeting was to discuss:

1. The narrow interpretation being applied to Section 8 of the Charter by some Department of Justice personnel. Different applications of this section in various jurisdictions across the country.

2. Plea bargaining. Allowing an accused to plead to NIP only when there is evidence to support PPT. The judge should hear the evidence and make that determination.

3. Sentencing. Totally different sentences being given across the country from very lenient in BC to quite stringent in Alberta.

4. Judge Cronin. It is our feeling that he should be appealed on every occasion where sufficient grounds are present to support that appeal.

5. Use of certificates of analysis only. Drug to be destroyed. (Trial period to start April 16th, 1990.)

We found Mr. Purdy very sympathetic to our concerns. He however stated that because he had an insufficient number of prosecutors handling an extremely large case load, he could understand why they occasionally…

[*Occasionally!*]

…looked for ways to reduce the case load. He informed me that he would be meeting with Mr. Danbrot who had

recently been appointed Director of the National Drug
Prosecution Strategy Task Force, and asked me if I would be
interested in discussing these matters with him. I immediately
responded that I would and a meeting was arranged for
90/04/18.

On that date I met with Mr. Danbrot and Mr. Purdy and
discussed fully items 1, 2, and 3 and touched upon our
problem with Judge Cronin.

Mr. Danbrot agreed that there should be more consistency both
in the interpretation of the law and in sentencing, particularly
in those cases where the convicted party has shown a
propensity to re-offend.

Mr. Danbrot will be meeting with various agencies and
individuals prior to making some recommendations to the
Federal Government. I am hopeful, from my meeting with
him, that those recommendations will help alleviate some of
our concerns.

I recommend that both the Canadian Association of Chiefs of
Police and the British Columbia Association of Chiefs of
Police give serious consideration to making presentations to
Mr. Danbrot regarding these issues.

D.W. Keith, Insp. 211
i/c Vice Section.

And what came of this…?

Gee, well…can you fill in the blanks in the following sentences?

"My _____ is in the mail."

"OF COURSE I'll _____ you in the morning!"

"Trust me, I'm a trained _____!"

And…in case you think this is just a Vancouver problem and
what can you expect from those Spandex-wearing pot-smoking
leftover-hippie-dippie trance-channeling crystal-hugging gra-
nola-munching freakazoids out in British Columbia…well, in
December of that year, we have this exchange of letters between
the VPD and Metro Toronto Police. It seems the Metro Toronto
area isn't doing much better and the cops are very worried…

METROPOLITAN TORONTO POLICE
40 COLLEGE STREET
TORONTO ONTARIO
CANADA
416-324-2222 FAXLINE 324-6345

December 17, 1990
Mister RJ Stewart,
Chief of Police,
Vancouver Police Department,
312 Main Street,
Vancouver, BC
V6A 2T2.

Dear Sir:

The Metropolitan Toronto Police Force is attempting to streamline its drug enforcement initiatives in order to better serve our community in the nineties.

It is with this in mind that I am requesting your assistance in this endeavour. I have compiled four (4) areas of concern which I would appreciate your agency responding to at your earliest convenience.

1. Would you kindly give us a brief overview of the current drug problems (both licit and illicit) within your jurisdiction.

2. I would appreciate it if you would detail some of the initiatives implemented by your Force to combat the drug problems with special emphasis on STREET LEVEL ENFORCEMENT.

3. How many drug prosecutional buys are required within your jurisdiction in order to ensure a successful prosecution?

4. I am requesting a perspective on Narcotic Control Act sentencing within your jurisdiction on the following substances:

Cannabis Derivatives—Marihuana [sic]
      Hashish
      Hash Oil
Cocaine Hydrochloride
Cocaine Base (Crack)

am looking at a general range for Possession, Possession for

the Purpose of Trafficking and Trafficking Charges that deal
with these substances.
I would like to thank you in advance and assure you of our co-
operation and mutual concern.

Yours truly,
Julian Fantino
Superintendent,
Detective Services.

Which prompted this reply...

Chief Constable's Office
Vancouver Police Department

William J. McCormack
Chief of Police,
Metropolitan Toronto Police,
40 College Street,
TORONTO, ONTARIO,
M5G 2J3.

91/01/07

Attn: Supt. J. Fantino.
Dear Sir:
In regards to your letter dated 90/12/17, as you are well aware,
British Columbia and more specifically, Vancouver, has a
major illicit drug problem which impacts on all of our citizens
in some way.
Possibly, because drug abuse has been a problem in this area
for such a long time, it is one of the reasons why the judiciary
in BC have come to treat most drug cases in a relatively
permissive manner.
Attached is a 1989 BC Court of Appeal case, REGINA v.
LESLIE SULLIVAN, in which that court basically stated that
the rehabilitation of addicted substance abusers, even those
who are repeat offenders, with extensive records, must be
considered over incarceration. This landmark decision

probably best demonstrates the attitude of the courts in BC regarding possession of narcotic charges.

Our comments on your four areas of concern are as follows:

1. CURRENT OVERVIEW OF DRUG PROBLEMS:

Marijuana and hashish are readily available throughout the city; little hash oil or weed oil is encountered. Marijuana and hash are sold on the street in the core area, in most bars, in many restaurants, at private residences, at many work sites, as well as at many schools and universities. Much of the marijuana seized is home grown and most of that is hydroponically grown indoors. Hydroponic cultivation is a booming business and it is estimated that as many as a thousand such operations may be in operation in the greater Vancouver area. THC levels vary from 7% up to a high of 22% with the average being approximately 10 to 12%. Imported marijuana is often considerably lower.

Although we have yet to obtain sufficient evidence to link any of our hydroponic houses to organized crime, we suspect that many are financed by biker gangs and other criminal organizations. These organizations will hire low-key individuals to monitor and harvest the crop. As a result, usually the accused have either a very minor or no criminal record. In 1989, thirty-three (33) individuals charged with cultivation were dealt with in our provincial court. The results were as follows:

STAY OF PROCEEDINGS	19	(58%)
DISMISSED OR ACQUIT	4	(12%)
SUSPENDED SENTENCE	2	(6%)
FINES $500 OR LESS	1	(3%)
FINES OVER $500	4	(12%)
JAIL ONE DAY	3	(9%)

HEROIN: The greater Vancouver area has a heroin addict population estimated at between six and ten thousand. Although heroin is not a "socially acceptable" drug, the addict population appears to be on the increase. Seizures of heroin are up over 800% from 235 grams in 1989 to 1,926 grams in 1990. The most apparent cause of this increase is the use of

heroin by cocaine addicts who are strung out and use the
heroin to counter the effects brought on by the heavy use
of cocaine (insomnia, extreme excitability, paranoia etc.).
Many of these individuals were not criminals prior to
becoming addicted unlike the traditional heroin addicts who
usually were introduced to drugs through their criminal
associates after they were entrenched in criminal lifestyles.
When they become addicted, they quickly compile long
criminal records.

Heroin is in plentiful supply in Vancouver and easily obtained
if you are known by the trafficker or "sponsored" by a trusted
user. A large number of addicts score their heroin in the core
area of the city where users and traffickers congregate.
However it can also be purchased at a few other locations
throughout the city—private residences, restaurants. Most
heroin is sold in caps with the usual street price being $35.00.
Almost all of our heroin addicts take it intravenously.

COCAINE: Cocaine is readily available throughout the city. In
the core area, it is sold indiscriminately to almost anyone who
asks and often non-users are solicited by traffickers or their
agents. This is a fairly recent phenomenon with cocaine only
becoming prevalent as a street drug since 1987. Cocaine is
usually sold by the deck in amounts from 1/8 gram up to a
gram. The most usual price is $120.00 a gram. Although little
cocaine is sold on the street in the form of "crack" or rock
cocaine, many users convert their cocaine to this form so they
can smoke it. In Vancouver the majority of our criminal
cocaine addicts take their cocaine intravenously.

What is truly disturbing about cocaine is that a great number of
users are able to use cocaine undetected by police until their
use is out of control and other criminal acts are perpetrated to
finance their addiction. Cocaine unlike heroin is used by
individuals in every walk of society and often taken in the
work setting. Police receive little intelligence on individuals
who traffic or use in the social or work environment. Up until
very recently, cocaine was considered socially acceptable by
many and we suspect its use is even more widespread than as
yet reported.

2. STREET-LEVEL ENFORCEMENT INITIATIVES:

Currently the VPD have only twelve operations members
working our Narcotics Squad. Six work as a group on
marijuana cultivation cases as well as on other soft drug
trafficking and cocaine trafficking cases while the other six
work with nine RCMP members as a unit and are assigned to
investigate street level heroin and cocaine trafficking (seven
more members will be assigned in 1991).
The Narcotics Squad is responsible for 30% of the total
number of narcotics charges produced by the Vancouver
police. In 1989, that amounted to 1,207...

[By 1992 it was closing in on 1,500...]

...which were almost totally divided between NIP and PPT.
The remaining 70% of drug charges were handled by our
Patrol members operating both in Plainclothes and Uniform.
Narcotics Squad members also seized over three million
dollars in narcotics in 1989.

[And close to four million in 1992. The whole of the VPD is
approaching a record 12 million in seized drugs for 1992.]

In our opinion constant pressure by our Narcotics Squad is
required in the core area where most of our street trafficking
occurs. We find that this pressure minimizes the negative
impact on that community and that when we remove these
policemen from this area for any length of time, crime
escalates.
Having said that, in the past year, we conducted one major
Conspiracy investigation into a local restaurant that was
selling heroin across the counter. The investigation required
all our manpower for seven weeks and virtually lost us one
man for a year.

[An injury—a bad one, but the judges don't see that kind of
thing; it might impair their purity.]

Wiretap and Surveillance both were used. The case culminated in the charging of eleven individuals with Conspiracy to Traffic in Heroin and another eighteen individuals with NIP. Approximately a half-million dollars in assets were seized.

Buy and Bust Operations are conducted several times a year in a variety of active locations. These usually run for four days. In both 1989 and 1990, the RCMP supplied undercover members for operations which lasted two and three months respectively. We average about twenty arrests in each Buy and Bust and we charged 58 individuals in one UC [undercover] operation and another 69 in the other UC operation.

It is an unfortunate fact however that our courts treat most of these cases as minor misdemeanors and we are flooded with repeat offenders.

The VPD are constantly looking for new ways to have an impact on street crime and the illicit drug trade. However to date we have found that the traditional route of keeping constant pressure on the street trafficker from both our plain-clothes Drug Officers and our uniform members gives us the best results, considering the resources available.

3. NUMBER OF BUYS TO GET A CHARGE:

The Department of Justice (DOJ) will prosecute on one buy if the case is solid. If the case makes it to court, usually a conviction is obtained. The sentences however are often in our opinion inadequate.

4. SENTENCING: MARIJUANA AND HASH-OIL:

The sentences for these substances would usually be similar and we will deal with them as one.

CRACK COCAINE and COCAINE HYDROCHLORIDE would also usually be dealt with by our courts in a comparable way and will also be dealt with as one here.

Drug	Charge	1st Convict.	2nd Convict.	Addit.
Grass	NIP	Discharge/SS	SS or fine	SS/jail
		[Suspended Sentence]		
	PPT	SS or fine	SS or short time	SS/jail
Coke	NIP	Dis/SS/fine	Fine or short time	SS/jail
	PPT	Dis/fine	Fine and/or short time	

The key word is "inconsistent." Minimum sentences should be legislated based on both the number of previous convictions and the amount of drugs involved.

For example, one individual, who prior to 1990 had accumulated 10 convictions for NIP, 5 convictions for PPT or Trafficking (Cannabis) and 4 convictions for Assault was charged with a variety of drug charges on TWELVE occasions during 1990. A few charges are still pending; however four separate counts were dealt with on 90/09/17 and convictions registered in each instance. The sentence was 30 days in custody on each count, CONCURRENT.

[To be served in one 30-day stretch, as opposed to consecuve, which would mean a total of 120 days at 30 days per count.]

Then again on 90/10/12, four more convictions were registered against this same individual and he was sentenced to 45 days on each count, concurrent.

I sincerely hope this information will be of some assistance to your department. If more material is required, I encourage you to contact Inspector Keith of our Vice Section direct as he is familiar with the issues and can no doubt be of some help in your endeavors.

Yours truly,
S.A. Ziola,
A/Deputy Chief Constable,
Bureau of Operations.

And so it goes...

You know, while I've got your attention, does it ever occur to ou that maybe the human race is just too stupid to live? Recently ey've discovered some fairly convincing proof of the Big Bang heory, which tends to confirm our intuition that everything in e universe was at one time contained in a single proton-sized nit and is now getting farther away from everything else in kind of meta-cosmic exploding cloud of probabilities and articles. Whenever I consider this, I get this brief vision of

some primeval God handing a human a very small and pro
foundly beautiful box and saying, "Now look, Gorg, this is ver
fragile and if you drop it a whole lot of things are going to hap
pen that you won't be able to control," and Gorg nods and wrap
both his paws around it and watches God drive off in a brand
new Galaxy, and as he watches God leaving, his nose starts t
itch. Makes you think, right?

Well, maybe not.

At any rate the situation continues to deteriorate, and Metr
Toronto has become the murder capital of Canada, due mostly t
gang wars over drugs, no matter what the hate-mongers are say
ing about cop racism and systemic economic unfairness.

(Why is it that stealing a stereo and smashing all the window
at Bloor and Yonge has become an acceptable form of politica
expression? Would Martin Luther King have approved, even i
they'd promised him a 500-watt pre-amp and a set of Bozes tha
could cause hair-loss and cardiac arrhythmia in a yak at six hur
dred yards? You see what I mean about too stupid to live?)

Montreal, Calgary, Winnipeg and Vancouver are also seeing
major increase in most drug-related crimes, many of which ar
hidden under the anonymity factor of the Young Offenders Ac
either because these juveniles are not easy to track through th
mazes of the juvenile justice system or because many of th
crimes never make it to a court and so avoid becomin
reportable statistics.

One last chart...

ESTIMATED COSTS OF OPERATING THE VPD
 NARCOTICS SQUAD FOR 1992:
SALARIES:

1	Staff-Sergeant @ $4,878.00 a month:	$58,536.00
2	Sergeants @ $4,534.00 a month:	$108,816.00
11	Detectives @ $4,155.00 a month:	$548,460.00
2	Constables @ $3,613.00 a month:	$86,712.00
1	Civilian @ $2,423.00 a month:	$29,076.00
1	Civilian @ $2,122.00 a month:	$25,464.00
1	Civilian Temporary:	$13,500.00
Benefits for members:		$165,591.00

Benefits for civilians:	$7,908.00
Court Overtime @ 3,860 hours avg:	$114,910.40
(Court costs do not reflect On-duty appearances)	
Lease Vehicles @ $400.00 a month:	$19,200.00
Rental Vehicles:	$1,357.00
Pagers @ $36.00 a month:	$324.00
VPD Drug Warehousing/Staff:	$146,936.00
VPD Drug Warehousing/Space: [est]	$150,000.00

TOTAL COST OF VPD DRUG SQUAD $1,476,466.00

Now by this time, we're hearing a few noises from the back of the room, where the social workers and the psychiatrists are sitting: drugs are a societal problem, a manifestation of a deeper malaise, a rotting at the heart of North American culture or a human reaction to the concept of mortality, or a release from the grinding poverty and durance vile imposed upon the commoners by a privileged and arrogant oligarchy. Some of them are whispering darkly of our own fears about pleasure, and the more mean-minded of them are suggesting that the cops like to inflate our fears about drugs so they can buy more really neat stuff from the military suppliers and turn the screws on the Vice Grip a little more.

And from a small crowd who has just returned from the bathroom wiping their noses and feeling a little feisty, the old song floats over the assembly…"Legalize it!"

Most of our police departments would agree that anywhere from 40 to 60 percent of all crime is drug-related. The Strike Force experience right across Canada (and in the United States as well) is that 90 percent of the people they pop for various crimes—B and Es, Armed Robbery, Theft, Assaults—are chronic drug-users. That means that, on average, our police forces are spending about 50 percent of their time trying to handle the various consequences of drug-related crime. I won't trouble you with the calculations, but that means that we, as taxpayers, are spending roughly $5 billion a year fighting "the Drug War."

Does that mean that if we just make the stuff legal, we can split $5 billion? That would mean $200 every year for every living citizen in the country. Or, if we just set it against th deficit, we might be able to dent that monster! And all we hav to do is...I mean, wow, this is really exciting!

Okay, first thing, we'd have to set up something like th Ontario Liquor Control Board—a great place to cram those ou of-work senators and auto workers. Then we'd have to get som sort of national ID run up, so we wouldn't have kids trying buy heroin underage. We'd have to decide how much we coul tax the cocaine—now there's a thought, a tax on the cocain trade, meaning more money, some of which we could set asid for those few undisciplined types who can't handle their drug And we'd have to have mandatory Crank-Free Areas in all th restaurants so nobody would have to watch some FNG* hurl h cookies because he was new to skag. Some trouble there wit the No Smoking zanies, probably, but that's why God made P agents. Next we hand out a few franchised dealerships—mayb Labatt or Molson or Seagram—hell, no—more like Starbucks Tim Horton Donuts! We set up a few federal guidelines abou purity and that sort of thing—can't have the Feds backing infer or crank or selling stepped-on skag, there'd be questions in th House! Hell, there'd be tie-ins and point-of-purchase items lik Designer Stash Bags or Personalized Silver-Plated Needle Complete With Safe-T-Flush Sterilizer System, only $59.95 o your VISA, American Express or MasterCard—no COD please. And, *my God*, think of the *advertising!*

CHINABONE MENTHOL
For that just-blissed feeling—freshens as you snort!

Or...

CRANK LITE
What We Shoot Around Here

* Fucking New Guy——from the Vietnam War

Or...

HAPPY VALLEY ORGANIC MARIJUANA
Promotes Cosmic Regularity—It's The Right Shit To Do

And...

LULLABY LUDES
When Reality Is Just Too Damn Much Work

The spin-off possibilities are endless, and think about all the money the so-called caring professions are going to make from all that drug counseling and therapy and hospital treatment and Gestalt therapy and Co-dependency Counseling, the federal grants that they'll get for Drug Education and Enhanced National Focus, the massive expenditures that will be necessary for Treating all these new addicts and users, the building and the new employment! Hell, a lot of jobs will become vacant just as soon as some new user connects with that pesky massive cardiopulmonary incident sometimes brought on by even one hit of cocaine. There might even be a major boom in mortuary services...the benefits go on and on...

Hello...is anybody out there...?

First of all, anyone who imagines that a drug like heroin can be put in the same context as a snifter of Remy after backgammon is either a fool or only a few days into his habit. I've seen the middle-class connect with heroin and no matter what they were saying about their habit, the results were always the same: one year later they were either dead or in treatment.

That goes in spades for cocaine and its derivatives.

Now there may be a few heroically balanced and highly evolved individuals who have such a superb moral and spiritual gyroscope that they can dabble in drugs such as these without spinning off into the pit, but bitter experience has taught the rest of us that all mood-changers are risky, and we don't need to legalize the more virulent ones to please the deluded—or criminal— posturings of a few elitist academics.

If anyone out there needs verification of this, think about

those years you wasted smoking dope back in the 1970s. How many of the insights that seemed so persuasive while you were stoned survived even the following ten years?

Hard to face, isn't it?

The Flower Children withered fast, didn't they? In spite of all that Age of Aquarius bullshit, the drug culture of the 1970s has left nothing more lasting than crystal therapy, Margaret Atwood books, a few poli-sci profs around the nation and the odd gathering of wet-brain New Age loopazoids on Galliano Island and up in the boondocks north of Barrie.

The point is, drugs were in a kind of de facto legalized state in the late 1960s and early 1970s—a period that is fondly recalled by far too many of the people who are currently in positions to influence the justice system. And all that came of that was a cloud of political and moral casuistry that blew away on the chilling winds of the first recession back in 1980. Even Amsterdam is regretting its position on heroin and cocaine.

The only reason I can think of to legalize a drug—and the drug would be marijuana—is that I'd much rather be trying to arrest a criminal who happened to be stoned on grass than a criminal wired on coke or speed. If you don't get that, ring up John Belushi and ask him to explain it to you. What is really underlying the legalization position is contempt; they can handle their drugs and they really don't give a shit if you or your kid can't.

Even if legalization had value, no one but a fool or a publicity hound—or someone drunk on his own hubris—would seriously expect our current crop of politicians to enter such a radical proposal.

Right now, we are in the middle of one of the most anti-vice, anhedonic ages in the history of the planet. You can get spray-painted for wearing a raccoon coat on King Street. You can get sued by your kids for second-hand smoke (people in restaurants will beat you senseless with their Hermès bags just for thinking about lighting up a smoke three tables over). Even the beer companies are running ads about controlling alcohol intake. Aside from the sheer stupidity of the idea, anyone out there who seriously thinks that a civilization as litigious, as self-righteous, as out-and-out puritanical as this one is about to legalize any further means with which to blow our brains out, ruin our livers, throw Olympic-class strokes in public places and generally red-line our psyches into total Pablum is NOT PAYING ATTENTION, and maybe we ought to turn around in our seats right now and check this guy's pupils. Or his pulse.

I'll wait here...and while I'm waiting, I'll tell you something else. Don Keith quit the cops. Even he had had enough. And before he left, he had a few things to say:

> ...We are of the opinion that each of the following pieces of legislation in some material way hampers effective drug enforcement and together with current sentencing practices are partly responsible for a declining drug situation in our city and throughout Canada:
> 1. The Charter
> 2. The Privacy Act
> 3. The Young Offenders Act
> 4. Bill C-61, Seizure of Assets
> 5. Bail Reform Act
> 6. Administrative policies.
>
> ...The Charter...the interpretation of the search and seizure section that is being applied calls for police to have a reasonable belief that an individual has drugs on his person at the time he is searched. Crown is not proceeding with cases where, in the absence of specific information, the police search a known drug user when he is seen leaving a place where drugs are known to be distributed...even when his actions are consistent with those of a person transporting drugs...What I believe would be a more realistic test would be a test on the balance of probabilities. I fail to see how a search in these circumstances could bring the administration of justice into ill repute...
>
> ...Needless restrictions are being placed on police officers. For instance, let's say the police have received information that drugs are being sold from a particular address. Surveillance shows that three individuals have visited that residence in a short period of time. This is consistent with persons making drug buys. The third person is stopped by the police, found

with drugs, and admits purchasing them from the suspect address. Justices are not issuing warrants and the police investigation is stymied and complaining citizens are left frustrated and angry.

…Drug investigations require that police deal with informants on a regular basis. Full disclosure as interpreted under the Charter has led to some informants being identified in court. This is very dangerous to the informant—life-threatening—and has resulted in many potential sources of information refusing to continue…and police are reluctant to use information that could result in the informant being identified in court and subsequently…killed. Surely a procedure could be set up that would protect the informant in all cases where he was not a principal in the offence…for instance, the judge could be given the name of the informant but would only reveal it to the defence after the defence was complete…this would prevent the defence from going on a fishing expedition to identify the informant…

…About Bill C61, the Seizure of Assets…it doesn't go far enough to have a major impact on most traffickers… Banks should be required to report all transactions over $10,000…The accused should not be allowed to use seized assets to pay for defence…it makes no sense that assets obtained by crime should be used to defend that individual…Now the courts must prove that the assets were obtained by the illegal enterprise…but once a case of trafficking against an individual has been proved, it should be incumbent upon that individual to PROVE that any assets he has were legitimately earned, otherwise those assets should be forfeited to The Crown. The same situation should apply to vehicles being used to transport drugs…

An illustration: suppose a bank clerk were to be discovered in an embezzlement, and the amount missing was substantial, and the investigation disclosed that this clerk had recently bought himself a T-Bill and a raft of blue-chip stocks. Should he be allowed to use the T-Bills and the stocks to finance his defence?

…In the States, buildings used as shooting galleries…are liable to seizure by the State…

…In the Privacy Act…this legislation made it illegal for anyone to monitor private conversations…Although police can make application to a Judge through the Solicitor General…to monitor…the process is complicated and restrictive…If a twenty-four hour available Justice was empowered to authorize short-term interceptions of traffickers…the chances of success would be greatly enhanced…

…The Young Offenders Act…requires a reporting procedure that is cumbersome, restrictive, and lengthy, together with courts that fail to deal effectively with accused parties…[it] leads to few young offenders being charged with drug offences…

[Which enables Stats Can to report a *decrease* in juvenile drug arrests!]

…even though a good number of school children do abuse drugs…

…Sentencing…to have any effect, sentences have to be fair, consistent, and trials have to be heard soon after the charge is laid, preferably within three months. Quick trials may not be attainable…but should be a goal…Fair and consistent sentencing could easily be obtained if minimum sentences were legislated into the applicable Acts…for example:

FOR POSSESSION…

First Offence: Sentence Suspended if Mandatory Drug Rehab is successfully completed.

Second Offence: 30 days jail/drug rehab

Third Offence: 90 days/drug rehab

Fourth Offence: 180 days/drug rehab

FOR MINOR TRAFFICKING…

First Offence: 180 days minimum/rehab

Second Offence: One year—mandatory rehab

Third Offence: Two Years less a day/rehab

If the Trafficker is not a user, the sentences should be longer, since the plea of drug addiction cannot be entered as a mitigating factor.

...Some other helpful things...Let police lay their own Informations. There are not enough prosecutors and we often perceived that they do not present the case as strongly as it deserves...

...Have JPs available at least until two in the morning, because the call-out system is lengthy and fraught with difficulties...

Have prosecutors present the full records of accused drug offenders...one judge refuses to listen to any details except previous drug convictions...I get the feeling that the judges do not understand the gravity of the matter and put the drug abuser into the category of being victims...They may be...but they are the authors of their own misfortune and in turn victimize countless others...

...Serious remedies are required.

Yes, they are.

Are we going to get serious remedies?

Probably not.

Why not?

Because no one with authority to change these things is listening to you or me.

Why not?

Simple. They're not afraid of us.

You and I can be had for a jig and a tale of bawdry. As I said in the beginning of this book, we have been sheep, and the coyotes do not fear sheep.

Not that our judges are coyotes. I think of them more as llamas and giraffes, placid ruminants with necks long enough to let them overlook the chaos and the ruin all around them, long enough to let them see "the Big Picture."

And the funny thing about the Big Picture is that all the real people in it are very, very tiny and easy to miss.

Those little tiny things there?

That's us.

ELEVEN

The Sheep Blink

I've been having a lot of fun here, over a serious issue, partly because, after watching the results of our silly-ass dithering over drugs and crime, I was in desperate need of a laugh.

The people who want to make certain drugs legal (and the choices are usually grass and cocaine, although some of them have mentioned heroin and morphine base) have it in mind that the driving force behind a lot of the crime we've been talking about in this book is a desire for illegal drugs.

The documents I've cited would tend to support this thesis. Even the cops are running charts on drug-driven crime, some of which we've taken a look at here.

So, are they right? Would legalization stop chronic drug-abusing criminals from committing crimes?

Simply put, no.

They're wrong—and I know I've said this before, but some things need a heavy-hitter—because they are making a fundamental error in their assessment of the criminals in the drug culture. They imagine that the only reason these guys steal cars and boost credit cards and run hookers and mug pensioners is that they need to feed their habit. So, they reason, make the habit less expensive and BINGO, these rounders will suddenly find regular jobs and stop hanging around the schoolyards and they'll stop breaking into houses and they'll stop mugging pensioners. If they can pull down enough money slinging burgers at Mickey-Dee's to finance their skag habit and keep their nasal cavities raw and their brain-stems anesthetized, then they'll see no need to get into other crimes. Ergo, the crime rate drops and we can put our money into better causes, such as rehabilitation and tennis lessons for sex offenders.

Wrong.

It should be a condition of employment (we have them for pilots and surgeons and anyone else entrusted with vital and far-reaching social responsibilities) that each and every serving judge, each social worker, each Crown and each and every last lawyer working in the criminal justice system anywhere in North America be required to spend one shift each month riding along with a good beat cop in a patrol car.

Because we are not in a university lab here or a moot court. This is life for us out here, and it's getting a little hairy, and these guys don't seem to be getting it.

And what they're not getting is that most criminals are in crime because *it pays*. Most criminals have no fear of jail. It's a chance to get caught up on the latest professional developments, sort of like a criminal convention paid for by the taxpayer.

They can lift weights and get fit and clean up their habits a bit, meet old friends and eat regularly, and in the fullness of time, they get back on the street and go back to work.

They're in it because *they like it*.

What does it pay for?

It buys booze and it buys women and it buys clothes and it makes a nice supplement to welfare.

It pays for lawyers.

It pays for trips to Palm Springs.

It buys guns.

It buys knives.

It buys police scanners and dent-pullers and it pays off girl-friends with access to CPIC records.

It rents hideout apartments and it buys off paramedics and it buys off the odd rape victim.

It pays for the baby food and the Kraft Dinner and the security system and the red 'Vette and the black Camaro.

And crime pays for drugs, which are lots of fun.

I mean, think about it…

Heroin…they say it feels like a warm shower of golden light from the inside out.

I knew a guy who said it was a winter drug, and I've watched one of my old girlfriends red-flag her way to Oz. It takes away the cold and it takes away the chill of reality. It snakes up your arm like a golden viper and it bites right into the core of your being and it opens you up and out comes all that easy graceful timeless warm soothing peaceful calmness, and it runs down your lungs and floods into your belly and it loosens all those knots and corded anxieties and it melts away your fear and your sense of being too damned SMALL to survive and it say no...nooo...you're fine you're just fiiine...you're okay you're safe you're...you're...you're feeling just a little anxious here...no...no, you're fine...no...yes...yes, well, it has been a while since the last hit and...just a little more now...just a little more...

And freebase cocaine (the up-market brandname for crack)?

Forked Blue Lightning.

Bang it into your lungs and suddenly you are the brightest, the absolute best and the brightest, and you can feel your muscles like electric wires and your brain-stem BURNS with brightness and wit and the thoughts come so FAST and the world opens up like a black dahlia and YOU CAN DO ANYTHING you fucking well please and you can GET WHAT YOU WANT NOW and...and...and who the fuck are YOU looking at, asshole? You looking at me...?

You looking at ME?

And dope...kick back and cut back and ride it down the far side...feel the easy slow tide take you down...feel warm blue water like Jell-O...feel the tide take you away...hear your voice in your throat where it purrs and rumbles and throbs...slow your heart...watch the women move across the room...watch the light change in the window...watch your life from a long way away...

...wake up in a cheap hotel room with some asshole you don't know standing in the doorway with your wallet and your shoes in his hands saying thanks for the loan, dipshit...

To someone in the Life, drugs are just one of the perks.

Make the drugs legal and they're just going to keep right on breaking into homes and running credit scams and sizing up the vics because *that's what they do.*

They're like the seagulls or the tigers or the coyotes. Born to be the predators.

They're in crime because it beats working.

They're in crime because they think you and I are jerks.

They think their lawyers are jerks.

They think the cops are jerks.

They think anyone who isn't in crime is a sucker, a wage-slave, a drone, a putz, a mope.

They think the judges are brainless assholes who can be conned by sharp talk. (Hard to argue with that opinion.)

They think the law is a chain you jerk when you want to flush away some serious shit. (Also hard to dispute.)

Legalizing drugs will not change that belief in the slightest.

Legalize drugs and these guys will just laugh and think to themselves…we were RIGHT! The jerks are AFRAID.

And they'd be right.

We are afraid.

TWELVE

The Thing About Guns

If we're not afraid, then why are there so many guns?

Anyone who watched Reginald Denny get his lights kicked out on a street in South Central L.A. last year will have gone through a number of spiritual changes, beginning with horror and revulsion—feelings that peaked when that asshole with the brick came up and smashed it into Denny's head and proceeded to dance—literally *dance* away on one foot, pointing at the ruined skull of an innocent man as if he'd just slam-dunked the winning basket at a Knicks game. It was a moment in every way as vile as the beating of Rodney King, which is supposed to have sparked the assault in some obscure interaction of social dynamics.

Bullshit, by the way.

That kid was having fun, a kind of fun he had probably experienced many times before. Providing specimens like that with a kind of generalized social licence by attributing their actions to racism is not only simplistic and an insult to the thousands of brutalized poor who would never contemplate such a savage act, it's also profoundly dangerous.

So, by the time I was sick enough to look away from the beating of Reginald Denny that day, I was thankful for only one thing.

I have a gun.

This may disgust you, but if you haven't gotten the message already, I'll make it plain for you right now.

You are not safe.

If someone decides to make a project out of you, there is not one damned thing the cops can do to stop him.

Sure, they'll drop around later to scrape up and bag the consequences, and they'll put out an All Points if they can get a description, but you personally are now fishwrap. Yesterday's news. Something for the parakeet to consider over his breakfast of seedball and suet.

The system does not operate to protect you or your family. It operates after the fact of violence, in an attempt to punish—or at least distract—the criminal who has shattered your complacency.

Sure, it's terrible that there are so many guns around, and if I could believe that through some marvelous necromancy the cops could magically conjure away all the weaponry now in the hands of the bad guys, I'd take my piece to the crusher with a grin.

In the meantime, things being what they are, I'm keeping mine, and I'll bet you thirty pieces of silver that almost everyone who watched the video from L.A. spent some time thinking exactly the same way. One of the nice things about being a devolved reactionary middle-aged white male is being able to say things like this and then sitting back to watch the rest of the sheep hit the far side of the pasture at a dead run.

Say what you want about gun control (and Canada is just now trying to pass some new legislation), if the crime rate continues, more and more citizens will buy and maintain weapons.

As a matter of fact, it's kind of hard to blame people for that. The social contract is a promise from government to the governed. We'll keep you safe, and in return you give up some basic freedoms. If the government defaults on that promise—as we have seen judges do—then, logically, all bets are off.

The Feds and their compadres may have the power to keep the citizens from having weapons, but they don't have the moral right. Not any more. They blew that deal the first time a criminal did it the second time. The Supreme Court blew it the first time they let a criminal walk on a technicality.

The rest is sound and fury, signifying the operations of power or the unexamined prejudices of the privileged class or the delusion of those citizens who have not yet learned a bitter lesson by having it burnt into their skin.

THIRTEEN

The Sheep Do Math

Why go over all this stuff?

Because what is going on out in the street right at this moment is directly related to the kinds of decisions and diversions that our judges are using to beguile their tedious hours and astound the intelligentsia.

It is my honest and deeply felt belief that most judges and all civil liberties lawyers profoundly misunderstand the nature and causes of criminal behavior. I have to believe this because the only alternative is to believe that they do understand the criminal heart and they're lying to us about it.

Nothing else explains their actions.

As for the rest of us, we're buying security systems and handguns in record numbers, we stay in the house, we get used to losing our car stereos every other Tuesday and we leave the survival of our fellow citizens, our friends and our neighbors, to chance and the probability curves.

I think John Donne had something telling to say about that sort of behavior.* Go down to the stockyards and see how well it works for the rest of the ruminants. Nor does it help to withdraw into vicarious fantasies of affront and vengeance, in books and television and films, where we can find a transitory illusion that truth and goodness prevail, where every madman and sadistic killer finds his swift and appropriately painful end.

There is little chance that any of these measures are truly effective for any but the most naive and unobservant. The rest of us, in our millions, grow a carapace, like a skin over a wound, and go on about our lives, trying to ignore the profound suspicion that evil is not punished, that good does not prevail, that we re fundamentally and continually unsafe in our homes and

---

"Any man's death diminishes me, because I am involved in mankind, and therefore never send to know for whom the bell tolls; it tolls for thee." Meditation XVII, *Devotions upon Emergent Occasions.*

streets, that in our cities dead-eyed armies of the night run in the shadows and do whatever the hell they please.

Those of us who feel this way may in fact be quite right.

Just look at the numbers.

Crime statistics are a shaky foundation upon which to base any theoretical edifice. Take these with a caveat because, like all statistics, they are usually compiled to further the purposes of the government paying for them. But they suggest, at least, the scope of our problems.

Let's take the United States first, since, as we've seen, crime trends there tend to lead Canada by about ten years. (For example, the drug crack, which is virtually everywhere in America, has just now begun to be a sizeable problem in Canada.)

In the United States, crime statistics are compiled by the Federal Bureau of Investigation and the Bureau of Justice Statistics. Bearing in mind that crime stats are never developed without a political subtext and, like polls, are extremely vulnerable to manipulation, the figures are nevertheless memorable and persuasive.

Drawn from the Uniform Crime Reports, the stats, called Crime Index Offenses, are divided into violent and property crimes. Violent crimes are murder, non-negligent manslaughter, rape, robbery and aggravated assault. Property crimes are burglary, larceny and theft (effectively synonymous), motor vehicle theft and arson. The figures show a two-year lag, due to reporting delays and FBI insularity.

Between 1978 and 1990 Crime Index Offenses increased by 25 percent. There were some variations in the growth rate. In 1981, there were 14 million Crime Index Offenses in the United States.

Remember, we're talking only about *reported* offences here. Most experienced street cops will tell you that there are roughly ten unreported offences for every reported one. In other words, any criminal you catch has probably pulled at least ten offences you'll never hear about. As a working theory, let's say that all the figures here could be multiplied by a factor of ten to indicate the actual crime frequency for any year.

After 1981, there was a slow decline up to 1984, when there were only (*only?*) 11.8 million Index crimes reported to the FBI. However, things warmed up after that, reaching the 14 million mark again by 1987, and all trends suggest that the figures may reach 18 million by 1993.

Another way of looking at it would be as crimes per 100,000 people. In 1980, for every 100,000 people in the States, there were 5,950 crimes. In 1987, the per-100,000 rate was 5,550, a slight dip, and now the numbers are on a sharp rise again for 1989, 1990 and 1991.

An aside to our fellow Canadians here: it's time to stop feeling superior to our American cousins in the matter of Index crime rates. In Canada, in 1991, the rate of Index offences (that is, crimes per 100,000 people) ran like this:

Newfoundland	6,062 crimes per 100,000
PEI	7,222 crimes per 100,000
Nova Scotia	8,987 crimes per 100,000
New Brunswick	7,491 crimes per 100,000
Quebec	7,925 crimes per 100,000
Ontario	9,340 crimes per 100,000
Manitoba	10,608 crimes per 100,000
Saskatchewan	10,834 crimes per 100,000
Alberta	11,836 crimes per 100,000
BC	14,981 crimes per 100,000
NWT	28,831 crimes per 100,000
Yukon	20,410 crimes per 100,000

In other words, in Canada, famous for clean cities and safe streets, there are roughly twice as many crimes committed for every 100,000 people as you would find in the United States, and the farther west you go, the worse it gets. So much for Canadian complacency and condescension.

Murder rates, by the way, are currently rising dramatically. What a shock, eh? Overall, the crime rate in Canada went up 8 percent from 1990 to 1991.

As might be expected, large cities had higher per 100,000 rates. Cities with populations over fifty thousand had a crime rate of 6,294.5 per 100,000 people. The only exception to this trend was, again, in murders, where rural areas and small towns showed slightly higher murder rates than large cities. (Why that would be is beyond me, but there it is.)

As I said, most street cops know that for every reported crime, at least ten have gone unreported. And I want you to remember, there are always political agendas implicit in any gathering of statistics. Remember the phrase "Lies, damned lies, and statistics"?

As we have seen earlier, crime costs. In the United States, in 1991, all three levels of government (state, federal and local) spent a combined total of $70 billion on law enforcement. It was, however, only about 4 percent of all government spending. In the United States, the federal government spent about fifty times as much on defence spending and "international relations" (an intriguing locution) as it did on law enforcement.

Of that $70 billion, roughly $35 billion was spent on police departments, another $20 billion on prisons and correctional institutions and the remainder, about $15 billion, on judges and District Attorneys and courtroom expenditures.

The main product of all these expenditures is, of course, prisoners. Inmates. Convicts serving an infinite variety of time in a wonderful array of "correctional" environments, from jails to federal prisons.

Jails are usually a local facility dedicated to the containment of prisoners awaiting trial after an arraignment (people who could not make or were not granted bail or an "Own Recognizance" release); prisoners serving terms of less than one year in the United States and two-years-less-a-day in Canada; and those prisoners carrying state or federal sentences for whom there is, quite simply, no more room in a state or federal prison. Many corrections officers with whom I spoke said that, roughly speaking, they have to release at least one inmate before his time for every one they have to commit. The bulk of the overcrowding comes from the massive increase in jailing for drug-related offences.

In some cases, violent offenders are being released to make room for drug-dealers and drug-users. It's a simple mechanical response: garbage in, garbage out. Just different garbage. If w as a society, decide that, say, financial crime is just as dangerous to society as violence, then we end up by putting more stockbrokers in jail and getting an equal number of violent offenders back on the street, unless we plan to raise taxes to build more prisons, which is something that is currently being considered in the United States and will probably be considered in Canada. Washington authorized $4 billion for prison construction in 1990, on top of the $4.4 billion it had authorized in 1988. (It's illuminating to note here that the United States has budgeted zero dollars for new public housing in 1993, a clue to their priorities. You're free to die homeless as long as you don't break any laws.)

Once again, the figures lag, but roughly speaking, there were slightly more than 650,000 inmates in federal and state institutions in the United States in 1989, and about 20,000 in various Canadian corrections facilities. The rate of increase in prison populations has been steady and dramatic, from a little over 300,000 in the United States in 1981 to a projected high of 700,000 by the end of 1991. In Canada, the figure is projected at 25,000 by the turn of the century. Even "diversion programs" like electronic bracelets, halfway houses and increased supervisory probation, all of which are usually reserved for non-violent offenders, have not been able to compensate for the spectacular increase in drug-related violence offences.

By the way, according to a Bureau of Justice Statistics bulletin, overcrowding had forced the storage of some 15,000 federal prisoners in state or local jails throughout the United States.

How do these figures break down? Exactly who are these people?

By sex, in the United States, 96 percent are males; in Canada, roughly the same, at 92 percent.

By race, in the United States, 50 percent are white, 45 percent are black and the remainder are Hispanics, Orientals or Native Americans; in Canada, it's split between white, black and Natives.

20 percent are married.

19 percent are divorced.

7 percent are separated.

55 percent have never been married or in a long-term legal relationship.

The average age of an inmate is twenty-eight. Most of the violent offenders, both recidivists and first-timers, are younger than the non-violent offenders.

Most have had about ten years of education.

Before their arrest, 70 percent held jobs, 20 percent were looking for jobs and the rest had no apparent job and did not claim to be looking for one.

In 1991, in the United States and Canada, 80 percent of all prison inmates were repeat-offenders—that is, people who had previously been jailed, paroled or on probation for other offences. Of all the inmates in our corrections facilities, approximately 70 percent have been imprisoned two or more times, 50 percent have been in prison three or more times and a hardy 30 percent have come back to prison six or more times.

There seems to be only a slight increase in length of sentencing for repeat-offender, and again only a minimal increase in sentence length for violent offences over non-violent offences. The average sentence length for a violent first-offender in the United States is 30.6 months. In Canada, it's likely to be much less, frequently six months and probation. The average sentence length for a repeat-violent-offender in the United States is 32 months. In Canada, it varies wildly but can reach 44 months in a federal facility. Provincially, it's two years less a day.

Something to keep in mind when looking at racial breakdowns in prison populations in both countries is that, while white males and non-white males are roughly equally represented in prison, white males outnumber non-white males in the general population by ten to one. What exactly this means, with reference to inherent cultural or biological tendencies, is unclear. Either non-white males commit more crimes than white males, or non-white males are ten times as likely to go to prison for their crimes than are white males.

My guess would be a combination call: violent crimes tend to be committed by an underclass, currently black or Native, since the upper class has devised any number of legal ways to steal and plunder (remember Charles Keating, Jr., and the Savings and Loans bandits, who cost us all about $500 billion in 1989 and 1990). Underclass males also tend to get busted harder than white males because they're a damn-sight more visible against an all-white judicial background.

And then you have prisoners out on parole or probation or in some kind of halfway house with, supposedly, supervised and limited access to the streets. Corrections Canada, currently under siege for some monumental screw-ups resulting in highly publicized tragedies, has slithered under the rock of "client privilege" in the matter of numbers and locations, but the best estimates put the parole and probation population at around 90,000 men and a few women.

In the United States in 1990, there were close to 4 million people under some kind of "correctional supervision," which includes people still in various prisons. Of that number, roughly 2 million were on probation (an interesting area of judicial incompetence we can set aside for now) and 362,192 were on parole.

Parole usually implies some kind of regular supervision—reporting to the case man, staying away from some locations or groups of associates, a prohibition against firearms or drinking restrictions—but the overloaded system frequently leaves a parolee effectively unwatched from the second month out, unless he's attracted the interest of street cops who remember him from his glory days.

In the United States and Canada, juvenile males account for roughly 60 percent of all property crimes and about 15 percent of all violent crimes—especially rape and murder. Canadian juveniles have a slight per-capita edge over their American cousins in both categories. All in all, juvenile offenders constitute the single largest offending population in both Canada and the United States, a fact that bears closer examination, since the Canadian government and most state authorities have special systems in place for dealing with offenders under the age of eighteen, and some form of special consideration for criminals under twenty-five.

Regarding property crimes—Break and Enters, car theft, vandalism, arson, smash-and-grab offences—the single most active age group is sixteen years old. Before that, they're usually into petty crimes and schoolyard power politics. After that, they're on their way into more demanding and complex crimes. Or they're on a work farm, learning the basics.

Crime and punishment find their most troubling nexus on death row, an area where governments in Canada and the United States have shown as much steadiness of purpose as a stork on skates. Currently, Canada does not allow capital punishment under any circumstances, although in the early 1970s it was still on the books.

In the United States, since the US Supreme Court decision in 1976 allowing capital punishment, the various circuit courts around the nation have been wildly erratic in sentencing criminals to death. Between 1970 and 1990, there were 143 executions carried out, one of which was carried out on a woman.

Here's a chart showing the most recent figures for capital punishment in the United States:

State	Total to 1991	Death Row Prisoners
Texas	375	320
Florida	224	299
Louisiana	172	31
Georgia	395	98
Virginia	117	45
Alabama	152	117
Nevada	40	57
Missouri	76	72
Mississippi	162	47
North Carolina	269	84
Utah	19	11
South Carolina	169	42
Indiana	45	48
Arkansas	124	33
Illinois	93	128
Oklahoma	63	118
California	292	280
Ohio	172	105
Pennsylvania	152	121
Kentucky	103	26

Tennessee	93	84
New Jersey	74	10
Maryland	68	19
Washington	47	10
Colorado	47	3
Arizona	38	91
Federal system	33	0
Connecticut	21	2
Oregon	19	10
Delaware	12	6
New Mexico	8	1
Wyoming	7	2
Montana	6	6
Nebraska	4	11
Idaho	3	19
South Dakota	1	0
New Hampshire	1	0
New York	329	No Death Penalty Now
Massachusetts	27	No Death Penalty Now
Iowa	18	No Death Penalty Now
Vermont	4	No Death Penalty Now
Rhode Island	0	No Death Penalty Now
West Virginia	40	No Death Penalty Now
Dist. Of Columbia	40	No Death Penalty Now
Kansas	15	No Death Penalty Now
North Dakota	0	No Death Penalty Now
Michigan	0	No Death Penalty Now

Of the states listed, no state below Oklahoma has executed anyone since 1977, except Washington State, which recently executed Westley Alan Dodd, a child-molester and killer who actively pursued his own execution. Taken overall, the trend in the United States seems to be toward few capital executions, in spite of the fervent entreaties of many victims groups.

By the way, current liberal activists are maintaining, usually the top of their lungs, that non-white males are statistically more likely to have the death penalty imposed and carried out than are white males.

Taking the long view, there's some truth in the claim. In the first place, non-whites are overrepresented in prison populations, the group from which death row inmates are drawn. And during the period in the United States from 1930 to 1987, 53 percent of those executed were black males, another 46 percent were white males and the final 1 percent classified as "Other" (female or another minority group).

But in recent history, for example the period from 1977 to 1989, 64 percent of those executed were white males, 5 percent were black males and the rest were women or Hispanic males.

This whole discussion, of course, sets aside for the moment the larger question of the ethical substructure of capital punishment. We'll struggle with that dragon in a later chapter.

The regional variations indicated by the Circuit Court sentencing records depend upon far too many factors to be casually disposed of in a few pages. Perhaps the most salient factor is financial.

According to the American Civil Liberties Union (ACLU), a staunch (many would say maniacal) opponent of death penalties under any circumstances, it costs the State and its minions about $5 million to execute a death row inmate. The process takes up to ten years, as lawyers and special interest groups push the appeals all the way to the governors' mansions. By contrast, it costs about $40,000 a year to keep a man in prison, and some of that cost can be defrayed by using his labor for the benefit of the State.

Let's suppose that a man is convicted of a capital crime at twenty-eight (the median prison age). To arrange his death will take from three to ten years, depending upon his skill at manipulating outside interests, his repulsiveness-factor and the resources of the ACLU and the Public Defender's office. It will cost the State, as we have said, about five million by the time the hammer comes down.

But warehousing him costs $40,000 a year for the average duration of a life sentence (a rather inaccurate term, which actually means a maximum-security term of ten to twenty years).

Let's put it at twenty, the outside limit. That's still only $800,000, a net savings of $4.2 million. Given the willingness of the opponents of the death penalty to fight it long and hard (a factor perhaps affected by the fact that most lawyers bill by the hour, whether or not they're successful), the price of revenge and visceral satisfaction seems rather high.

The United States and Canada have always had mixed emotions about the death penalty. In the United States from 1930 to 1989, 4,017 executions were completed by state or federal authorities. Capital punishment was ruled unconstitutional in 1972, but reinstated by the Supreme Court in 1976, as concerns about the rising crime rate replaced the liberal agendas of the 1960s.

(As usual, and it's something we should all bear in mind when we approach the bench for any reason, the structure and attitudes of the justice system are as susceptible to political and social pressures as any other branch of government—possibly more so. The recent pitched battles over *Roe v. Wade,* an area many thinking observers thought was settled, and of course the Clarence Thomas hearings, illustrate the old axiom that the price of freedom is eternal vigilance…each and every year. It seems that some battles are never won for the ages, only settled for the moment.)

By the middle of the 1980s, thirteen states and the District of Columbia would not authorize a death penalty. Maine, Minnesota and Wisconsin have not allowed a capital sentence statute since 1932. Neither have Alaska and Hawaii. It was declared unconstitutional in Michigan in 1963, in Iowa and West Virginia in 1965, in Kansas and the District of Columbia in 1973, Rhode Island in 1979, Oregon in 1981 and Massachusetts and New York in 1984. In California, the state Supreme Court found the death penalty in its current incarnation "partly unconstitutional."

All in all, the debate over the death penalty is at the epicenter of a larger disturbance, a fundamental and continent-wide disagreement about the very nature of crime and punishment.

Citizens in every town and village from Nova Scotia to southern California carry profound doubts about the quality and effectiveness of the justice system. The sheer numbers of crimes and criminals, the attendant (and wildly uneven) press coverage and the simple discontent felt by anyone with a clear mind and a little common sense have brought the administration of justice into disrepute in every jurisdiction in both countries. The statistics show the size and breadth of the problem but reveal little of the essence.

We can all see that it's not working.

It's harder to see *why* it's not working.

I made a reference earlier to an old street cop rule that only one out of ten crimes comes to the attention of the justice system and therefore finds its way into StatsCan or the Bureau of Justice Statistics. The Ten Beef Rule has a number of corollaries.

It usually takes ten crimes to bring an offender to the attention of a cop, effect an arrest and get him registered in the system with a fingerprint number and an arrest record.

Now…it will take at least ten arrests before that person will actually stand up before a judge in a juvenile or adult court. Before he gets that far, he will have been case-managed in one way or another by harried juniors in anterooms, netting a simple dismissal, or a suspended sentence, or probation, or a release under a bond, or assignment, to a juvenile worker, or a simple scolding from a street cop (sometimes a simple beating from a street cop), or he'll turn into an informer, or any one of a series of other events will prevent him from reaching a judge.

Sometimes, as happens in any overloaded system, his file will get lost or the witnesses will fade away or he'll take "Greyhound Therapy" and split for another county; or the court will issue a "non-returnable warrant," a "get-out-of-town" warning, which means that if this person is caught in another county or province, the issuing court won't pay to get him back. Usually, the arresting officer won't pay for the return himself, so the fugitive walks.

So, where were we? Back to the Ten Beef Rule.

Ten crimes before he gets noticed.

Another ten crimes before the system takes him seriously enough to drag him into the jammed-up court system. Judges want a clear dock at the end of the day, and they don't react well to having to deal with trial cases that could have been disposed of at a lower level.

And, so say the cops and Crowns and DAs who work the courts, a judge will ignore the guy another ten times—we've seen this already in the previous chapters—before he'll take the kid seriously enough to give him a jail or a prison sentence.

What's the score so far?

Say ten crimes of various degrees before he gets caught. Then he has to get caught ten times before he'll be taken seriously by the justice system. So, according to our count, that's an even *one hundred* crimes before he faces a non-judicial penalty such as probation or assignment to a juvenile worker or a social worker or gets caught up in the informer network.

And, finally, ten non-judicial dispositions before he sees a judge, who will likely not propose a jail term unless he has seen the kid nine times before. (Or ninety, if he's Judge Cronin.) Even judges get nasty when you don't listen to their fatherly advice. They don't like to see the same faces too often. After a while, they'll do something to make sure they don't see this particular face again for a few months.

If the formula holds up, the judge could be looking at a person who has committed *one thousand* crimes of varying degrees of severity when he finally decides to do something dramatic about him. (In the Gordon Watson case, we saw a man who admitted to *fifteen thousand* B and Es in the Vancouver area.)

If this sounds a little high to the civil libertarians, I'll compromise. Let's say the judge loses his patience easily, and he gavels the prisoner in the dock after five appearances. Possible, even in a dense urban area.

So we could place a conservative estimate of five hundred crimes on the criminal's conscience on the day he finally gets off the bus in a hobble and heads in to the bug-spray room and the big yard. And I'd like to remind you that only a third of these offences will be Possession or Trafficking beefs. The rest are B and Es, Assaults, Armed Robberies, Rapes, Car Theft...*ad nauseam*.

(Cops I worked with in New York City cited cases where the suspect was implicated in two thousand minor felonies before they got a good case on him, so the five hundred figure is very conservative. In Toronto and Vancouver, I've heard cops say it's closer to seven or eight hundred.)

In prison, as we have seen, he will probably do no more than thirty months, and possibly less, given the overcrowding in all the prisons and jails in both countries.

Where does this take us?

It suggests, for one thing, that the huge number of crimes reported to the Bureau of Justice Statistics in Washington and the Solicitor General's office in Ottawa may represent the diligence and energy of far fewer criminals than we might infer from the numbers.

Yet the numbers are very high. Let's test the hypothesis.

Again applying the rule of ten, the total number of crimes committed in the United States, let's say in 1987, works out as follows:

Murders	20,100
Rape	91,100
Robbery	517,700
Aggravated Assault	855,090
VIOLENT CRIME TOTAL:	1,484,000
Burglary	3,236,200
Theft	7,499,900
Auto Theft	1,288,700
PROPERTY CRIME TOTAL	12,024,700

TOTAL INDEX CRIMES 13,508,700 serious crimes in 1987
RULE OF TEN FACTOR x 10
TOTAL CRIMES COMMITTED 135,087,000 reported and unreported in 1987

Now we divide the total number of crimes, reported and unreported by five hundred, which is the number of crimes we think we can assign to each person who walks in the front gate of a jail or prison. That gives us:

$$\frac{135,087,000}{500} = 270,174$$

Now if the rule of ten has any validity, we have found the number of people who were sentenced to a jail or a prison in the United States sometime during or at the end of the year 1987. If they all got the average sentence of two years and change, the prison population for the whole state and federal system should be:

$$\begin{array}{r} 270{,}174 \\ \times\ 2 \\ \hline 540{,}348 \end{array}$$

We've multiplied by two because a roughly similar number of crimes were committed in 1986, and those prisoners will have received the usual two years and change, so they'll still be in the system in 1987. So, we should find that the justice system was holding at least 540,348 people during 1987.

Well, well. In 1987, according to the Bureau of Justice Statistics bulletin, there was a total of 581,609 prisoners in their various institutions in 1987. That's a surplus of 41,261.

I suspect that the numbers would average out over a ten-year period. And we have to bear in mind that the latest figures for prison populations in 1990 and 1991 are running close to 700,000. But the basic point of the exercise was to lend a little statistical validity to what might otherwise be perceived as street-cop voodoo. As a general principle, the Ten Beef Rule seems to hold up.

To save some time, I've done the same calculations for Canada, and the numbers break down the same way. In Canada, we end up with a hard-core recidivist figure of 40,000 or close to one-tenth of the hard-core crowd in the United States.

Now the question you ought to be asking yourself is: *Who are these guys?*

We tend to look at the statistics and develop some vague idea that a hell of a lot of very irritating people are out there doing extremely bad things with little chance of punishment. We also imagine these people to be unknown, faceless, foot soldiers in that dead-eyed army of the night we spoke of earlier.

But many experienced street cops, and I've known a lot of them in the last fifteen years, will tell you that they have a pretty good idea who is doing what in their neighborhoods. And the little math exercise we used to check the Ten Beef Rule leads us to another interesting question: *How many criminals are there?*

Based on the numbers we've developed in this chapter, logic would suggest that there may be far fewer career criminals operating in Canada and the United States than we imagine. Probably as few as the current population of the federal and state prison systems in both countries—say around 600,000 men and some women.

How could that be, since the people we're talking about are currently in prison, and unless we're all working under a serious delusion about prisons, those guys are not free to rip up and down the side-streets pulling crimes and keeping us up late. They're inside, right? So who got your VCR last night?

Good question? So, we say that in the United States and Canada there are 600,000 guys inside right now. For two years, roughly. But some of the 600,000 guys who were in two years ago are out now, and the odds are good that one of them either has your VCR or knows who does. The odds are even better that some street cop knows a guy who knows the guy who has your VCR. It's all connected. (The trick is not in the knowing. It's in the proving!)

And some of the 600,000 criminals are getting out early, and some more are being paroled, and some others are waiting for appeals, and some more are in work-release…in other words, that 600,000 figure is rather like a photograph, a picture of one moment in time. Just as in a picture, the action only seems frozen; each of these men has been caught mid-stride, in a passage through the justice system. Some of them won't be back; single-timers do exit. Not many, but they do happen.

So…how many full-time criminals are there, based on our numbers? How many guys are in the Life, more or less committed to a lifetime of various illegal activities, known to the street cops, known to the DAs and the Public Defenders and the parole officers and the victims?

Ballpark? United States and Canada? And we're including the beginners and the retiring pros and the wannabes?

Well…we need 600,000 to keep the prisons full.

And we need 300,000 just getting off the bus and headed for the disinfectant chamber.

And the same number of guys standing by the side of the road in a shiny prison suit with fifty bucks in their pockets, blinking at the outside again.

Adjusting for anomalies like one-time offenders, innocent people wrongly convicted, those who have killed or maimed in a burst of rage but who are not habitual offenders, the profoundly stupid or unlucky, and a certain subtraction in the interests of conservative projections...let's say...

One million.

That doesn't sound like a lot of criminals, considering that the populations of the United States and Canada add up to 282 million people. It's about one-half of 1 percent of the population...*carrying out 99 percent of the crimes.*

(Remember we're not including corrupt politicians and connected bankers who know how to work the system for a half-billion and still keep their estates in Connecticut and Westmount.)

So...once again, we are looking at a fundamental question: *Why doesn't somebody stop these guys?*

If most of the misery in this world, the terror in the streets, the paranoia and depression we all deal with as honest citizens, the impotent rage we have to suppress on a nightly basis is being caused by such a tiny percentage of mean-minded sons-of-bitches, why do we put up with it? Why can't we slam the gates on them all and make the cities fun again?

Well, maybe we don't really understand the criminal mind. Maybe all the academics and all the shrinks and all the people currently billing the Feds for consultant work and all the undergrads in criminology courses and all the young idealists studying to be social workers and anger-management therapists and all the rabid civil libertarians like Clayton Ruby and Susan Eng, Phil Rankin, and even Alan Borovoy don't know what the hell they're talking about.

Why do you think they call it Corrections Canada? Because the experts are convinced that they know the criminal mind better than we do, and they are going to fix it.

Unfortunately, while they are trying to figure out how to fix it, the rest of us are being driven off the streets and chased into our homes and cornered there, because so far what they are doing to rehabilitate the criminal is simply not working.

Why not?

I've been trying to illustrate the ways in which the isolated power of the justice system works against us all. It has been my thesis all along that the justice system does not truly understand the nature of the beast they are paid to deal with, which is why the unanswerable authority of our judges ought to worry you as much as it worries me.

I've used the drug scene to illustrate the ways in which this kind of judicial hubris affects us, but what underlies the entire issue is something far more serious than the needless proliferation of petty criminals and the ruinous effects on our sense of community.

I don't believe that the experts who create legislation and the lawyers who juggle it and the judges who twist it know the first thing about evil.

I think the cops do, and I think some of the psychiatrists who work with criminals are getting an idea of it, and certainly the victims know, in ways that I hope none of you ever share, but these people are a lot like the stoker shoveling coal into a ship's boiler; what counts is who's at the helm.

True evil is something like an iceberg in the darkness out beyond the sweep of the searchlight; most of it is under the surface, all of it is cold.

And when you hit it, believe me, you know it for what it is.

FOURTEEN

Yellow Rope

The crutch is the part that gets to you, that single crutch and the trips the kid would make, back and forth to the Orangeville Secondary School every day of that frantic final week. Four trips a day and each one, each long stumble-and-hop with the grate of that rubber tip on the asphalt, went right along Center Street past Number Nine, the red-brick box where the Orangeville Police Force and the OPP were going over and over the reports.

Ray Holden, the chief, was sitting at the head of the board-room table with the officers coming and going: Tom Rosser, Frank Love, Joel McArthur from the OPP, all the harness men in and out like it was some kind of Feydeau farce and not a murder investigation at all.

Four times a day this kid would hobble past that window: in the morning after breakfast, then back home for lunch, thinking God knows what while he's there at the kitchen table, his crutch down on the floor, then off to school again for afternoon classes and out again in the red riot of fall under a bleak and distant sun in a grey wool sky. Hoppity-scrape to the front of Number Nine, where, as always, he'd stop for a minute and look across the road at the station-house windows, third one from the left, where, behind the tinted glass, Ray Holden and his men were trying to figure out just who in holy hell could do such a thing, and not in New York or Washington or Toronto either, but here! in this place, this small town in the valley, in the heartland, where good people worked hard days in the fields and factories and there was a wide main street with feed stores and donut shops and old town men on the bone-bleached benches outside the courthouse under a snapping flag, in this little heart's-blood town of Orangeville, Ontario.

And one of those days when the kid was doing that, stopping on his way home from school to stare into the windows, Holden can't remember exactly which day but it was early in that bad week after they found the children, Holden looked up from the papers in front of him and out over the bent shoulders and the smoke and the talk in the long room, through the window out into the grey November day, and he saw the kid on his crutch staring in at them, trying to see into the room, and it came to him—a silent magnesium flower exploding in his mind—that maybe, maybe…there was that day—was it last month?

Holden is classic police chief material, a big man, seamed in his face and hands, soft and straight in his talk, the kind of man who would never curse in front of a woman but who could take a layer of skin off the side of your face with a look if you crossed him. Holden lives for hockey and works for the town of Orangeville. He says that when he dies they're going to bury him at the blue line of the town rink, where he can feel the Zamboni going over and listen to the crowds cheering for the nine o'clock Friday games. He answers his own phone and any people in the town can just walk in off the street and talk to him if they've got something on their minds.

So the day comes, that day last month, he hears this call from the duty desk and there's this kid, big, maybe five-ten, one-fifty, Holden's seen him around, he's in grade nine or something over at Orangeville Secondary. Holden takes him into his office, where the kid sits down and speaks right up, cool and straight.

There's drugs at school, Chief Holden, street drugs. Kids are smoking it and dealing it. Also some chemical stuff. This isn't right, Chief. It's wrong for them to do that. I can see that and I'm in grade nine.

What's this? Holden is thinking. What have we got here? Bells are going off in the Chief's mind. Wait and see what the kid has to say.

What he has to say is that the school, no, the town, could use something like what that Sliwa guy in New York did, a guardian society, like deputies or vigilantes, only they could work with the Orangeville police as undercover operators. Me and some of my friends, we could take down names, you know? See who's dealing what, who's doing what, getting into trouble? It's wrong, they should do those things, and I, me and my friends, we could be a kind of secret investigating force for you. What about that?

What I think about that, the Chief is saying to himself, is that

I'd rather slam my hand in a car door than take you up on that type of offer, and what the hell is going on with you, kid?

What he says is, Hey, that's a very interesting idea. I feel our own officers are doing a fine job for the community, but citizen help is always welcome. I'll have to think about that. See what the law says. And I thank you for coming in, son. What was your name again?

This scene came back to Holden as he was sitting in that boardroom and his officers were going through six hundred interview forms and the room was filling with smoke and heat and frustration and that kid, the same kid, was out there leaning on that crutch and staring at the window like it was the screen at a drive-in movie and some horror film was running on it, something very bad. Something vile.

Marcel and Jeannine Babineau came home from a hockey game at 7:45 on Sunday evening, November 4, 1984, and found their youngest son sitting in the dark house watching the television. The other two children, Monique who was nine, and Daniel, who was eleven, were not in the house.

For a while the Babineaus were merely angry, in the way parents get angry at children who do something silly that they have been told a hundred times not to do. They were a strong Catholic family, regular members of Saint Timothy's Church over at Center and Dawson, not far from the house. They weren't harsh people, and the search for the two young children was, in its early minutes, concerned but not frantic. But it's not a big town and there were only so many places to look. They didn't call the police until 8:41.

The police dispatcher gave the call to Officer Murray Storey, who was out in one of the blue-and-whites. Storey spent some time looking for the children, on foot and in the car, using the back-light to sweep the bushes and the yards in the Babineau neighborhood. After a while, he asked for some help.

By 9:30 that night, a lot of people, townsfolk and police officers, were looking everywhere they could think of for the two Babineau children.

The kids were well liked in the neighborhood, a suburban

tract-home development on the west side of town, a neat grid of bungalows and trimmed lawns and aluminum doors and carports and gas barbecues and split-rail fences, a school, a church with a steeple, a playground.

Murray Storey found the kids in that playground behind Saint Peter's Catholic School on Dawson Road. Monique was on her side, on the ground outside a school portable. Daniel was close by, on his back, with his hockey jacket pulled up on his body so his face was covered. They had clothes on. There was no obvious sign of sexual assault. But there was some blood.

Storey left nothing to chance. He called the station and an ambulance was there within two minutes. A little after 10:00, Dr. David Knox, who was working in the Emergency Room of the Dufferin County Hospital, pronounced both children dead. The coroner, Dr. Austin, arrived a few minutes later to make the thing official. A family friend of the Babineaus made the ID.

Chief Holden stood in the Emergency Room and waited for the identification to be done with two officers standing a little apart and the nurses with faces as white as bone inside the soundless immensity of that moment. Holden thinking about what he was going to say to the parents.

After a short while, he walked out to his car and drove up First Street to the lights and made a right and then a left under a shaded avenue of oaks. He drove along a side street and then he got out of his car and walked up the driveway to the Babineau house, to the front door, where there was somebody standing backlit in the soft, warm, yellow light that comes from homes like this in neighborhoods like these.

It was like the kid had an on-again, off-again knee. It had been operated on the week before...before this week, the week those kids were killed. He's on the street around and about all that week, along with everyone else in town. The talk is "transient" and "psycho killer." The streets are full of rented Chevys and Lincoln Town Cars from out of town, stuffed with newspeople from all over the country. Here and there we're getting man-in-the-street interviews, carrion-crow snippets for the uplinks.

"Are you afraid for your own kids?" The woman with her

hands full of shopping bags outside the Safeway, blinking in the lights, two kids hiding behind her legs, what the hell does she tell them? Of course she's afraid.

"How do you feel about capital punishment?"

"How do you feel about child molesters?"

"How do you think the mother feels about this?"

"Are you safe in your beds?"

For the teens in town, it's like a circus has come down Main Street, like Alexandria is finally getting sacked and all the quotidian tyranny of clocks and cops and hallway prefects is over. Like nobody is happy that those poor kids got it, but it's …like it's *intense,* you know? School? Nobody's thinking school. There's a killer on the streets, man, like it's a movie. Jeez, there's whatsername? The broad from Channel Three. And Jim Junkin with a whole camera crew, a Betacam BVP-Three, and the sound guy. Is that make-up on Jim, man? What a homo!

And his hair, the foam-rubber hair. All the press and video pack. Scurrying this way. Racing that, full of witless, avid purpose, like things feeding in a ditch, rooting for the newest taste sensation. Lights are popping on and off down at Center Street by the cop shop and up at the Babineau house it's like the Apaches have the place surrounded. The curtains are pulled and a blue-and-white blocks the driveway, hot white lights play across the brick façade, black shadows flicker and twist as the lights go across…

At the school! Vans and rent-a-cars and guys with steno notepads interviewing everybody, stopping moms in the streets and sticking those fuzzy mikes in their faces, the newsguys all bright eyes and breathing through their mouths, the camera guy and the sound man hanging back, having a smoke, saying things to each other in low voices about whoever it is that Media Man interviewing now, the kids hanging around in the back of the picture, jumping up into the frame, waving, grinning, getting on TV. No shots of the kid on his crutch. But he was there.

On the crutch, going to the high school, then down to Country Donuts on Main Street…Hey, how's the knee, man? Isn't it wild about those kids? In-*tense,* man! Those kids, eh? I hear they were really cut up, man? Waddya think, man? Waddya think?

What does he think? That's the whole thing, isn't it? That's the major question in all of this.

On November 6, a Tuesday, he was thinking about helicopters at around 12:30, lunch hour. This was one of those days when the kid with his on-again, off-again knee injury was taking his four daily trips past Ray Holden's office to his house, which was right next to the playground where they found the Babineau kids.

This day, this Tuesday, the kid is standing in his own backyard watching the police helicopter floating around doing aerial photography, of the crime scene, and there's an Orangeville squad car parked on the grass by the gate, guarding the scene, as they say.

The officer, Mike Robinson, sees this kid on a crutch, taking it all in, in the rearview mirror of the cruiser. Robinson gets out to talk to the kid, see what he wants.

So nothing, really. They chat. Bad stuff, right? Weird, he says, the kid says, leaning on his crutch. How's the leg? says Mike. Okay, says the kid. A silence.

Did they go in the school? asks the kid. Then, without waiting, he adds, I heard they did.

This catches Robinson's attention, because nobody—*nobody*— knows that the forensic guys are dead certain that both kids were killed inside Saint Peter's School and then dragged outside.

Well, son, says Robinson, I wouldn't know about that. And then he walks away and gets back into the squad car and takes out his notebook and he writes it all down.

And on the next day, November 7, the kid was thinking about medallions, about God and punishment perhaps, like a good Catholic kid, because he turned up on that crutch at Baxter and Giles Funeral Home, where Monique and Daniel were laid out in their coffins and where Marcel and Jeannine Babineau were doing all those busywork funeral things that we've come up with to distract ourselves from this cataclysmic and abysmal horror that has opened up at the dead center of things and into which everything there ever was or ever will be is sooner or later going to disappear and…oh, yes…now he comes…hippity-hop on his little crutch with his little burden of secret thinking, and in his hands, in those particular hands, he has gifts. For the…deceased

Catholics lean towards talismans, relics, rosary beads, prayer cards, votive candles, burning sandalwood, little wooden crosses, little scruples we like to fondle at the edge of the great salt sea of eternity. The kid brought two of them.

A medal and a palm cross. Palm crosses are very strong medicine in the Catholic Church. When Christ arrived finally in Jerusalem on that Sunday, which was only seven days from the next Sunday, by which time he'd been dead three days already—so much for fame—on that first Sunday, the people of Jerusalem spread palm fronds in his path, and we now call this day Palm Sunday and try not to think about the fact that these were the same people who milled around under Golgotha hill the following Friday, muttering and grumbling no doubt, but other than that doing not very much of anything—so that since then some of us think of palm leaves as a sign of faithlessness, of betrayal. Of course, the Church disagrees.

Well, he brought them, palm crosses and a scapular medal, and he asked Jeannine Babineau if he could give these…tokens? Mementos? Coins for Charon? On his crutch he asks this.

Yes, of course, says Jeannine, her mind full of cut earth and new grass and the smell of flowers. (Did he look her in the face? Did I see what there was to see there?)

So over he goes, hippity-hop, to the coffins, and we see him on that crutch, looking down at the powdered doll faces in their best clothes, hands folded across their breasts, rosaries, flowers, the scent of flowers in his nostrils, a hint of corruption perhaps, and the tidal hush and rumor of soft voices all around, the polished wood, the brass, the pale silk, and the kid, standing there.

Was there, in some dimension, in some distant place, a lacuna of breath? Will he? Does he have the nerve? With those particular hands?

He put the scapular medal into Daniel's hands. Monique got the palm cross. We can assume they have them still.

Thursday was the funeral, at Saint Timothy's, where they all went to Mass each Sunday. Now white candles are burning, and the air is thick with grief, rage, the smell of hot wax and flowers and people breathing.

The kid is here at 9:55 in the morning, a little late, since he's an altar boy and supposed to serve with Father van Item. Well, look at this...today there's no crutch. On-again, off-again. In-again, out-again. *Dum affligit me inimicus,* Protect Me from Harm.

He shows no emotion this day, praying for a while at the back of the church, alone. Then he and his older brother lead the procession, in their surplices and soutanes, the older boy carrying the cross and the kid carrying whatever he was carrying, into the yellow breathing space of Saint Timothy's Church.

They said a Requiem Mass for the Babineau children, in which everyone was assured that God in His Infinite Wisdom would suffer the little children to come unto Him, and then they sang and their voices went up into the rafters of Saint Timothy's, through the roof and into the dull grey sky and a cold November wind took the sound and blew it out over the valley until it faded and died out there. And when the song was over the Babineau kids were still dead.

The kid and his older brother led the procession again, this time out the front of the church and down onto the lawns, and there was no limp but his left hand was bandaged.

Out onto the threadbare lawns of Saint Timothy's Church, where the media were waiting in a brutal crush, videocams and fuzzy mikes and boom mikes and light-racks thrust into faces, mouths working. You can watch this video, see the kid in the middle of it in his altar boy outfit, see him watching it and taking it in and nothing shows in his face. Shouts. Scuffles. Cover this! Get that? There's the family! Get the mother? Lady, how's it feel? Are you angry? Get the father!

Now, over at the side, Ray Holden faces down one of the haircuts in a jostle of mediapersons; the Chief is very angry, saying hard things to all of them in a low, carrying voice, and they're still filming him—it's news! The Chief is swearing at them—that's a picture! Jesus, is he pissed off! Get the face, get me a tight shot of his face!

At the grave site, the kid stayed away from the cut earth and the mound covered with a blanket of fake grass. There was a wind, they say, though others aren't so sure. It was a fall day and there was no warmth in the sun.

The kid left early, without the crutch. Various people saw him leave, but only the cops were making notes.

There's nothing magical about police work. In the homicide squads there are a few rules. Nearest and Dearest is probably the first rule. If someone is dead, the chances are good that someone near and dear has swung the hammer or insinuated the blade. Homes in a row on a residential street are like little kettles on a griddle. Some of them are so hot you can feel it through the front door or see it in the scalded faces of the children in the yard. When they go, they don't blow, they fall inward.

Twenty-Four, Twenty-Four is another rule. The first twenty-four hours of the investigation, before the blood dries and the weapons are hidden, and the last twenty-four hours of the victim's life, where he went, who saw him.

Look for the motive—*cui bono,* who gained? But above all, think of Opportunity. Find out who was around. Who had the chance? To find that out, you do what's called a canvass. You send officers around to everyone anywhere near the crime scene and you ask them what they saw. Usually, they tell you that they didn't see anything, but what they don't know is that they're telling you where *they* were.

The Task Force did six hundred interviews. Every detail, every alibi, was checked and cross-indexed. Discrepancies were followed up with secondary interviews by the senior investigators.

You say you were at the OK Bowling Alley? But they didn't see you there.

No. They're sure.

No. They'd have noticed. That crutch stands out.

Are you sure that's where you were?

Well, by this time the kid has to know he's being watched. Discreetly, from a distance. We can see him down in the basement of his house, where he liked to play Dungeons and Dragons, where he had a kind of workshop, and there in the basement, with its high slit windows and the smell of old concrete, the kid had to wonder where he'd go from there. Should he do something? Should he help them, go to the cops and say, look you've got it wrong. It wasn't me, it was somebody else?

What does he think? Watch the videos. Use the freeze-frame to catch him again, coming out of Saint Timothy's Church, part of a spill of townsfolk and police officers, just another blurry white face in the press—hold him there—a scintillating cloud of white static and black dots on the television screen. Look at him hard and try to see it there in his face. What were you thinking, kid? What was in your mind that cold grey day?

The Orangeville cops were up against a problem now. The kid was being watched. There were inconsistencies in his statements. He said he was at a friend's house on that Sunday, but the friend never saw him. He said he was at the bowling alley, but no one at the alley saw him around. Why lie about it? His own statements placed him the schoolyard at 4:50. A witness saw the Babineau children walking towards Saint Peter's School at 5:10.

The kid—well, now he's a suspect and not just a kid—the suspect says he was somewhere else at 5:30 and home again at 5:45. His father was home when he came in, so that time's all right. But where was he between 4:50 and 5:45? That's fifty-five minutes. Where was he? What was he doing?

The cops took their problem to Tony Williams, the local Crown. Tony Williams, a tall well-set man in his early forties, grey-bearded and fit, a cool and earnest man, looked at the forensic evidence and the contradictory statements and he looked up at Holden and Rosser and Joel MacArthur and said, yes, dammit, we do have a problem, a problem with the Young Offenders Act. Because, at that time, the act said that no kid under fourteen could be transferred to adult court, where adult responsibilities and adult sentences could be laid upon him. The act said that no kid under fourteen could go to jail for longer than three years. What the act was saying to Tony Williams and the cops was that even though it looked like the kid might have strangled two little children for no apparent reason the most they could hope to see him get was three years. You see, the kid was just thirteen years old. Apparently, it had never occurred to the people who framed the Young Offenders Act that a thirteen-year-old kid could commit a double murder. It had, however, occurred to the kid.

The kid was home on Saturday, November 10, six days after the discovery of the dead bodies of Daniel and Monique Babineau in the playground behind the kid's house. The cops had been to see him a couple of times that week. He must have known they were checking out his story. He was—he is—by all accounts, a very intelligent boy. When Craig Hall of the Identification Branch showed up at his door along with Tom Rosser of the Orangeville police, he must have felt...something. Shame? Guilt? Remorse? Fear?

He was thirteen years old, an altar boy, a friend of the Babineau family, a good Catholic, a straight arrow. He had wanted to be a guardian, an undercover agent for Chief Holden, a force...a force for *something* in the community. And he was.

It was 6:35 in the evening and here they were in his living room, talking to his dad, and what they wanted him to "volunteer" were his fingerprints, some hair samples and a pair of his running shoes. The running shoes he'd been wearing last Sunday. Saturday night, this was, and the evening of the sixth day.

Tomorrow was Sunday. The eleventh of November. Remembrance Day. Veterans' Day. A day for remembering.

Rosser noticed something on the kid's arm as they were going through the routine, getting the prints, the hair-cuttings, the shoes. The kid had four parallel marks, scratches, on the inside of his right forearm.

They came to get him at 12:35 on the Sunday, right after Mass, and all of them—the kid, his father, Frank Love and Tom Rosser—went down Center Street to Number Nine, where they introduced the kid to a new guy, Wayne Frechette from the OPP. Frechette was a polygraph examiner for the OPP, one of the most experienced polygraph examiners in the country.

They all kicked some stuff around for a while. How come you said you were at the OK Bowling Alley and nobody saw you there? How come the marks on your arm? You understand the cautions you've been given? You want to talk this over in private with your dad? You want a lawyer here? You understand there's no fear or favor offered? Where'd you get the marks? Where were you last Sunday between 4:50 and 5:45?

I'm trying to see this as it must have been, the soft voices of the cops, the coming and going of officers and the smell of coffee, the boy sitting in that wooden chair, doing what he can. Parrying this, ducking that, trying to see what was coming, thinking hard about his answers, about what he'd already said and what he should have said. Trying to hold it together, feeling fear, maybe? I'd say yes, there was fear, because nobody tries that hard to keep the thing together unless they're afraid of something. And over here somewhere, in the room, up against a wall and leaning on a filing cabinet, the kid's father, his face a bleak grey blue and his stomach full of glacier ice and acid, staring at the back of his kid's head, hearing the lying words come out full of truth and conviction and vulnerability, that little tremolo he always used when he was telling the *truth,* Dad, *honest,* Dad. Don't you *believe* me, Dad?

Forty-five minutes of this, going back and forth. The kid gives up nothing. He's a rock in a riptide, shaky but rooted in the earth. He looks them right in the eye, all the cops, even his father. He alternates between misery and anger. How can this be happening? Why aren't you guys doing something about the *real* guy? Man, he's out there, right now. Why is this happening to *me?*

Finally, they ask him to submit to a polygraph test. Wayne Frechette comes forward, explains the way it works.

How about it? says Holden. It'll be your chance to clear this all up.

Yes, says the kid, after a brief period of silence. Yes, I'll do it.

Frechette carried out a preliminary examination of the kid from 1:15 to around 3:45 on the Sunday afternoon. Halfway through the examination, staring at Wayne's impassive face and listening to the machine's low hum and the scratching of the needles on the rollout, the kid finds himself in a thicket of contradictory statements and he stops…Okay, yes. I was there when they died. But it wasn't me that killed them. It was another guy, this stranger. Like a drifter, you know? Who was he? Well, I never knew him, you know? He just come out of somewhere. He says look kid, I'll kill your family if you don't help me do the Babineau kids.

Frechette went after this in the approved style, taking the story as true, asking for details: what did the guy look like? how old? where did you first see him? what did he say? And the kid, he's got his balance back now, he's giving it more of the tremble, looking Wayne in the eyes, the good kid now coming clean, like he was just trying to save his family and like he's really a hero who's been through a hard time but now he's coming home again, setting it all straight.

Frechette came out of the interview room at 3:45, leaving the kid in the room with the machine. He took a coffee from Holden and shook his head, looking back into the interview room at the kid.

Hard kid, says Frank Love, one of the Orangeville cops.

Yeah, says Frechette, who's done this kind of thing for years.

That kid, says Frechette, sipping his coffee, shaking his head. He's thirteen going on thirty-five. Right out of prison.

A silence. What now? says Love.

Hey, says Frechette. We do it again.

It took a while—another statement, some persuasion from his father and from the kid's priest at Saint Timothy's, Father van Item. A waiver of rights and a Caution—all the moves in the dance forensic, but by the end of Sunday night, November 11, the kid dropped the story about the "stranger" who had forced him to help with the killings.

A final statement was signed in sequence by the boy, his father, by Father van Item, by Inspector Frank Love and Constable Tom Rosser.

The legal definition of the document was "an inculpatory statement." What it added up to was that last Sunday, a week ago, this kid, the kid on the crutch, the altar boy and stand-up straight-shooter, the high school freshman, who'd never been in a spot of trouble and who was liked by almost everybody, had lured two young children into a deserted school where, after some consideration given to means and location, he had separated them and strangled them both, in different rooms, with a two-foot section of yellow nylon rope that he had found in the work shed in his own backyard. And that he had no idea *why* he had killed them.

None at all.

"The collective conscience does not allow punishment where it cannot impose blame"—a quote from *Holloway v. the United States* in 1945. In the United States and Canada, this proposition, now approaching the status of a first principle, is sometimes presented in court as a plea for Diminished Capacity, sometimes Insanity, sometimes for Reduced Culpability because of age, or sex, or social position, by which we mean to say race. In the courts, these facets of guilt and innocence fall under the shadow of *mens rea,* the question of the guilty mind.

In the United States and Canada, the ideas of Diminished Capacity and Antecedent Causes have created havoc in the justice system. In a noble effort to codify the enigma of the mitigating circumstance, legislators have wound the edifice of justice in vines and brambles of semantics and subjective interpretation, to the point where a clear view of the connection between crime and punishment is nearly impossible.

Roman law regarded a child of less than seven years as incapable of guilt. Hobbes first proposed the theory of the social contract, wherein man renounced the rights of personal vendetta in exchange for freedom from the caprices of his neighbors and a presumably more equitable system of legal accountability. Bentham developed a "felicific calculus," an algorithm by which he imagined he could calculate the end result, the goodness or badness factor, of every social act. It was Lombroso who read Darwin and deduced that criminals were atavistic biological specimens who were not like you and me.

The end result of these disputations was the creation, in each of Canada's ten provinces and in the fifty states of America, of laws directly addressing the question of *mens rea,* known as Insanity pleas, Diminished Capacity pleas and Juvenile Offender laws. In most states and provinces, the age at which a youth can be held completely responsible for his crimes varies from sixteen to eighteen. In all of these legal jurisdictions, any child aged thirteen or under is generally considered incapable of criminal intent and exempted from punitive consequences, regardless of the nature of his offence.

In Canada, the Young Offenders Act (YOA) was proclaimed on April 2, 1984. Presented to the public as a bold initiative the way Canada chose to deal with children and young people who became entangled in the law, it was intended to improve on the inadequacies detected in Juvenile Delinquent laws in the United States and Canada. Singled out for special attention under the YOA were offenders under the age of sixteen.

In the YOA, a distinction is made between a "child" and a "young person." A child is any person who, in the absence of evidence to the contrary, appears to be younger than twelve, and a young person is anyone who appears to be older than twelve but under the age of eighteen.

The compassionate intent of the act was clearly articulated in Section 3, the Declaration of Principle, in which Canadians heard more clearly than ever before the voice of current liberal sociological thought:

"While young persons should not in all instances be held accountable in the same manner or suffer the same consequences for their behavior as adults, young persons who commit offences should nevertheless bear responsibility for their contraventions."

Section 16 of the YOA makes it clear that no child under the age of fourteen can be transferred to an adult court, regardless of the offence. Other sections decree that the maximum allowable sentence for any crime that a young offender might commit will be no more than three years. Three years and no more. For *any* crime. Including murder.

The trial? Well, you may have trouble with the trial, perhaps more than with the kid, because you understand evil but stupidity gives us all a hard time. It's said by some perhaps jaded veterans of the bar that the courts exist not to provide justice but to provide a chance for justice, and that all the trappings of the courts, the flags and the oaths and the rituals, are nothing but a crystallization of our wish, our hope as a society, that somehow, some way, by some judicial alchemy, the base metals of ordinary human souls might be transmuted, however briefly, into truth and compassion and...understanding.

The kid was first arraigned on two charges of Homicide under section 218 (1) of the Criminal Code, a charge of Murder in the First Degree. The first arraignment took place before

Judge K. Wang in the Young Offenders Court in Orangeville on November 14.

The kid's defence attorney, Geoffrey Mullin, immediately petitioned the judge to have the courtroom closed to the public under Section 39 of the YOA, which allows the judge to exclude all members of the public from the courtroom if he sees such a move as being in the interests of the young person or the proper administration of justice.

The arguments for and against a Section 39 closure of the court took eight hours. Judge Wang then delivered himself of a forty-two-page oral decision on this matter on November 26, refusing to close the court to members of the public.

A court date of December 31 was set to hear the actual case against the kid, Judge K. Wang to preside.

Then a lawyer named David Tilson, hired by the local newspaper of record, *The Globe and Mail*, contacted the court clerk to obtain a written copy of Judge Wang's decision not to close the court. Tilson was acting for *Globe* reporters who wanted to be sure they had access to the trial, since most of the people in the country were anxious to see what was going to be done about this kid.

The court clerk said no, sorry, can't do that.

Why?

Well, it seems there's a distinction between what's said out loud to court and the typed record thereof. The clerk suggested that Tilson write a letter to Judge Wang about the difficulty.

Tilson did, sending it on December 27.

Judge Wang read Tilson's letter into the court record on December 31, the day the kid's trial was supposed to begin in earnest, and suggested a formal hearing into Tilson's request on February 1, 1985. The actual trial was postponed.

Fine. Only Tilson showed up on that day in time to hear Judge Wang disqualify himself from sitting as the trial judge. seems that he had inadvertently read an educational assessment form concerning the defendant and therefore considered himself to have been prejudiced unfairly against the boy. So a new date had to be set, and the townsfolk had to wait some more.

In the meantime, Crown Attorney Tony Williams and Geo

Mullin, the defence attorney, had been receiving verbal reports from various psychiatrists, psychometricians and social workers at the Syl Apps Youth Center in Oakville, where the kid had been sent for a full assessment of his mental state.

Things were narrowing down to two choices, neither of which looked good to either man. Mullins could plead the kid not guilty to the charges, but the evidence was overwhelming and would almost certainly result in a conviction on two counts of Murder One, with a maximum sentence under the Young Offenders Act of three years in a juvenile facility. Since the kid had first been committed to custody on November 11, 1984, and the YOA started the clock on confinement right away, that would mean a mandatory release date of November 11, 1987.

Or the second choice, a plea of not guilty by reason of insanity, under Section 16 of the Criminal Code. Mullin would maintain that the kid had "a disease of the mind" that kept him from knowing that the killing was wrong or from fully understanding the nature of the act.

Tony Williams was prepared to cooperate with an insanity defence. First of all, it didn't please him that all the kid would get for a double murder was three years in a fenced playground and a total blackout of all his records as soon as he got out.

Second, an insanity plea would ensure that the kid was held in a psychiatric facility like Syl Apps, where it might be that he would get some treatment and society might be a little safer when this kid got out. But he'd have to be convinced on the matter of insanity. That was vital, for his personal standards as a man of the law and for the protection of the legal system.

Technically, he needed to be persuaded by qualified experts that, on the balance of probabilities, there was at least a 51 percent chance that the kid was legally insane.

Mullin was going to go along with this tactic because he and the kid's family felt that it was the best thing for the boy. The father in particular wanted the boy in treatment so he could be cured and, so the theory goes, made whole again.

Mullin knew that a conviction, even under the YOA, was something that would stay with the kid for life. But an acquittal, even a Section 16, was an acquittal. As far as the justice system was concerned, the kid could walk away from a psychiatric hospital sometime in the future, presumably cured, and no record or trace of his—crime is the wrong word now; we can call it a *mistake*—would remain to prevent him from living a normal life.

Well, the Babineau family would remember, of course. But, in the eyes of the law, that was really beside the point. The courts are too pure to trouble about something as vulgar as vengeance and retribution. In many trials, judges have thrown out members of the victim's family for crying in court. Crying might be prejudicial to the defendant. It might influence the jury

At any rate, Mullin agreed to allow the evidence against the kid to enter the record unchallenged, thereby simplifying what promised to be a truly horrendous affair involving some sixty witnesses. If Tony Williams could be convinced of the fairness of a Section 16 plea, then the trial could be reduced to three witnesses: Constable Tom Rosser, who would testify to the evidential chain, and two expert witnesses from the local psychiatric community, who would assess the kid carefully and, presumably, make such a compelling case of legal insanity that the boy could be held, theoretically, indefinitely at the pleasure of the Lieutenant Governor.

Subject to the statutory yearly review, of course.

Well, the kid finally came to trial on February 25, before Judge A.R. Webster of the Family Court in Orangeville. There was some preliminary byplay between lawyers acting for various local newspapers and Judge Webster. The newspapers wanted access to every record handed up to the judge by the clerk of the court and the judge disagreed. Under the Young Offenders Act, information about the defendant *or* his victims *or* anything else the judge doesn't want you to hear about can be declared privileged

Which is, in case you're wondering, why you haven't seen the kid's name yet. You see, you can't be told his name. Under the YOA, if I do, or if anyone gives you enough information about him to make an educated guess at his name, then that person goes to jail. For two years.

So, in a wood-lined room, under the flag, with all the news people present feeling the heavy presence of the YOA at the shoulders, the field was at last clear to actually try the case, to arrive at a just disposition of a terrible enigma.

To accomplish this, all that was required of them—the judge, since there was no jury, and the lawyers and the expert witnesses—was to answer as best they could one simple question: what went wrong with this thirteen-year-old boy?

He'd been trying to make a wooden sword, but the thing kept breaking. And the knee, the crutch, kept him from riding his bike or going for a long walk, which is what he did when he felt…like this. He slammed his hand into a bench, a big, strong, thirteen-year-old boy, blood rising in his face, a red veil.

Sundays with the family. We can see the kid moving about in the basement of his house. The family is here and there, doing whatever it was they did on Sundays, whatever most families do. The kid says the thought just came into his head. The idea was just…there.

What do you mean? What do you mean, it was just there? There like you see a spider on the basement window? There like your breath is there? Well, he's not saying. The thought was just…there. He had to kill someone.

This too might trouble us.

Someone. Not *something.* And not any particular person. No loathed nemesis from the schoolyard, where the young first learn the laws of the jungle. Not some cat or dog or bird or frog, the usual proving ground for developing sadists. The free-form miasmic nature of his decision won't leave us at peace. He had to kill something human. Anything *human.*

He told the doctors that he thought about who he would kill.

Perhaps his little brother, upstairs watching television. No. Too many people in the house. They'd catch him.

One of his buddies, maybe? Too far to walk, with his bad knee and that crutch. Well…let's see…

Round and round she goes, folks. Vanna waits for the letter.

Kill Danny. The Babineau kid.

Okay. How?

Call him up. Say, Hey, Danny. Meet me at the school. I got to some stuff at the school. Saint Peter's. I need some help, on account of my knee is fucked.

This he does. He calls the Babineaus', and we get the idea that the Babineaus are already out of the house, because surely if Marcel or Jeannine had answered the phone, heard his voice, they'd have remembered his call. So the phone rings in the Babineau house on that slow Sunday afternoon, and the kids are sitting around doing pretty much nothing, a small-town kind of day in the fall, and the phone rings again and little Danny gets up and walks over to it—it's sitting there on the hall table or stuck to the wall, like a fat black beetle, burring with possibilities.

Hello, says Danny, into the phone, into the mouthpiece grid, and in his ear...there's the voice, the one Wayne Frechette will hear for hours just seven days later, a familiar voice, a friend's voice.

Sure, says Danny, perhaps a little thrilled that one of the older guys wants to see *him,* a lousy eleven-year-old. I'll come. I'll be there.

So now the phone goes down, and okay, Danny is on his way, so quick now, the kid is out of the house, on that knee but covering the ground, out the back gate and across the brown field to Saint Peter's School with his dad's screwdriver in his pocket, and he takes a plate off a door lock. Now he has access to keys for the school, because someone else (whose name is known but can't be spoken because it will infringe upon the killer's rights) has a set of keys to the school, and the kid knows where they're kept.

But he figures, no, don't use the keys. They'll know who has keys. It'll lead them straight to you.

So he makes it look like burglary, taking the door plate off with his father's screwdriver, working away at the screw-heads, scraping the paint out of the head, getting the blade in, working fast but well, doing the groundwork.

He goes into the school and looks around, trying to figure out where to do it. He already knows how. He has the yellow nylon rope with him. Brought it along with the screwdriver.

Well. How about the girls' change-room, off the gym? No windows. Solid walls. Good soundproofing, in case something goes...wrong. Okay, do it in the girls' change-room.

So the best-laid plans, right? What happens?

He goes back outside, pulling the door shut, and who comes around the corner but Daniel, little Danny, and what the fuck is this?

Danny brought along his sister! His little goddamned sister. Look at her, toddling along after her older brother, Jesus. Man, what're you gonna do now?

He decides he'll have to kill her too.

Now all through this, no one can detect any sign that he ever asked himself why, or thought about stopping. Not that there wasn't calculation in him, calculation about the place, about who might have the keys and what the keys would tell them. About the method, and the possibility of…difficulties…of noise.

Somehow he got Monique to wait for them, for Danny and the kid to come back. Then he got Danny into the girls' change-room…and now it was in front of him—to do the thing or not.

There's no need to tell you all the details. Danny fought. Danny did what he could. But the kid was big. Even then, he was close to one-fifty. Now, he's full-grown. Close to six feet. Heavy. Danny was a small kid. He wasn't going to get any more time to build himself up. Time was up for Danny's childhood.

You should know that strangling someone isn't a matter of seconds, nor is it a simple compression of muscles. It takes effort, and will, over a matter of minutes, sometimes six or seven.

Six or seven minutes of intense muscular effort, face to face with the victim. Eye to eye as the changes take place.

One.

Two.

Three.

Four.

Five.

Six.

Sev—So now Danny was down. He hadn't expected blood, but there it was. He went along the hall to the washroom and pushed open the door, and there was Monique. Waiting for him, doing what she was told to do by her brother's older friend. Monique—was—we have no way of knowing the correct word here.

Easier?

Faster? Little lungs give way. Tiny hands fluttering.

The cord tends to cut into his hands. It hurts him. His shoulders are cramping as well.

This is work.

Monique is over.

More complications. Back in the hall, he hears Danny calling.

Danny *calling?*

Well, we have seen that strangling someone isn't easy. It's something you have to work at. Do just right. He found Danny in the change-room. he got it right this time; the practice helped.

Will? Yes, he found the will, the determination. Both of the expert witnesses agreed to that: Dr. Clive Chamberlain, of the Thistletown Regional Center, and Dr. Robert Coulthard, of the Clarke Institute, a famous national center for psychiatric research and treatment, specializing in forensic psychiatry.

After several lengthy interviews with the kid, and hypnosis, and psychometrics, and family interviews, and electroencephalograms and full medicals, after more interviews, and consultations, and due consideration, and recourse to the Diagnostic Statistical Manual Number Three, it was their opinion, their expert opinion, that the kid was suffering from…latent schizophrenia, and a component of obsessive-compulsive behavior.

Oh…well…*that* clears it all up, doesn't it?

Neither expert could say with any certainty whether such an…episode…might ever happen again. But neither doctor had any doubt that the kid had been under a compulsion to kill that Sunday, a compulsion of such strength and dominance that drove all other considerations from his mind.

Was there any physical—psychological—genesis or component to the …episode? Nothing organically wrong with the boy

Not that science could detect.

It was a disease of the mind, then? Latent schizophrenia?

Yes.

Did the doctor come to the conclusion that it was a disease the mind to the extent that it renders the young person incapab of appreciating the nature and quality of an act? Or of knowir that the act is wrong?

Yes. That would be Subsection 2 of Section 16 of t

Criminal Code.

The experts were reminded that Section 16, Subsection 2 makes a distinction between "appreciating the nature" of an act and "knowing that it was wrong." The word "or" in the code is vital. Did the boy have a disease of the mind that rendered him incapable of recognizing that he was doing murder, or of knowing that it was wrong. One or the other. Not both.

To sustain a plea under this section, the defence need only prove one of the two qualifying states of mind.

Did the experts feel certain that the boy was "incapable of appreciating the nature" of his killings?

Yes, they both did so believe.

In his judgement, released March 20, 1985, Judge Webster accepted "on the balance of probabilities" that the accused had a disease of the mind that rendered him incapable of appreciating his act, the act being the murders of Daniel and Monique Babineau on November 4, 1984. The judge was not persuaded that the accused was unaware that his murders were wrong.

Under the Young Offenders Act, a young person who is not found guilty in a Young Offenders Trial—and the kid was found Not Guilty By Reason Of Insanity—will have all records of his case destroyed. Fingerprints. Polygraph records. Police depositions. Psychiatric assessments. In this case even the trial transcript. It would be as if the trial had never taken place.

Up until 1988, the kid was in custody at the Syl Apps Youth Center, the juvenile facility where he was sent to be assessed by the court. He's not there now. I don't know where he is. The police are not allowed to know where he is. No one may know. After all…he's innocent. Cured. Responded to treatment.

In May of 1991, the Supreme Court declared that indefinite deferrals are unconstitutional. So we can pretty well assume that, as of 1992, this kid is out on the streets, and I guess we had better hope they cured him, because no one can know his name or find out anything about his background. Perhaps Wittgenstein would find this amusing.

Maybe we'll never find out where he is, and what he's doing now. Or maybe we'll hear from him.

Why the crutch? He was strong enough to strangle two healthy children. Why the arrogance and coldness during his interviews with cops and psychiatrists? In this layman's view, no very convincing case was made that the boy was truly insane, whatever the hell *that* means, McNaughton Insanity Rules being what they are.

Initially, it was a struggle for the Crown Attorney to persuade himself that an insanity defence was justifiable. It took a three-hour session in camera with Dr. Coulthard before Tony Williams and the detectives could accept the plea offer with a clear conscience.

And if they had not been able to accept it, the kid would be long gone from some juvenile summer camp, and where he went after that would be none of your damned business. For that matter, in the judgement of the government, in the judgement of those legislators and child-care workers who framed the Young Offenders Act, none of this *is* any of your damned business.

Chamberlain and Coulthard called the kid a "latent schizophrenic," and that's fine with me, although latent schizophrenia is an inside joke. In essence, it means that, well, yes, this kid is an obvious wacko, but we have no idea what the hell is wrong with him.

They might have called him a "psychopath," that 1 percent of all sociopaths who do harm to others, but again these are all just names, and it's a failing of the modern world that we imagine we have understood something when we can think of a name for it. It would have made as much sense in this kid's case to call him a white rhino or a banded krait.

Psychopaths. The argument rages about them. Are they born? Are they made by disturbed families? Do they make themselves, fashion themselves out of the rough stuff of plasma and bad intentions that compose most infants before the civilizing influence of society touches them?

The grim reality is that, to someone like this kid, we are nothing but images flickering on the bone at the back of his skull. If he blanks, we cease to be. If it pleases him to watch the images dying, then he'll reach for the yellow nylon rope and what it takes, and do it twice if he gets the chance. They ne come in, they never get tired, they don't want to be caught, and they're damned good at what they do. There's no cure for this condition, and we're a long way from understanding it. You can't get a lizard to tell you his dreams.

What's left to us, standing in the hallway outside the courtroom while we imagine that better minds than ours are dealing wisely and justly with these enigmas?

Maybe we want the kid to be insane, not for the sake of a Section 16 plea, but for our peace of mind. If we can look at what he did, at what his kind do and have done and will do tomorrow, look at the cruelty and the brutality of it, at the will to do harm that flowered like a black orchid in that boy's mind, if we can look at this and say, hell yes, he must have been crazy, because only a crazy person could do such a thing, then we have placed him outside, away from the fire of civilization, out in the darkness past the edge of town, something different from you and me. The Latin root for "insane" is "unclean."

So we can see him there still, standing before the white coffins, an enigma on a crutch, a crippled spirit, images of dying children flickering on the wet bone inside his skull, a monster with the glacial chill to touch his victims, to put tokens into their hands and then hobbledy-hop on that crutch out into the crisp fall air and off home, hoppity-scrape, to dinner with the family, and to judgement, and the rest of his life, carrying his burden, his mystery, away with him, and the night coming on behind him like the closing of a door.

FIFTEEN

The Lost Boys

Now I don't know how it strikes you, but it seems to me that the people who had to deal with the kid-killer in Orangeville didn't have the foggiest idea of what to do with him. So they were left with no choice but to try to hammer him into one of the pigeon-holes they had handy—in this case the one labeled LATENT SCHIZOPHRENIA—and nobody who watched it happen was under any illusion that the experts were doing a good job. They were all making it up as they went along.

Why?

Because what they had in front of them was something that the framers of the law had never imagined in their worst nightmares. They had something truly evil, and true evil is *not supposed to exist.*

After all, hasn't psychiatry and sociology pretty much explained all this stuff? I mean, it's all down there in black and white in the Young Offenders Act.

Sure...

DECLARATION OF PRINCIPLE
POLICY FOR CANADA WITH RESPECT TO
YOUNG OFFENDERS—act to be liberally construed.
3.1 It is hereby recognized and declared that
(a) while young persons should not in all instances be held
    accountable in the same manner or suffer the same
    consequences for their behavior as adults...

[...a pivotal assumption. Remember it.]

...young persons who commit offences should nonetheless
    bear responsibility for their contraventions;
(b) society must, although it has the responsibility to take
    reasonable measures to prevent criminal conduct by young
    persons, be afforded the necessary protection from illegal
    behavior;

[Oh, yeah? Watch…]

(c) young persons who commit offences require supervision,
   discipline and control, but, because of their state of
   dependency and level of development and maturity, they also
   have special needs and require guidance and assistance;
(d) where it is not inconsistent with the protection of society,
   taking no measures or taking measures other than judicial
   proceedings under this Act should be considered for dealing
   with young persons who have committed offences;

[That means they don't have to go to jail.]

(e) young persons have rights and freedoms in their own right,
   including those stated in the Charter of Rights and Freedoms
   or in the Canadian Bill of Rights, and in particular a right to
   be heard in the course of, and to participate in, the processes
   that lead to decisions that affect them…

[Now here it comes. Pay close attention because this is why
ou don't have your VCR any more…]

…and young persons should have SPECIAL GUARANTEES
   of their rights and freedoms.

This is vital. What the YOA says is that juvenile offenders
ave special rights that, in effect, outweigh the rights of ordinary
tizens. That's one hell of a packet to pass without serious pub-
: debate. Under the YOA, kids who commit crimes are, in a
:ry real way, provided with special privileges that will be
:fined by justice system professionals.
In case you're wondering, that doesn't mean *you!*

(f) in the application of this Act, the rights and freedoms of
   young persons include a right to the least possible
   interference…

[Are you getting this down?]

…with freedom that is consistent with the protection of
society…

[That's the theory. The practice is to ignore the consequences
to society's safety because, after all, we have proven we can be
safely ignored in matters that are best left to our legal masters.]

…having regard to the needs of young persons and the interest
of their families;
(g) young persons have the right, in every instance where they
have rights and freedoms that may be affected by this Act, to
be informed as to what those rights and freedoms are: and
(h) parents have responsibility for the care and supervision of
their children, and for that reason, young persons should be
removed from parental supervision either partly or entirely
only when measures that provide for continuing parental
supervision are inappropriate.
2. This Act shall be liberally construed…

In other words, if there's a judgement call to be made about
kid, the Act *mandates* the milder judicial response. The court i
required to go easy on him.

The Young Offenders Act had its origins in the same kind
psychological and sociological study-groups that rendered suc
disastrous judgements as the release of Melvin Stanton and th
ongoing lenience shown to drug offenders in our courts.
    The general theory behind the YOA and all other theorie
about criminal offenders is the largely unsupported belief th
crime comes from environmental and genetic sources beyon
the criminal's control. This theory easily takes the inquiri
agency back beyond the date of the criminal's birth and ther
fore assigns to his actions a series of antecedent causes f
which he cannot be blamed. This sort of thinking has given ri
to the popularity of the Wounded Child Theory, the idea that
are, all of us, in one sense or another the victims of some kind
original abuse and deprivation. As Hobart Mowrer put it:

At three I had a feeling
of ambivalence toward my brothers
And so it follows naturally
I poisoned all my lovers.
And now I'm happy,
I have learned the lesson this has taught:
That everything I do that's wrong
is SOMEONE ELSE'S FAULT.

In his phenomenal bestseller *Homecoming,* John Bradshaw provides a checklist that will help his readers diagnose themselves to determine whether or not they are carrying this Wounded Inner Child in their hearts. Answer yes or no…

I experience anxiety and fear whenever I contemplate
anything new.
I'm a people-pleaser and have no identity of my own.
I'm a rebel. I feel alive when I'm in conflict.
In the deepest places of my secret self I feel there is
something wrong with me.
I'm a hoarder, I have trouble letting go of anything.
I feel inadequate as a man or a woman.
I'm confused about my sexual identity.
I feel guilty when I stand up for myself.
I have trouble starting things.
I have trouble finishing things.
I rarely have a thought of my own.
I continually criticize myself for being inadequate.
I have trouble identifying what I'm feeling.
I have communication problems.
I try to control my feelings.
I cry when I'm angry.
I rage when I'm scared or hurt.
I have trouble expressing my feelings.
I worry.

And the answer of course is *who the hell doesn't?*
It strikes me that there's a fallacy in Bradshaw's thesis

regarding the Wounded Inner Child; he makes his feelings towards this child clear in the following passages.

On page five of *Homecoming,* Bradshaw quotes a poem by Christopher Morley. It's about the apparently innocent and pure delights of childhood, ending with these lines:

> And Life, that sets all things in rhyme,
> May make you poet too, in time,
> But there were days, O tender elf,
> When you were Poetry itself!

Bradshaw has this to say:

> What happens to this wonderful beginning when we were all "Poetry itself"? How do all those tender elves become murderers, drug addicts, physical and sexual offenders, cruel dictators, morally-degenerate politicians? How do they become the "walking wounded"? We see them all around us; the sad, fearful, doubting, anxious, and depressed, filled with unutterable longings. Surely this loss of innate human potential is the greatest tragedy of all.

And, deeper into the forest...

> ...Children, naturally filled with wonder, are spontaneous and live in the now. In a sense, they are exiled in the now. Using the word WONDERFUL, I'll give you a profile of the wonder child. Each letter stands for one of the natural traits.

> Wonder
> Optimism
> Naiveté
> Dependence
> Emotions
> Resilience
> Free Play
> Uniqueness
> Love

Bradshaw's vision of the Proto-Child (somehow I can't bring myself to use his phrase, the Wonder Child, without feeling a little queasy, as if I'd just eaten far too much cotton-candy) is not a new one. It has its roots in Dionysian mythology, Judeo-Christian Garden-of-Eden remembrances and various brands of Enlightenment Theory that are echoed in the Peter Pan stories and various—much less coherent—New Age writings.

The basic assumption seems to be that children are fundamentally inclined towards goodness and sweetness and wonder, and that somehow it is their exposure to the world of adults—to the terrible Fruit of the Poisoned Tree—that makes them do bad things. It's the original self-exculpatory argument, elevated here to a first principle.

So there is no such thing as the Bad Seed, and if somehow the Wonder Child...excuse me, I have to shudder here for just a second...if the Wonder Child does something so mindnumbingly evil that just reading about it will burn out your brainstem, then it follows that this evil act was a consequence of some terrible intrusion from the Dark Side.

Which is wonderfully nice to think, and deep down inside it makes us all feel warm and cuddly and...nice.

Unfortunately, anyone actually engaged in the study of childhood development and childhood behavior—for instance, daycare workers and school-crossing guards and parents—has a world of empirical evidence to the contrary.

As much as we may dislike it, people such as Abraham Maslow, Desmond Morris and Jane Goodall have accomplished some very persuasive studies—studies with high predictive values—that suggest that we all, as humans and as *human animals,* come into life with a whole range of hard-wired tendencies, and many of them are not at all pretty to watch. I could go on in this vein for a hundred pages, but it's simpler if you just take a trip to someplace like a zoo or a preschool playroom; you'll get the point.

Alfred Adler himself suggested that the will to power is one of the most basic of these hard-wired urges, and it's usually expressed in dominance, and dominance is accomplished by aggression, and aggression is ugly as hell.

Deluding ourselves with heartwarming fairy-tales about the innate goodness of children is comforting and soothing—kind of an epistemological cuddle-blanket—that can keep out the chilling realities of human nature, but carrying Bradshaw's principles into the arena of the justice system is like taking a Nerf Bat to a bar fight; you're just not going to last very long.

Accepting Bradshaw's Wounded Inner Child theory (and millions have) leads you by an ineluctable (and extremely tedious) logic directly to the idea that We Are All Victims, and victims deserve care and nurturing and understanding (and extra cookies).

It's a very powerful place to occupy, as Barbara Findlay makes very clear in her pamphlet *With All of Who We Are: A Discussion of Oppression and Dominance.** What follows is her Oppressor/Victim index:

Are you:

OR	
• raised working class or poor?	• raised middle-class?
• a woman	• a man
• a lesbian or a gay	• heterosexual
• survivor of physical abuse	• not a survivor of physical abuse
• under 25	• over 25
• over 45	• under 45
• Francophone	• not Francophone
• a Native Person	• a non-Native person
• someone who had a language other than English or French as your first language	• someone whose first language was English or French
• a survivor of sexual abuse	• not a survivor of sexual abuse
• a survivor of mental hospitals	• not a survivor of mental hospitals

* Barbara Findlay, *With All of Who We Are: A Discussion of Oppression and Dominance* (Lazara, 1991).

• of Jewish heritage	• not of Jewish heritage
• a parent	• not a parent
• a survivor of alcoholism	• not a survivor of alcoholism
• a survivor of drug abuse	• not a survivor of drug abuse
• disabled	• able-bodied

She goes on to suggest that people in the left-hand column are likely to be "oppressed"—read victims—and people in the right-hand list are likely to be "oppressors"—read *white Anglo-Saxon heterosexual able-bodied males in their forties.*

(I guess at this juncture the Disclosure Law requires me to admit that I am a white, Anglo, male heterosexual in his mid-forties. Further, I have blue eyes, blond hair, I have no physical or mental disabilities, I can bench-press my own weight, I own several weapons and I am fairly skilled in their use, I like football and beer and cats and I have never been in a mental hospital, I've never had a drug problem, I was raised middle-class and English is my first language. I now stand ready to accept my punishment, which, for most of the Professional Victims out there, will be an immediate expulsion from the debate on the grounds that only true victims may write about victimhood.)

Anyway, now we recognize that most of you—I exclude myself and others of my ilk—are carrying Wounded Inner Children, at which point Bradshaw and the rest of the faith-healers applaud your courage and welcome you into the fold.

It's a wonderfully liberating concept, and it's not hard to understand why it would have such a tremendous (and, not coincidentally, profitable) appeal to the millions of Worried Well, for whom these symptoms are part of everyone's existence, perhaps are even part of the fabric of being…I have no problem with any of this.

Well, just one.

Surely some of the people buying into this Wounded Inner Child business are Not Very Nice; the odds alone argue for this.

And perhaps some of them are actually sort of rotten.

Rotten to their kids, their wives, their subordinates at work.

Maybe a few of them are rapists or wife-beaters or killers.

Maybe they *are* Wounded Inner Children. But they are also Grown-Up Assholes.

I'm not comfortable with lumping all of you out there into the same category as Grown-Up Assholes, and I don't think you should be either. So before you climb aboard for the Magical Mystery Tour back to the Wonder Womb—no, I won't be coming along—just do one thing for me?

Check the passenger list.

Other than that, I think this is all cute and sweet and really...really...*nice!* The reason this stuff sells is the same reason that everything New Age sells, and diet books sell and co-dependency books sell and Shirley MacLaine sells, and that's because the *star* of each and every one of these books is (*Ta-daah!*)—*you!*

These books are all about *you!*

Your body, *your* mind, *your* past, *your* future, *your* boyfriend, *your* girlfriend, *your* toxic parents, *your* karma, *your* aura, *your* past life as a Mesopotamian concubine...of course they sell.

And perhaps the world *will* be a better place when all the Worried Well finally get their chakras under control and their Inner Children crammed full of self-esteem and their bowels working like a Rolex Oyster.

Why?

Because perhaps then these self-absorbed whiners will lift their heads up and take a look around the neighborhood and see some *real* victims—under the bridges, on the dole, in the ghettos and the barrios and the flophouses, even in the jails.

So, as I've said, I think all this Wounded Inner Child talk is very nice, and I think it's a nice idea to try to make your kids think well of themselves, within reason, and it's nice to try to be spontaneous and not to worry too much.

What it has to do with law enforcement, however, escapes me completely. Because nowhere in my copy of the social contract can I find the clause that says:

WE THE STATE
PROMISE TO SAFEGUARD

YOU AND YOUR LOVED ONES
UNLESS THE PERSON
WHO HAS STOLEN YOUR VCR
OR RAPED YOUR DAUGHTER
IS A CERTIFIED
WOUNDED INNER CHILD
IN WHICH CASE
WE OWE IT TO HIM
TO MAKE IT ALL BETTER
REGARDLESS OF THE RISK TO SOCIETY
AND BY THE WAY
HERE'S THE BILL
WILL THAT BE VISA OR AMEX?

Although compassion and nurturing are important in this life, and self-esteem is a good thing to have, they have their limitations. Self-esteem is a phrase we hear far too much.

The schools say they want to give the students self-esteem.

Parents talk about giving their kids self-esteem.

Everybody says how important and vital it is for our kids to have lots and lots of self-esteem.

I don't hear anybody suggesting that these little dears might have to *earn* this self-esteem, perhaps by being good students or by actually excelling at some difficult art, or by doing hard community work for someone who needs it.

Drop in at your local school someday and hear what the latest learning theories are. Kids don't *learn* math, they are supposed to *experience* it. We don't give them grades any more, because it might damage their self-esteem. We don't debate any more because it's important to show tolerance for differing opinions. Kids don't have to worry about spelling or phonetics because the idea is to be creative, to let them experience language without stuffing them into little boxes where they might suffer a loss of self-esteem.

This nonsense comes straight out of Montessori and the 1960s left-wing academic cadre that has been screwing up the education system ever since they scrapped the Departmentals and made all the classrooms "Open Concept."

We talk about self-esteem as if it were a vitamin supplement that helps to build healthy souls, and perhaps that's true. But it has to be the real thing, a sense of competence and pride that comes from attempting something challenging, dealing with it and achieving a degree of mastery over it. Self-esteem is not given to children. Children acquire it for themselves. What we offer instead is merely flattery, and flattery is toxic, corrupting, corrosive and, finally, condescending.

Ask any parent.

For that matter, go to the bookstores again and check out the number of books with titles like *Spoiled Rotten* or *Toxic Teens* or *Living With Children.* And ask yourself, how different was your relationship with your parents? How different are the standards for politeness around adults? What has just hit you in the back of the head, much to the delight of your kids, is a pendulum.

I'd like to take this moment to warn any young mother out there who sees herself as a kind of fountain of light and goodness to her children that if she works very hard at convincing her kids that they're the center of the earth, the best thing that ever happened to her, that each and every little burp and gurgle is music to her ears, and she keeps it up for a few years, what will happen is…*they'll believe you!*

And when that happens…you're toast.

You'd better get used to catering to their whims and pandering to their ugly moods, because as far as they're concerned, *that's your job!*

They'll have so much self-esteem you'll choke on it. In the Adlerian sense, you have rolled over and bared your throat and as much as this may repel you, your kids are *brain-wired* to accept this as a sign of their dominance over you.

In the fullness of time, you and every other adult they see will be reduced to shadowy background figures in the Imax movie of their lives. You'll be free to pay and pony up and pick up, but don't expect thanks, because, after all, you *said* they were just the cutest little things and you pumped them so chockfull of self-esteem that their little skulls were bursting with it.

There were two faxes making the rounds of the police station and federal enforcement offices while I was researching this book. One was a typical cop meditation.

STRESS
IS THE FEELING YOU GET
WHEN YOU WANT TO
BUT CAN'T
CHOKE THE LIVING SHIT
OUT OF SOME ASSHOLE
WHO
DESPERATELY
NEEDS IT

Something any honest parent will admit to feeling from time to time during moments of quiet contemplation of their teenagers. And the other one must have been sent in by a parent:

TEENAGERS!
Tired of Being Hassled
by your stupid Parents?
ACT NOW!
Move Out!
Get a Job!
Pay Your Own Bills!
DO IT WHILE YOU STILL
KNOW EVERYTHING!

So first we've let these deluded academic twits screw up the schools...fine...it's a done deal, and anyway, who needs to be part of a powerful economic and creative nation-state? Maybe it'll be FUN being a Third World backwater dishing up peameal bacon—you want fries with that, sir?—and maple-syrup candies and devolved hockey players to tourists from better-educated and more competitive nations.

But then we let these people take on the justice system. They promptly served up the Young Offenders Act. And now, notwith-standing their continuing delusions about teenage criminality, we have teenage criminals with self-esteem.

If we can agree that one of the components of self-esteem is confidence, then they have lots and lots of self-esteem. Wounded Inner Children they may be, but they had enough moxie left to commit the following offences in just one year—1990.

(By the way, these are just Young Offenders who were charged, so keep in mind that, according to the Ten Beef Rule, what we're seeing here, with the exception of the murder charges, is just one-tenth of the number of kids involved in crime.)

25	Young Offenders committed first degree murder
23	Y.O.s committed second degree murder
6	Y.O.s committed manslaughter
62	Y.O.s committed attempted murder
30	Y.O.s committed aggravated sexual assault
54	Y.O.s committed aggravated sexual assault with a weapon
2,321	Y.O.s committed sexual assault
12,507	Y.O.s committed assault level one
3,643	Y.O.s committed assault bodily harm/or weapon level two
314	Y.O.s committed aggravated assault level three
384	Y.O.s committed assault unlawful bodily harm
23	Y.O.s discharged a firearm with intent to wound
306	Y.O.s assaulted a police officer and got charged [Most just get a severe slapping around.]
56	Y.O.s assaulted a peace officer or security guard
330	Y.O.s committed other types of assault and got charged
275	Y.O.s committed other sexual offences and got charged
9.	Y.O.s abducted a person under fourteen and got charged
3	Y.O.s abducted a person under sixteen and got charged
326	Y.O.s committed robbery with a firearm and got charged
621	Y.O.s committed robbery with other offensive weapons

1,329 Y.O.s committed other forms of robbery and were charged

10,458 Y.O.s broke into a business premise and got charged

15,469 Y.O.s broke into private homes and got charged

5,331 Y.O.s committed other forms of B and E and got charged

6,317 Y.O.s were convicted of car theft

1,780 Y.O.s stole a truck and got charged

903 Y.O.s stole a motorcycle and got charged

966 Y.O.s stole some other kind of vehicle and got charged

39 Y.O.s were charged with stealing a bicycle worth over $1,000

755 Y.O.s were charged with stealing valuables worth more than $1,000 from a car

214 Y.O.s were charged with shoplifting over $1,000

1,335 Y.O.s were charged with other thefts over $1,000

2,199 Y.O.s were charged with stealing bikes under $1,000

8,057 Y.O.s were charged with stealing goods worth less than $1,000 from a car

38,346 Y.O.s were charged with shoplifting goods under $1,000

In case you missed that…*thirty-eight thousand three hundred forty-six kids* were *charged* trying to steal something from a store. And any parent will tell you that almost all kids caught shoplifting are sent home with a stern warning, either by the security people or the patrol cops responding. So no matter how you slice it, there are a hell of a lot of kids out there ripping off the stores. No wonder that security guards in the plazas are always harassing the mall rats!

Anyway, where were we…?

13,834 Y.O.s were caught stealing other items under $1,000

6,888 Y.O.s were caught in possession of stolen goods

1,274 Y.O.s committed check fraud

1,171 Y.O.s committed credit card fraud

1,678 Y.O.s committed various frauds

By the way, that's a total of *one hundred and seventeen thousand and fourteen* (117,014) *property crimes*.

Let's interrupt this depressing litany to do some math. I guarantee you that the figure we have read represents at most one-tenth of the property crimes committed by Young Offenders in Canada in 1990. So that brings it to...

$$
\begin{array}{r}
117,014 \\
\times\ 10 \\
\hline
1,170,140
\end{array}
$$

...or *one million one hundred seventy thousand one hundred and forty property crimes committed by young offenders in* 1990.

Now you know who got your VCR. Feel better? And you also know why household insurance and car insurance are more expensive than ever before.

      7 Y.O.s were busted for prostitution
    13 Y.O.s were popped for procuring
  380 Y.O.s were popped for other kinds of prostitution
  122 Y.O.s were charged with possession of explosives
  668 Y.O.s were charged with possession of prohibited weapons
  122 Y.O.s were charged with Possess Restricted Weapon
1,803 Y.O.s were charged with other weapons offences

Now that's a total of 2,715 kids charged with weapon offences, and if we use the Ten Beef Rule, we get *twenty-seven thousand one hundred and fifty* times that police officers found weapons in the possession of Young Offenders. Nine times out of ten, the charge will be dropped or plea-bargained down in exchange for some promise of remorse and community service. Once again, if you doubt this, spend a few nights on the beat with your local cops. If anything, it's a conservative estimate. Face it; the kids are *armed*.

     949 Y.O.s committed arson and got charged
   5,051 Y.O.s jumped bail and got charged [most are simply
          returned to a group home or lectured]
      24 Y.O.s dealt in counterfeit currency and got charged
   3,152 Y.O.s were charged with disturbing the peace
   1,593 Y.O.s escaped custody and got charged

   Again, the YOA must be "liberally construed," so nine times
out of ten a kid who runs and gets caught is simply returned to
whatever agency is supposed to be watching over him.
   While I'm on that subject, you should know that one of the
main reasons the Young Offenders Act doesn't work is that none
of these so-called diversionary avenues is enforceable. A youth
court judge can insist that a Young Offender carry out some sort
of community service, or go to some counseling sessions, but if
the kid ignores these instructions, nothing happens! He just gets
brought up again and given a scolding, which he'll ignore again,
because, in the long run, he knows that there's really not a damn
thing they can do other than to drag him into court now and
then. The act has no teeth at all.

     258 Y.O.s committed indecent acts
      38 Y.O.s committed kidnapping
      12 Y.O.s were charged with a breach of public morals
     651 Y.O.s were charged with obstructing police
   1,133 Y.O.s were charged with being unlawfully at large
     684 Y.O.s were charged with trespass at night .
   2,306 Y.O.s were charged with property damage over
          $1,000
  16,435 Y.O.s were charged with property damage under
          $1,000
  10,614 Y.O.s were charged with other Criminal Code
          crimes
       2 Y.O.s were charged with Heroin Possession
       5 Y.O.s were charged with Heroin Trafficking
       2 Y.O.s were charged with Heroin Importation [IMP]
     123 Y.O.s were charged with Cocaine Possession
     131 Y.O.s were charged with Cocaine Trafficking

4	Y.O.s were charged with Cocaine Importation
205	Y.O.s were charged with PPT, NIP or IMP Other Drugs
2,517	Y.O.s were charged with NIP Cannabis
644	Y.O.s were charged with PPT Cannabis
17	Y.O.s were charged with Cannabis Importation
11	Y.O.s were charged with Cultivation
11	Y.O.s were charged with PPT Controlled Drugs
179	Y.O.s were charged with Possession or PPT restricted
22,365	Y.O.s were charged with liquor offences

Now that's just for 1990. According to the latest reports, all these figures are showing an increase for 1992.

What's truly staggering about this chart, taken from the most recent StatsCan publication, is that it doesn't in any way reflect the number of Young Offenders who either were not charged for an offence because of some other diversionary response mandated by the Young Offenders Act, or those who were never arrested at all because of the difficulties the Young Offenders Act presents to police officers. If we apply the Ten Beef Rule to this question, we get the following estimate of the number of Young Offender crimes the citizens had to deal with in some unofficial way in 1990:

$$\begin{array}{r} 224{,}676 \quad \text{total Y.O.s charged} \\ \underline{\times\ 10} \quad \text{undetected crimes per Y.O.} \\ 2{,}246{,}760 \end{array}$$

TWO MILLION TWO HUNDRED AND FORTY-SIX THOUSAND SEVEN HUNDRED AND SIXTY crimes pulled by Young Offenders that they got away with ABSOLUTELY CLEAN.

If you find this hard to believe, ask around. If you can't find at least two of your friends or family who have had something stolen or a car window smashed or a child harassed, then call me up and tell me. The fact is, these kids are very hard to bring into the station-house for anything.

For example, let's say a police officer has information that leads him to believe that a certain young male known to the neighborhood is carrying out a series of daylight B and Es. He's been seen going into homes, he's talked about it to his buddies, and he has been observed by other agencies selling VCRs and stereos to a known fence.

(You'll have no doubt guessed that this has actually happened and that I watched it happen. And no, I'm not going to give you any names, because I haven't forgotten that if I so much as hint at the kid's identity, I could be put away for two years.

Next step: the police officer attempts to get some information about the kid. He has to make a special request for this kind of information, since it comes under the control of the YOA and therefore cannot be sent over the air.

If the reporting system is up-to-date (which is hardly ever) and *if* he can get permission (hardly ever) the police officer is now in a position to figure out where the kid lives and—oh, no—the kid is now a resident of a group home and nominally under the control of one of the many diversionary agencies employed by the State to provide shelter and guidance to Y.O.s.

So off he goes to the group home, where he knocks on the door and waits politely, cap in hand, for someone to answer it.

The scene runs something like this:

Five minutes pass…
Some kids arrive and brush past the officer.
He says: "Say, kids, can you get someone out here?"
They say: "Why the fuck?"
He says: "I need to talk to someone in charge."
They say: "She's out."
He says: "Someone must be here…is [NAME OF KID] here?"
They say: "Why you hassling HIM?"
He says: "Can you send out a worker?"
They say: "Fuck off."
The kids go inside. They make very loud pig-snorting sounds, which are soon buried under an avalanche of techno-house punk-rock so loud it's literally painful.

Since this is a real residence and the cop has no warrant and this is just part of an investigation, he rings again.

Three minutes pass.

Finally, a young woman appears, looking very official. She radiates impatience and contempt. She is closely followed by a dissipating cloud of grass smoke. Ordinarily, the cop would do something about the presence of marijuana, but bitter experience has taught him the futility of such an action where it involves a diversionary residence operating under the YOA.

The young woman gives him the kind of look usually reserved for stuff that sticks to your best Ferragamo pumps.

She says: "What is it?"

He says: "I'd like to speak with [NAME OF KID]. Is he in?"

She says: "What about?"

He says: "Just some questions…can I see him?"

She says: "Can't you leave him alone? Why are you always on his case?"

He says: "Ma'am, I just want to ask him about some thing that have been—"

She says: "Is it about an offence?"

He says: "It's just some questions. Something he might hel us with."

She says: "Something stolen?"

He says: "Yes, ma'am…can you ask him to—"

She says: "I'll have to call his lawyer. You can't talk to hi without a lawyer present."

He says: "Well, I understand that, but I'm not charging hi with—"

She says: "He's had enough bullshit from you guys. You' just trying to dig up some shit. Don't you guys have anythi better to do than go around trying to fuck over [KID'S NAMF He's had a rough enough life and he's trying to go to school a all you can come up with is another piece of bullshit—"

He says: "Ma'am, have you seen him carrying anything li radios or a VCR or anything?"

She says: "I'm not going to answer that."

He says: "Look, the kid's back into B and Es and people getting a little angry about it. Someone's going to hurt h

Maybe if we just talk to him, we—"

She says: "You come back with a warrant and I'll see his lawyer is here and if he wants to then maybe you can talk to him."

He says: "It's just an investigation right now."

She says: "So go investigate."

He says: "Have a nice day, ma'am."

Clearly, this young professional woman's agenda was different from the investigating officer's agenda. That's what the YOA is all about, that's why it was created. This exchange is a direct result of the spirit and the language of the YOA. This young kid, who was at the time sixteen years old, had run into the law many, many times. He was almost famous around the station-house for the sheer bravado he demonstrated in his pursuit of other people's stereos. The youth court judge, sitting as is the custom, in camera, had assigned this kid a worker and his lawyer had agreed to have the kid entrusted to the custody of a group home. Apparently his home life was less than perfect (like the home life of many kids who don't go after your stereo), so it was decided to divert him from the criminal justice system.

The young woman who came to the door is someone who has been indoctrinated with the beliefs and principles of the social-work cadre, one of which is that this kid was somehow Wounded and what he needed was time to "get his shit together"—along with a lot of other people's shit, apparently—to "find himself."

This is a position that she holds in all sincerity, almost as a point of honor. Time may soften her, but it's unlikely to change her elemental beliefs about boys and men and women.

Now the cop has another agenda.

It's his job to do something when a citizen comes to him and says, "Hey, man, somebody just bagged my Sony!" As much as the social worker, he is the product of his education and of the institution that has shaped him.

His sense of honor is also on the line.

Further, as a cop, he knows that one of the things that keeps him safe on the street is the respect he commands. Not fear, because fear creates resentment and resentment can lead to some kind of assault, and not necessarily a frontal one either.

So one of the items on his agenda is to tolerate the jibes and sneers of the young boys in the house without losing his temper or his position. In other words, he needs to take just enough shit to seem professional but not so much that he'll be perceived as a mark, someone who can be had.

Because, sooner or later, someone will try him out, and no matter what happens, the cop will be risking more than the guy who's trying him on: physical injury, legal charges, professional censure, peer-group ridicule. No matter what happens to the guy who takes him on, unless he dies, he wins the respect of other criminals and a reputation for toughness.

Another reason the cop doesn't want to provoke fear-based confrontations is mathematical: for the guy attacking him, it's probably the only time he'll try it; for the cop, it'll be just one of a whole lifetime of assholes who want a piece of him.

Another thing on the cop's mind is a genuine desire to solve this crime. Not so much because it's a particularly important crime, or because he feels he owes something personal to the victim (though he might) but because he signed on to do something good for society.

People who don't know cops find that hard to believe, but it's true. This cop believes in his heart that it is wrong for a citizen to have his stereo taken unlawfully—stolen—and he further believes that the kid who stole it should not get away with it. To the cop, it seems obvious, something about which we could all agree. And solving crimes will get a beat cop elevated to one of the squads, to promotions and better pay.

So he has a lot of reasons for wanting to solve the case and get the man's stereo back, one of which is his honest belief that if the law doesn't stop this kid, someone from the neighborhood will.

Now he and the young woman are on the steps facing each other, as far from understanding each other as any two people can be.

She sees one of *them*, the cops who slap the kids around and bully them in the alleys and chase their asses for no good reason. A thug in a uniform, with no sympathy or understanding, someone without the brains or the education to see the complexity the issue. After all, she has a degree, a certificate, a college education, a Master's in Social Work or Psychology or Sociology; she's one of the elite, the best and brightest, down here on the street to Make a Difference, to protect the downtrodden and the abused from undereducated steroidal jocks without any real learning.

She's wrong about that.

Cops who want a future on the job are taking law degrees, psychology degrees, college-level courses, a lifetime of additional study. And not many people know what a candidate has to go through just to get the job:

- A high-school diploma with good marks
- No criminal record of any kind
- A complete background check that takes months
- A complete credit rating check
- Supply thirty unrelated personal references
- Write a detailed ten-page personal autobiography
- Pass the police exam—an all-day affair
- Pass an extremely challenging physical skills test
- Undergo a three-hour polygraph examination
- Undergo a drug test
- Submit to a detailed psychiatric profiling
- Submit to a hostile interview with three detectives
- Undergo an all-day scenario-reaction test
- Undergo a three-hour physical examination
- Complete three years of intermittent on-the-job training at a Police College or Justice institute
- Pass a complex firearms-training course
- Qualify monthly on a firearms-scenario course

How many social workers or law students or lawyers or even erving judges could pass even a few of these requirements? Iell, the polygraph test alone would send shivers down the pines of half the criminal lawyers in North America.

So the cop standing in front of the social worker also considrs himself a trained professional, and carries not only his own cord but the record of every cop, including the bad ones. And the social worker is carrying the record of every other social worker this cop has ever spoken to.

This confrontation is typical and is repeated *ad nauseam* every hour of every day of every year, in the United States and Canada. Multiply it by the number of times a Young Offender comes to the attention of a cop, and you begin to see the scope of the problem. Because while the social worker—read MOM— is standing on the front porch confronting the cop—read DAD— Junior is sliding out the upstairs back window with somebody else's VCR under his arm.

Now I ask you, is this really how we want things to go?

Apparently, it's how the people who designed the YOA want things to go, because they're still resisting major changes in the basic assumptions of the YOA. Like most insulated academics who are high enough on the food-chain that their personal butts are not in danger, they cannot—or will not—admit that the YOA is creating a criminal subculture that will trouble the counsels of the Small and the Silly for decades to come.

Let me give you a few illustrations, from my own experience.

TORONTO

In the Jane-Finch corridor, an elderly Jewish woman whose family had moved to Israel was living alone in an apartment near a mall. Each month she made her way, with difficulty, to the local trust company to deposit her pension check and a small subsistence from her relatives in Israel.

After having stalked her movements for a time, seven young boys assaulted her as she left the bank, stole her keys and cash and left her bleeding on the ground. While she was in the hospital, the same group of boys entered her apartment and completely trashed it. Trashing it included defecating on her bed, jerking off on her pillows and stealing everything of value.

Upon her return, she suffered a heart attack. She died a few months later. The boys were located and charged on the insistence of the police, but the charges were later stayed on condition that the boys perform several days of community service.

The community service order was never complied with and no further action was taken.

VANCOUVER

In the city's southern suburbs, a gang of teenaged boys had been operating untouched for many months, in spite of frequent resident complaints to the police. Students were being beaten and robbed on the way to school, cars were being vandalized and robbed daily, elderly residents were afraid to go into their own yards.

Finally, the gang, in an attempt to steal a car, pushed it down the street. It got away from them and smashed into a pole, causing extensive damage. After an investigation, the police arrested one of the boys involved. The boy admitted, in spite of counsel, that he had stolen the car, and he named the other boys involved. The Crown refused to prosecute the other boys because there was no corroboration of the accused boy's testimony.

Crown decided that it would be unfair to charge the boy who had admitted the theft and not to charge the others, so all charges were dropped.

TORONTO

A fourteen-year-old Young Offender who lived at home with his drug-addicted parents and who was stealing from local stores and houses to finance their habit and his own was arrested in possession of a large quantity of drugs and stolen property. He demanded and got legal representation. The lawyer advised him to say nothing and made several challenges to the evidence on a Charter basis.

While the judge was considering the Charter arguments, the two detectives who were investigating the case made a personal plea to the boy's lawyer. They said the boy was in a severely disturbed family, that he had been taught to use drugs by his parents, and that if the lawyer's defence was successful, the boy would be returned to a dangerous home environment and would continue in his criminal activities until something serious happened. They asked the lawyer to persuade the boy to plead guilty and they guaranteed that the Crown would argue for leniency and relocation to a safer environment.

The lawyer angrily refused and prevented any attempt at direct contact between the boy and the two detectives, to the point of demanding a judicial direction, which she got.

The judge accepted the Charter challenge and ruled the evidence inadmissible. The boy was freed and returned immediately to his home and his criminal activities.

Four years later, he was no longer a Young Offender and he was convicted of Theft Over $1,000 and sent to a remand center pending a pre-sentencing hearing. While in custody he was repeatedly raped by two other prisoners. He attempted suicide but failed.

He is currently serving a sentence for Armed Robbery and PPT Cocaine.

He is represented by the same lawyer.

VANCOUVER

A young boy had been harassed by a local teen gang for refusing to become a member. His parents went to the police to see if something could be done to prevent the harassment.

Two of the teen gang members were under diversionary treatment mandated by the YOA. The police attempted to interview these boys in a group home. The operator of the group home refused access to the boys. The police then asked the operator to take care that the boys under her control not be allowed to harass an innocent boy. She refused to take responsibility for this, saying that to do so would be to admit that the boys were doing something wrong and that would be a betrayal of her relationship with them. It would undermine their trust in her and interfere with their rehabilitation.

The harassment continued and escalated. Finally, the boy agreed to go along on a series of robberies. He now has a criminal record and has dropped out of school.

WINNIPEG

Two Young Offenders butchered an eighty-three-year-old man, slitting his throat, stabbing him many times with knives and broken bottles before finally chopping him into pieces with a hoe. They then ransacked his house and stole a small amount of money. They did this, according to their own words, "to see how it felt to kill someone."

They expressed no remorse when caught. Psychiatrists for the defence argued that the Young Offenders were "victims of grandiose thought patterns" and therefore unable to formulate intent. One of the psychiatrists testified that his opinion was based on several examinations of the boys over a period of weeks.

The detectives involved in the case did some checking at the cells where the boys were being held and discovered that this doctor had visited the boys only once, for no longer than twenty-three minutes, according to jail records. When confronted by the detectives, the psychiatrist refused to alter his testimony.

During their incarceration, the two Young Offenders obtained psychiatric manuals and discussed plans to "act crazy" so they could be put into an institution and "get healed" and go back to the street.

They were moved to adult court and given twenty-five years each.

VANCOUVER

In East Vancouver, several organized gangs of teenagers were breaking into parties thrown by residents of the neighborhoods. The parties, usually school parties for classmates and friends, were infiltrated at first by one or two of the female gang members, who would then station themselves at the doors of the house. At a pre-arranged time the females would open the doors of the house and allow twenty or thirty male gang members into the house.

The gang members would then go through the rooms of the house stealing whatever was in sight. If they encountered resistance, several gang members would "swarm" the person and beat him brutally. Knives and guns were shown and frequently sexual assaults would be part of the attack.

When parents formed a vigilante group, the police informed them that organized citizen response that led to violence would be prosecuted.

The gang continues to operate, in spite of the arrests of many of its members, because the leaders are not being placed in secure custody. Community service orders and court-mandated counseling have been unsuccessful and not complied with.

Under the existing restrictions of the YOA, according to a police spokesman, "There's not a damned thing we can do to stop them."

TORONTO

Teenagers traveling on Toronto's subway system were advised by authorities not to wear expensive running shoes or the popular Doc Marten's boots that were in style because the youths were vulnerable to assault and robbery. Gangs of youths were entering the subway cars and "swarming" any teenager who was wearing these items. Teens who refused to surrender their shoes or boots were brutally beaten in front of the public.

TORONTO

Due to the increasing number of weapons being found on students in the city's high schools, a proposal has been made to install metal detectors at the entrances and to train teachers in the correct way to "negotiate solutions" with threatening and violent teens.

Teachers' groups are resisting the idea that, in addition to all their other responsibilities, they now be required to perform duties best left to police officers and corrections workers.

Weapons offences under the YOA are not routinely a jailable offence, so teens found in possession are frequently returned to their communities because detaining them would "interfere with their education."

TORONTO

Elderly residents of Toronto were advised to avoid the subway and to find alternate ways to do their banking and shopping since they have been targeted by youth gangs. Multiple incidents of attacks by teenagers on elderly and crippled people have created intense fear and depression among the city's aging population.

"Young Offenders are resistant to law enforcement threats since there seems to be little that the courts can do to dissuade juveniles from engaging in crime." (A ranking Metro cop)

In his powerful article "Growing Up Scared"* (it should be required reading for every graduate of a course in Social Work) Karl Zinsmeister quotes Daniel Patrick Moynihan on the subject of juvenile crime:

> "From the wild Irish slums of the 19th century eastern seabord to the riot-torn suburbs of Los Angeles, there is one unmistakable lesson in American history; a community that allows a large number of young men (and women) to grow up in broken families, dominated by women, never acquiring any stable relationship to male authority...that community asks for, and gets, chaos."

Zinsmeister's basic point is that although left-wing activists view tougher juvenile laws as a male, conservative, even fascist fixation, the real victims of Young Offender crime are children. Which should make it a liberal crusade as well.

Homicide is now *the* leading cause of death for children in American ghettos, and the odds are nine to one that the killer will be another child. I've made the point again and again that we are *not* insulated from what happens in the United States. What happens there happens here ten years later.

Zinsmeister closes with these words:

> If we are to have any chance of preventing young criminals from infecting a class of successors, and from stalking an innocent public, then we must see with clear eyes what they have become; sad cases, but now unambiguously part of the problem. Unless this new crop of teenage marauders is incapacitated, the vicious cycle of youths preyed upon and then preying upon others may become unbreakable in our cities. And blameless children, never having known the protections and sanctuaries that are civilization's original justification, will be hurt most.

Karl Zinsmeister, "Growing Up Scared," *Atlantic,* June 1990.

Zinsmeister—through Moynihan—cuts to the heart of the Young Offender problem; the disenfranchisement of male authority.

The female social worker—and thousands like her whom I have met and tangled with personally—are typical of a very modern female sensibility, which I'll state, for reasons of brevity, as the Dworkin Thesis.

The Dworkin Thesis holds that all male power is vile and corrupt, and that all female power is quintessentially pure and life-affirming. In varying degrees, this idea has saturated our culture, to the point that there's a pretty wide consensus that anything to do with men is probably ugly and certainly regressive. There are a hell of a lot of men who buy this as well, for reasons that completely escape me but that may have something to do with impressing female undergraduates and sucking up to a certain kind of female fascist mind-set.

The Dworkin Thesis has taken a particularly virulent form in our universities and law schools, where most of the consultants and professionals who work in the justice system first formed their basic belief systems.

Naturally, this hatred of anything male has had far-reaching effects in the framing and execution of our juvenile laws, since it is part of the Dworkin Thesis that children are corrupted and made evil by exposure to masculine beliefs and value-systems.

Punishment, retribution, denunciation, revenge—all of these are seen as male constructs that contribute to an endless cycle of abuse and violence. Although developed by women and men and passed into law by a predominantly male legislature, the essence of the Young Offenders Act is pure feminist dialectic. The YOA embodies the supposedly female values of compassion, nurturing, forgiveness, rebirth and renewal. In order to save the Wounded Inner Child, the child must first be protected from masculine belief systems and something called Male Rage. And who personifies these Jurassic-era values better than a uniformed cop?

That's why you'll hear sophomoric observations about "guns as penis-substitutes" and "the homoerotic semiotics of police uniforms" and "sado-masochistic rape fantasies objectified billy-clubs" and "the bondage archetype of leather belts and Sam Brownes." This comes from the same people who say things like "LIVE is EVIL spelled backwards," AIDS is a CIA plot" and "WOMEN ought to be spelled WIMMIN," deluding themselves that they have done something important in the world.

There are facile but popular locutions that have become thought-terminating clichés. Their purpose is to degrade and devalue masculine qualities.

There's little one can say in the face of the Dworkin Thesis, other than to observe that nature seems to have required some male participation in the reproductive cycle and it looks as if that's not going to change anytime soon. So eliminating males from the gene pool is going to take several millennia or simply-*ons* and *tons* of rat poison. Sorry, but there it is.

How politically incorrect of Nature.

By the way, in Vietnam, it was the women who did the cutting, as it was with the Plains Indians, as it was in Afghanistan, as it was in Africa and Madagascar and ancient Britain and in Gaul and China and…well…as Rudyard Kipling put it:

When you're down and wounded
on Afghanistan's plains,
And the women come out
to cut up your remains,
Just roll to your rifle
and blow out your brains,
And go to your God like a soldier.

And I don't think anyone out there with a mind yet unclouded cant and witless dogma would argue with the fact that at least percent of the world's *emotional* abuse is committed by women. I suppose what I'm getting at is that the Dworkin Thesis ay be a useful tool for prying some power and privilege out of e hands of greedy men, but as a first principle it's nasty, lammatory, revisionist, profoundly ahistorical, stupid and, imately, just another form of brutish prejudice.

The male values of strength, protection, justice and punish-nt are important for the creation of a soul in true equilibrium, and absolutely vital when it comes to making men out of boys. To imagine that you are helping adolescent males by keeping them isolated from the influence and judgement of men is a dangerous delusion. To carry this baseless prejudice into the field of law and enforcement and justice is not just dangerous, it's criminal negligence.

All prolonged criminal behavior is basically adolescent. The essential criminal mind-set is that of a boy trapped somewhere between infancy and adolescence, between the protection of his mother and the judgement of his father.

In the modern world, sometimes the only exposure a Young Offender is going to have to the restorative and healing power of masculine judgement and forgiveness is in his conversation with police officers. Any system that prevents any attempt at genuine communication between police officers and Young Offenders works against the rehabilitation of the child. Young men are hard-wired to push the limits of behavior. But when they encounter no limits, only unceasing approval and forgiveness, the resulting vertigo destabilizes and destroys them. Then they are truly The Lost Boys. And we all pay the price.

Which, by the way, is very high.

SIXTEEN

Cui Bono?

In one year, the Greater Vancouver Region listed the following estimate of damages and costs incurred by Young Offender crime:

ESTIMATED Y.O. INVOLVEMENT IN ALL B AND Es
  AND VANDALISM: 95%
ESTIMATED TOTAL VALUE OF Y.O. RESIDENTIAL
  THEFT: $3,000,000.00
ESTIMATED MAN-HOURS Y.O.s COST THE POLICE:
  $500,000.00
ESTIMATED COST OF Y.O. INTENTIONAL DAMAGE:
  $600,000.00
ESTIMATED COST OF Y.O. DAMAGE TO BC HYDRO:
  $710,000.00
ESTIMATED COST TO VANCOUVER PARKS:
  $350,000.00
ESTIMATED COST TO BC TELEPHONE: $660,000.00
ESTIMATED COST OF GRAFFITI ALONE: $30,000.00
ESTIMATED COST OF PROPERTY STOLEN IN
  VANCOUVER: $200,000.00
ESTIMATED TOTAL Y.O.-RELATED SHOPLIFTING:
  $6,000,000.00
ESTIMATED TOTAL Y.O.-RELATED ARSON COSTS:
  $5,000,000.00

t's very difficult to extrapolate these figures to obtain a national
r international total. The political ramifications of such a dis-
losure might be rather incendiary. I think it's safe to say, how-
ver, that Young Offender crime in Canada must cost taxpayers
nd homeowners and car-owners millions and millions of dollars
at could be going into deficit-reduction or social programs.
ut it's not. A lot of this money is going into salaries for people
ry much like the young woman who didn't want us to talk to
e kid who had been boosting VCRs and stereos from around
e neighborhood.

Which reminds me...about a week after we gave up trying to reach this kid, we finally found him. He was in the Emergency Room at Saint Michael's Hospital in downtown Toronto. He had been discovered stepping through the back window of a man's house a little way up the street from the halfway house where he was living.

He had the guy's television set in his hands.

He tripped on the way out and lay stunned on the ground outside. He lay there long enough for the householder to reach him. The householder kicked the boy for a very long time—long enough to get tired of it.

The neighbors called the cops and an ambulance came to take the kid to the hospital, where we finally got a chance to say hello. He recovered after a few weeks and was released.

No charges were laid against him.

However, the home-owner was charged and convicted of Aggravated Assault. Since he was not protected by the Young Offenders Act, he spent three months in jail, lost his job and is now permanently marked with a criminal record, a record that may interfere with such basic freedoms as shopping in another country or applying for work with a bank or a securities firm, or as a courier, or in any other bondable occupation.

By the way, he didn't get his TV back either.

Now as far as the kid is concerned, how long did *his* record stay around to bother him?

Section 45 of the YOA, Non-Disclosure and Destruction of Records...

Subsection (4): A young person shall be deemed NOT TO HAVE COMMITTED any offence to which a record is kept pursuant to sections 40 to 43 relates when the circumstances set out in paragraphs (1) (d), (e), or (f) are realized in respect of the record.

Say *what?*

You know, it occurs to me that part of the reason the lawyers and the legislators get away with so much silly-ass jurisprudence is the way they write. This stuff is not only deadly-d and boring, it's nearly impossible to comprehend. So we stay away from it, and these guys get to do pretty much whatever they want.

What Subsection 4 means is that if the Young Offender is guilty of a crime but is diverted into some other line of treatment, then all records of his crime are destroyed two years later, and if he got convicted on a summary conviction or an indictable offence (including murder), they're destroyed five years later, and as far as the law is concerned...*it never happened!*

By the way, the social worker who got in the cop's face over this kid was probably pulling down around $30,000 a year plus some overtime, and the agency running the house was getting around $200 per day for each Young Offender in the house, and if the kid's lawyer had showed up to protect his client's interest, the lawyer would probably have billed Legal Aid or welfare something in the are of $75 for the trip.

Now it's been my experience that whenever a large group of people are engaged in an activity that is, on the face of it, quite absurd and counter-intuitive, then you should dig a little deeper, because somewhere under all the manure is a cash-cow. And the name of the cash-cow in the YOA is diversion.

Once again it gives me great pleasure to trundle out yet another stolen—I mean confiscated—document for your edification and amusement. In this case, it's a confidential Crown Counsel Policy Manual extract from the British Columbia Attorney General's office, Criminal Justice Division:

CROWN COUNSEL POLICY MANUAL
1-1-91 file number 55360—00 DIVISION 1
Reference PMC 8-16-90 CONS/REV JRC #83—#85
For the purposes of this policy, diversion is defined as a pre-
    trial procedure whereby a Crown Counsel uses his or her
    discretion on a case by case basis not to prosecute an alleged
    offender. Instead the alleged offender is referred to an
    individual or agency...

[Pay attention now—someone's about to score big at your pense!]

...with the intent of establishing an agreement by which the prospective divertee undertakes to accept, and is given the opportunity to demonstrate, personal responsibility for the alleged offence.

[Sounds nice, huh? Here's the catch.]

Participation in a diversion programme is voluntary, and, if a diversion agreement is reached, the Crown relinquishes its right to prosecute the divertee for the offence which gave rise to the decision to divert, *regardless of whether or not the conditions of the agreement are met.* [Emphasis added.]

By the way, remember that under *Askov* the Crowns are de-emphasizing almost all Failure to Comply charges, which effectively removes any motivation the divertee might have had to cooperate with the diversion program. Once he gets the diversion agreement, it's fuck you and the horse you rode in on. This is madness!

The diversion programme emphasizes the importance of providing an alleged offender with the opportunity to act in a responsible manner...

[Like *hell* it does...]

...the diversion agreement enables the divertee to assume responsibility for his or her behaviour by honouring the negotiated conditions.

[Or what? Or nothing, that's what.]

Those conditions may include making restitution to the victims or society for loss suffered as a result of the offence, undertaking to affect a reconciliation with the victim, voluntarily participating in various counselling programmes...

[More taxpayer-funded group-gropes!]

...or a combination of these.
It must be emphasized that the purpose of diversion is not
  retribution...

[That's pretty obvious.]

...or, except in an incidental way, deterrence.

[So's that.]

Diversion should be viewed as a positive and humane
  alternative which, for some cases, has the potential to provide
  greater benefit to the offender...

[Like getting away scot-free.]

...the victim...

[Yeah? Like how?]

...and society than would be expected from further processing
  through the criminal justice system.
Diversion programmes...are not viewed as part of the criminal
  justice system, but are administered through the Corrections
  Branch of the Ministry of the Solicitor General.

Which means that these programs are federally funded. The
whole point of this is that the courts are overloaded and "diversion" is a way of dumping cases that no one except the victims
akes seriously. And who gives a shit about them?
  There are some "guidelines" listed. I'll give you the most
musing ones...

The Crown must be of the opinion that to divert the alleged
  offender would not endanger the community.

[Hah!]

The offence must not have been of such a serious nature as to
threaten the safety or tolerance of the community.

[In other words, if we let this asshole walk, will the press
raise hell and will we get in shit with our bosses...?]

Conversations between the prospective divertee and Crown
counsel...shall not be used at trial should a diversion
agreement not be concluded.

[Which means that the guy can confess to the crime and talk
about it all day and bitch about his luck, but if he finally says,
hey, no, I'd rather go to trial, then *bingo,* he's a born-again innocent and the Crown has to prove he did it.]

A...divertee shall not be charged with the offence which gave
rise to the diversion or to any other offence arising from the
same circumstances *nor shall proceedings be re-instituted in
the event that the divertee fails to honour the terms of the
diversion agreement* [emphasis added] (see *R. v. JONES,*
1978 40 CCC).

[Which means he gets a free ride for everything he did in connection with the crime and even if he never shows up for the
counseling or he never pays the money back or he wags his
willy at everyone in the room, *nothing happens to him!*]
Is it just me, or does this seem like a world-class piece of
lame bullshit?
Anyway, that's Diversion.
Okay, diversion. Diversion *where?*

Group homes
Youth farms
Foster homes
Contract homes
Treatment centers
Assessment centers
Counseling

Education programs
Community Service Plans

And who staffs and runs all these diversionary facilities?

Social workers
Psychiatrists
Psychologists
Counselors
Guidance professionals
Anger-management consultants

And who helps the government decide what to do with Young
Offenders?

Law professors
Criminologists
Social workers
Psychiatrists
Psychologists
Counselors
Consultants
Guidance professionals

For reasons that I'm sure are very persuasive (but that have
somehow eluded me) the diversionary agencies in all of our
cities, in the United States and Canada, are reluctant to release
the amount of money they are given each year to guide, counsel
and correct the behavior of Young Offenders. Many of them cite
client confidentiality as the reason. Others have just suggested
very nicely that I piss off like a good boy.

But I did get that figure of $200 a day for each Young
Offender in the system. So let's take that as a basis.

In 1990, as we have seen, a total of 224,676 Young Offenders
were charged with various offences under the Criminal Code and
other statutes. The justice system is very reluctant to say just
how many of these kids were placed in some kind of custody,
it is true that custody is legally the last resort under the YOA.

Consider:

...S.24.1
...The principle to be applied in considering whether custody
should be imposed involves balancing the gravity of the act
with the needs of the youthful offender, bearing in mind the
statement of policy in s.3 [act to be liberally construed] which
means that custody is to be ordered after all else fails.
The traditional principles of sentencing such as deterrence,
punishment, retribution or denunciation are not to be
considered; R v RCS (1986)...
...Neither the court's convenience nor concern about the
young offender's disruptive influence in the small community
warranted the court in proceeding to impose a custodial
position...
...this subsection imposes a mandatory duty on the judge and
his failure to comply with it renders his order of committal to
custody a nullity: R v MSS (1985)...

Which seems to me to suggest that all that blather about "th
protection of society" was just a smoke screen for the mandate
legal requirement that Young Offenders never be subjected
such unpleasantries as "deterrence, punishment, retribution
denunciation"—how regressively *male*—unless the crime is
massive and disgusting that it's politically explosive to do an
thing but jail him.

So, we had 224,676 Young Offenders charged in 1990. Of th
number—and it's only a guess based on my Ten Beef Rule—
say that only one-tenth of these kids got any kind of jail time.

That's 22,467 kids who got some sort of jail time. The ma
mum jail time for any offence under the YOA is five years
recent amendment; it used to be three, remember?) and ther
no way that anyone other than a few of the most violent kids
that. The average sentence, in my experience, would run
three months with two years' probation and some kind of "c
and control" order sending the kid to one of the "diversiona
agencies.

Let's say that, out of the 22,467 kids who got jail time, 22, of those were back in a diversionary agency within six months. So it would be fair to include them as part of the profit picture for the diversionary agencies.

Where are we now?

We have, say, 200,000 kids somewhere in the Young Offender system, but not in jail, and another 22,000 in some sort of custodial situation (many of which are privately owned) and about six months away from freedom, which gives us the total of 222,000 *young offenders* who are somewhere in the machinery of the justice system, but not under the direct control of Corrections Canada or the cops, and that means under the control of one of the diversionary agencies.

Now, not all of these 222,000 Y.O.s would be in an agency residence. A hell of a lot of them are back home with Mom and Dad, sitting in front of the TV and wondering what—or who—to do tonight. How many?

The Ten Beef Rule suggests that nine-tenths of them would have gotten virtually no supervisory orders other than probation or community service. That leaves 10 percent in some sort of diversionary court-ordered taxpayer-funded program. That's 22,200 *young offenders*.

Now we know that, on the average, the diversionary agencies pick up around $200 per day for each Young Offender in their care. So...

$$
\begin{array}{r}
22,200 \\
\times\ 200 \\
\hline
4,440,000
\end{array}
$$

Follow me here...are we saying that the *daily* pay-out for all these Young Offenders is *four million four hundred and forty thousand dollars*. How much for the year?

$$
\begin{array}{r}
4,440,000 \\
\times\ 365 \\
\hline
1,620,600,000
\end{array}
$$

Am I right?

Are we looking at *one billion six hundred and twenty million, six hundred thousand dollars* going to various diversionary agencies in 1990?

Well, it's not as simple as that. Of the 22,200 kids, not all of them are in residences. Many are in some kind of program or counseling program, but as a general rule I think we're in the right territory. If the diversionary agencies aren't billing $200 a day for residential care, they're billing an equivalent amount for the time they spend counseling the kid, or trying to find him, or testing him psychometrically, or asking him if he resented his toilet-training, or trying to get him to understand the concept of private property and why you shouldn't kick other kids in the head. So I think it's fair to say that there's at least *one and a half billion dollars* to be made yearly out of the trade in Young Offenders, (which buys a lot of social workers like the young lady who didn't want us to talk to the stereo thief in Toronto).

And how much are the lawyers making out of the Young Offenders Act? Legal Aid won't say, and neither will Health and Welfare. I guess we'll have to do it ourselves.

The average lawyer's bill for counseling a Young Offender upon his arrest is $75.

The lawyer will bill around $400 for a trial, if it's a simple one. That includes trials where plea-bargaining or Stays are considered, any straightforward trial. We'll leave the sensational and complicated ones aside because they're rare.

If the lawyer attends for an adjournment, he'll bill around $150 for that.

So the bill comes in, and I'll be conservative...

PRELIMINARY ATTENDANCE	$75.00
ADJOURNMENT ONE	$150.00
ADJOURNMENT TWO	$150.00
REPRESENTATION AT TRIAL	$400.00
REPRESENTATION AT DISPOSITION	$250.00
	$1,025.00

That's a bill to Legal Aid or a federal funding agency $1,025.00 for a simple YOA proceeding.

And in 1990, we had 224,676 Young Offenders, almost all of whom would have been represented by a lawyer. (The act allows for some proceedings to go forward without a lawyer, but the general practice in any criminal proceeding is to have a lawyer present. My experience is that lawyers are *everywhere* in the YOA.) So I'm going to let the figure run at a conservative 200,000.

$$\begin{array}{r} 200{,}000 \quad \text{Young Offender cases} \\ \times\ 1{,}025 \quad \text{fee} \\ \hline \$205{,}000{,}000.00 \end{array}$$

So there's another $205 million in business, this time for the lawyers who bill Legal Aid and the Feds. By the way, try to get a law firm to tell you how much they billed Legal Aid for Young Offender trials in any year. They'll look at you like something they found at the bottom of a martini and duck behind client confidentiality.

Now I'm pretty well convinced that my estimate of $205 million in basic YOA billing is very conservative. I expect that it could run as high as $500 million. And if $205 million doesn't seem like a hell of a lot of money to you, then $500 million won't impress you either.

Mind you, that's $1,025 for one lawyer billing one time for one charge under the YOA. Multiply that fee of $1,025 per trial by the number of YOA clients a lawyer will average a week, if you can find that out. In Vancouver, years ago, there was a law firm called Gove and Senior, which specialized in Juvenile cases. Tom Gove, now a judge, steadfastly refused to say how many kids he handled each week, but he was there almost all day and almost every day, so you can draw your own inferences.

In general, I'd say that the average lawyer whose specialty is Young Offender law will have a caseload of forty or fifty Y.O.s a month, each of whom is on some point in the arc of the justice system. He'll be billing for a variety of services, the least of which will be $50 for a phone call and a follow-up letter and the largest of which will be $400 for a trial. Even if he only bills each client once and he bills them $50, he'll still be billing $2,500 a month. What is far more likely is that he'll be billing an average of $300 per client each month, for a gross income of $15,000 a month, or $180,000 a year.

By the way, at a rough estimate, 60 percent of chronic Young Offenders go on to become full-time career criminals, and guess who'll get their business then?

There's a real incentive for a lawyer to keep his Young Offender out of any truly rehabilitative program, because once he's convinced the kid that he can get him off anything, that kid will remember him when he hits the big time and needs help with some serious charges.

One of the delights of being a lawyer is that the longer you take to do something and the more complicated you can make it, the more money you can bill. Lawyers have no incentive to be efficient in any individual case, only in the management of office time. Billing is the blood of the business. And in the twisted world of the Young Offenders Act, the better you are at keeping a kid out on the street committing crimes, the more money you'll make off him. Perhaps this is not intentional, but it is the ultimate consequence.

Looking at the figures has given me an idea.

Obviously the Young Offender problem is costing the country a truly depressing amount of money. Maybe billions, if you consider increased insurance costs, the price for municipal property damages nationwide, hospital and medical treatment arising from Young Offender assaults and brutalities of various stripes.

So let's follow the Young Offenders Act mind-set to its logical conclusion. Let's *pay* these kids *not* to commit crimes.

Let's take all the money we're putting out to fund endless studies, to pay for all the legal fees, to employ thousands of social workers and psychiatrists and psychologists, to run hundreds of diversionary-care homes and farms, and the money we pay to clean up after Young Offenders and patch up their victims, and simply hand it over directly to the Young Offenders, in exchange for a promise never to be bad again.

Clean. Simple. Direct. A monthly check, let's say.

Naturally, if they do commit another crime, why, then we stop payment on their monthly check. No messy trial. No counseling. No diversion. Just a straightforward deduction. We co⟩

include the cost of any property damage or personal injuries to the victim in that deduction.

Of course, then we'd have all these unemployed lawyers and social workers and counselors and youth workers. Collateral damage, I guess.

Regrettable.

Really too bad.

Well, I'll try to live with it.

SEVENTEEN

The Insolence of Office

Okay, where are we now?

I think—I hope—that I've made a pretty good case for my contention that the justice system doesn't seem to have any really clear idea of what evil actually is. Certainly the outrageous repeat-offender stats, the staggering numbers of kids getting into crime and the fumbling, ineffectual responses we get from the diversionary agencies all add up to a system without much of a system to it. If they knew what they were doing, *thing's would be getting better!*

And they're not.

Well, what exactly are the best theories around on evil, on the criminal mind? Are criminals made, like chocolate-chip cookies and the Lada?

Or are they born, like wolverines and bats and law students?

Are criminals crazy?

Well, as far as the legal definition of insanity goes, we have seen the troubles it presented in Orangeville. Not surprisingly, a lot of psychiatrists are unhappy with the position of the law on insanity.

The legal definition of insanity in the United States varies from state to state. The generalized view of the insanity defence is that it is a kind of compromise device that allows the law to make value judgements, avoiding convictions in crimes where the accused is obviously incapable of forming a criminal intent (such as a clear case of psychosis or severe mental retardation) and yet defending the law from the legal absurdity of regarding all criminals as "sick" persons who need treatment—a view that is held with maniacal intensity in many universities and psychiatric institutions.

The fact of the insanity argument, according to experts such as Abraham S. Goldstein*, compels the courts to engage in presumably healthy psychodramatic exercises that...

* Abraham S. Goldstein, *The Insanity Defence* (1967).

...can play a part in reinforcing the sense of obligation or responsibility. Its emphasis on whether an offender is sick or bad helps to keep alive the almost forgotten drama of individual responsibility. Its weight is felt through the tremendous appeal it holds for the popular imagination, as that imagination is gripped by a dramatic trial and as the public at large identifies with the man in the dock. In this way, it becomes part of a complex of cultural forces that keep alive the moral lessons, and the myths, which are essential to the continued order of society...If the choice between the two sanctions (Guilty and Sane or Not Guilty but Insane) is to be made in a way that will not only be acceptable to the larger community but will also serve the symbolic function... *it is important that the decision be made by a democratically selected jury rather than by experts* [emphasis added] because the public can identify with the former but not the latter...

In the Orangeville case, a very energetic attempt was made to keep information away from the general public entirely with a press ban. This is a trend that has accelerated over the years as judges find themselves less and less patient with the messy intrusions of the public.

The Orangeville case presented us with a tragic example of failure of foresight because the framers of the Young Offenders Act were either too stupid or too naive to imagine that a child could commit such an obscene crime. Crippled by the surreal restrictions of the act, the courts and the people of Orangeville were forced to undergo a legal circus where, among other things, the name of the accused, known to the entire town, could not be printed in the local paper, while the names of the victims—also legally proscribed from print—were reported from coast to coast, and finally, where intelligent men and women had to fumble desperately for some psycho-legal fiction that would allow them to keep the little bastard in jail for an amount of time that wouldn't cause a riot and a lynching in the town.

Concerning the basic question of insanity, which, reduced to its essence, means, "Is this guy snake mean or crazy?" we have the text of the insanity law:

16. (1) No person shall be convicted of an offence in respect of an act or omission on his part while that person was insane.

(2) For the purpose of this section, a person is insane when the person is in a state of natural imbecility or has a disease of the mind to an extent that renders the person incapable of appreciating the nature and quality of an act or omission or of knowing that an act or omission is wrong.

(3) A person who has specific delusions, but is in other respects sane, shall not be acquitted on the ground of insanity unless the delusions caused that person to believe in the existence of a state of things that, if it existed, would have justified or excused the act or omission of that person.

(4) Every one shall, until the contrary is proved, be presumed to be and to have been sane.

Although the phrasing brings to mind the various pitfall mapped out by Wittgenstein regarding "an unearthly precision the insanity law, as it is applied in Canadian courts, is distinct better than some of the more ridiculous judgements allowed the United States.

For instance, the CCC on sociopathic personalities:

Although personality disorders or psychopathic personalities are capable of constituting a disease of the mind the defence of insanity is not made out where the accused has the necessary understanding of the nature, character, and consequences of the act, but merely lacks appropriate feeling for the victim or lacks feelings of remorse or guilt for what h has done, even though such lack of feelings stems from a disease of the mind; R v. SIMPSON, 1977, 35 CCC (2nd)...

And on Diminished Capacity:

Our Criminal Code does not recognize the defence of diminished responsibility and even though the accused may have been ill at the time of the offence he is technically sane if he was able to distinguish between right and wrong... CHARTRAND v. THE QUEEN (1975) 26 CCC...

And on "disease of the mind":

The term "disease of the mind" is a legal concept and it is therefore a question of law for the trial Judge what mental conditions are included within the term as is the question whether there is any evidence that the accused suffered from an abnormal mental condition comprehended by that term. Any malfunctioning of the mind, or mental disturbance having its source primarily in some subjective condition or weakness internal to the accused (whether fully understood or not), may be a disease of the mind if it prevents the accused from knowing what he is doing...the ordinary stresses and disappointments of life, though they may bring about a malfunctioning of the mind such as a dissociative state...

[The Orangeville killer, perhaps?]

...do not constitute an external cause...which takes it out of the category of a disease of the mind and could not form the basis of a defence of non-insane automatism: R. v. RABEY... ..."Disease of the mind"...excludes self-induced states caused by alcohol or drugs as well as transitory mental states such as hysteria or concussion. Thus personality disorders may constitute a disease of the mind. The word "apppreciates" imports a requirement beyond mere knowledge of the physical quality of the act and requires a capacity to apprehend the nature of the act and its consequences: COOPER v. THE QUEEN...

Seen in that light, it becomes pretty clear that regardless of the protestations of the court, the kid in Orangeville got a free ride. He obviously "appreciated" the consequences of his act, since he did his level best to avoid them; his suggestion of automatism doesn't fit the legal standard; and the diagnosis of

"latent schizophrenia" is so vague as to have no substance whatsoever. A convincing argument can be made that the verdict
would not have been possible if the trial had been held in front
of a jury. The defence lawyer clearly understood that a jury
would be highly likely to reject the insanity defence and convict
on Murder One.

The justice system just didn't know what to do with him.

They still don't know what to do with him.

His name can't be spoken or written. I know his name, as do
most of the citizens of Orangeville. But unlike the citizens of
Orangeville and the rest of Canada, I have a pretty good idea of
where he is, and believe me, I'd dearly *love* to write it down,
because I believe that this boy—hell, he's in his twenties now—
this man *needs* to be named. I'm not persuaded that the consequences to him of being publicly named are at all relevant, nor
do I give a damn about them.

On the other hand, the effects on all of us, on our sense that
justice is something we all share in and control, a sense that we
are active and empowered members of an honorable State, this
privilege has been arbitrarily taken away in the name of some
elusive principle understood by our betters, one presumes, and
one that not many of us share.

We are, despite the protections described in the case law contained in Section 16, at the mercy of whatever defence a skilled
lawyer cares to propose.

Remember Lord Brougham's edict and consider this case—
case of somnambulism.

The Globe and Mail, 31 May, 1988
(unattributed)
TORONTO, Ontario

> Kenneth James Parks, 24, of Pickering, Ontario, became last
> night the first Canadian acquitted of murder on the grounds
> he was sleep-walking at the time of the killing.
> An Ontario Supreme Court jury of eight men and four women
> deliberated nine hours before finding Mr. Parks Not Guilty
> of second degree murder in the May 24, 1987, stabbing death

of his mother-in-law, Barbara Ann Woods.

The jury was told that Mr. Parks drove 23 kilometers from his home to a townhouse in Scarborough, where he attacked Mrs. Woods, 41, and her husband Dennis, 46, in their bed, stabbing his mother-in-law five times.

However, five psychiatrists called by the defence said the man's activities and statements to police that he had fallen asleep at his house and awakened only after the killing were consistent with a major episode of somnambulism.

The defence evidence went unchallenged when the Crown produced no expert witness to dispute the sleep-walking theory, apparently because a psychiatrist hired by the Crown reached the same conclusion.

The medical witnesses told the jury they found Mr. Parks' activities consistent with what might be expected of an aggressive sleepwalker, and that they had ruled out all other possible explanations for his conduct...In his charge to the Jury, Mr. Justice David Watts said the only verdicts still open to the jury were Guilty or Not Guilty, since the evidence did not support findings of Not Guilty by Reason of Insanity or of the lesser charge of Manslaughter.

On May 24th, 1987, Kenneth James Parks, twenty-three, climbed into his car at around two in the morning, leaving his wife asleep in their home, and drove fifteen miles through freeway traffic to his mother-in-law's house. He used a delicate professional lock-pick to break in and made his way up to the master bedroom, where forty-one-year-old Barbara Woods lay sleeping beside her husband, Dennis Woods.

He bludgeoned Barbara Woods to death with a tire iron he had brought with him for the purpose. He also attempted to kill his father-in-law as he came to his wife's defence, stabbing him repeatedly and strangling him into unconsciousness.

The matter came to trial in the Ontario Supreme Court in May, under the gavel of Mr. Justice David Watts. The trial made a quantum leap into the forefront of the local media when defence counsel Marlys Edwardh introduced the argument that Kenneth Parks could not be held legally responsible for the attack, which she did not dispute that he had committed, because Mr. Parks was, at the time of the assaults, sleepwalking.

Five forensic psychiatrists appeared for the defence in this case and each of them described somnambulism as a sleep disorder, but most definitely not a form of insanity under Section 16 of the Code. They each contended, persuasively as it turned out, that Parks was "effectively in a coma" as he drove the miles of freeway between his home and his mother-in-law's house, as he skillfully and silently picked the lock on the front door, as he climbed the stairs with a tire iron in his hand, as he pounded into ruin the skull of a sleeping woman.

The psychiatrists confidently, and persuasively, maintained that his lower-brain functions would allow him to perform these apparently conscious acts, but he was, in psychiatric terms, "completely out of control."

Edwardh, who seems to have made something of a specialty out of the Diminished Capacity defence, introduced the records of thirty previous instances in medico-legal literature wherein a person had murdered under the influence of aggressive somnambulism. The experts admitted that in none of these instances, going back as far as 1848, had the killer traveled so far, and in such a complex manner, from the place where he had fallen asleep.

They also maintained that Parks was predisposed to sleepwalking, having had two previous episodes. The likelihood of the attack was increased by the fact that Mr. Parks went without sleep for three nights before the killing, and exercised heavily on the day of the attack.

Crown counsels argued that somnambulism has never been accepted as a successful defence in a murder charge in the United States or Canada. But their position was weakened fatally when their own witness, another forensic psychiatrist, found it impossible to disagree with the opinions of his peers on the defence.

On Friday, May 27, 1988, after deliberating for nine hours, the jury returned with a verdict of Not Guilty. Simply Not Guilty, not "by reason of insanity" or through extenuating circumstances. Barbara Woods was bludgeoned to death by a man who was simply sound asleep.

Parks went back to court on June 27 to face a charge

attempted murder in the assault on his father-in-law, Dennis Woods. To no one's surprise, the same defence was presented, with identical results.

Parks was also delivered up in District Court on June 13 to answer charges that he defrauded his employer of $30,000. Apparently in the grip of a gambling mania, Parks had lost his family's life savings and $30,000 from the electrical firm that employed him.

June Callwood wrote an eloquent, compassionate and completely wrongheaded book about this affair in 1991, after being given exclusive access to the details of the case by the members of the Parks family. Not surprisingly, her book became a sympathetic apologia for what she obviously viewed as an unavoidable tragedy, a position quite consistent with her larger social agenda.

Callwood's take on the story was no doubt fairly predictable and must have influenced the Parks family's decision to let her have the inside story, or as much of it as they felt she could handle. Unfortunately for the dead and the wounded, Callwood's book became yet another in a long line of verdicts on a violent act that consigned the victims to the role of collateral damage, rather like the victims of "friendly fire"—dead, yes, but tricked into death by a run of bad luck, by being in the wrong place at the right time—while the killer was allowed to usurp the role of the victim. Parks is free now, separated from his wife. He has no criminal record, and he is not even under medical supervision. It's hard to tell which of the consequences is the more obscene.

The essential "wrongness" of the decision in the Parks case has far-reaching psychological effects for our entire society. Regardless of the niceties of the argument, what emerges from the Parks decision is the failure of the State to cherish its dead. Parks may have had some transitory disorder that led him to kill in such a brutal manner. My argument is that what was in his *mind* is irrelevant; his *body* committed a savage assault resulting in death, traumatic injury and a lifetime of suffering. For which he was, effectively, forgiven and freed without censure or restriction.

The subliminal message from the courthouse to the rest of society is that the fact of the death carries little weight in the scales of justice; what mattered was a possibly specious psychological theory proposed by members of a profession that cannot pretend to any predictive reliability. The psychiatric assessment of violent offenders is, by the profession's own admission, an area of intense debate. Their record of success in threat assessment is no better than fifty-fifty. You can say the same for astrology.

And on the other side of the balance, the need we all have to feel that justice is a force in the world, that a human life is more than just a pawn in an adversarial exchange of arcana and supposition—this carried no weight at all.

Parks should have been required, once the facts of the case were established according to all the safeguards and rights extended to any accused, to accept a level of responsibility for the killings. A pronouncement of "existing and ongoing threat" could have been filed.

I'm not concerned about his moral guilt here. Neither was the court. That's fine with me. What was needed was an action by the courts that would have given the rest of us what we need to reinforce a valuable ethic: that life is cherished and honored by the State; that a successful defence of somnambulism places upon the killer a legal and moral requirement to prove that it won't happen again.

Parks could then have been invited by the court to prove, in a separate venue, and one less weighted to his advantage, that, on the balance of probabilities, he posed no further threat to society. Since he'd already been judged dangerous, the onus would be on him to make that case. His defence would then be free to call upon whatever expert witnesses it could afford to attempt to persuade the State that he was *not* dangerous.

In front of a jury of his peers.

Instead, the issue turned on *mens rea* and his ability to formulate intent. The State's duty to censure violence and to consider the safety of innocent citizens who may share converging trajectories with Kenneth James Parks was merely a minor element in the drama. In cases of murder, where an argument of temporary insanity, automatism or lethal somnambulism has been put forward, it ought to be the court's first duty to ensure that the killer will not kill again.

This was not done in the Parks case.

As far back as the infamous "Twinkie" defence in the murder of Harvey Milk in San Francisco, juries and judges have been called upon to weigh the validity of thousands of Antecedent Cause or Diminished Capacity cases. In most of these trials, the arguments of forensic psychiatrists have been decisive factors in the determination of guilt and, more important, disposition.

In a recent Canadian case, a man charged with embezzling several hundred thousand dollars of research funds from the federal government allowed his lawyers to put forward the defence that he was suffering from Chronic Fatigue Syndrome. Apparently, the adrenaline-charge he got from the thrill of the fraud was the only way he could counter the effects of his syndrome.

Apparently, the judge in this case did not think that allowing such a contemptuous and clearly specious argument to be placed before the court would "bring the administration of justice into disrepute."

Forensic psychiatrists have been called upon to make similar judgements about thousands of violent offenders, in courts of law, as advisers to parole boards, as experts in pre-trial and pre-sentence hearings, as keepers and healers of society's most puzzling and repellent members—rapists, murderers, the habitually violent and aggressive.

It's rough road, strewn with traps and pitfalls, but one they travel with a reasoned confidence in their science, in their judgements and in the correctness of their vision of the human heart.

Unfortunately, the one area with which they do not have to contend is the area left to the rest of us, those of us who have wives or children or husbands, many of whom will be killed, maimed, raped or beaten by violent offenders, whose diagnosis from a skilled psychiatrist allows them back out into society, where, to the amazement and horror of all concerned, they repeat their crime often more chillingly and more brutally than before.

It's not difficult to cite cases where this precise scenario has been played out. It happened again in London, Ontario, when two criminals on a day-pass from Saint Thomas Center kidnapped and raped a fourteen-year-old girl. They threw her naked body into a creek under a bridge, thinking she was dead. She crawled two hundred yards to a farmhouse and got help. She is now alive and physically recovered. About her emotional life, about her hopes for future peace and serenity, the doctors are less willing to speak forcefully.

A man attacked an acquaintance of mine, named Tema Conter, after following her home from a shopping excursion on Yonge Street in Toronto.

She was raped and tortured and, finally, beaten to death by this man, who was on a day-release from a halfway house at Yonge and Eglinton in Toronto. Melvin Stanton, a psychopath with a forty-year history of sexual assault and murder in the United States and Canada, had been undergoing "anger-management counseling" in the penitentiary.

The psychologist "treating" Stanton, Lynn Stewart, became concerned that Stanton was "depressed and suicidal" because he saw little hope of being released into society. He had shown some "progress" in courses such as "anger-management" and she decided to attempt to place him in a treatment program for sex-offenders run by The Clarke Institute in Toronto. The cost of the course was roughly $62,000. Her decision to do so was based on a number of professional observations made while Stanton was in prison and closing in on his mandatory release date.

The Canadian health insurance plan would not pay for the cost of the treatment because Stanton was an inmate of a prison and not, technically, eligible for health insurance.

Dr. Neil Conacher, a senior Corrections psychiatrist, expressed the opinion that Stanton was deeply despairing and any treatment that helped him to confront and deal with his inner demons might take away the anger that was sustaining him. Conacher recommended that Stanton be given no further treatment, since his anger was all he had to keep him going and take it away might result in his suicide.

Conacher also made the observation, later, that no one who has not been exposed to a man like Melvin Stanton could have any conception of what men such as this are really like.

Dr. Stewart disagreed.

Dr. Stewart, anxious that her "patient" not descend dee

into his suicidal despair, arranged for Stanton to be released into a low-security halfway house in order that he might qualify for health insurance and thus have his sex-offender course paid for by the people of Canada.

A long line of prison shrinks had examined Stanton during his years in the system. They had all concluded that Stanton was "gaining in insight and motivation."

A young female doctor, Arunima Khanna, expressed the opinion that his violent nature was a form of self-expression, arising from his resentment at being mistreated by life. She wrote that:

> Stanton feels there has been a burn-out in his psychopathic behavior, that he is tired of fighting the system—and there is reason to believe this. He now recognizes the value of prosocial behaviour and constructive coping and is trying to improve himself.

At the hearing, Khanna appeared wonderfully free of any sense that her professional insights into Stanton had somehow contributed to the terrible death of an innocent woman. She went through the whole inquiry with one of those thin-lipped half-smiles you see on people who know in their hearts they're really pretty neat and they've got their heads straight about things. By the end of the week, she had been voted "Most Hated Witness" by the press gallery, a tribute I'm sure would have bothered her not in the slightest. She had that stainless-steel sheen in her eyes, the kind of look you see in overintellectualized college kids who have mistaken an "A" average for genuine understanding. In her dealings with Stanton, Khanna was either profoundly condescending or unforgivably stupid. Probably both.

The Parole Board members are vague about the discussions they had among themselves while considering Stanton's release, but one of them mentioned that had she known that Stanton had raped a sixty-two-year-old woman when he was twelve and killed a girl when he was fourteen, she might have decided differently. The YOA mandates that all criminal records relating to a Young Offender be destroyed when he has reached the age of twenty-three.

Certainly the Parole Board treated the Stanton case carelessly, ignoring his recent behavior in prison (he had pulled a knife on another inmate at Warkworth and had trashed his cell). Stanton's case-management team contradicted itself in various appearances before the Coroner's Court, essentially blaming anyone and everyone else for the mistaken decision to grant Stanton a Temporary Absence Pass.

I was at the hearings, and all I saw was the same old bullshit from a group of supposed corrections professionals; they didn't know the whole story, or they weren't in agreement, or somebody lied to them, or it seemed like a good idea at the time. It's the kind of conduct that defines and pervades our corrections system.

Thirty-six hours after his arrival in the halfway house, he must have lost his grip on "prosocial behaviour" and the value of "constructive coping" because he was busy sending a young black woman to her grave in what has to be a death beyond any of our worst nightmares. I have seen the crime scene photos, and I have had many years of experience with violence and murder. knew this woman. Her death was a hard and terrible one by any human standard.

Stanton is back in the penitentiary. He is, by all reports, very sorry for what he has done, according to the same kind of professionals who let him out in the first place. He is undergoing therapy at this time and is reported to be "coming to terms" with his violent nature. Tema Conter's family is doing less well.

Dr. Stewart is unavailable for comment right now. She retained a lawyer to safeguard her interests at the Coroner's inquest, after which the outraged Coroner excoriated every professional connected with the case.

But I'll tell you right now that I've watched her and I've watched Arunima Khanna and the rest of their colleagues, and they have learned nothing from this experience.

They are all quite serenely and quietly certain that they did nothing wrong. They're making the same noises about this now that they always have. If you want my personal opinion, think psychiatrists and psychologists are, by training and in their souls, totally incapable of comprehending the nature of beasts with whom they deal.

I think Tema Conter would agree with that.

In a case I became involved with while working at the Four Eight Detective Area Task Force in the South Bronx, we caught a man who was killing and raping young boys in a ghetto neighborhood. He had a long history of severe psychiatric disorders. He had been in and out of many therapeutic institutions. When he was released into our precinct, we were not warned. Nor were the citizens. He tortured five boys to death before we caught him.

At his trial, a defence witness, a forensic psychiatrist, testified that the savagery of the assaults might indicate a desire on the killer's part to "appear insane," as no sane person could ever kill in such a way. But he contended that there was a disease known as Ganser's Syndrome, a psychiatric condition wherein an insane person imagines that he is faking the symptoms of insanity in order to escape punishment, and that this fakery is in itself a form of insanity. The defence later maintained that their client was not guilty, by reason of Ganser's Syndrome. A noted forensic psychiatrist was produced in support of this contention. The defence was unsuccessful.

The killer was allowed to plead guilty to lesser charges and was confined to Attica for ten years. He'll be out in seven. He is forty-one now. He'll do it again. They always do. It is in their nature to do these things, as it is in the nature of a gull to fly and a lizard to dream reptile dreams.

Well…it's easy to see why this issue affects all of us so strongly. What is less easy to discern is what, if anything, can be done about it.

I've talked to forensic psychiatrists who are beginning to have doubts about the ethics of their testimonial contribution to the release of dangerous persons. I've seen District Attorneys and police officers threaten to resign after expert witnesses have persuaded juries that there was some overriding psychosis, some transitory dissociative state, some bizarre interlude of aggressive somnambulism that lifted the burden of guilt from the killer and placed it on the shoulders of his parents, or society, or genetics, X-rays from Melmac—anyplace, so long as it's over there and not...here, in this room, at the defendant's table, staring at his hands and containing the mystery of violence within his soul.

Well and good...but resentment is easy, and comforting, and a balm to the affronted, but no kind of solution. Ultimately, the issue must be confronted in the parliaments and the legislatures. The governments in Canada and the United States are being pushed towards this question by hundreds of events similar to the ones described in this book.

I believe that the public's emotional sense in these matters is not being addressed in any direct way. The courts confine themselves, rightly, to questions of law and interpretation. The lawyers do what lawyers do best, arguing persuasively for whoever pays the bills. And the police do not concern themselves with motivations beyond the most rudimentary calculations of the homicide detective: who stood to gain, who was the nearest and dearest, who hated, who was spurned, who likes to kill this way?

And the psychiatrists, troubled by the issue, are divided among themselves and unwilling to speak too soon on such divisive and dangerous principle, although there is groundswell of sentiment within the psychiatric disciplines that they should withdraw from the arena of violent psychosis and confine their work to the treatment of the Worried Well.

The Stanton case, and hundreds of others, has proven to complex and puzzling a phenomenon for the psychiatric community. Realizing that they have no true maps of the territory they are falling back on psychoactive drug treatment. We'd call it warehousing. And because the warehouses are full, many these people are being pronounced "cured" and sent out into the world again.

At the heart of these issues are perhaps some of the most troubling and fundamental questions to face a civilized society. Where does violence come from? What feeds it? What nurtures it? How can we begin to detect and predict it? And how does society predicated on the principles of mercy, of redemption, forgiveness and healing, how does such a compassionate society confront the killer who does it for no other reason than he likes it and he can get away with it? When the thing he does is shocking we will turn ourselves inside out trying to get some distance from it, to label and file it.

The phrase "limits of personal responsibility" is an illuminating one. I ought to admit at this stage to a personal feeling—I can't in honesty use a word any more concrete than feeling—that there are two elements to any violent crime.

The first is that inchoate urge to do harm that has its wellspring in the abyss of all souls, in the impenetrable mist of millennia that obscures our origins in the Olduvai Gorge and our lives on the savannah in the morning of the world, the record of which is woven into the endless living cable of our DNA. Dominance. Aggression. Fear.

But the second element in any violent crime is the moment of choice, that single, fleeting moment in which the killer feels the weight of society and the pressure of the sea of morals in which we all swim, and he has that transitory chance at redemption.

In that moment, I believe, even the most driven and ruined heart, the most opaque and occluded mind, sees that flash of light and reason wherein lies his choice. I believe that evil men and women will *choose* to do harm, will *choose* to pass on the burden of pain (real or imagined pain is a meaningless distinction), will, in short, perform one conscious act of decision, and in that act of decision is the basis for punishment and censure.

A detective I worked with used to say that he pitied the child that used to be, the child who was abused or hurt or ruined by careless or cruel parents, but as for the man who grew from that child, the man who chose to pass that pain on...he deserved nothing but a fast and merciful killing, as you'd kill a cockroach in a kitchen or a rat in the cradle. A hard rule, I admit, but a rule that most ordinary people would find fundamentally sound and understandable.

The burden of forensic psychiatry is to justify compassion, and in its present construction, it fails abysmally to do that in any manner that is accessible to the general public. It's a bedrock of the social contract, which binds us all to the rule of law: that justice must not only be done, but should be seen to be done. An even more crucial factor is that society quite literally creates responsibility and nobility in its members by declaring and sustaining the expectation of responsible and noble lives. To remove guilt from the social calculus demeans and diminishes every human being. Where antecedent causes and blind urges can be argued for every vile act, the soul will rot.

Clearly, there is an antipathetic tension between the operations of the justice system and the academic inquiries of psychiatry, and perhaps psychiatry, being by far the junior science, ought to give way here.

As one well-known psychiatrist, Bernard Diamond, put it, in a kind of manifesto:

If and when the time comes when the following conditions are approached, I would freely abandon the adversary system insofar as it applies to problems of mental illness:

WHEN each defendant, rich and poor, rural and urban, in enlightened communities and backward communities, can be reasonably guaranteed the type of exhaustive clinical investigation that is now available to only a few unfortunate defendants.

WHEN all expert witnesses are highly trained and experienced and adept in transmitting their findings to court.

WHEN observation hospitals are staffed with dynamically oriented psychiatrists who fully appreciate the important role they play in the administration of justice.

WHEN such psychiatrists, through their own enlightenment and self-understanding, can be relied upon to detach themselves from their own prejudice and refrain from homogenizing their moral judgements with their medical opinions.

WHEN our whole profession of psychiatry is less preoccupied with its own omniscience and sufficiently secure in its public status that it is unafraid to expose its deficiencies of knowledge about some of the most fundamental problems of human nature.

WHEN the forensic psychiatrist is permitted to operate within a legal framework which allows him to apply his professional judgement to appropriate questions of psychological reality and not to philosophical and theological rules and syllogisms—when he can apply his knowledge to human reality instead of legal fiction.

WHEN society is able to leave behind its archaic need for vengeance and retribution and learn that its own best protection is inextricably woven in with the rehabilitation of the individual deviant; that to degrade any member of that society with either the formal vengeance of punishment or the stigmata of legal insanity is to degrade only itself…"*

Presumably Diamond would have regarded the Orangeville kid and Melvin Stanton as intriguing challenges to his libertarian principles. One thing about Olympus, the air is fresh and you can see for miles.

The question of *mens rea* is too complex an issue to get into here, even if I were capable of assessing it adequately, but you should know that it is the single most complicating issue that the courts have concerned themselves with since they disbanded the Inquisition. Because to know, fully and completely, what was in another person's mind, at any point in his actions, is a spiritual and literal impossibility, as anyone who's married can tell you.

Now, it's reasonable to ask the courts to give due weight and consideration to the degree of intent that an accused may have harbored prior to or during the commission of a criminal act. We get into difficulties, however, when we decide that someone who was legally insane—such as this kid in Orangeville—was not guilty at all, because he was unable to formulate an intent to kill that was clear and unaffected by a mental disorder.

That case turned on a persuasive diagnosis of this mental disability—latent schizophrenia—which pleased no one, least of all the people of Orangeville, who do not pretend to Dr. Diamond's purity of professional ethic. They found it hard to accept that a boy from the town could plan and execute the purposeless thrill-killing of two children and, in their view, walk away without even the "stigmata" of a public proclamation naming him a murderer. Although finer souls such as Dr. Diamond's have no need

The Fallacy of the Impartial Expert, Archives of Criminal Psycho-Dynamics, 1-226, 1959.

275

of it, it's a basic and enduring fact of human nature, and will continue to be long after you and I are dust in the wind, that vengeance is a salutary and healing balm, and it is the business of the justice system to regulate and apply vengeance and retribution in a public and orderly way.

It has not been, historically, the business of the justice system to provide a kind of enforced psychoanalytic forum in which the acts and omissions of certain individuals can be held up to the light streaming from the eyes of expert psychiatric witnesses in order that their cognitive imperfections may be projected upon the *tabula rasa* of the jury for the edification of us all and the rehabilitation of the miscreant.

All this is changing, and you can hear the agenda in Diamond's manifesto. Actually, Diamond has made a pretty good case for one thing that he may not perhaps have anticipated…

Let's ban the use of psychiatric testimony in trials and limit it solely to an advisory role at the time of sentencing.

And, further, let's ban psychiatric testimony from Parole Board hearings until psychiatry can demonstrate a degree of reliability that has so far eluded it completely.

And let's keep young female psychiatrists out of the prison system, because they clearly don't know what the hell they're doing in there.

Now seems like a good time to point out that our Supreme Court, in its wisdom, has recently decided that the custom of placing insanely violent criminals under the care of the Governor General for an indeterminate amount of time is (*Ta-dah!*) unconstitutional. So we can expect to see a lot of these guys calling up their lawyers and taking their cases to court after all, just because a guy has a taste for kiddie-porn or is in the habit of stalking and raping young women, that doesn't mean he ought to be locked up forever.

And the effect of that ruling on killers who fall under the YO is too depressing to contemplate, as these examples will illustrate.

TIME, 8 May, 1989

…on a clear April night in Central Park. Looking, they said, for something to do, they…came upon a 28-year-old woman jogging alone past a grove of sycamore trees…they chased her into a gully, then spent the next half-hour beating her senseless with a rock and a metal pipe, raping her and leaving her for dead. When she was found three hours later, she had lost three-quarters of her blood and had lapsed into a coma.

Dr. Diamond? Dr. Diamond, please come to Emergency! We need you to help us rise above our archaic need for vengeance here…

I was around when the six kids were brought into court on this case, which became famous as the Central Park Jogger Rape. The boys, Raymond Santana, 14, Kharey Wise, 16, Yusef Salaam, 15, Antron McCray, 15, Steve Lopez, 15, and Kevin Richardson, 14, were supported by a mob of black activists and apologists who at one point accused the rape victim of inciting the attack, calling her a "white whore" and a "cunt," and calling the trial "a lynching." Others called out, "Where's the boyfriend who met her at ten o'clock…lynch the boyfriend…lynch *all* her boyfriends, she had *lots* of them!"

Very unattractive.

In his statement to the cops, Santana admitted that he and his "wilding" brothers had forced her to the ground, pulled her pants down, told her to "shut up, bitch," hit her with a brick to get her to stop resisting, hit her twice in the face with that brick, dragged her farther into the brush, naked, over glass and rocks, repeatedly raped and sodomized her, "grabbed her tits," punched her in the face and then stood up and "jerked off on her." Then they walked away, laughing. The attack lasted fifteen or twenty minutes.

By the way, the defence lawyers put up a vigorous challenge on constitutional grounds, including *Miranda* and *Escobedo* and citing early social deprivation, poverty, even dysfunctional group dynamics, anything but genuine remorse.

Again, I found it hard to live up to Diamond's manifesto, especially when I heard various expert witnesses tell the court that these children were "victims" as much as the jogger was a victim, that "overwhelming societal forces" had driven these kids to this act as a kind of protest against the desperation of their lives, or a cry for help, or even as a kind of "rite of passage" similar to Masai warriors hunting lions.

By the way, the boys were convicted under the juvenile law and almost all of them will be back out by the time you read this.

And this…

LOS ANGELES NCIC TELETYPE

A fifteen-year-old girl was kidnapped at knifepoint by two men, held captive for five days and repeatedly raped. She managed to escape and was picked up by a passing car with three teenaged boys inside it. She asked them for help. They drove her to a park in East Los Angeles where the oldest boy raped her again.

And…

WEST VANCOUVER PD TELETYPE

Brian Wilhelms required 12 stitches in his neck after he was attacked by 10 youths at Ambleside Beach. Wilhelms also lost $400 in cash. One of the youths stood over Wilhelms with the man's wallet and called him a "wimp…only wimps bleed."

And…

RCMP FRASER VALLEY

Leny and Karsten Madsen and their two children were hacked to death by their foster son Tyrone Borglund and Michael Peever.

RCMP SURREY

The body of 12-year-old Shawn Tirone was finally located in a park months after his killing at the hands of local teens in a drug transaction "gone wrong." Local teens kept the location of Tirone's body a secret for reasons of loyalty and group solidarity.

METRO TORONTO POLICE

In what they describe as "swarming," gangs of teenagers have been roving the downtown streets of Toronto assaulting individual citizens, beating them, and stealing watches and cash. These gangs are of mixed racial composition and are all under the age of eighteen. As one member who was apprehended said, they are "not afraid of the pigs" because the YOA protects them.

WEST VANCOUVER

In the Lock It or Lose It campaign, West Vancouver police warned shoppers at the upscale Park Royal Center that there has been an uncontrollable rash of car break-ins and car thefts and people are being asked to put all visible belongings in trunks, to lock all doors, and not to leave their cars unattended for too long. In one day, twelve cars had their windows broken and their contents stolen. Teenaged gangs and individuals looking for money and goods have been reported in the area, but juvenile laws make it impossible to keep these gangs under control.

METRO TORONTO

In an internal memo, Metro Police are citing the rise of milk store robberies by children under the age of thirteen. Investigators have reported that older teenagers, aware of the limitations imposed on the police by the YOA, are using younger children to carry out the robberies in the knowledge that no legal steps are possible against them.

METRO TORONTO

A young boy who came to the aid of a fellow student who was being attacked by youth gang kids in the schoolyard was punished for his intervention when the gang kids hunted him down and knifed him repeatedly, warning him not to interfere when they were dealing with defiant outsiders.

There are many many similar stories, and, frankly, if I list
n all here I'll be too depressed to finish the book...

I've presented these cases in such detail to make a few im tant points about the criminal mind and the justice system, an first of these is that the phrase "justice system" is an oxymo It's not really a system. It's more of a territory, a zone ir which we all expect—hope—things will happen for the That people who serve in this...territory...will do it with best that is in them, in accordance with the best that is in us. All of us in the territory.

And I ought to point out here that cops aren't operatin anything but instinct and experience either. It's just that wl cop fucks up he or she may die, so they tend to be careful a their judgements and they try to keep them reality-based.

Civilians would like to imagine that there's a course s where that street cops take, maybe a classroom in a big cop versity, where they have a slide show complete with drive houettes and voice-overs, and the cadets sit in their seats press STOP or FORGET IT or FOLLOW THEM or GO DONUTS and the instructor grades them and gives them a tificate.

That's not the way it works.

Not to say that modern law enforcement professionals go through intensive and repetitive training, some of it a degree level in universities across the country, in order to d op an understanding of the terrible complexity of the justice tem. They do, more and more every year. But all the sc training in the world isn't going to make them good cops.

What does?

Maybe you'd have to call it a kind of cop Zen.

It all seems so...random. Accidental. Too much luck and chronicity and not enough professional skill. Not enough. enough of a *system* to it. Hell, if cases get solved, on a s cop's hunch or a detective's gonzo determination, if that's some guys get caught, then it's a damn wonder that any *ever* goes to jail!

Exactly the point.

And to this instinctual and chaotic scene, we now injec arcana of psychiatry? What can psychiatry say about inci such as these...?

CP and *The Globe and Mail,* 21 November, 1991
By Nina Aprile
STRATFORD, Ontario

The mother of a slain 11-year-old boy wept openly in court
yesterday as a letter written by her son while his killer
watched him was read into the record. "Dear Mom and Dad,"
began the letter read by Peel Regional Police Detective Gene
Inglis at the first-degree murder trial of Joseph Fredericks, "I
am writing you this note," it says, and then the ink fades out.

The letter was written to Anna and Jim Stephenson by their
son Chris, who was repeatedly raped, tortured and viciously
murdered after he was abducted from a mall in Brampton,
Ontario, in June.

Mr. Fredericks, 46, of Brampton, has pleaded Not Guilty by
Reason of Insanity.

Detective Ronald Bain testified yesterday that in a statement to
police, Mr. Fredericks said, "I didn't mean to hurt him. It's
over now. Things got carried away. I didn't mean to kill him.
You can't understand the hate and hell I've had to deal with
since I was eleven years old."

According to Detective Bain, Mr. Fredericks sobbed while
giving the statement.

Fredericks was a convicted sex offender who had been in and
out of various prison facilities for many years. In his
statement to police, Fredericks claimed that he had killed the
boy to get even with the justice system for not giving him
adequate psychiatric treatment...

...Two senior parole officers denied responsibility for their
failure to properly supervise Fredericks. They also denied
knowledge of much of Joseph Fredericks' history of sexual
offences against children, his long internment in maximum
security under a Mental Health Act, and a doctor's
recommendation that he undergo drug therapy to control
his sexual urges.

an Carmichael, a supervisor with the Guelph office of
Corrections Canada, said that because of a splitting of
caseloads between two regions, his office was not technically

responsible for Mr. Fredericks when Christopher Stephenson of Brampton was murdered.

Mr. Carmichael said Mr. Fredericks failed to telephone him as arranged the day before the accused abducted Christopher at knifepoint from a shopping mall in Brampton in June, 1988.

Fredericks, 46, led police to the boy's body in a wooded area near railway tracks in Brampton. He admitted confining the child in his rented room for about 24 hours and sexually abusing him before taking him to the remote area, where he strangled and stabbed him.

Mr. Carmichael also said he did not know that Fredericks, on parole from a provincial reformatory, had anal intercourse in a secluded area with a child in Ottawa in 1984, on his first day of freedom from a group home.

"I really didn't become privy to that information until a later date. I wasn't aware of many things because of the quickness of his release," Mr. Carmichael said.

Mr. Fredericks was released on Mandatory Supervision on March 11, 1988.

Mr. Carmichael said there is now a National Parole Board inquiry into Mr. Fredericks' case.

Brian McKegney, a parole officer in Hamilton, Ontario, when the boy was killed, said Mr. Fredericks moved from his jurisdiction to Brampton just two weeks before the killing.

Mr. McKegney also denied detailed knowledge of Mr. Fredericks' long history of sexual offences against children, which included sexual assault of a mentally retarded patient in a Saint Thomas psychiatric ward, and of a young boy in a Kingston hospital.

In other testimony, a police witness said that after killing the boy, Fredericks said he returned home, drank a glass of milk, and washed a dishcloth that he happened to notice was dirty.

Fredericks was quoted as saying "I didn't sleep all that well." The trial continues.

SEATTLE, Washington

A Dennis Riches, 24, of Seattle, was arraigned in court today on charges that he raped a six week old baby girl.

Riches, a repeat sex offender whose history of sexual dysfunction was a matter of client privilege, was acting as a babysitter for the victim's family when the assault occurred.

The baby girl underwent surgery today and is reported as in fair condition.

Lawyers for Mr. Riches commented that it is likely that a plea of Not Guilty by Reason of Insanity will be entered.

WINNIPEG, Manitoba

Winnipeg police failed to respect the rights of a twelve-year-old boy who was convicted of the murder of two women in June, a provincial judge ruled yesterday.

Judge Marvin Garfinkel said the police violated two sections of the Young Offenders Act by failing to give the boy a full explanation of his right to have a lawyer or an adult at his side during police questioning.

The boy was isolated in a police interview room for almost six hours after his arrest. The evidence suggests the youngster was tired, groggy, and frightened as he endured police questioning from 3:08 am until 7:31 am, Judge Garfinkel said.

The boy, who is now thirteen, is the youngest person to face a murder trial in Manitoba's history.

Judge Garfinkel refused to allow the trial to hear two statements taken from the boy by police officers after his arrest. A statement by an accused person must be made by a "voluntary mind" and not by a person who is "dulled by fear or lack of sleep," the judge said.

The second statement, taken from the boy a day later, was ruled inadmissable because the police again failed to give the boy a proper explanation of his rights, Judge Garfinkel said.

The police knew that the boy did not want to talk to them, yet they went to a Winnipeg youth detention center and asked him to give another statement, the judge said.

He said police exercised "not only psychological control but also physical control" over the boy.

There is psychological pressure on anyone in police custody, and a twelve-year-old child does not have the same "inner strength" an adult can muster to withstand the pressure.

Because of his age, the boy cannot be named or tried in an adult court.

(continues...Canadian Press Serv.)

"He's one of the nicest little kids I've ever met"...

Mary Kate McDonald (Defence Lawyer)

He stands just over five feet tall–a shock of dark hair atop his slight frame.

To some, he's just a nice boy gone astray. To others, he's a cold-hearted killer who took the lives of two elderly women during a break-in at their home in the summer of 1988.

At 13, he ranks among the youngest children ever convicted of murder in Canada...

...Among the few experts in Canada specializing in children who kill is Dr. Clive Chamberlain, a psychiatrist at Thistletown Regional Center, near Oakville, Ontario, who has treated youths between nine and 18.

"We're talking about a very rare situation," he said.

"I've probably seen more kids who have killed than most people and I've only seen 40 over the past 20 years."

...On July 1, the boy broke into the home of Kiyo Shimizu, 89, and her 59-year-old daughter Chieko. For more than 30 minutes the two quiet women were repeatedly beaten and stabbed. At 1:15 am, police arrived, responding to a desperate emergency call from one of the victims.

When they found the youth, he was descending the staircase, his clothes and shoes stained with blood.

Chieko died that night, Kiyo five days later.

During his trial, the boy displayed little emotion. Small and meek, he barely acknowledged his parents, who weren't aware of the murder until four days after the arrest.

His few smiles were reserved for his lawyer, Mary Kate McDonald...

The boy was convicted of two counts of second-degree

murder. The maximum sentence he can receive under the
Young Offenders Act is three years in a juvenile facility. If
the boy had been under the age of twelve at the time of the
killings, no charges would have been laid against him.

Dr. Chamberlain said a child who commits murder does not
immediately realize the consequences of his actions.

"They know that they killed someone," said Chamberlain, who
testified at the trial of a 13-year-old boy in Orangeville
accused of killing Monique and Daniel Babineau, "but I think
many of them are unaware of it at a more complex level."

TORONTO, Canada

First-degree murderer René Vaillancourt said yesterday that his
inability to get a good job "forced" him to squander every
break the justice system has ever given him and culminated in
the murder of a policeman.

"I did not choose [crime], I was forced into it...I was forced by
the general pressures of living in society and paying rent and
getting food," the 40-year-old man said at his parole hearing.

He added that these social pressures caused him to violate bail
conditions, probation conditions, and some of the training
opportunities he had in prison.

Asked by Crown Counsel Paul Culver if these same pressures
led him to the murder of Toronto Police Constable Leslie
Maitland, Vaillancourt replied "Yes, but I am very remorseful
about taking a life and I have made every effort to prepare
myself to become a productive citizen. I realize what I did
was very wrong. I have always acknowledged that I was fully
responsible for it...I am not the same person anymore. I have
completely changed my way of thinking. I just want to
become an honest citizen."

...Vaillancourt was convicted of murdering Constable
Maitland during a botched getaway from a bank robbery in
1973. He fired two bullets into the police officer at close
range and then chased his partner into the police cruiser,
shooting four more bullets.

Mr. Vaillancourt testified (at his parole hearing)...that the petty thefts that dominated his adolescence could be traced to the high unemployment rate in Quebec.

"I looked for jobs, but there weren't any." Pressed by the Crown, he acknowledged that he had held several jobs, but left most of them because they were "unsatisfying."

"Mr. Vaillancourt, everyone in this room has to pay rent and buy food," the Crown said quietly. "Are you saying we should all resort to a life of crime to do that?"

Mr. Vaillancourt simply repeated his rationale. Mr. Culver then asked why, at his 1973 trial, Mr. Vaillancourt pleaded not guilty by reason of insanity to the Maitland murder.

"I must have been insane to do what I did."

...Earlier in the hearings, Correctional Services Canada security officer Richard Blasko testified that Mr. Vaillancourt probably had an easy time establishing (his) drug trade (in prison) because "cop killers" have a high status in the prison community.

But Mr. Vaillancourt testified he only sold enough drugs to pay for his own supply. He said he only began to take drugs...[to be like other inmates. I had to find some form of escapism, so I started doing drugs. And if you don't do the same things as your supposed friends, you are cast apart."

[Mr. Vaillancourt's parole request was denied.]

And, finally, an illuminating study of the limits of psychiatric understanding...The Green River Killer...

Vancouver Sun, 14 July 1989
by Mark Hume
SEATTLE, Washington

A massive seven-year police hunt for the killer of more than 40 women in the Pacific Northwest is now focused on a former Spokane law student who was known as a brilliant public speaker—but who Task Force detectives say talked privately of an urge to cut up and kill prostitutes.

The huge police investigative team are searching for the Green River serial killer named William Jay Stevens, Jr. as a "viable suspect" in the string of slayings that have claimed 41 known victims in Washington, Oregon, and Idaho. Another eight women are missing and presumed dead.

Unsolved murders of women in British Columbia are being studied by police for possible links to the killings that have been under investigation since 1982.

US police say Stevens made frequent trips to Vancouver.

Captain Bob Evans of the King County Police Department said Stevens is just one of the more than 1500 suspects who have been investigated in the worst case of serial killings in US history.

In a 39-page affidavit filed with a search warrant at King County Court, police place Stevens in proximity to many of the slain women.

...The police affidavit, filed to support a search of Stevens' Spokane home on Wednesday, portrays him as a man with multiple personalities who often dressed as a police officer, had an unmarked police car, and who went on driving odysseys throughout the Pacific Northwest.

He told friends he worked for the police, hinted at involvement with the Central Intelligence Agency, and would go out of town on "secret missions."

...Police state that gas receipts, telephone records, credit card bills, and statements from individuals were used to place Stevens in Portland, Seattle, and Spokane at the time of many disappearances.

"Records obtained thus far have failed to provide him with an alibi for any of the 49 suspected Green River homicides," states the affidavit.

Vancouver Sun, 15 July 1989
by Mark Hume
SEATTLE, Washington

Merv Ortmann told investigators about a bizarre meeting he had with Stevens.

Ortmann, an acquaintance, said Stevens came into the house "acting very macho and attempting to give the appearance of a Mafia figure."

During the conversation Ortmann related to Stevens how he had recently been in hospital after a brown recluse spider had bitten him in the house.

Ortmann said when Stevens heard the story, he began to get nervous and was anxious to leave the house.

Ortmann said that he seemed to witness Stevens' progress through several personalities, eventually ending up helpless, almost an infant, demanding to leave but incapable of doing so. He had to be taken out before he could regain his composure. This experience convinced Ortmann that Stevens had multiple personalities.

So Ortmann, whoever the hell *he* is, thinks that William Jay Stevens had "multiple personalities." Based on one mildly hysterical interlude with arachnophobic overtones. Surely this cannot be the stuff of forensic brilliance?

Yet, in a way, it is exactly information of that sort, possibly apocryphal, frequently malicious, that leads detectives to their solutions. The case of the Green River Killer is worth looking at because of what it teaches us about our national sense of what the "law" really is.

I have quoted press coverage of the Green River suspect for a reason. A look at this particular lament of the justice system, and of the interaction that developed with the media, is a telling lesson in the fragile infrastructure of justice in our society.

Vancouver, Canada, is less than forty miles from the United States border with Washington State. According to Washington State laws and local press protocol, no media outlet in the United States would have actually named a suspect in such a notorious case, in accordance with the principle that a man is innocent until he is proven guilty, and ought not, therefore, to be subject to the psyche-shattering and irreversible effects of public connection with such a series of vile acts.

And, as a matter of fact, aside from a few early slips by field correspondents, no Washington State media sources did use William Stevens's name in their reports. They referred to him as an "unidentified suspect," or "an unnamed Spokane man"

However frustrating that may have been to the people of the Pacific Northwest, for whom the Green River Killer had become a kind of mythic Vlad the Impaler, it was the right thing to do. It was the compassionate thing to do, since the man had only been named in an affidavit to a justice, and had not even been charged with the crime.

But, due to an accident of geography, there existed, a few miles to the north of Seattle, a major population area jam-packed with energetic media agencies who were in no way shackled by an American judge's press ban in this case. And these media agencies, newspapers and television outlets were widely read and watched throughout the northern part of the Washington State. They were in the Canadian city of Vancouver, a city of almost two million people. As you have read, in these outlets, the name of William Jay Stevens, Jr., was not only mentioned, it was *shouted*. It was skywritten across the front pages of every paper, and it was the lead story in all the television and radio news programs.

Your reaction to this phenomenon will of course be affected by your personal feelings about the right to privacy and the protections of the law as they collide with the natural desire a threatened public has to know the names of bad men.

As a working journalist, with stories published in the United States and Canada, I would have done precisely as my colleagues in the Canadian news agencies did.

Why? Partly because putting a name to the Green River Killer would have been so damned cathartic. The worst serial killer in the history of the West. A force for fear and paranoia since July of 1982. A man who had brutally murdered nearly fifty young women, and the hell with the idea that they were "only" prostitutes. They were young, vital women, and this werewolf had hunted them down and killed them like livestock, in the nastiest way he could manage. The people needed, *I* needed, a name, a face and a resolution of this horror.

And, perhaps more important, in the mind of every experienced newsperson working the crime beat, the case against William Jay Stevens was dead solid perfect, the result of some of the best police work either country could bring to bear on a case like the Green River killings. Stevens fitted the profile like a snake fits its skin.

Which brings us by a roundabout route to the most recent attempts to understand the criminal mind. Anyone who saw *The Silence of the Lambs* will recognize these guys.

The FBI's Behavioral Science Unit (BSU), situated at Quantico, Virginia, has studied the criminal career of serial killers for over twenty years. Nineteen agents and one hundred profile coordinators work out of a presidential bomb-shelter hidden in a stand of heavy Virginia oaks. Assisted by a $500,000 computer system, and drawing on reports filed with the related Violent Criminal Apprehension Program, also based in Quantico, the BSU has gathered information on hundreds of multiple murderers in Canada and the United States, including Richard Chase (the Vampire of Sacramento), the Tylenol poisoner, the Atlanta child killings, David Berkowitz (known as The Son of Sam), Ted Bundy and John Wayne Gacy, who tortured and killed thirty-three young men in the Chicago area between July 1975 December 1978. (The Gacy case was brilliantly detailed in Tim Cahill's stunning book *Buried Dreams*.*) And you can bet they have already begun to "debrief" Jeffrey Dahmer.

The BSU has pioneered a system of criminal investigation known as Profiling, the aim of which is to draw on a combination of field experience and psychiatric knowledge to develop a loose but directed description of a possible killer.

Each serial killer has an idiosyncratic pattern, a systematic way of going about the selection, pursuit, killing and disposal of his victims. Each of his victims will show characteristic damage or be placed in a ritual manner, or taken from a social group such as prostitutes or nurses or hitchhikers, having special sig nificance to the killer.

No two are exactly alike, but serial killers in general conform to a limited number of types.

Most serial killers:

• are single white males from twenty to forty-five

* Tim Cahill, *Buried Dreams* (New York: Bantam, 1986).

- have better-than-average intelligence
- appear socially competent
- have the respect of their peers in the workplace
- seem to be sexually competent
- are usually heterosexual
- are the eldest child in a family
- had a relatively stable childhood
- had inconsistent childhood discipline
- seem to be under tight control during the crime
- frequently use alcohol during the crime
- have secret fantasies of power and violence
- have some kind of girlfriend or steady partner
- are mobile and seem to travel a great deal
- have one or more vehicles at their disposal
- follow the crime story carefully in the media
- change jobs often and move from town to town
- seem to give the killing careful planning
- learn from their earlier mistakes
- target a specific stranger
- observe the potential victim for several days
- sometimes arrange a casual contact with the victim
- develop a personality assessment of the victim
- control the victim as soon as intercepted
- control the time and place of killing
- demand total submission from the victim
- use ropes, handcuffs or other restraints
- engage in some pre-killing abuse or torture
- kill in the same manner every time
- conceal the body after the crime
- leave no weapons at the scene or in the victim
- show a sophisticated understanding of evidence
- dispose of the body after a delay
  transport the body some distance from the scene
  may return to the scene of the killing to reminisce
  may return to watch police at the crime scene
  may offer unsolicited advice at scene
  may gather information on police investigators
  are frequently authoritarian in their views

- may have once applied to be a police officer
- frequently collect police equipment
- usually live in the neighborhood of the scene
- are disciplined and cautious
- systematically review and adapt their tactics
- seem to have a cycle of pressure and release
- do not suffer from any guilt feelings
- have no empathy or mercy for their victims
- enjoy their sense of power and accomplishment
- do not want to be caught
- will employ every legal defence if caught
- will firmly and consistently deny their guilt
- may successfully pass a polygraph test
- will actively resent police accusations
- may have had a minor police record or contact
- will not stop unless stopped

Obviously, many of the listed details would apply to perfectly normal citizens, and no single characteristic is a reliable indicator in itself. But a short review of the press information on William Jay Stevens, Jr., shows a number of correlations, and is exactly those correlations that increased the attention of the Task Force, once a "Crime Stoppers" tip phoned in to Detective Myrle Carner of Seattle had suggested his name.

All the BSU Profiling system can do is help the officers focus their searches, and all of the 1,500 men interviewed as possible suspects over the past years were types that conformed to the BSU pattern.

Few of them conformed as closely as Stevens.

1. He was in the right age group (twenty to forty-five).
2. He was a white male.
3. He had a better than average intelligence.
4. He was socially adept (twice head of student council).
5. He was respected and admired at Gonzaga law school.
6. He had no apparent sexual dysfunction.
7. He was the oldest child in the family.
8. Although adopted, his childhood was stable.

9. Informants reported that he had secret fantasies of violence.
10. He maintained various personae and posed as a CIA operative.
11. He was highly mobile and traveled often in the target areas.
12, He followed the Green River news stories closely.
13. He changed jobs and moved from Spokane to Tacoma to Seattle.
14. He was known to reside in areas where bodies had been found.
15. He frequently expressed authoritarian views.
16. He had been a military policeman.
17. He had stolen a great variety of police equipment.
18. He was known to impersonate a Seattle police sergeant.
19. He was a convicted thief and a prison escapee.
20. He had expressed a violent dislike of prostitutes.

That's twenty hits on the BSU profile computer. That alone would make Stevens a Grade One suspect for the Green River Task Force. But Motive is only part of the equation the justice system needs to take a case to court. The police must also satisfy the District Attorney that the suspect had Opportunity, and that he has special knowledge of the way in which the victims had died, in other words, that he had the Method.

In the matter of Opportunity, again the match-ups were remarkable. VISA bills and gas receipts placed him in the area of many of the killings at or around the time of the killings:

December 23, 1983. LISA YATES is last seen in Seattle.
December 23, 1983. STEVENS uses his VISA card in a Seattle hotel.

May 8, 1983. JOANN HOVLAND last seen in Seattle.
May 7, 1983. STEVENS uses his VISA card in Seattle.

August 11, 1982. CYNTHIA JEAN HINDS last seen in Sea-Tac strip.
August 12, 1982. OPAL CHARMAINE MILLS last seen south of Seattle.
August 16, 1982. STEVENS sells car in Seattle.

May 22, 1983 MARTINA AUTHORLEE last seen south of Seattle.

May 23, 1983. CHERYL WIMS last seen in Seattle.

May 19, 1983. STEVENS uses VISA in Seattle suburb.

May 22, 1983. STEVENS uses VISA in another Seattle suburb.

October 20 to November 7, 1982. SHIRLEY MARIE SHERRILL last seen in Seattle. Her body is found in TIGARD, Oregon.

October 22, 1983. STEVENS buys gas in Seattle.

November 4, 1983. STEVENS buys gas in TIGARD, Oregon.

October 8, 1982. DENISE DARCEL BUSH last seen south of Seattle. Her body is found in TIGARD, Oregon.

October 8, 1983. SHAWNDA LEEA SUMMERS last seen in Seattle.

October 3, 5, 6, 8 and 11, 1983. STEVENS buys gas in TIGARD, Oregon.

October 13, 16, 20 and 22, 1983. STEVENS buys gas in Seattle.

April 10, 1983. GAIL LYNN MATTHEWS last seen in Seattle-Tacoma.

April 14, 1983. STEVENS uses VISA in Seattle.

November 10 to 11, 1982. KIRSTEN SUMSTAD found in box in Seattle.

November 8 to 13, 1982. STEVENS buys gas and food in Seattle.

Kirsten Sumstad's body was found in a cardboard box behind the Magnolia Hi Fi store in Seattle. At that time, Stevens was living in Spokane. Yet his gas receipts show that he was in Seattle when Kirsten Sumstad disappeared, and that he had taken some electronic gear into Magnolia Hi Fi around the same time.

One of the victims lived one block away from Stevens when he was a student in Seattle. Another one lived near Stevens parents in Spokane. Four of the bodies were found, nude, bound and gagged, a couple of miles from a house Stevens owned in Portland, Oregon. All of this added up to Opportunity.

About the Method? The Task Force wasn't talking.

So Method was a question mark. Nobody outside the loop knew whether Stevens had shown any special knowledge of the manner of the killings. And it was highly unlikely that Stevens's lawyer would ever let him volunteer that kind of information. There were constitutional protections against self-incrimination.

So now the Task Force is looking at one of two things: 1. A string of unrelated coincidences that defy probabilities, or, 2. A very, very viable suspect in the Green River killings.

Add to this weight of circumstantial evidence the testimony of various friends and acquaintances of Stevens, concerning his fantasies about CIA work and "secret missions," his supposed hatred for prostitutes (reported second-hand, of course, and not confirmed by Stevens), the reports of his torture fantasies involving prostitutes and his allegedly erratic personality, and you cannot avoid the obvious inference that William Stevens is somebody you want to question very hard about the Green River cases.

All of this information came out in the press reports a couple days after Bob Evans asked for a search warrant. Obviously, someone on the Task Force leaked the information to the press, at least, leaked the fact of the affidavit. This was, perhaps, regrettable. It was also regrettable that the press ran with it as enthusiastically as they did.

That's easy to say in hindsight. At the time, you couldn't have filled a phone-booth with people who thought Stevens was innocent or with people who thought the trial should be anything more than a drumhead formality, followed immediately by a public execution, preferably televised. Perhaps in the Seattle Kingdome with a national uplink and satellite coverage.

I would have bought a front-row seat. With popcorn.

So you can imagine my...shock...horror...and shame...when the Green River Task Force, at the very last minute, on the eve of Stevens's release from jail at the end of his prison term for theft, declined to lay charges against him.

Declined to lay charges!

What about the *evidence?*

What about the Behavioral Science Unit and that $500,000 computer and nineteen FBI agents and a hundred assistants and all those high-powered detectives and the incredible correlation between Stevens and the typical serial killer?

What about all those bodies damn near on his doorstep?

What about his alleged hatred for prostitutes, and his phony police badges, and his CIA fantasies? What about his secret god damn missions?

What about all the times he was in town when women were missing?

What about all the stuff everybody has been writing about and talking about all over the damned media?

I felt *cheated.* I also felt…suddenly mean and small. Like man who feels the will of the people at his back and who turn around suddenly with the insight that he's not leading the peo ple; he's heading up a lynching, and a lynching of a man wh may be innocent!

A lynching of a man who is innocent, under the law.

So all the science, all of the skill and study and learning, t PhDs and the criminologists and the computers and the who high-tech circus of the FBI, all of that came together to pitch innocent man to the wolves?

What this chapter boils down to is this.

Question: Are criminals crazy?

Answer: Who knows?

If we can't figure out one man's mind, how can we e expect to understand the minds of criminals in any way, how we presume to make predictions about their behavior, to eng in legal discussions of *mens rea* and Diminished Capacity spend taxpayers' money trying to "rehabilitate" sadists and s offenders, or to pay for the "professional assessments" of pri psychometricians and psychiatrists like Stewart and Arun Khanna and all the rest of them in the United States Canada?

And should we even try?

EIGHTEEN

New Maps of Hell

I got into the Green River case because I think a hell of a lot of people these days are forming their opinions about the nature of evil on the basis of the recent film *The Silence of the Lambs*.

In the movie—a brilliantly realized adaptation of Thomas Harris's book—Hannibal Lecter is portrayed as a brilliant and diamond-hard intellect placed at the service of monstrous appetites. And the other killer, the one named Buffalo Bill, is depicted as driven by uncontrollable compulsions and a confused sexual identity.

It was great entertainment, although, as I have said before, I'm beginning to be a little uncomfortable with such graphic and powerful portrayals of human brutality. A lot of homicide cops I know are telling me that they think some killers see the popularity of movies such as this one as a kind of tacit condoning of crime.

I don't know if it's true, but if it might be true, don't we owe it to the women in our nation to be very careful about the things we glorify?

One problem with the definition of evil in the film is that it's based on psychiatric theories no different—and no more predictive—than the ones we discussed a while back.

Let me give you an example of the FBI Psychiatric Profiling Unit at work. Then you decide how much weight to place on their opinions of evil.

In the March 1990 issue of *Harper's* magazine, the Readings section reproduced a transcript of a Senate investigation into the tragic explosion of Gun Turret Two on the battleship USS Iowa, in which forty-seven crewmen were killed. The Naval Investigation Service (NIS) had concluded that the explosion was an act of suicidal rage on the part of the one seaman, twenty-four-year-old gunner's mate Clayton Hartwig.

Part of this investigation involved the employment of the FBI's Behavioral Science Unit (BSU) to do "an indirect personality assessment" of Clayton Hartwig, post-mortem, to "see what made him tick." To see, by inference, what had led him to rig the explosion.

FBI agents Richard Ault and Robert Hazlewood, founding agents of the BSU Profiling methodology, described the process as a "Gestalt-like examination of Hartwig's life and last days." Here, as in the case of the Green River Killer, the BSU was looking at a named suspect in an atmosphere of intense political pressure. In this instance, it was clearly in the interests of the Navy to find the Iowa explosion an act of sabotage. To do otherwise would expose the Navy to a severe criticism of battleship operations in a climate of defence-spending reevaluation. Not to mention the hundreds of personal lawsuits that would inevitably follow a clear revelation of endemic naval incompetence.

The *Harper's* transcript focused on an exchange that took place between Agents Hazlewood and Ault and Senators William Cohen, Alan Dixon, Sam Nunn and John Warner. It's worth looking at here because it clarifies the reasoning behind judicial resistance to Profiling as evidence. You will recall that the *deus ex machina* the Navy was conjuring here was Hartwig' alleged homosexual relationship with another sailor, and hi rage at a supposed rejection, a reading that bears some similarit to the Green River Task Force against William Stevens.

Hazlewood: During Clayton Hartwig's childhood, he was a loner and was largely estranged from his family. While in the eleventh grade, he formed his first close friendship, with a male two years younger. In one incident, this friend purportedly took a knife away from Hartwig, after Hartwig made a suicidal gesture with the weapon. Hartwig considered that the action had saved his life, and after joining the Navy, he gave this friend $200 a month for a year and a half.
While in the Navy, Hartwig had low self-esteem and had only two close friends, one of whom, Kendall Truitt, served with him aboard the USS *Iowa*. In January of 1988, Hartwig took out a $50,000 double-indemnity life insurance policy and named Truitt as the beneficiary. Truitt married in December 1988, and Hartwig was reported to be deeply depressed as a result. Hartwig and Truitt ceased all communication aside from orders that Hartwig gave in the line of duty. The

insurance policy was in effect at the time of Hartwig's death.

Nunn: You said he had motives for sinking the *Iowa,* but I didn't hear facts that led to that conclusion.

Hazlewood: Approximately one week prior to his death Hartwig discussed suicide with his shipmate David Smith. In addition, a female acquaintance says that Hartwig had always closed his letters with simply "Clay" but that the last letter she received from Hartwig closed with "Love always and forever, Clayton." Another female acquaintance had written to Hartwig, telling him he should quit hiding in the Navy, and he wrote back, "I don't think the 1,200 men that went down on the USS *Arizona* were hiding, or the 37 sailors that were killed on the USS *Stark!* I could become one of those little white headstones in Arlington Cemetery any day!"

In another instance, a chief petty officer discovered a piece of paper, captioned "Disposable Heroes," in the sleeping area occupied by Hartwig, Truitt, and others. Whether or not it was written by Hartwig, it is quite clear that he saw it. It read "Sailor boy, made of clay, now an empty shell, finished here, greetings death, you coward, you servant, you patriot, more death means another crow." Hartwig also told a shipmate he wanted to die in the line of duty and be buried in Arlington Cemetery.

Dixon: My understanding is, the information that you had in the form of exhibits, statements, and other things was given to you by the Naval Investigative Service. You did not develop those yourself?

Ault: No, sir. We didn't do our own investigation.

Dixon: Okay. Now the poem "Disposable Heroes" that you refer to, is it in handwriting?

Ault: Part of it.

Dixon: Have you analyzed the handwriting to determine who wrote the poem?

Ault: No, sir. We didn't do any of the investigation. That would have been the Navy's problem.

Dixon: Has anybody?

Hazlewood: I believe that NIS experts looked at it and were unable to ascertain whether it was Hartwig's writing.

Dixon: Well, surely the FBI could make that determination. There is evidence that another person killed in the action wrote poems all the time, and it is the view of the crew that "Disposable Heroes" was not the work of Hartwig at all.

Hazlewood: Whether he wrote it or not really has no bearing. The point is that he could have seen it because it was posted in his area.

Dixon: And David Smith, whom you mention specifically, you know that he has recanted substantial parts of his testimony?

Hazlewood: It's my understanding that he's recanted a portion of his testimony, sir.

Dixon: Did you ever subject Mr. Smith to polygraph?

Hazlewood: We did not conduct any investigation whatsoever, sir.

Dixon: No. Now its it a correct characterization of what transpired that the FBI, for whom I have the firmest respect, actually itself talked to nobody, interviewed nobody, analyzed no fingerprints, analyzed no handwriting, and otherwise did no investigation to determine whether the explosion might have been an accident?

Hazlewood: We don't do that type of investigation for this type of request, sir.

Dixon: Now Mr. Hazlewood, it was you who suggested that the relationship between Truitt and Hartwig had soured to the extent that their conversations consisted solely of orders given in the line of duty aboard the ship.

Hazlewood: Yes, sir.

Dixon: And Truitt was not present when Hartwig was in that gun turret?

Hazlewood: No, sir.

Dixon: Now, isn't it remarkable that a man who hated another man would not cancel a cancellable insurance policy rewarding his enemy and would contemplate suicide with the full knowledge that his suicide would benefit this person?

Ault: No, sir. I don't think so. There are decisions that are made before a suicide that look absolutely silly when an investigator arrives on the scene. Why would a man jump off a bridge and leave his shoes sitting there?

Dixon: I recognize, of course, that the documents you have used were given to you by the NIS. But other than these statements, letters, the poem, have you any hard evidence that would support the idea that Hartwig carried out this act?

Ault: No, sir. This opinion that we submitted is based on a half-scientific, half-art form.

Cohen: But the Navy said, "We don't think it was an accident."

Ault: Yes, sir.

Cohen: Did they indicate to you that they had a predisposition that Mr. Hartwig had in fact—

Ault: Yes, in fact, they did.

Cohen: Well, that's what I'm asking.

Ault: Well, they said to us that the forensic evidence showed that something happened very rapidly in that turret and that the only one in a position to make those things happen was Clayton Hartwig, and they asked if we would take a look at him.

Cohen: Did you have access to the records of all the others who were in the turret?

Ault: No, sir. We didn't ask for them.

Cohen: Okay. In this particular case, you did not review the Navy's statement that they thought it was not an accident. You accepted that?

Ault: We accepted it.

Cohen: In your judgement, as professionals, if there were other individuals who were inside the turret, shouldn't it have been of interest to you to make an assessment of their personality profiles?

Hazlewood: No, sir. Whenever we are requested to do a case for an investigative agency, we make the assumption that we are dealing with professionals. They provide us with the materials for review, and that's what we review.

Cohen: Now, about the poem "Disposable Heroes," is there, in your experience, a feeling among men in the Navy that they might feel like disposable heroes? In other words, someone's out on a ship, they read about the USS *Stark,* and they say, "Hey, that could happen to me."

Ault: That's right.

Cohen: Now someone else writes a poem and they post it on a bulletin board or in an area where others sleep, and you use that as an incriminating piece of information?

Ault: We threw that in because you never know what the triggering incident's going to be in a case like this. You never know whether or not just reading that poem might have been the thing that sparked some decisions on his part.

Cohen: Now I believe you indicated that he had a stack of Bibles on his bookshelf—

Ault: One shelf had seven, eight Bibles on it.

Cohen: The fact that someone has seven Bibles on his bookshelf doesn't mean anything to me.

Ault: It wouldn't to you, sir, but it does to me. I'm the expert.

Cohen: Well, tell me what it means to you then.

Ault: Well, this man's whole record reflects a preoccupation with death and violence. He made bombs, read *Soldier of Fortune* magazines, carried a 9 mm pistol with him. We go through his room at home and we see books on death and violence and we see Bibles. Now if he were a strong practitioner of a certain faith or went to a seminary, then I would be inclined to form an opinion that he wasn't suicidal. But he didn't. He went from that room into the Navy, worked as a gunman, continued with this process of death and violence until he reached the point where an explosion occurred in the turret where he was in charge.

Cohen: Let me ask you, is it abnormal for members of the Navy to have subscriptions to *Soldier of Fortune* magazine?

Ault: I recall very few of my fellow Marines who subscribed to *Soldier of Fortune* magazine.

Cohen: Very few of your fellow Marines were driven to violence? Didn't they teach you a lot of violence at Marine boot camp?

Ault: They teach us to hate the enemy.

Cohen: You indicated that he had only three close women friends.

Ault: With whom he never had any sexual contact, as far as anyone could tell. He proposed to one woman on their second date. She turned him down.

Cohen: Well, what's so unusual about that?

Hazlewood: She was a dancer in a strip joint.

Cohen: Aren't there some sailors who, after having been out to sea for some time, see someone who's attractive—might be a stripper—and make a proposal, maybe under the influence, maybe just suffering from a lack of companionship?

Hazlewood: That's quite possible.

Cohen: Okay. Who was the second?

Hazlewood: She was a woman who had had sex with the high school friend he'd been sending $200 a month to. When he found that out, he ceased the payments to his friend and, in fact, wrote that same girl and accused her of letting him down.

Cohen: Would you find that an extraordinary reaction?

Hazlewood: I would find that a very unusual reaction.

Cohen: Okay. Let me go through the other characterizations. You drew some significance from the fact that he signed one of his letters "Clayton" rather than "Clay." What's the distinction?

Hazlewood: He signed it, "Love always and forever, Clayton"—much more formal than simply "Clay," as he had signed his letters in the past, with no "forever," no "love," nothing.

Cohen: Another factor I think that you drew some significance from was that he said he could hide his hurt and never reveal it.

Hazlewood: That's what he said, yes, sir.

Cohen: Is that unusual?

Hazlewood: When you combine that with the fact that people reported never seeing him angry, never seeing him violent, that to us is a danger sign. We've seen it on too many occasions where they've just stored it up and then went out and murdered 14 people at a college or blew up a ship or killed a lot of people in shopping centers. Yes, sir.

Cohen: I find that there's a lot of reaching here. A couple of more questions. In a letter, he said "I could become one of those headstones any day." Why is that so unusual?

Hazlewood: It was a response to the young lady who accused him of hiding in the Navy, and it was an over-reaction on his part. Combine that with a statement that he made to a shipmate that he'd like to be killed in the line of duty and be buried at Arlington. Then this statement becomes significant, yes, sir.

Cohen: Well, I must tell you, I find it hard to arrive at that judgment. You take a young man, he's out on sea duty, he receives a letter from a young woman who says he's hiding out, either emotionally or physically. He writes back and says, "Hey, wait a minute. I'm not hiding from anything. I'm out here working with thousands of people in a very dangerous environment, and I could become like any one of those hundreds of headstones that occurred in Beirut or on the USS *Stark*." And then he makes a statement to a friend and says, "If I go, I want to go in the line of duty." Is that unusual?

Hazlewood: I was in the Army for 11 years and never once did I or any of my friends make the statement "I'd like to die in the line of duty." No, sir. I didn't want to die in the line of duty.

Cohen: If you took a look at the personality traits of the individuals who volunteer for the Navy, I suppose you'd find a number of loners who played with toys and pistols and collected them during childhood.

Ault: Sir, the whole turret may have been full of suicidal people. We accepted evidence from the Navy that there was no accident; we also accepted the same kind of evidence that the only guy in a position to do any damage was Clayton Hartwig. It's as simple as that.

Cohen: You indicated that his letters show that he was extremely egocentric. What do you mean by that?

Ault: Self-absorbed, narcissistic.

Cohen: Can you give me an example?

Hazlewood: To one friend, he wrote, "So your girlfriends thin I'm good-looking, huh?"

Cohen: You've got to be kidding me.

Hazlewood: No, sir. We're not kidding you.

Cohen: This is a twenty-four-year-old, relatively immature individual, who says, "Do your friends think I'm good-looking?" And that's egocentricity?

Ault: Yeah, I would say so.

Cohen: Here's a man looking for compliments. Is that unusual in a twenty-four-year-old sailor?

Hazlewood: Not just looking for compliments; fishing for compliments.

Warner: You mentioned that the man apparently was, in your judgement, alienated from his family. Can you clarify that?

Ault: The sister herself stated in an interview that he was largely estranged from other family members.

Warner: Yet he goes back home at Christmas.

Hazlewood: First time in five years.

Ault: And in addition to that, he leaves a letter stating that he loves them.

Hazlewood: Which he'd never done.

Ault: And he didn't say it face-to-face.

Cohen: The man went off to the Navy, had some hard times with his family, comes home after five years, leaves a note, "Mom and Dad, I love you." That'd be unusual?

Ault: Could be an indication that he'd decided that he was going to do himself in. Could be a lot of things. We chose to conclude that it was probably an indication that he'd begun to make up his mind that he wasn't happy with his life and wanted to end it.

Cohen: So it would have been a more normal course of conduct for him to continue the alienation with his family?

Hazlewood: Yes, sir.

Warner: Thank you, gentlemen. Tough job that you've had to perform.

Hazlewood: Thank you.

Months later, an independent federal investigation absolutely onerated Clayton Hartwig, eviscerated the Naval Investigation rvice smear and charged the Navy with a deliberate coverup endemic incompetence and faulty procedures on board its bat-ships. Kendall Truitt and the rest of the survivors of the *Iowa* losion were given an official apology, and the editors of *The*

World Book Encyclopaedia were ordered to recall and correct the "Year in Review" story that named Clayton Hartwig as "the most probable cause" of the disaster in Gun Turret Two.

The Navy is currently attempting to upgrade its training procedures and has, tacitly, accepted the pronouncement of the independent General Accounting Office inquiry. No one, outside of those people in the Department of the Navy and the NIS whose jobs and reputations are at risk, still thinks that Clayton Hartwig was anything other than one of the tragic victims of a seagoing disaster on the USS *Iowa*, a disaster that was most likely caused by an over-ramming error in the gun breach that put three bags of powder under far too much pressure. Laboratory tests supported that conclusion. So it was naval incompetence and plain bad luck, not a homosexual snit-fit that left forty-seven men dead.

In defence of the FBI, it's only fair to emphasize that the BSU is accustomed to working with accredited and presumably disinterested police forces involved in a criminal investigation. The FBI is not naturally going to assume that the requesting agency has an animus against a particular person, that it will selectively develop shaded information or that the fiscal well-being of the requesting agency depends upon the selection and public immolation of a scapegoat.

In this case, intelligent analysts who have done brilliant work in the field were saddled with a politically charged and arguably one-sided dossier and left in the dark, like mushrooms, to come to the most useful and politically correct conclusion.

But the tenor of the document rings clear. You can see how any man's past, when read through the dark lens of hindsight, can give the appearance of deviation. Any psychiatrist will tell you that the white-bread-two-kids-and-a-Volvo-I'm-Home-June-In-Here-Ward quintessentially serene American family just doesn't exist. There isn't anyone reading these words, or writing them, who has not done things he or she would just as soon keep under wraps. And if you haven't, I don't want to meet you.

As an aside, about the FBI and their Behavioral Science Unit in general, most regular cops I know have very little interest in the BSU beyond a kind of careful curiosity. Cops usually refer to anyone from the FBI as a "Feeb."

Despite the representations in *The Silence of the Lambs*, a film that was in many ways a very long and highly unreal advertisement for the BSU, the insights that the BSU have achieved have very little relevance in the field. And the conceit that a Quantico freshman would be called in on such an important—and career-making-case, in any capacity, flies in the face of years of my own personal observations. It just wouldn't happen.

For that matter, Hannibal Lecter bears as much resemblance to real serial killers I have met as Bambi does to Godzilla. Lecter is charming, brilliant, insightful, sleek—utterly unreal. Most serial killers are dull, pathetic slobs with as much charisma as a bag of hammers. Regarding Profiling, there's a parallel with the Fingerprint Files. The FBI maintains a massive and technically marvelous fingerprint record, but until you can put some kind of name on your fingerprint request, there's not a damn thing the FBI can do for you. You have to narrow the search, and that's what the "art-science" of Criminal Profiling can do. It can take the details of an individual case and tell you whether it fits—in a general way—into the pattern of similar crimes. You are then free to pursue your investigation along the lines they suggest, or not.

Many departments do not, and they still have the same clearance rate as departments that adopt the FBI process completely. And the harsh reality is that almost all of the cases that the FBI cites as having been "solved" through the application of BSU techniques were actually solved by ordinary detective work, informants and a liberal helping of plain good luck. It's typical of the FBI to race in at the kill and claim responsibility for the entire hunt. After all, they're Feds.

So psychiatry, this time on the enforcement side, once again presents a more persuasive picture than the facts support. Or at least, that's how it strikes me.

I admit I'm no more immune to error than any professional shrink or psychometrician.

It's just that nobody dies when I get it wrong.

NINETEEN

Bones and Runes

Every now and then, something very evil is taken alive and turned over to the shrinks for study.

And the shrinks get it wrong.

And somebody dies...

Here's an extract from some FBI Behavioral Science Studies conducted by Agents Robert Ressler and John E. Douglas, in cooperation with Ann Wolbert Burgess, a well-known authority on the subject of serial killers.

RAPE AND RAPE-MURDER:
ONE OFFENDER AND TWELVE VICTIMS*

This study analyzes data pertaining to 12 rapes and rape-murders committed by one male adolescent offender over a four-year period. All offenses except the first were committed...

[Get this, my friends...]

...while the offender was under psychiatric and probationary supervision...

...The offender's antisocial behavior was first recorded when he was age nine...He was sent to a state psychiatric facility following his first felony of rape and burglary at age 14. During his 18 month stay he received individual insight-oriented...

[Read Freudian-Jungian psychoanalysis]

...treatment and the discharge recommendation was that he live at home, attend public school, and continue psychotherapy on a weekly outpatient basis, with his mother actively involved in his treatment.

* *American Journal of Psychiatry*, 140: 1 (January, 1983).

Three weeks after returning home from the residential facility, he was charged with attempted armed robbery, an act intended to be rape.

[Great…just perfect…good work, Doc. I'm impressed.]

It took one year for him to come before a judge for sentencing on this charge…

[*Excellent!* At least we're consistent!]

…and in that time…

[Are you ready…?]

…he had committed his first rape and murder, but had not been charged for that offense. The disposition on the attempted armed robbery was probation and outpatient psychotherapy.

[Of course! If at first we don't succeed, try try again.]

He had served eight months of his probation when he was apprehended for the five murders. His psychiatric diagnoses according to the DSM-II…

[The Diagnostic and Statistical Manual, a big book that rinks have on their desks where they can look up what's rong with someone and find the correct label.]

…included adolescent adjustment reaction, character disorder without psychosis, and multiple personality. He was given 5 life sentences…After two years of incarceration, he admitted to six additional rapes for which he was never charged.

[By the way, I've seen some of the crime scene photos in this se. They look like a slaughterhouse floor.]

TABLE ONE:
ESCALATION OF CRIMINAL BEHAVIOR IN THIS CASE:

Age	Offence	Victim's Age	Sentence
12	theft		probation
12	mischief		probation
13	drive/no licence		stay of proceedings
14	rape & burglary	25	state psych. center
14	larceny		state psych. center
14	B and E		state psych. center
16	Rape	25	never charged
16	Rape	25	never charged
16	B and E Rape	17	never charged
17	Attempt Armed Rob	22	probation/therapy
18	Rape	25	never charged
18	Rape & Murder	24	Life in prison
19	Rape & Murder	22	Life in prison
19	Rape & Murder	34	Life in prison
19	Rape	25	never charged
19	Rape & Murder	27	Life in prison
19	Rape & Murder	24	Life in prison

I know I said that it was probably wrong to get into the gri
details of murders of this sort, but you need some idea of t
cost of this kind of psychiatric malfeasance to innocent livi
beings. I know the cost because I've seen it and walked throu;
it and paid to have it removed from my pant-cuffs. This kid w
one of the worst I've ever run into.

For example, in his own words:

She asked me how I wanted it and I started to think she was a
whore so while I was raping her I was thinking do I kill her
don't I because of what she was, a whore, and while I was
thinking that, trying to figure what I should do, she took off
running down the ravine. That's when I grabbed her. I had h
in an armlock. She was bigger than me. I started choking
her...she stumbled...we rolled down the hill and into the
water. I banged her head against the side of a rock and held
her head under water...

And again, another victim…

I go into the woods after, I see her run from behind a tree and
that's when I go after her. From then on I knew I had to kill
her. She trips over a log and that's when I catch up with her
and I just start stabbing her…

The victim was stabbed fourteen times. And with his next victim…

I was thinking, I've killed two, I might as well kill this one
too…something in me was wanting to kill…I told her to stop
trying to talk to me because when she talked I had to think
about her and I got soft…I tied her up with her stockings and
I started to walk away…then I heard her through the woods
kind of rolling around and making muffled sounds and I
turned back and said "No, I've got to kill her. I've got to do
this to preserve and protect myself…"

The woman died from twenty-one stab wounds to the left side
f her chest and her stomach.
And again…

We were walking along through the culverts underneath the
highway…that's when I pulled out the knife and without even
saying anything I stabbed her…maybe one hundred times.

Why did he do these things? In his own words…

And this woman judge she sent me to a diagnostic center.
That's what started me resenting authority…nobody could
tell me what to do or when to do it or how to do it…and the
killing, it was a real turn-on to realize that the women I raped
weren't reporting me so I knew they were scared and that was
a turn-on…The cops and the doctors, they were all assholes,
I was too slick for them, I could tell them anything, tell them
it was all my mother's fault or that I was angry at a judge or
something… anything to get them off my case…they were

all assholes who'd believe anything...

One of the most maddening things about this sorry exercise is that we're only reading about it now because the killer is *still being studied* by the same profession that didn't know what the hell to do with him in the first place.

One last comment from the file on this kid, from the panel of psychiatrists who reviewed this case later:

> ...rape and attempted rape behavior should be viewed as serious and chronic and thus repetitive. The interviewer should not assume that a patient with a history of sexual assault has committed it only the number of times for which he is charged. When the patient has been under stress and especially at times when he has been charged with other criminal acts (breaking and entering, stealing cars, larceny) the interviewer should *inquire* about concurrent assaultive behavior or rape fantasies...Groth and associates' study of convicted sex offenders...reported that each offender had committed an average of five sexual assaults for which he was never apprehended.

By the way, here's another place where we could spend som time thinking about the Ten Beef Rule. How many killers ju like this kid went the same route—in and out of state hospital into probation and therapy, conning the docs and the worker filling their nights with hideous brutality?

Hell, even I don't want to think about *that!*

There's a tremendous amount of theorizing about the root this kind of evil. It's rather like a vast plain, where many diff ent organizations have sunk wells or dug mines deep into t question. Depending on where in this terrain the well has be sunk or the shaft has been driven, the information that comes the surface is gathered up by the relevant inquiring agency made a part of whatever orthodoxy they adhere to. None of th seem to recognize that they have all cut into the same dark s stance, and that it has been with the planet for as long as life been with this planet. So they come up with various different names for it.

The clerics blame the subsiding of the sea of faith, and the loss of religious structure in modern life.

Feminists blame men.

Conservatives blame the liberals.

Liberals blame the fascists.

Citizens blame the politicians.

Sociology attributes evil to poverty, social deprivation, endemic transactional dysfunctions related to socio-economic theory, attitude dissonances and a fundamentally Marxist dialectic.

And Psychiatry, which has the highest pretensions to relevance in this arena, blames early abuse, or the Oedipal complex, or any one of fifty different explanations, all of which are mutually exclusive and antithetical.

Psychiatry uses jargon to complicate and isolate the inquiry, imagining that by labeling the various incarnations of evil they have somehow magically understood it. They use tests such as the Rorschach ink-blot test, the Thematic Apperception test, inventories such as the Minnesota Multi-Phasic Personality Inventory. They come up with classifications out of the Diagnostic and Statistical Manual, such as "dissociative reactions" or "fugue states," all of which are intriguing and suggestive, none of which deliver any predictive value whatsoever.

(The American Psychiatric Association has recommended that psychiatrists refuse to participate in legal procedures until the rules of evidence can be changed to allow them to express their diagnoses completely, and not just those portions which are of use to the defence or the prosecution.)

As an example of the primitive nature of psychiatric insight into deviant criminal behavior, a short excerpt from…

THE BEHAVIORAL TREATMENT OF RAPISTS AND CHILD MOLESTERS—(Behavioral Approaches to Crime and Delinquency, Plenum, 1987)

Vernon L. Quinsey, Terry C. Chaplin, Anne Maguire and Douglas Upfold.

…Modification of Inappropriate Arousal.

…At Oak Ridge, several forms of behaviorally oriented
laboratory treatment procedures are offered in order to modify
sexual arousal patterns, as manifested by changes in penile
circumference to inappropriate stimuli. Basically, the aim is
to lower patients' penile arousal to inappropriate stimuli…
…Four basic treatment procedures are used; biofeedback,
signaled punishment, olfactory aversion, and masturbatory
satiation. All treatment occurs in the sexual behavior
laboratory described previously.

Biofeedback is used with either auditory or visual stimuli…It
involves the illumination of lights inside the chamber that
informs the patient of the state of his arousal. In this
procedure a patient either views slides or listens to tapes
while his penile circumference is monitored. Plethysmograph
output is sent to a Schmitt Trigger (an analog-to-digital
converter) that illuminates lights when a certain preselected
criterion is surpassed…
…In the case of visual stimuli, several sets of slides are
generated from our pool. Each set consists of 10 slides of
adult females, and 10 slides representing each of the patient's
deviant categories as determined by the assessment. Audio
stimuli consist of six scenarios describing consenting
heterosexual activity and six scenarios describing
nonconsenting heterosexual activity (rape). Scenarios are
either chosen from the pool of previously recorded tapes or
are generated by the therapist with the aid of the patient to
reflect the relevant inappropriate fantasies.

In a treatment session, a patient views slides and/or listens to
tapes while his penile circumference is being monitored. If
penile circumference surpasses the preset criterion during
presentation of an appropriate stimulus, a blue light is
illuminated. Alternatively, if the criterion is exceeded during
presentation of a deviant sexual stimulus, a red light is
presented. A patient would normally participate in a series of
biofeedback sessions involving a different set of stimuli,
presented in a random order each day.

Signaled punishment uses the same stimuli and the red and blue lights as described above...a mildly painful (but harmless) electric shock, however, is associated with arousal to inappropriate stimuli. During the recording interval for a deviant stimulus, a brief shock is delivered via a probability generator at the end of 40% of the 5-second intervals in which the patient was above criterion (ie: the red light was on). These shocks are delivered via an arm band that is attached to the upper part of the patient's left arm. Shock intensity is determined by the patient before each session.

Olfactory aversion is similar to signaled punishment but, rather than using a shock, an aversive odor is associated with arousal to deviant stimuli...we have experimented with several noxious odors including those obtained from rotting meat, valeric acid, and ammonia. During a session, the patient is instructed that when the red light is illuminated, indicating that his penile circumference has surpassed the preset criterion during the presentation of an inappropriate stimulus, he is to inhale deeply from a squeeze bottle containing the odoriferous substance. The therapist can monitor the patient's behavior via a one-way mirror to ensure compliance with the instructions.

Masturbatory satiation is the final method of modifying sexual arousal that is used in our laboratory...unlike the preceding treatments, penile circumference is not monitored throughout this procedure. A patient is taken into the assessment chamber and is seated on the reclining chair. The therapist sits outside the chamber where he can see the patient through the one-way mirror and hear him via the intercom. The patient is instructed to masturbate while verbalizing a consenting (and age-appropriate) heterosexual fantasy until ejaculation. At this point the patient continues to masturbate but now verbalizes his deviant fantasies. The patient masturbates and fantasizes throughout a long series of hour-long sessions. The goal of the treatment is to satiate the patient with his inappropriate fantasies through their extensive rehearsal in a state of low sexual arousal...

About which the professionals had this to say...

RESEARCH REPORTS Vol VII No 1 March 1990

Psychopathy, Sexual Deviance, and Recidivism Among
  Released Sex Offenders

Mental Health Centre, Penetanguishene, Ontario

...In conclusion, the level of prediction attained in this study
was high enough to be helpful in the policy area but, as in
other prediction studies conducted by ourselves and
others...not high enough to reduce the false positives rate to a
level where one would be comfortable using the predictors
identified in this study to make longterm decisions for
individual offenders. In addition to their relation to risk of
recidivism, however, deviant sexual interests and degree of
psychopathy have, respectively, obvious treatment and
supervisory implications. Because of their theoretical
relevance, these variables are more helpful to policy-makers
than simple "tombstone" predictors. In the future, the key to
reducing sexual recidivism is likely to lie more in the areas of
developing more effective treatments and better supervisory
methods than in better prediction...

And in another Quinsey document...

...With respect to the treatment of rapists, there are,
unfortunately, no comparative evaluative studies of different
treatment types. Behavioral methods of treatment appear very
promising and antiandrogen treatment may be effective with
hypersexual rapists but there are no longterm followup data
relevant to either treatment method. Castration appears to be
related to low recidivism rates but is ethically problematic...

All of which seems to suggest that sitting one of these pigs
down in a chair, strapping a sensor around his pecker and showing him porno pictures while he sniffs a can of dead meat

be *interesting* and *diverting* and even fun to watch, but it sure as hell doesn't seem to have any real-world applications, other than keeping sex therapists and psychology researchers well-supplied with donuts and pocket change.

(By the way, at the end of this book I provide the complete text of this research report. You've got to read it; it's one of the most persuasive arguments I've ever seen for getting the psychiatrists out of the legal system entirely. It's a compendium of half-assed socio-mechanical Behaviorist thought-control, dim-witted parlor games and federally funded undergraduate arrogance, nearly beyond belief. Don't miss it!) The image of a therapist sitting in a room making notes and going Hmmmmmm while some pervert rubs his dingle to a slide show featuring pictures of little boys in garter-belts REALLY redlines my gag reflex. Putting "professionals" like these up against the kind of primeval horror that these criminals represent is like sending Clayton Ruby and Marlys Edwardh in to clean up the South Bronx. Perhaps I'm not alone in this...

The Province, 13 March 1992
TOWN BACKS RCMP ALERT
SEX OFFENDER WARNING GETS
CITIZEN SUPPORT
By Salim Jiwa
VANCOUVER, B.C.

The town of Creston is rallying behind its police force's decision to warn the public that a convicted sex offender on mandatory supervision has moved into the community.
RCMP ran into a barrage of criticism from civil libertarians and the Correctional Service of Canada after a warning bulletin was plastered around the town three weeks ago.
The Creston Child and Youth Committee, made up of RCMP and community groups, published the posters about convict Garry Noel Tilley, 48.
He was convicted of nine counts of contributing to juvenile delinquency in 1971 and convicted in 1988 of eight counts of sexual assault.

Tilley was serving a six-year sentence when released on
mandatory supervision in January.

He is now living in Boswell, near Creston.

"Those civil liberties people can stick it in their ear," said
Creston Mayor Lela Irvine yesterday. "…Tough shit."

…John Westwood, executive director of the BC Civil Liberties
Association, said he met RCMP brass in Vancouver to
express his concern.

"The fact a man was convicted, no matter how bad an
offence…he doesn't automatically lose all rights to privacy,"
said Westwood.

Really, John?

I hope you can hold on to that noble detachment if Garry Noel
Tilley decides to drop by YOUR house and party with YOUR
kids. I have a feeling no one would be howling louder for blood
and ruin than John Westwood, Executive Director of the British
Columbia Civil Liberties Association. This rigidity of thinking
arises from a kind of intellectual Pavlovian response whenever
someone says the word "rights." Civilized societies have been
making discriminatory judgements about rights for centuries. For
example, the right to defend your home and your children has
been rather severely hampered by the legal prohibition against
being adequately armed to do so with some degree of assurance.

It seems that the civil liberties that Westwood and his ilk are
trying to defend are not those of the innocent general population.
They can argue this until their veins pop, but as long as they
cling to a principle in the face of any consequence for society
they will be seen as nothing better than puffed-up fools and dim-
witted ideologues.

And nowhere in any of this undergrowth have we seen a
insight that enables us to do something about evil. And my contention is that we don't know what to do about it because we
have no clear idea what the hell it is. All we know is that whenever we cut into the psychic terrain of humanity, in drug-dealers
or Young Offenders, in B and E specialists or armed robbers,
abusive husbands and tyrannical wives, we find it, and sometimes, in killers, we find it very close to the surface.

I've given the matter a lot of thought, as you may have gathered by now. I've seen far too much of it, and I've spent a hell of a lot of very long, very empty nights staring into a glass and trying not to think about what I have just driven away from.

It won't come as a surprise to you to find out that I have my own view of evil. Nor will it amaze you that I'm about to tell what I have come to believe about it.

TWENTY

Dante's View

On the basic issue of evil, I offer the following, and final, narrative.

A few weeks ago I was sitting in my office, staring at the computer screen with a head full of ozone and sparks, when I got a call from Rick Crook, a Major Crimes detective down at Vancouver Police Headquarters. Crook's message was brief and to the point.

"Stroud, I'm down here at Powell and Salisbury. I think you need to be here."

It was a Monday morning. The city was grey and cold. When I got down to Powell and Salisbury, the yellow ribbons were already up and the local print and television media were all over the place.

It was the dock area, down by the tracks, under the shadow of a row of grain silos. Across the tracks an old factory blocked the view of the water. I could see men standing out on the roof high above us, watching the little cluster of uniformed cops and the detectives in suits and trench-coats.

Next to a low blue-and-red building, beside a loading dock, shape lay in the mud, under a brown woolen blanket.

I stepped through the media cordon and slipped under the crime-scene ribbon, looking for Crook and his partner, A Cattley. I saw them in a conference with Staff Sergeant Ra Biddlecombe, the Commanding Officer of the Vancouve Homicide Unit, and a couple of RCMP investigators. I staye clear of that. I walked over to the site and looked down at t shape under the blanket.

I saw a pair of hands just visible at the edge of the blank already bagged in brown paper. A few bloodstains were visib soaking into the mud. There were thousands of wheat grai imbedded in the mud, and tire tracks. White cards with numbe on them had been placed around tiny bits of debris, scuff mar drag marks, a coffee cup.

It was a woman, I supposed, from the feet. They were sm

and neat and naked. It was a saddening sight. It made her seem so vulnerable, lying on the cold ground, covered with a dirty blanket, her bare feet uncovered. A detail like that brings it home hard. You don't get used to it.

I waited around for Crook and Cattley to get free. While I waited, I watched the media people and the crowd around the outside of the crime ribbon. I saw the same look on each and every face—an avid, stunned curiosity. Nobody seemed to be having a good time, but nobody was leaving either.

I stayed away from the media. I was wearing a suit and a trenchcoat. If they found out I was just another journalist, there'd be some strong pressure to either let them in or to throw me out. After a while, Crook and Cattley walked over.

Rick Crook is one of the city's better cops, and a nice illustration of the kind of cop that we get these days. A solid man with a thin mustache and wary brown eyes, he has a wry and cynical manner but misses nothing. Like all homicide professionals, he's quiet, careful, polite and direct. He knows as much law as any defence counsel and as much about the human body as most pathologists. What he knows beyond that is what every good cop knows about the human heart, but he doesn't let it show.

Cattley is a big, hard-faced blond from England, another professional, but different from his partner, maybe a little more outspoken about criminals and perhaps a little angrier than Crook about the justice system. He gives the impression of reserved aggression, a kind of balanced tension between his sense of humor—which is strange—and his controlled anger at the things he has seen, at the things he has had to investigate, at the kind of people he runs into every day.

Crook filled me in briefly.

A young Native female had been sexually mutilated. There was considerable blunt trauma to the skull. She'd been dumped early that morning. They were talking to possible witnesses. The crime-scene technicians were building a blackout tent down the street. When it was ready, they'd truck it up here, uncover the body and start taking some photographs. Stay away from the press and they'd keep me informed.

While he was talking to me, I was thinking about Charles Ng, about the Green River Killer and all the other killers we have all been studying and thinking about for years.

I thought about them for a long time, all through the arrival of the crime-scene technicians, the removal of the body, through the press conference downtown at police headquarters, thought about it while I sat in a chair in the squad room and watched Crook and Cattley go through the information.

What I thought was, *It's never going to end, is it?*

Late in the afternoon, a railway cop came in with some interesting information. He'd been on patrol around the Powell and Salisbury area early the same morning, say 5:00 a.m. He was in a uniform car, cruising the blocks, trying to keep the hookers and the johns on the move. He'd turned the corner onto Salisbury and saw a dark-blue van parked beside the dock, right down by the tracks. Figuring that some john was getting his money's worth, he stopped the cruiser and got out.

As he was walking towards the van, he saw some movement in the front seat. Then the engine started and the van pulled away, tires spinning in the mud and the grains.

He turned back and ran for his cruiser, fired it up and went off in pursuit, hard on the van's tailgate, heading up towards East Hastings.

It was winter, a long, dark night. He had never looked for anything beside the van, on the ground. Why would he?

He chased the van up Salisbury. The van ran the lights. He lost it. Well, he figured, it was just some john, and all he really wanted to do was chase the johns off, so what the hell. He went off shift a little while later, went home, went to bed. It wasn' until he woke up that he heard the news.

He came right down, feeling a little stupid, sorry about losing the van.

He had done one thing, however.

He had gotten the plate number.

The plate number came back with a registered owner by the name of Brian Allender, with an address of 2831 East Broadway in Vancouver. Allender had no record of sexual violence. Record came up with a picture of him: a beefy, red-haired man with broad, slightly chubby face, very ordinary, just another citizen.

Crook sent the VPD Strike Force out to establish surveillance at 2831 East Broadway. It was a small, neat bungalow on a long block of small, neat bungalows. Strike Force sent a car around the back and down the access lane. They found the blue van parked behind 2831. The plates were off.

The windows of the van were heavily tinted; it was impossible to see inside. The house looked occupied. A trike stood on the back porch. Lights were on.

Strike Force took a look at the van. The tires were muddy.

Imbedded in the mud and the treads were hundreds of grains of wheat.

Back at the squad room, things went promptly into overdrive. I found a seat away from the action and looked for a time at the picture of Brian Allender. He was in every way unremarkable.

I found this depressing.

Later that evening, Crook and Cattley and I drove over to the parking lot of Vancouver General Hospital. Knowing what was coming, I turned down Cattley's offer of a bite from his sandwich.

We walked through a slow, soft rain towards the ground-floor elevator entrance that leads to the pathologist's office and the morgue. Carm Zenone, a fine-featured and good-humored Italian man who was one of the pathology assistants, was outside having a smoke, leaning back in a metal chair and watching the rain.

He offered me a smoke, a Winston, and although I quit smoking a few years back, I accepted one. Crook and Cattley and anone and I went up in the elevator. As soon as the door opened I was back in the South Bronx, smelling what all morgues have to offer. I drew in on the Winston and walked along with the others past the metal lockers where the bodies are stored and into the bright, spacious autopsy room. The victim wasn't laid out yet. She was still in a purple bag on a gurney in corner.

I was introduced to Dr. Laurel Gray, lean and attractive, with the auburn hair and a direct, amused manner. Crook and Cattley ted casual business with her while we all climbed into our gical robes and plastic booties.

And, eventually, the victim was wheeled over, taken from her wrappings and covering and laid on her back on the stainless-steel table. A wooden block was placed under her head.

Gray and Crook and Cattley gathered around her. Gray switched on an overhead light and the victim—we didn't know her name at this point—was suddenly and terribly revealed.

Up until this time, my only look at her had been inside the black-plastic crime-scene tent. That had been difficult.

This was more difficult.

Now, I intend to keep my promise. I'm not going to get into the grim details, other than to say that I have seen about 150 murdered humans and this was one of the worst. I know this will bring pain to her family, if any more pain can be imagined, but I need to make a point here, about evil and how I have come to see it.

Crook and Gray and Zenone and Cattley stood for a while in silence, looking at the young woman's body. I stood back a few feet, watching them.

For a little time, they had nothing to say. No grim jokes. No cynical comments. No professional commentary. For a few seconds, they were just four good people, staring into the pit.

They looked suddenly old, and tired. The hard white light bleached all the color from the scene. Their eyes were bleak and their shoulders bent. Cattley looked over at me for a moment and I could see something very hard in his face—a kind of anger, perhaps hatred, but banked down and bottled up and under tight control. Crook's face was solemn, compassionate, even gentle. Gray and Zenone seemed momentarily stunned.

Finally Gray shook her head slightly and something changed in all of them. Zenone went to get some water to bathe the woman. I watched him sponge her and wipe the mud from her face.

She looked very young, very calm, at peace. Head slightly raised, her eyes closed, she seemed to dream over the ruin of her body. I looked down at what had been done to her.

I felt many things then, most of them familiar.

And something new.

I thought this was *hard* to do. What was done here was work, something that took effort and a kind of brutish dedication. The had been spent, and a twisted sort of logic was in play. This was a work of hands, something to which some thought and planning had been given. The man who had committed this obscenity was no animal, tearing at prey, reckless and savage.

This was a kind of intelligence.

I have seen many killings, and some of them are obviously the work of psychotics in some terrible ecstatic convulsion of violence. The FBI calls them "disorganized killers." You can think of them as animal killers, although few animals kill for sheer destructive joy. But this one...I knew this for what it was. I had seen it before, many, many times.

This was true evil.

True evil because a decision to do harm had been made, in a cold mind, under a pale winter sky, with a clear intention, with a plan, steps taken, equipment ordered, a site chosen, a class of victim identified, cover stories worked out, evasive maneuvers considered. Choices made.

And the plan had been carried out.

Executed.

And like all plans, it had been composed of a hundred different decisions. And each decision was contributory, part of the design, a step along the way. And the destination had been visualized, imagined, fantasized, but coldly, with a careful, incremental logic in place.

And I knew then what evil was.

Clearly, the object here was power, dominance, even hatred.

But the means were purely rational, a consequence of a prolonged period of reflection and contemplation.

Each day, in some small way, this killer had done what was needed, had foresworn his heart, had betrayed his humanity, had constructed a cold room in which to grow his chilly fantasies away from the light of reason. And it may have been that, in the beginning, he did not fully understand where he had decided to . But somewhere along the road, as he came up a long slope and reached a kind of crest, he could see it. He knew it was re, waiting for him.

That's the moment!

That's where evil is.

It comes when you stand in the middle of your passage, far enough from your beginning to have left yourself behind, not yet at the end of your intentions, but at the midway point. You have as far to go as you have to return. Everything trembles in the balance.

And you consider, for a moment or a year or an hour.

And your foot lifts and you set it down again, but farther down the road. At that point, everything that was merely possible becomes probable, and in a little while, it becomes inevitable.

That's what evil is.

The rest is bookkeeping.

It was 3:00 the following afternoon. I waited in my car, watching the front door of the bungalow at 2831 East Broadway. It was a clear, sunny day, the first breath of an early spring in the soft blue sky. The trees stood bare and brown, skeletal against the cropped lawns and tidy porches. Men were positioned at each side of the house, at the rear, by the front door.

One large man in a jacket and jeans stood away from the front door, hesitated and then lunged forward, striking the door with his heavy boot. It flew open, and the Strike Force men rushed in with Crook and Cattley, Ray Biddlecombe, the rest of the squad.

When they took him, the man was not surprised. After all, he had seen this moment in the distance, a very long time ago.

But he was very tired, because the road was very long, and he had walked its full distance, step by single step.

TWENTY-ONE

The Sheep Get a Word In

Since then, at an uncertain hour,
That agony returns,
And till my ghastly tale is told,
This heart within me burns.
— Samuel Taylor Coleridge,
The Rime of the Ancient Mariner

Well, it strikes me that I have been tiresome, and have held you from your supper. If you'll give me a few moments more, I'll try to make some sense out of this...extraordinary outburst!

Last things first: if I am in any way correct about the incremental nature of evil, if it is true that someone can quite literally wander away from the path of reason by a sequence of intentional steps—and I think it is—then it follows that our society should be very clear about what it considers to be right and what is wrong.

This is not what we are doing. I have spent the majority of this book trying to illustrate that fact.

We've looked at the Charles Ng case and the deliberation of our Supreme Court concerning him. What inferences can we make from that case?

I think there are two...

First of all, no matter what you are accused of, the Supreme Court will go to any lengths to safeguard your legal rights. This may sound just fine, but in the Ng case, the Supreme Court was also dictating to a foreign and sovereign nation what *they* could or couldn't do.

They have no business doing so, and certainly no business doing it on my time and with my tax dollar.

No one but a lawyer would see anything wrong with sending a cockroach like Charles Ng back to judgement by the first available flight. Although the arguments were intricate and the deliberations very fine, the issue was profoundly vulgar and useless, and any system that assigns so much time and cash and spiritual force to a pursuit that is basically vile and against the clear and expressed wishes of the people has no reason to exist.

The second inference that a careful observer might draw from the Charles Ng case is that despite our protestations to the contrary, the law exists for only one practical reason, and that is to protect the accused.

Okay, I can accept that.

On one condition.

I'm a law-abiding, tax-paying citizen. I give you permission to go on about this business of Due Process in my name, provided that the results are the results you originally promised me.

Specifically, that the rule of law will make all things civilized possible, including life, liberty and security of the person. That's fair; those were the reasons you talked me into this in the first place, the arguments you used to get me to put my sword down and stop engaging in duels and vendettas, to forego personal vengeance.

But as soon as that changes—and it's looking pretty dicey right now—then, in the vernacular, it's time to get out of my face. All bets are off. *Hasta luego, compadres.*

And if you're sitting on your padded leather bench and thinking, well, hey, the hell with HIM, it's too late now, we've got him under control, look up towards the back of your courtroom over the bowed and cowed, to the back wall, where these words have been spray-painted:

IN OPPIDO LUSOR SOLUS NONE ES
(Roughly, "You're Not the Only Game in Town.")

And don't think of it as a threat. It's more of a polite reminder.

On the theme of moral guidance and example, arguments such as Diminished Capacity, the insanity defence and other psychoforensic constructions contribute in every way to a generalized and quite logical inference: if I can cite an antecedent cause that predates my birth, or is at least beyond my own control, then no matter what I have done, I must be considered guiltless, and must not be punished.

I have no doubt that there are instances when this may be a valid argument, may in fact be as good an explanation for what was done as anything else we can propose. But in general, society needs to accept the fact that allowing such an exculpatory argument to stand in a court of law does extensive damage to the broader social consensus as to what is evil and what is merely unfortunate.

We need to rearrange our priorities here.

Compassion and charity require us to deal gently with people whose aggressions are the product of organic neurological convulsions, no matter how prolonged. You do not punish a child whose reflexive action has resulted in a boot to your kneecap. A sneeze is not an assault.

But in crimes where there has been a clear and sustained series of conscious steps taken, no matter how minor, that have resulted in a violent act, then the first requirement of the justice system ought to be to censure that as firmly as possible.

I was never convinced by John Hinckley's insanity defence. You can see in all his letters and in the map of his travels a willful refusal to accept the burden of being an adult. He was feckless, puerile, alternately sullen and grossly expansive. He consistently refused every attempt to help him. He set out on a dimwitted and vulgar campaign to achieve a stupidly adolescent goal by means that were, even to him, so transparently asinine that he denied any responsibility for them after the fact.

And, on another day, another court declared Jeffrey Dahmer to be perfectly sane.

Obviously, there's something quite wrong here, and until we get better maps of Hell, we ought to confine ourselves to defining Heaven in such a way as to promote moral and ethical behavior. In other words, unless there's a clear and demonstrative organic reason for violent behavior, scrap the insanity defence entirely. Limit the trial to a simple question:

Did the body in the dock do the deed?

If the facts are incontrovertible, then convict the body.

If the lawyers representing the body wish to present mitigating evidence regarding the provocation or the contents of his all, let them do so at a sentencing hearing, held to determine the potential threat of the convicted aggressor.

If the needs of society, especially the need to reinforce the idea and the practice of polite and honest behavior for all citizens, do not interfere, then a sentence or a direction should be imposed that fits the case. And once imposed, it should be carried out without variance or subsequent dispute.

At this hearing, by the way, psychiatrists would be free to diagnose freely and at length, to discuss and debate fully, free from the arbitrary and distorting rules of the adversarial system. It's what they wanted, isn't it?

Psychiatry has shown itself to be entirely incompatible with legal process. Everybody knows it. The only reason it's in the courts at all is that it provides lawyers with manipulative devices that help them win cases.

That's all.

So ban it.

You will have realized that I have a problem with the Young Offenders Act. I have either made my case or failed to make it. I just want to reinforce one fundamental point about the "diversionary treatments" that are mandated by the Young Offender Act, that are, in fact, the very reason for the existence of the Act.

We do not know if diversion is effective because there's no way to force the Young Offender to cooperate with it. Regardless of what the people running it tell you, I have seen it fail a thousand times. Once the Young Offender figures out the ropes with the help of his attorney and other Young Offenders, he can duck any court-mandated diversionary treatment with impunity. He just won't show up.

So, after a long delay composed of the sum total of the incompetence of each person and each agency involved, there will be a direction to a police officer to go out and find the Young Offender and bring him back before the court.

We have seen how difficult that is, but let's say it happens.

The Young Offender will have his lawyer there.

The judge will be stern, but the YOA must be liberally construed.

And custody is not an option.

So there's not a damn thing the judge can do to force the kid to do what he's told.

And the kid knows it.

So he makes whatever promises and remorseful declarations that he thinks the court will swallow, he puts on a solemn face, and when he's out in the hall with his buddies, he'll shoot the cop a finger, laugh and hit the streets with his pack.

This result is built into the YOA.

The officials will deny it, of course. They have to.

They'll say, well, if the cops would only do their jobs, catch these brats, things would be different.

And it's true that some of the cops I've known will go out of their way to avoid having anything to do with a Young Offender. Who can blame them? Certainly not I. Certainly not anyone who has seen how *pointless* it is to catch one, bring him in, go through all the paperwork and the extra bullshit, only to see nothing at all happen. It's a total waste of time, and the little rats smell bad, and they're mouthy, and they know every twisting turn of the YOA, and by the time you've done the paperwork, they'll have been back on the street for hours. Now this truth is obvious to anyone who has ever had any dealings with the YOA. It's a profoundly stupid piece of legislation and it ought to be scrapped entirely.

Suspend it pending an overhaul. In the meantime, treat any kid older than twelve like an adult offender.

I guarantee you, you'll have their full attention.

Regarding prisons…criminals are not afraid of prisons because *they run them*. In prison, they can deal drugs, shank their enemies, butt-fuck the youngsters, pump iron, make phone calls, read the law books, discuss the latest advances in armed robberies or B and Es, find out who's planning what, meet old buddies, make new friends and generally have a hell of a time until they have served one-third of their so-called sentence, at which point, they're *free!*

This is neither correction nor deterrent.

So take back the prisons.

Run them like the Marines run Leavenworth. Your ass is run

by the book, you don't talk, you keep yourself in order and God help you if you don't.

There's no parole, no shanking the stoolies, no sodomy in the showers, no day pass, no Temporary Absence, no Compassionate Leave, no conjugal visits. You don't vote. You don't fight. You don't get out of your cell unless you behave.

It's no fun at all.

Now a lot of corrections officials will object to this. They'll say that unless you can offer a prisoner some motive for good behavior, some reason to cooperate with prison programs and institutional rules, he'll suffer a catastrophic loss of hope and become troublesome. Unless we bribe him with Early Release or Temporary Absence Passes or Mandatory Supervision or Conjugal Visits, he'll lose self-esteem and start to create problems for the guards and the staff.

So give him the following motivation:

Give him no freedoms whatsoever. Run his ass from dawn to midnight, under strict guard and unceasing supervision, with no free time, no weight-rooms, no law libraries, no ball park, no swimming pool, no fun at all. Run the prisons the way they run them in Singapore—clean, quiet, safe, orderly *and hard as steel*.

I guarantee you, you'll get a lot fewer convicts back for a second or a third stay. Right now, we have a 60 percent recidivist rate. That'll stop.

And the ones who are in will have one very powerful motivation to cooperate: if they don't, their sentence is extended for every infraction.

What this is is a lesson in something called "the Majesty of the Law." By the time prisoners get out of places like this, they never want to go back. They have a recidivist rate that is hardly visible on the scale.

What the hell. If we have to pay for the damned prisons, then maybe we should get to run them.

On the subject of capital punishment:

While I agree that the one demonstrable and inescapable result of an execution is that the guy will never commit another crime, I'm still against it.

Not for any reason of compassion, or because I think the S

suffers morally from the act. States and nations quite often sanction killings. They call them wars, and the best killers get medals, and the thanks of the regiment, and make the cover of *People*.

No, I'd forbid capital punishment because in no way has the justice system shown one-tenth of the efficiency, the consistency and the simple good judgement to deserve a power such as this. If the justice system behaves properly for, say, twenty years, then I'll reconsider it, as long as they ask me nicely.

Until then, forget it. The justice system has no more right to the power of death than a toddler has to the car keys.

Well, that brings up prison overcrowding. If we follow these suggestions, there'll be no room for all the new prisoners, and all the prisoners who will have to serve all of their sentences.

True.

So stop jailing for white-collar crime.

Jail for violence and chronic drug-dealing.

Jail for violence because violence is the common denominator of almost all serious crime, and therefore it's the kind of behavior we need to step on very hard.

Jail for drug-dealing because, more than any other criminal enterprise, drug-dealing creates crime and supports criminal behavior.

As for Fraud and Fiduciary Malfeasance and the thousand other crimes that cost us all more money than blood, make those criminals live at home, wearing electronic collars, going to a day job, paying their own rent, paying taxes, even paying off the people they defrauded or otherwise deceived.

Don't even jail for B and Es. Make the kid pay for everything he stole by working it off. If he defaults or evades, he goes to a workfarm under guard, where he can continue to work—for a lot less—until he has paid off his debt to the people he hurt.

But if a kid is violent, or uses a weapon, or threatens, or commits any kind of aggressive act, then he goes to jail.

First time, a year.

Second time, twice that.

Third time, five times that, or ten years.

No parole, hard, clean time, no time off, no nothing.

Very simple and straightforward.

I'm sure there'll be lots of reasons that we can't do this, but what I would like to hear are reasons that we *shouldn't*.

And I'm sure that if I *do* hear it, it'll be a judge saying it. About the judges…I'm confused as to why the rights of an accused under the Charter are somehow more important than the rights of an un-accused citizen to "life, liberty, security of the person and enjoyment of property." It seems to me that society suffers far more damage from the ruination of these freedoms than it would if the rights of an accused were regularly disregarded. For one thing, there are a hell of a lot fewer accused people than there are un-accused people.

We make discretionary judgements about rights and freedoms all the time. While I am persuaded that Due Process is, by and large, a good thing, I am not persuaded that what the judges are doing is anything but contributory negligence leading to the erosion of our freedoms under the Bill of Rights.

I may have promised you that I'd stop dragging out examples of this, but, dammit, the Supreme Court is just so busy it's hard to resist.

Just one more. It's called *Stinchcombe*.

Stinchcombe was handed down on November 7, 1991, the judgement rendered by the Honorable Mr. Justice Sopinka, a man who made his mark—so to speak—as a defence lawyer. I think his reasons for judgement in the matter of William H. Stinchcombe are a very powerful illustration of my argument that judges are only human, that they carry the prejudices of their private labors into public office, and that, sometimes, they need to be brought to heel before they pass bad laws and cause intolerable harm in the justice system.

It starts out simply enough. A Calgary lawyer named William Stinchcombe was alleged to have misappropriated some financial instruments from a client by the name of Jack Abrams. He was charged with thirteen counts of criminal breach of trust, thirteen counts of theft and one count of fraud.

The Crown argued that Stinchcombe had in effect stolen

property held in trust for Abrams. The defence didn't deny that Stinchcombe got the money for the property, but it was their contention that Abrams had altered the client-trustee relationship and made Stinchcombe his business partner, and Stinchcombe had, as Abrams's partner and not his trustee, acted legally and was not guilty of breach of trust.

So far so good.

At the preliminary inquiry, Stinchcombe's secretary, Patricia Lineham, gave some evidence that favored the defence. Exactly what she said nobody seems to have recorded.

After the preliminary, Lineham was interviewed by an RCMP officer, who taped her statement.

In line with the disclosure rules, the Crown notified the defence that the taped statement had been taken, but Crown did not say what was in the statement because Crown had decided that Lineham was a not a credible witness and had therefore decided against calling her as a witness in the actual trial.

Crown was acting on the assumption that disclosure rules required Crown to reveal only those elements that will be used against the accused in the actual trial.

Defence saw it differently.

Defence tried to get the trial judge to force the Crown to reveal what was said in this taped statement.

The trial judge, acting in keeping with established disclosure rules, dismissed the application.

The trial proceeded, and the accused was convicted on all twenty-seven counts. Defence appealed, arguing a breach of the disclosure law.

And, in the fullness of time, the appeal reached the Supreme Court, where Mr. Justice Sopinka got his teeth into it.

In his judgement, Sopinka quoted Justice Rand in *Boucher v. the Queen* (1955 SCR 16):

It cannot be overemphasized that the purpose of a criminal
    prosecution is not to obtain a conviction, it is to lay before a
    jury what the Crown considers to be credible evidence
    relevant to what is alleged to be a crime. Counsel have a duty
    to see that all available legal proof of the facts is presented; it

should be done firmly and pressed to its legitimate strength but it must also be done fairly. The role of the prosecutor excludes any notion of winning or losing; his function is a matter of public duty than which in civil life there can be none charged with greater personal responsibility. It is to be efficiently performed with an ingrained sense of the dignity, the seriousness and the justness of judicial proceedings.

At least, on *his* side of the room. The defence is not required to disclose a damned thing and can actually play any silly-ass game it wants to, including demanding all sorts of nuisance disclosures and rooting about in the Crown's briefcase for whatever it thinks will be troublesome. The prosecution, already placed at a considerable disadvantage by the Charter restrictions on admissible evidence, on Reasonable Search, not to mention the burden of proof, must now contend with a fractious and unpredictable defence-driven disclosure process that allows innumerable delays and enables the defence to ransack an entire investigation and expose witnesses to the possibility of harassment at the hands of accused persons who might be free on bail pending the actual trial.

And Sopinka agreed.

As a matter of fact, he went even further than any previous judge in extending the disclosure rights of the defence to include the identity of informers, the names of anonymous witnesses who might be at risk by their exposure and, in all practical terms, a free ride through any and every element of the investigation at any stage.

Sopinka would argue that he created and defined solid parameters, but our own experience has shown us that any sweeping change in the rules will always have far-reaching and totally unforeseen consequences.

Sopinka just made it about a hundred times harder to informers to come forward with evidence about a crime, because he took away the Crown's right to protect him from exposure during the disclosure process.

Now, most informers are not coming forward out of the goodness of their hearts and a sense of civic duty. Most informers criminals themselves, who have cut a deal with the cops in exchange for information leading to the arrest of some person more dangerous than they.

That's not pretty, but it's how almost all serious crime investigations are solved.

Discourage police informants and you severely, perhaps fatally, handicap the ability of the police to actually solve crimes.

Sopinka, being a former defence lawyer, knows that very well.

Now why in the name of God would a sworn representative of the State want to go so far out of his way to further cripple the prosecutorial function? Could it be that Sopinka is aiming for the judgement of history, in the tradition of Oliver Wendell Holmes and Learned Hand? Might it be possible that Sopinka seeks "the bubble reputation" by ramming the rest of us into the cannon's mouth?* Or is he just so damned impressed by his heroic stand against a fascist police state that he has forgotten his blood oaths and promises, one of which was a promise to uphold and safeguard all the laws of the land and not just those that appealed to the knee-jerk liberal in him?

Sopinka *desperately* needs to reconnect with the real world!

But that didn't stop him from kneeing the Crown in the nuts.

He was, after all, taking the high ground.

The same high ground they took in *Askov,* in *Duarte* and *Vong,* and in the *Ng* and *Kindler* decisions.

And if a few informers in, say, drug cases, get their throats cut and their tongues pulled out through the slit, well, that's the price we all pay for Liberty, Freedom and nine chauffeur-driven overprivileged and well-protected aging lawyers in black dresses.

This is not right.

How to fix this?

As I said, any judge who shows a sustained and prolonged reckless disregard for the actions of people he sets free on charter technicalities ought to be held morally and legally culpable. He ought to be abruptly and unceremoniously *canned.*

...then a soldier,/Full of strange oaths and bearded like the pard,/Jealous of honour, sudden and quick in quarrel,/Seeking the bubble reputation/Even in the cannon's mouth..." William Shakespeare, *As You Like It* (II, vii, 150–54).

For that matter, judges should also be declared vulnerable to a lawsuit in civil court, for damages and punitive costs, if someone freed under an insubstantial and capricious Charter technicality then commits an assault or a serious crime.

In other words, if a judge screws up a case for no good reason, sue the bastard.

For that matter, we should be able to sue any public official who, by negligence or incompetence, contributes to the release of a criminal who then re-offends in some heartbreaking way. Judges, parole board members, corrections officials, prison psychiatrists, prison guards—anyone in the causal chain.

Even the lawyer who got the guy off.

Finally...we ought to close the law schools for at least fifteen years. We have too many lawyers. Two-thirds of the world's lawyers work in the United States and Canada. Somebody tel these guys, you can't *sue* a nation to greatness.

If you're a young student considering a career, choose teaching, or medicine. Even social work. But for Christ's sake, don' be a lawyer.

We need more lawyers like we need more three-eyed carp i the drinking water. Much as I hate to quote him, Lee Iacocc had a point when he observed that the Japanese have only on lawyer for every ten thousand people, while we in Nor America have one for about every three hundred people. Th more lawyers a nation has, the more work these lawyers w generate. It is the business of lawyers to divide and double-bi Lawyers create laws and then make their profit from confou ing them. What they do is inherently reductive, parasitic, di sive. And far too many of them are ending up running the cou try, or sitting on the Supreme Court.

For that matter, maybe it would be a good idea to appoint f mer cops with law degrees to the Supreme Court, just for balance. I'm not convinced that letting lawyers and forr lawyers occupy all the positions of power in the House and Supreme Court is doing anything good for Canada. We being crushed by the spiritual deadweight of lawyers, mos whom stand for nothing but a good argument, a two-mar lunch and an itemized bill sixteen pages long. Let's run the bastards out of Ottawa.

Of course, this is not going to happen. Lawyers won't let it.

So compel all lawyers and judges working in the justice system to serve three shifts a month as reserve police officers or jail attendants. If they refuse, bar them from the court.

It would be a reality-check they DESPERATELY need.

I realize that Due Process is important. But so is the right of the people to move freely and without fear in the streets and the parks.

Important too are the rights of the victims of crime to some sense that they matter, that their nation values them and shares their horror, their shame, their grief.

We need to find a balance in this country—in all countries where Due Process and individual rights are valued—a balance between rights and reason, between the rights of the individual and the rights of all individuals.

We have not found that balance. And all of us are left standing at the edge of a long drop, struggling against a kind of vertigo that can and will ruin this nation. Justice is not the preserve and domain of lawyers, and their intuitions about the law are no more likely to be correct than are the intuitions and conclusions of any thoughtful citizen. There is no mystery here, hidden in the labyrinthine syntax of legal writing. These are eternal verities, and they can be phrased in simple and compelling language. I quoted Marcus Aurelius at the beginning of this book:

> Waste no more time
> arguing what a good man should be.
> Be one.

The truth is there for anyone to discern.

The problem is not with what's written on the page.

The problem is there's a lawyer standing in your light.

And one final comment…to all the victims of crime.

I regret what has been done to you, not only by the criminal, but by the justice system, which operates in my name, and which I have tolerated for far too long. For that, from my heart, I truly sorry.

Resolutions

Since the publication of the hardcover version of this book in April 1993, Canadian criminals have been busier than ever, and the Canadian justice system has been scrambling to keep up with them. In the late summer of that year, the Ontario government released a report from their statistics department, triumphantly announcing a three or four percent decrease in violent crime in the city of Toronto. Assorted critics of the police and various rabid critics of this book jumped onto the public stage to back up the report, including the University of Toronto criminologist Anthony Doob, whose choleric review of *Contempt of Court,* in *The Toronto Star* blistered the book pages and depressed my mother for hours. So there! Crime rates *are* falling, just as we said. Look at the figures!

Now it has been a long-standing contention of mine that all stats are suspect, and in particular stats that seem to show that your government really does know what it's doing. Chief McCormack of the Metro Toronto Police Department, who was in Halifax at the time at the Chiefs' convention, fired back a letter saying that the government stats were in error, and that his departmental figures showed an increase in the rate of violent crime in the Toronto area.

Doob and his cronies dismissed the Chief's comments as self-serving—related to a bid for more money—and went on to dismiss as semi-hysterical anyone who had an opinion about the numbers that they didn't like. Which made it all the more sweet when about three days later, the same government office issued a retraction, admitting that their figures were in error and that the Chief's statement about an increase in crime was correct. Doob and the rest of the bureaucratic experts were inexplicably silent on that development, but most of the ordinary citizens of the town enjoyed a transitory moment of satisfaction when their own observations of street crime were, for once, confirmed official sources.

In another development, the case of Brian Allender—cited this book in the chapter "Dante's View"—finally arrived in fi of British Columbia Supreme Court Justice Thomas Braidwood. It was in September, and the case drew a lot of local attention. The victim, Cheryl Joe, had been a member of the First Nations, and part of a large band of friends and family centered in the town of Sechelt, on the BC coast. The accused, Allender, was a hockey coach and a minor community leader, with a wife of fourteen years and a thirteen-year-old son who played on one of his teams.

The trial was an illustration of everything that's wrong—and a few things that are right—about the justice system. Allender's lawyer, Larry Myers, offered no argument to the fact of the killing, officially admitting that Allender was the man who bludgeoned Cheryl Joe to death—with a propane tank—and who waited for her to die so he could remove her external sexual organs with a saw and a Swiss Army knife.

What he did want to contest was the issue of *mens rea* and Allender's ability to "formulate intent," terms that we have examined in great detail in the body of this book, pesky considerations of the great intangibles of life that have proved extremely difficult to pin down in the adversarial arena of modern courts. It was the aim of the defence to create in the minds of the jury a reasonable doubt about the contents of Allender's heart— that Allender's brutal assault on an innocent young woman was the result of, primarily, his consumption a few hours before of a bottle of hundred-proof Jamaican rum, and also the result of some long-standing psychological problems arising from his ambiguous relationship with a possessive mother. If the Defense could make a case for these arguments, then the only charge Allender would have to answer to was Manslaughter, a crime that sometimes results in very minor penalties.

Now the Crown had to prove—again beyond a Reasonable Doubt—that Allender had intended the death of Cheryl Joe and had caused it by a reckless and criminal disregard of the consequences of his actions. In Canada, the defense of drunkenness is only "mitigating" and not "exculpatory," but it would be enough to bring the charge of First Degree Murder down to, at the very least, Second Degree, and possibly all the way down to Manslaughter. In sentencing terms, that would be the difference between life in prison with no possibility of parole for twenty-five years (First Degree), life in prison with the possibility of parole in ten to fifteen years (Second Degree), and ten years with parole a real possibility in one-third of that time (Manslaughter). As I've pointed out—some say tiresomely—this is the kind of tangle you get into when you require an adversarial court to consider such evanescent and subtle forces as evil intent and the fogging effect of alcohol or drugs.

Here's where it got very strange. In the chapter called "New Maps of Hell," I raised the possibility that movies such as *The Silence of the Lambs* were sending a dangerous message to some potential killers out there, the message that the public fascination with graphic and twisted evil implies a kind of public complicity, even a kind of moral licence. At least, that was how the argument might go. Sure enough, that's how it went in the Allender case.

The early days of the trial were taken up with establishing beyond any doubt that Allender had killed Cheryl Joe, that he had killed her by striking her seven or eight times in the front and the back of the head with a red propane tank he kept in his van, that it took Cheryl from one-half hour to two hours to die, and that the removal of her breasts and her pubic area was done *post mortem,* that is, after her death. A vital point.

Detectives Crook and Cattley gave their evidence, as did Dr Laurel Gray and the various forensic technicians. The basic narrative of the killing was laid down in a week and went unchallenged by the Defence, other than a few cavils about how long it took the woman to die and how much blood might have been shed while the killing was being done. On the following Monday, the Crown rested and the Defence rose.

Under Canadian law, an accused person cannot be required to testify during the trial, and Myers' main tactic was to keep Allender off the stand. At no point in the trial had Allender been asked a direct question. The man sat, silent, hunched, impassive behind a bullet-proof plastic screen with his back to the public watching the witnesses pass with no visible signs of emotion. Myers wanted to keep it that way. But he had a problem.

If he wanted to argue that Allender had killed in a blind paroxysm of drunken rage, then somebody had to actually say to the jury. Someone with views useful to the defense. And who might that be?

Well, by this time it will come as no surprise to you that this special someone was—a forensic psychiatrist! His name was Shabehram Lohrasbe, a heavy-set dark-bearded man weighed down with a heavy file and a great deal of personal *gravitas*. Myers wanted to introduce as evidence a twenty-eight page psychiatric report on Allender that Lohrasbe had generated after eight lengthy conversations with the accused, along with several standard psychiatric tests—the Minnesota Multi-Phasic, the Heterosocial Adequacy Test, the Taylor Manifest Anxiety Scale, the Social Avoidance and Distress Scale, the Fear of Negative Evaluation Scale, and the Assertiveness Questionnaire. Myers wanted to draw out all of this information under direct examination in order to establish the following arguments:

Yes, Brian had killed Cheryl Joe.

Yes, he had bludgeoned her into unconsciousness and waited around for at least a half-hour while she bled to death.

Yes, he had sawn and sliced off her external sexual organs.

But…

He had been blind-stinking drunk at the time and didn't know what he was doing.

Or…

If the jury can't buy that, then he was blind-stinking drunk and suffering from an uncontrollable urge to mutilate and eat—sorry, but that's what they were trying to prove—her sexual organs, and that this uncontrollable urge was brought on by a whole bunch of childhood problems and the malevolent influence of *The Silence of the Lambs*.

Hell of a coincidence, that. Why, it was right there in a recent book, a book that actually detailed the killing of Cheryl Joe and the arrest of Brian Allender, published six months before Allender actually came to trial. Well, whatever the source, the argument was that somehow or other all these factors, the rum, the movie, the fact that he had a lifelong fascination with pornography and violence (this is known as the Ted Bundy defence, a defence much loved by the Christian Right and the Radical Feminist movement), that the victim had angered him somehow and the tank was right there, and...well...golly. Oops.

Unfortunately for Larry Myers, the Honorable Justice Braidwood raised his hand as the lawyer was trying to get the expert witness introduced and on the stand and asked the Clerk of the Court to escort the jurors out of the courtroom. It seemed that a *voir dire* was going to be necessary.

After the jury filed out, Judge Braidwood turned his impressive basaltic facade towards the Counsel for the Defence.

He asked Mr. Myers if this was the sole witness that the defence intended to present.

Yes, it is, Milord, and that's why—

You understand that there is a considerable body of case law, Supreme Court decisions, that prevent you from introducing evidence based on hearsay without providing the court with an opportunity to question the primary source of the evidence.

In other words, my client?

Yes, that would be the primary source of this psychiatric evidence, the source for the formulation of Dr. Lohrasbe's opinions, would it not?

But, Milord, if I am required to present Mr. Allender...th Crown will wish to cross-examine...that is not to...we do no intend to allow Mr. Allender to be...

Then you can't introduce a witness whose evidence is base on access to a witness which is denied to the Court and th Crown.

Myers stared up at Judge Braidwood, his round tanned fa paling within a corona of silver-grey curly hair, his hands mo ing restlessly through the papers littering his desk.

But Milord, if I cannot present the evidence of Dr. Lohrasl then I am left with no defence whatsoever.

Then allow Mr. Allender to be called in support.

Myers looked...not exactly green. Perhaps *tourmaline* catch the shade. Milord, I cannot allow Mr. Allender to be called.

(Damn right. Because then the Crown can rip him to little l on the stand, something the entire court is literally *hunger* for.)

Then you cannot present this evidence. The case law is v clear.

At this point there was a recess.

When the court was reassembled, the judge heard final arguments and then restated his position. Unless Allender could be called in support of the doctor's evidence, then the doctor's evidence could not be introduced. (That meant that all of the juicy stuff about *The Silence of the Lambs* and the effects of violent pornography—headline-grabbers all—must remain wrapped up tight inside the good doctor's bulging manila file folder, and the jury would not even be informed of the existence of such a report.)

Myers bleated and fumed a bit, and then stood up and asked the judge to declare a mistrial.

The judge seemed to settle a little deeper into his chair and his face became, if possible, more granitic and forceful.

That I will not do, he said.

But Milord...

Clerk of the Court will bring the jury back in.

I was pleased and surprised to see a Supreme Court judge with the courage and the simple common sense to resist the fashionable in defence of the fair, and my respect for the profession rose a few notches. Provisionally, but palpably.

Myers was left with the argument that Allender was drunk when he killed the young woman and was therefore incapable of forming the sufficient degree of premeditation to fulfill the Code definition of First or Second Degree Murder, and [could] therefore only be convicted of Manslaughter.

Joe Bellows, the Crown, a lean dark-haired and intense young man with a calmly inexorable manner of prosecution, argued that Allender had waited at least a half-hour and possibly two hours after bludgeoning the woman, waited until she actually died before mutilating her, and that passage of time—during which he made no attempt to revive her or to get her medical help—that delay constituted a deliberate decision to let her die as a result of his assault. It was Murder in the First Degree.

The next morning, after a long and exhaustive charge to the jury during which Judge Braidwood tried to balance all the arguments and see them weighted correctly for the jury, the jury retired to consider what to do with Brian Allender. Crook and

Cattley and I retired to drink quietly but steadily in a black mood.

At 8:17 that evening, in front of all of the members of Cheryl Joe's family, the jury returned with a verdict.

Guilty of Murder in the First Degree.

Braidwood complimented them on their decision, complimented the Crown and the Defence, and turned to Brian Allender.

Stand up, he said.

Allender stood, with his lawyer beside him.

"The crime described in the evidence is the most appalling I have heard of in thirty-five years of practising law. The matter of sentencing is mandatory in a case of First Degree Murder. Brian Allender, I sentence you to Life Imprisonment, with no possibility of parole for twenty-five years."

Allender took it in silence. No one thought of a lamb.

As I walked out of the darkened atrium of the BC Supreme Court, a slow rain was falling and the sound of crying, the sound of a whole family mourning a death, and, perhaps, the sound of a kind of terrible healing filled the air. Although many people would say that Brian Allender deserved death—and I believe that he does—what he got was justice as it exists in Canada, and for the Joe tribal band, in my view the only people who really count in the matter, that seemed to be enough.

Meanwhile, back in Saint Catharines, Ontario, during the same week, lawyers for Paul Bernardo—currently known as Paul Teale—announced that they had no intention of asking for a press or publication ban on the April 5, 1994 preliminary hearing into the deaths of Kristen French and Leslie Mahaffy, two young girls found brutally butchered two years ago, in a case that had captured continent-wide attention.

Too much attention for our current justice system, apparently.

I've been an opponent of press and publication bans in murder trials ever since I covered the killings of Daniel and Monica Babineau in Orangeville years before. In that case, described in this book in the chapter "Yellow Rope," we were all treated to the Kafkaesque experience of a murder trial where the accused a thirteen-year old boy protected by the Young Offenders Act but known to everyone in town, could not be named in a single printed or televised report.

That's the kind of tangle you get into when you stray from the simple and ancient precept that justice must be seen to be done, a principle that seems to be making our justice system professionals very nervous. Take, for example, the matter of Karla Homolka and her involvement in the Bernardo investigation.

For those of you who have been trekking in the Himalayas for the last two years, most of the country was horrified by the apparently unrelated disappearance of two young Ontario girls within a few months, and the subsequent discovery of their bodies, naked, dead, and one dismembered, in two isolated parts of southwestern Ontario. Now although I have seen the photos and the files in these cases, and I know a fair amount about the investigation, the fact remains that only one of the two people charged with these deaths has been convicted, so you'll understand if I step very carefully here, in an effort to explain the principles involved without leaving myself open to a charge of…Contempt of Court.

What we're looking at in these two killings comes under the heading of Organized Premeditated sexually-oriented control killings, the kind of killings studied by organizations such as the behavioral Science Unit of the FBI and other centers of forensic medicine such as the Clarke Institute and the Oak Ridge center at Penetanguishene, Ontario. The experts have come up with a of classifications and definitions in an attempt to order and somehow explain the minds behind the killings.

Organized vs. disorganized. Psychotic and non-psychotic. Sociopathic. Affective disorders. Transitory or fugue psychosis. Organic and non-organic. Sado-masochistic. The labels run endlessly and, to many of us, pointlessly, since there seems to be no way that any of this insight leads us to a reduction or an eradication of this type of violence and murder.

In this case, it's a matter of record that Paul Bernardo (Teale) married to a young woman named Karla Homolka, and that the months following Bernardo's arrest in February 1993 to arraignment and trial and conviction of his wife Karla in

July, the investigation encountered several obstacles. It's also a matter of record that the trial judge imposed a massive and near-ly limitless gag order on everyone connected with the Homolka hearing. The gag order prohibited anyone from publishing any information whatsoever about the proceedings of the trial and about the nature of the evidence presented, even going so far as to specifically *exclude* an individual journalist who had signed a book contract to write a history of this sensational case. American journalists were also warned, without the possibility of enforcement, against reporting any of the details of the Homolka trial, a move which left Canadian journalists in the strange position of seeing US news media getting access to a Canadian case denied to them under penalty of imprisonment.

Further, the judge made a verbal distinction between the pub-lic and the press, asserting that nothing in the law made i mandatory for a trial to be perceived as public *only* if the pres were present. He maintained that not only could the press b excluded, but that even the public—ordinary citizens—could b excluded and the trial could still be regarded as taking place i public. How did he manage this judicial necromancy?

Well, if you've been following my thesis about the arroganc and elitism that runs rampant through our justice system, yc won't be surprised to hear that, in the opinion of His Honour, tl public is sufficiently represented by its appointed professional the judge, the Crown, the Defence, the cops, the members of tl jury and so on. In other words, leave it to the professionals, a we'll tell you what we want you to know when we're damn good and ready. In the meantime, go away and do not troul the councils of the wise.

Naturally the public outcry was loud and long, to the credit the citizenry. Christie Blatchford, one of the best of Canad crime reporters, went to the wall in protest with the backing her paper, *The Toronto Sun*, and other media outlets launcl legal challenges as well.

By the way, Canada's publishing houses should be fight this fight as well, since the trial judge made it a special poin say that he regarded book writers as even more irrelevant t members of the daily press, making the nonsensical distinc that a reporter covering the trial for a newspaper or a television station was somehow "official press," while the same journalist doing the same work for a Canadian book publisher under contract was merely a private citizen, and not covered by the traditional principles of freedom of the press. All in all, it was a pretty hysterical and dangerous gag order, and anyone interested in seeing our courts operate in the open had to view it as a very ominous abrogation of citizen access.

So why do it?

Speaking in theory, what kind of circumstances and pressures might account for the results we saw in the trial of Karla Homolka and the behaviour of the justice system professionals during the days and weeks before her trial? Since the gag order was actually *opposed* by lawyers acting for Bernardo, what would be so threatening about the evidence or the trial that such a Draconian and crypto-fascist diktat would be allowed to stand? Let's agree to tolerate some elliptical writing here.

We know that the police have access to a suspect's home for several months after his arrest. We know that the police have linked Suspect One, a male, to at least forty-eight cases of rape and assault in the Toronto suburb of Scarborough, assaults attributed to someone called the Scarborough Rapist. Since you and I are experienced homicide investigators with almost one hundred and fifty successful cases under our garrison belts, we are in a position to make some educated guesses about how such an investigation might have proceeded.

We have two bodies, located in separate, isolated but *not* remote areas of the province. Both are bodies of young females, both fit a certain physical somatype—they look alike. Let us say there are signs of sexual assault, certainly signs of brutality. One of the victims had a different haircut from the day of her disappearance. What can we deduce from the location and condition of these two bodies?

Well, first of all, whoever killed them probably meant for them to be found. Although the bodies were found in isolated areas, the areas were not deserted. The bodies were not buried, only discarded. So the killer could assume that they would be discovered, and probably in a short time.

What does this say?

It says that whoever killed them derives part of his or her pleasure from the notoriety of the crime, from the outrage and the pain caused. So the killer fits a certain profile, that of the serial killer who derives satisfaction from the exercise of control and domination, and from the sensation of defying and challenging established authority.

The location of the bodies is not the location of the killing. That also fits the profile of a thrill-killer. The haircut implies, tragically, a time of captivity and some sort of ritualism of the act, a period of obscene drama played out for the amusement and gratification of the killer.

The fact that the bodies were found in or near water also tells us something. Nothing destroys forensic evidence better than water. It washes away fibres, skin samples, fluids—anything from which some DNA or any locator evidence might be obtained. Serial killers know this very well, and the fact that both of our theoretical bodies were found there suggests that the killer knows something about police Ident procedures.

As investigators, we're faced with the worst kind of murder investigation—the random killing. No obvious connection between the victim and killer. We're left with doing a massive canvass of everyone who could have had anything to do with the victims—neighbors, passers-by, anyone in the vicinity where the bodies were found. And at the same time, we do a complete background check on all of the family members, in Homicide terms, the Nearest and Dearest, because experience has shown us that most victims have at least a marginal connection with their killers.

And we also know that, even in the worst serial killer investigations, the task force almost always generates the name of the killer within the first thirty days. It happened in the Bundy case; he was one of a massive list of people who were reported by citizens as owning the right kind of Volkswagon Beetle. Unfortunately, his name was buried under thousands of other possibles, and he went on to kill as many as fifty other people before he was run to earth in Florida.

Now what?

Now we do the hard grinding dirty-work of any police investigation. We pull together as many detectives and uniforms as possible, we ask for the help of the public, and we follow up every last tip, no matter how silly-ass or stupid, no matter how crazy the tipster might seem. We try to keep a record of people providing tips and cross-reference them by computer, mainly to trap the ones who call in several hundred times, as happened in the Bundy case, where one man called the task force three-hundred and forty times before someone noticed.

We also go through arrest records, looking for anyone with this sort of *modus operandi,* and we eliminate as many of them as we can, although Corrections Canada won't tell us who's in and who's out of their system, citing "client privilege." We also lie to the press about what we have and where we're going, because we know the killer is reading the accounts in the media, and we want him to have a false sense of security.

At least, we *hope* it's false.

And we squeeze the finks, the informants, every last doper and B & E artist and street punk we can think of, hoping for some clue, knowing in our hearts that killers like this rarely have criminal backgrounds and criminal associates.

We also see to it that our investigators get psychiatric counselling, that they don't go stale or get depressed or get too angry and push the law too far, or in any one of a thousand ways blow the operation.

And the core group tries to hold the family together, tries to make them believe that the case will break and that everything is being done.

And time passes…

And we get a break.

Finally.

We have been working the car, and the connections.

We have a short list and we work that short list. We cross-reference this person's movements with the trail of our victims, and other victim of any kind of sexual assault, because we know many of these killers are progressive, that they frequently move from one kind of sexual assault to more grievous and more brutal assaults.

Our list gets shorter.

We go back and look at our original list, our First Thirty Days list. We see some correlations. Perhaps we see a single name.

Perhaps we do Surveillance on this name, and we get a sense of the suspect and the suspect's circle.

Maybe we let our Surveillance get burned, just to see what happens. Put on the pressure. Make a normal life impossible. Shake up the family.

Divide the family.

Find the vulnerable one.

Put the weight on.

Look for cracks.

In the meantime, Forensic is getting not much, because Suspect One is either innocent or damn smart. Right now, w don't know which.

We do know we're running out of time.

And maybe, one cold day in the winter, we see a hairlin crack in one of the family members. We increase the pressur The crack widens.

And this person goes to a lawyer.

And after a long time, the lawyer and his client say to yo look, maybe this is what happened, and maybe not, but it loo to us like you can't make a case without us.

We sit there across the table and what we're thinking is over our faces, but the lawyer doesn't care about that. That's his job.

The lawyer knows we need what his client can give us.*

In our business, this moment is known as Let's Make a Dea

Now, we fast forward a few months. Our case is mu improved. We have taken our suspicions and some of our c roborating evidence to a judge, and the judge has signed a v rant, and we have gone out to pull in Suspect One. Now press is all over us, and the case is a runaway, and the media

* That a deal was made is the opinion of the author, deduced from publicly known facts—the eventual trial took 45 minutes and Karla Homolka was found guilty in that time.

in a feeding frenzy, and somewhere in the system, some official is getting nervous. Christ, this is a big case. Look out there in the street.

We need to cover...we need to control this trial, not let it turn into a circus. After all, we have the *big* one to follow. First of all, we need to nail this source, cut the deal, dispose of the road-blocks. Get the source convicted and sentenced and in a position to testify against Suspect One.

But we need to do it secretly. The public *hates* deals.

We need a gag order.

A *big* gag order.

In the best of all possible worlds, our justice system officials would simply say to us all, Look, we needed what this person had, and according to the rules you agreed to as citizens, we had to offer a deal. That's what we did. If you don't like it, if it makes you sick, well join the God-damn club. How do you think *we* feel about it. After all, we've seen the photos.

But that's not where we are. We are in a world of forensic cowardice and judicial arrogance. So instead of the truth, we get a gag order. We get told to go away and mind our business. We are dismissed. Herded out of the courtroom. Turned out to graze.

Like sheep.

Have a nice day.

The Behavioral Treatment of Rapists and Child Molesters*

Vernon L. Quinsey, Terry C. Chaplin, Anne Maguire, and Douglas Upfold

Crimes of sexual aggression, such as child molestation and rape, are common in Western societies. Although exact figures are difficult to obtain because of vagaries in victim-reporting practices and differences in legal definitions over regions, serious acts of sexual aggression are almost exclusively committed by males and constitute a serious social problem. A sizable minority of sexually aggressive men commit sexual crimes at high frequencies over long periods of time (Abel, Becker, & Skinner, 1985; Groth, Longo, & McFadin, 1982). These individuals, who are the primary focus of the present chapter, are infrequently arrested by the police or, if apprehended and incarcerated, often reoffend upon release (Abel *et al.,* 1985).

Clinicians and behavioral scientists have sought to develop methods that will modify the sexually aggressive behaviors of these men. Because of the seriousness and frequency of their crimes, each cessation of offending by a sexually aggressive person is important. Despite the importance of developing effective interventions for these offenders, however, not much evaluativ research on interventions has been conducted. Most of the methodologically acceptable literature is recent, and the field a long way from having definitive evaluations of any treatme methods. This chapter provides an introduction to the behavior treatment of sex offenders through the description of a particul program.

Traditionally, sex offenders have been treated using ps chotherapeutic methods, most frequently group psychotherap

* Vernon L. Quinsey, Terry C. Chaplin, Anne Maguire, and Douglas Upfold, Research Department, Mental Health Centre, Penetanguishene, Ontario, Canada, LOK IPO. This work was supported in part by a series of grants fro the Ontario Mental Health Foundation.

These psychotherapeutic methods have diverse rationales, but many appear to rest on the assumption that sex offenders have character traits that must be altered. Unfortunately, the search for unique character traits among sex offenders has not yet proved successful (e.g., Quinsey, 1977, 1984, 1986; Quinsey, Arnold, & Pruesse, 1980), and no trait theory has been able to explain the different sorts of sexual misbehaviors that offenders consistently exhibit.

More direct measurement of phenomena that are know or thought to be related to the behaviors of interest has proved useful, however. For example, sexual arousal, as measured by penile expansion to slides or stories, has been shown to be under stimulus control (Quinsey, Chaplin & Upfold, 1984; Quinsey, Steinman, Bergersen, & Holmes, 1975). The stimuli that occasion sexual arousal among sex offenders are related to their offense histories, so that sex offenders can be differentiated both from nonsex offenders and sex offenders with different offense histories by measurements of their sexual arousal to a variety of stimuli.

The findings of individual differences in sexual arousal patterns, together with advances in other areas of the behavioral literature, have led to a new rationale for the treatment of sex offenders and a new treatment methodology. Briefly, sexual behaviors may be conceptualized as behaviors like any others. In this view, undesirable sexual behaviors are assumed to be the result of skill deficits and/or inappropriate behaviors acquired at a earlier time, in particular, the acquisition of inappropriate or deviant" masturbatory fantasies. The task of treatment, therefore, is to provide the offender with the requisite skills and techniques for the self-management of his future sexual behavior. Broadly speaking, these assumptions are those of the social competence model (Rice & Quinsey, 1980).

In a social competence model, sexual behavior is considered be learned behavior, involving the acquisition of the specific behaviors involved in sexual activity, the association of particular stimuli and fantasies with sexual arousal, and the acquisition attitudes toward various sexual activities and sexual partners. all likelihood, the same processes underlying the acquisition of acceptable sexual behaviors underline the acquisition of inappropriate or aggressive sexual behaviors. Although the evidence supports the assumption that sexual behaviors are learned, the precise mechanisms are, at present, unclear. In addition, certain associations (such as an association of aggression with sexual arousal or an association of female characteristics or youthful appearance with sexual arousal) may be particularly easy to learn because of the historical influence of evolutionary selection pressures on reproductive behavior (Quinsey, 1984). The belief that sexual behavior is learned encourages the development of behavioral procedures in the treatment of persons who exhibit inappropriate sexual behaviors. As an aside, though, behavioral methods of treatment might be efficacious even if the behaviors were not learned or, conversely, nonbehavioral methods might be appropriate with behaviors that are learned.

The program to be described in this chapter was developed using an explicit logic. First, measures were sought that either had a prima facie theoretical relationship to sexual offending or differentiated identifiable subgroups of sex offenders from other offenders and from persons who had not committed an offense of any kind. After such measures were identified, interventions were designed that would change offenders so that they had post-treatment scores on these measures similar to those of nonoffenders or that would produce changes expected to be related to lower recidivism. The final task was to determine whether these measures were related to recidivism and whether changes on these measures were related to lower recidivism rates.

The Setting

Traditionally, treatment programs for serious sex offenders have been housed in correctional institutions or mental health facilities for forensic psychiatric patients. These typically all male, secure institutions are still the most common sites for sex offender treatment programs. Some of these institutions have different kinds of offenders, and others specialize in the housing and treatment of sex offenders alone. These institutions may not only provide custodial care and treatment but also may decisions about whether or when these men should be released. These decisions are related to complex issues of law and social policy. More recently, a number of programs have been implemented in the community; some of these programs treat persons under a variety of legal mandates, whereas others treat only voluntary clients who are under no legal coercion (e.g. Abel *et al.*, 1985).

The setting of any program provides a set of opportunities and constraints that structures the form the program can take (Quinsey, 1981). This section of the chapter describes the institution in which the treatment program highlighted in this chapter—the "Oak Ridge" Sex Offender Program—is housed.

Oak Ridge is a 300-bed, all-male, maximum security hospital in Penetanguishene, Ontario. It is operated by the Provincial Ministry of Health but is built in the style of an old prison. Patients enter Oak Ridge in several distinct legal categories: (a) persons under warrants of remand who are referred by the courts for a pretrial or presentence psychiatric assessment, (b) persons under warrants of the lieutenant governor who are referred by the courts after having been found not guilty by reason of insanity or, more rarely, unfit for trial, and (c) involuntarily certified patients who are referred from federal or provincial correctional institutions as mentally ill or from regional psychiatric or mental retardation facilities as severe management problems.

Oak Ridge is a second-stage institution that accepts and refers patients primarily to and from other institutions, and very seldom to or from the community. The patient population is very heterogeneous in its characteristics, including length of stay. Adequate staffing has always been a problem, and there are few professional staff, as is characteristic of such institutions. Although the program characteristics of Oak Ridge are complex, the programs themselves tend to be designed for all patients on a given ward, and include work placement, patient-run milieu therapy, or token economy programs. Phenothiazines and other medications are commonly used. A more detailed description of various aspects of Oak Ridge has been presented elsewhere (Quinsey, 1981).

Historical Reference

Although current behavioral programs for sex offenders are usually conceptualized in terms of social learning theory (e.g., Bandura, 1969), they are the historical result of early treatment efforts in the behavior therapy tradition (e.g., Wolpe, 1958), most particularly assertion training and studies on aversion therapy with homosexuals (e.g., Feldman, 1966). To a large extent, current behavioral programs for sex offenders represent the behavior therapy approach, together with Freund's (1981) psychophysiological method of measuring male sexual preference. An overview of the history of behavior therapy and early work with sex offenders has been provided by Yates (1970).

At the time the Oak Ridge sex offender program was started, in 1972, the literature on the assessment and treatment of rapists and child molesters was very limited. As time went on, however, more information became available from the literature and from our own studies that encouraged the modification of our treatment procedures. Reviews of the literature can be found in Abel, Blanchard, and Becker (1978), Kelly (1982), Langevin (1983), Laws and Osborn (1983), Quinsey (1973, 1977, 1983, 1984, 1986), and Quinsey and Marshall (1983).

We started measuring child molesters' sexual-age preferences using a technique pioneered by Freund (for a review, see Freund, 1981) and attempted to modify these preferences with classical conditioning techniques (Quinsey, Bergersen, & Steinman, 1976). We subsequently added sex education, heterosocial skill training (Whitman & Quinsey, 1981), and training in self-management techniques (Pithers, Marques, Gibat, & Marlatt, 1983). In addition, Abel and his colleagues (Abel, Blanchard, Barlow, & Guild, 1977) developed a technique to assess sexual arousal to sexual themes (e.g., force, bondage, etc.) that allowed us to include rapists in our treatment and assessment efforts. Finally, we have added treatment techniques such as signaled punishment (Quinsey, Chaplin, & Carrigan, 1980), satiation (Marshall, 1979), and olfactory aversion (Maletzky, 1980) in a continuing attempt to improve our ability to modify inappropriate sexual arousal. These procedures are described in more detail later.

This program, then, has evolved from the simple use of classical conditioning to modify child molesters' inappropriate sexual-age preferences to a multifaceted program of skill acquisition and self-control. Similar changes have occurred in other behavioral sex offender programs. These changes, we believe, have led to a much stronger treatment intervention. At the same time, however, the changes have made the overall program difficult to evaluate. Fortunately, the recent literature does contain some evidence that behavioral treatment packages of the kind described in this chapter are efficacious. Davidson (in preparation), for instance, has followed up sex offender inmates who had received behavioral treatment (sex education, social skills, and aversion therapy) and compared them with a cohort of similar inmates who were released before the availability of the behavioral program. Child molester inmates who had received treatment were convicted significantly less frequently for new sex offenses than child molesters who had not received the program; unfortunately, no differences were found between treated and untreated rapists. Kelly (1982) has reviewed 32 behavioral studies that used a variety of treatment techniques in the treatment of child molesters and concluded that behavioral techniques do lower sexual recidivism rates; fewer data, however, are available on the behavioral treatment of rapists (Quinsey, 1984).

At present, the sex offender program at Oak Ridge has five components: (1) laboratory assessment of sexual arousal, (2) problem identification, (3) heterosocial skill training, (4) sex education, and (5) modification of inappropriate sexual preferences. These components are described individually next.

The Program

Laboratory Assessment of Sexual Arousal

The assessment of sexual arousal, although not yet entirely standardized, is performed in a similar manner by a variety of laboratories. Laws and Osborn (1983) have presented a very detailed outline of how such laboratories operate.

Each sex offender who is referred to the Oak Ridge Sex Offender Program for treatment is first assessed in the sexual behavior laboratory. The laboratory is equipped with a sound attenuating and electrically shielded patient's chamber, a rearview projection screen, and apparatus for automatically scheduling slides and audiotaped material and for monitoring penile circumference and skin conductance. Penile circumference is monitored on a Beckman Dynograph at two levels of magnification and on a digital voltmeter.

Depending on the nature of the patient's offense history, he receives a slide test of sexual-age preference or an audiotaped test designed to measure his arousal to rape stimuli. Because the two methods of assessment are similar, the visual assessment method is described here in detail, and the methods for the auditory stimulus assessment are described more briefly later.

During assessment sessions, patients are seated in a reclining chair. Penile circumference is measured by means of a mercury-in-rubber strain gauge placed around the shaft of the patient's penis. The gauge is connected to a Parks Electronic Model 270 Plethysmograph. A desk top is placed across the arms of the chair to prevent the patient from seeing or manipulating his penis.

The patient is instructed to relax, remain as still as possible keep his eyes on the translucent screen, and try to imagine th person represented in each slide as a potential sex partner. A standard array of slides is then presented to the patient. Thi array consists of two slides of each of the following categorie: adult females, adult males, pubescent females, pubescent male: child females between the ages of 6 and 11, child males betwee 6 and 11 years of age, child females under the age of 5, ma children under the age of 5, explicit heterosexual activity, ar landscapes. Each slide is presented for a period of 30 second Penile circumference is recorded from 2 seconds following sli presentation until 30 seconds after the slide offset. The intersli interval is 30 seconds, although this is extended if the respon does not return to baseline (the starting position). The patien sexual arousal pattern is determined by the relative levels response to each of the 10 slide categories.

In the auditory assessment, stimuli are presented via an in com. On our standard tape, these stimuli consist of 18 aud taped scenarios describing various interactions with an a female, read in a man's voice in the first person. Five of th scenarios describe consenting heterosexual interaction, five describe nonconsenting heterosexual interaction (rape), five describe nonsexual violence, and three describe sexually neutral interactions. The patient is instructed to try to imagine that he is the person speaking on the tape. Maximum penile circumference within the interval from 2 to 180 seconds after stimulus onset is recorded. A 30-second interval precedes the next stimulus, during which responses are not scored.

We have conducted a lengthy series of studies designed to validate various aspects of our measurement of sexual arousal. In our first study (Quinsey et al., 1975), we found that penile responses to slides of persons varying in age and gender discriminate child molesters from normals (community volunteers and nonsex offender patients), whereas verbal reports do not. Penile responses also relate closely to the child molesters' histories of victim choice. Child molesters showed more sexual arousal to slides of children who were the same ages and genders as their victims than did others. Incest offenders exhibit less inappropriate age preference than other child molesters (Quinsey, Chaplin, & Carrigan, 1979).

Rapists exhibit relatively more sexual arousal to audiotaped descriptions of brutal rapes than to consenting sex stories in comparison to normal subjects (Quinsey, Chaplin, & Varney, 1981). Some rapists show sexual arousal to descriptions of nonsexual violence as well, and the amount of arousal is related to whether they have in the past physically injured their victims (Quinsey & Chaplin, 1982). Normal subjects show less arousal when the victim does not consent and very little when the victim is described as suffering. Rapists' arousal, however, is not affected by victim consent or suffering (Quinsey & Chaplin, 1984). Rapists are best differentiated from nonsex offenders on the basis of their sexual arousal when the rape stories are cruel and short.

Although penile response measurement is far superior to verbal report, sexual arousal measures can be faked by some persons and must always be interpreted with caution (Quinsey & Bergersen, 1976; Quinsey & Carrigan, 1978). Although faking is frequently not a problem in initial testing (Quinsey et al.,

1975), it becomes more of a difficulty in treatment. In treatment, this problem can be addressed, if not solved, by attempting to ensure that the results of psychophysiological assessment do not determine whether the offender is kept within the institution, which is sometimes difficult, and in presenting the treatment issue to the patient as not involving a "cure" but as learning to control inappropriate arousal. From a research or evaluative perspective, the issue of faking is bypassed by relating sexual arousal measures directly to recidivism.

Problem Identification

Within many institutions for the treatment of offenders, serious problems exist in the rational selection of suitable targets for intervention and in the assignment of offenders to various treatment programs. The emphasis in assessment is often on diagnosis and various legal issues rather than on the identification of offender problems that might be amenable to modification and much less on collaboration with the offender in the design of a individualized program that can address these problems. Quinsey and Maguire (1983) have found that, although experienced forensic clinicians agreed on psychiatric diagnosis and on whether an offender would benefit from phenothiazines, the exhibited little agreement as to the appropriateness of other behavioral and nonbehavioral methods of intervention. In addition, there was little agreement as to how much these various treatments (or any treatment) might benefit a given offender. Given this lack of consensus, it is not surprising that the offenders themselves are often skeptical and frequently resistive when offered the opportunity to participate in treatment programs various kinds.

The purpose of the problem identification program is for therapists and patients to reach the same view of what treatment appropriate and relevant before treatment proceeds. Therapeutic compliance and active patient commitment are seen to follow from a "theory" of sexual offending that is shared by the offender and the therapist.

The program is run in a group format with four to seven patients and two staff members. Patients are selected who h one or more offenses involving child molestation or rape, have sufficient verbal ability to participate in the group, and are at least potentially interested in treatment. The goal of the program is to produce a written theoretical account of each patient's sexual offense pattern to which all group members subscribe.

The first meeting begins with an elementary exposition by one of the therapists on the scientific method. Specificity of explanation is stressed with a variety of examples. Consistency between the evidence and the phenomena to be explained is advanced as the criterion for acceptance of a theory. An illustration of this issue is provided later. The accepted theories are, of course, acknowledged not to be absolutely true but are the best that can be developed given the state of our knowledge.

The second group meeting is concerned with a general discussion of why a man might rape a woman and later why a man might molest a child. Typically, group members advance explanations couched in dynamic terms that they have learned in group psychotherapy or idiosyncratic justifications for their behavior.

At the third meeting, a therapist hands out a sheet containing "personality profile" of each patient that is asserted to be a provisional explanation of the patient's offense history. Each profile is typed with the patient's name at the top and the therapist's signature at the bottom. Actually, the profiles are identical and are taken from Ulrich, Stachnik, and Stainton (1963). The profiles contain assertions that are true of everyone or so vague to be meaningless. The therapist asks for written feedback on the accuracy and adequacy of his preliminary effort. The purpose of this procedure is to vividly demonstrate the type of explanations that are not desirable and to indicate how one can check on the validity of explanations of behavior. Patients are typically enthusiastic at their acceptance of the profile's validity. After a very careful description of how the profiles were obtained, however, patients often see the nature of their task more clearly, particularly the need for specificity, and they become more skeptical of glib and vague explanations.

In the remaining sessions, each patient in turn presents an oral autobiography. Each autobiography takes from 2 to 6 hours. Notes are maintained and checked informally against the patient's history (e.g., relatives' accounts, police reports, etc.). At the conclusion of the history, a brainstorming session is held. The hypotheses that emerge from this session are systematically checked against the autobiography and eliminated where inconsistent with the autobiographical material. Sometimes, other information such as laboratory tests of sexual preferences are included as data. The therapist, working backward from the offenses, produces a theory of proximal factors (circumstances immediately surrounding the offenses) and distal or predisposing factors, which are more remote in time. This theory is presented to the group and the final revision (as amended by group discussion) accepted by the group. A copy of the theory is given to the patient, and one is put on his clinical file.

Theory construction is a difficult task. Where possible, the scheme put forward by Pithers *et al.* (1983) is used to organize the material. An example may clarify these points. A patient in one of the groups had committed a series of rape murders During the time in which the murders were committed, the patient was very depressed about his wife openly having an affair with another man. The patient naturally enough attributed these murders to his depression. Through the autobiographical material, however, we could demonstrate that the "depression, perhaps more properly labeled as anger, was only one of the proximal causes and that the explanation was much more complex and involved factors that had occurred much earlier in time The patient had, in fact, attempted to rape a woman many years before his marriage. This occurrence led to questions about sadistic sexual fantasies that the patient acknowledged and the were confirmed by psychophysiological assessment. The final list of relevant problems included assertion deficits, sadistic fantasies, and a number of other difficulties.

The procedures described here appear to resemble those used in any treatment program and, in particular, those used in psychodynamic programs. There is an important difference, however. Specifically, the explanations themselves are pitched at a low level of inference and are very data-oriented. The amount objective detail used to support the explanations is sufficient convince most of the patients of the explanations' validity w out difficulty, particularly because the data and often the theories are supplied primarily by the patients themselves.

Patients are usually pleased with the results of the program initially but later begin asking what the theory means with respect to their treatment. At that point, the therapist is in a position to inform the patient what can and cannot be addressed with existing programs. On occasion, an individual program has to be developed, or the patient may have to be referred elsewhere within the institution for programs (such as those for alcohol abuse) in addition to, or instead of, the sex offender programs. Because of the detailed knowledge of the sex offense pattern that the therapist has acquired, a program of self-management can often be advanced and elaborated upon in subsequent treatment.

The problem identification program is the newest module in our treatment program, and, as yet, no evaluative data are available.

Heterosocial Skills Training

It is widely believed that many sex offenders are socially incompetent in a variety of areas (Marshall & Barbaree, 1984). Thus, in addition to attempting to suppress inappropriate behavior, both behavioral and nonbehavioral treatment programs frequently incorporate methods to improve various aspects of sex offenders' social abilities. At Oak Ridge, the heterosocial skills program is designed to improve the social skills of rapists and child molesters and to reduce their heterosocial anxiety. The rationale for this approach is that offenders must be able to obtain sexual gratification in an appropriate manner in order for appropriate behaviors to be reinforced. The naturally occurring rewards in appropriate sexual interactions are probably critical in reducing recidivism. Heterosocial skill deficits, however, need not have played an etiological role, although they may have, particularly in combination with other factors. This point is important because of Stermac and Quinsey's (1986) finding that rapists show the same level of social skills in interacting with females as with males and are not differentiable from other patients who are not sex offenders. Both groups of patients were, however, less skilled than nonpatient, low socioeconomic status controls.

Patients are assessed before and after treatment using the same measures. Because not all sex offenders have social skills problems, the assessment is used to determine which sex offenders should be offered this treatment. The treatment itself is behavioral in nature and involves modeling, coaching, videotape feedback, and extensive rehearsal in a group context; more detail is provided later.

Assessment: Likely candidates are interviewed at some length regarding their dating history before formal assessment. The nature of the assessment and treatment program is explained in detail at this initial interview. The formal assessment begins with a 10-minute conversation with a female who is unknown to the patient. This conversation is videotaped. The patient is instructed to converse on any topic except the assessment itself. He is asked to behave as if the woman were a potential date but is not required to ask her for a date. The female is instructed to converse in a friendly but passive manner and not to initiate conversation. She is instructed to interrupt silences of 5 to 10 seconds with an innocuous comment (e.g., "Nice weather we are having"). The patient and female confederate subsequently fill out questionnaires that measure their perceptions of the conversation.

Two trained females later independently rate a videotape of the conversation according to patient anxiety, social skill level, and a variety of other measures. We have obtained good inter-rater reliabilities on these measures (Stermac & Quinsey, 198; Whitman & Quinsey, 1981).

The second phase of the assessment involves the Heterosocial Adequacy Test (Perri, Richards, & Goodrich, 1978). This measure has been shown to have high internal consistency, interrater reliability, ability to discriminate known groups, and sensible correlations with other measures (e.g., high correlations with subjects' self-ratings of heterosocial skill and low correlations with the Taylor Manifest Anxiety Scale). Our version of the Heterosocial Adequacy Test has been adapted for our population and consists of 20 audiotaped heterosocial situations. The situations involve interactions that are highly likely to occur, are of moderate difficulty, and prompt a wide range of responses.

patient is asked to respond as he would if the situations were actually occurring. The patient's verbal response (or indication of a nonverbal response) is recorded on a second tape recorder. These responses are evaluated on dimensions of social skillfulness by two independent raters following the methods of Perri *et al.* (1978).

Finally, the patient completes four questionnaires: The Social Avoidance and Distress Scale, the Fear of Negative Evaluation Scale (both developed by Watson & Friend, 1969), the Assertiveness Questionnaire (Callner & Ross, 1976), and a dating history questionnaire that provides information on the frequency, duration, and perceived success of past relationships. The psychometric characteristics of these questionnaires are acceptable and are given in the original references.

The assessment determines the extent to which the patient has difficulty in heterosexual interactions. For patients who exhibit substantial heterosocial skill deficits, the assessment data provide a pretreatment baseline with which to compare subsequent performance, together with a specification of which areas require improvement.

Treatment: A male and female therapist together with four to patients constitute a group. The first session is devoted to introductions and establishing rapport. Groups members state their objectives. The confidentiality of material discussed in the group is stressed. The remaining sessions focus on learning specific skills, following a curriculum that has been adapted from McGovern *et al.* (1975).

The first topic concerns asking a female for directions in an appropriate manner. This skill is intentionally simple and nonthreatening and is used to habituate patients to videotaping and giving videotaped and verbal feedback on their performance. It provides an experience of initial success. Each of the skills is introduced and taught in the same manner. The therapists first describe the technique and model the appropriate behaviors. Then each of the patients, in turn, role-plays the situation with a female. A videotape of the performance is then discussed. Feedback always starts with praise and ends with constructive criticism. Specific behaviors, such as posture, eye contact, spacing, clarity of speech, voice volume, and speech content are addressed.

The next few sessions are spent teaching the importance of listening in becoming a good conversationalist. A listening game is employed to demonstrate listening skills. Listening is a major focus of all the sessions that follow and is, therefore, discussed in great detail. Concentrating on listening also serves as a distraction from becoming anxious or concerned with how to respond when the other person is finished speaking. Patients are encouraged to use open (e.g., "What do you think about X?") as opposed to closed questions (e.g., "Do you like X?"). The emphasis is on asking questions that allow the partner to give an extended rather than a "yes" or "no" response. The patient is then expected to listen to the response so that he can ask another related open question. Other techniques that are taught include: (a) paraphrasing (a technique used to rephrase the statement the other person has just made in order to demonstrate that one is listening), (b) perception checking (a technique used for clarifying the other person's feelings on the topic being discussed), (c) elaboration (a technique used to express an opinion or experience similar to the one being discussed by the other person), (d) association (a technique used to switch topics in a conversation to a related topic), and (e) answer-ask (a technique used to encourage the other person to express feelings by offering one's own first). Everyone is expected to learn each new technique before progressing to the next technique. Each practice conversation in which the patient engages is expected to include the newest technique learned and, as applicable, any techniques learned earlier. By using this style of teaching, the length of each conversation increases in preparation for the topic of informal dating.

"Informal dating" is introduced next because it is very similar to the longer conversations the patient has been practicing. An informal date is described as a date that occurs on the spur of the moment. For example, the patient encounters a woman he knows and with whom he has had a conversation in the past and asks to join him for lunch or a beer. Such a date does not involve preparation and, therefore, prevents unnecessary preparatory iety. In a role-playing format, the patient is expected to engage in a short conversation with the woman and then ask her to join him for a beer. He constructs the scene for this encounter in accordance with his life-style. For example, if he often shops in a mall, then this is where the scene is set. The conversation they engage in while having a beer is exactly as it would be in the longer conversations that have been practiced. It is stressed at this point that beginning a heterosexual relationship is very similar to starting any friendship and can, therefore, be expected to develop slowly. The second and third dates are very similar to the first but can involve a more formal meeting (e.g., going out for dinner).

The other topics in the social skills program include phoning to ask for a date, introducing a woman to friends or family, complimenting a woman, and dealing with annoyance and rejection. At the completion of this 60-hour program, the patient completes the assessment procedure described earlier for a second time in order to measure his improvement.

Evaluation: Whitman and Quinsey (1981) have shown that blind ratings of sex offenders' heterosocial skills increase significantly from pre- to posttreatment. A sex education control condition that involved a similar amount of group time and interaction with a female therapist did not affect social skills ratings.

Sex Education Program

The rationale for sex education is much the same as for heterosocial skill training. In order for sex offenders to develop appropriate sexual relationships, they must have an understanding of appropriate sexual behavior and community values. Many offenders lack sexual knowledge and maintain beliefs that appear likely to encourage further sex offending (Abel *et al.*, 1985; Quinsey, 1977, 1984, 1986).

Assessment: Patients are assessed at the beginning and end of treatment on a variety of paper-and-pencil measures. The Sex Education Quiz examines the objective knowledge covered by the course curriculum. The quiz is divided into a section that requires patients to match biological labels with corresponding anatomical structures in diagrams of male and female reproductive systems, a section that contains multiple-choice items, and a section that requires patients to supply appropriate terms in paragraphs describing ovulation, sperm production, and pregnancy. A brief version of this quiz has been developed for patients with more limited academic skills.

The Cognition Survey (Chaplin & Quinsey, 1984) was taken from various sources in the literature; some of it was adapted from work done by Abel and Marshall and their colleagues. The survey consists of a set of statements relating to specific sexual beliefs and is organized into three categories of 36 items each. Patients indicate the extent of their agreement with each item. The child molestation category items involve beliefs that may serve to maintain sexual behaviors with children (e.g., "A child who doesn't physically resist an adult's sexual advances want to have sex with the adult"). The rape category is similar (e.g., "Many women fantasize about rape and privately hope it happens to them"). The general category relates to commonly held beliefs about sexuality (e.g., "Athletes make better lovers tha nonathletic people").

Further questionnaires measure attitudes toward rape (Field 1978), attitudes toward women (Spence, Helmreich, & Stapp 1973), social self-esteem (Lawson, Marshall, & McGrath, 1979 social anxiety (Record, 1977), and sex roles (Bem, 1974).

Treatment: The sex education program is divided into an object tive knowledge section and a subjective or value-related section The order of presentation, depth, and relative focus of the se tions are tailored to the needs of each particular group patients. Instruction is done in a group format with a male an female therapist and a group of four to six patients.

Each therapist takes responsibility for presenting specific ture material. Lecture topics for the objective portion include tory of sexuality, male sexuality, male sexual intercourse, fen sexuality, female sexual response, sexual intercourse, mastu tion, conception, pregnancy, childbirth, birth control, sex-rel diseases, sexual dysfunctions, and sexual variations and de tions. Value-related topics include relationships and marri sexual behavior, norms and parameters, sexual attitudes, sex and the law, sex and morals, and stages of moral development.

After each lecture, a question period is followed by a discussion of related issues. Whenever possible, audiovisual aides are used to present or clarify the material. Periodic quizzes are given to help assess progress.

An effort is made to relate the material to the offenders' own lives. Often, discussions deal with aspects of institutional life, such as lack of privacy, lack of access to females, and the stigma attached to "being a sex offender." A sense of group cohesion is developed, particularly in the early sessions, by the use of awareness exercises. For example, dilemmas involving competing values are presented to the group in a concrete situation. Members are then asked to choose how they would respond to the situation and present a justification for their choice.

Although the intent of the course is essentially instructional, some time is spent addressing group process issues and dealing with interpersonal issues among group members and, occasionally, helping with current problems the patients may be having on the wards.

Evaluation: Large increases in factual knowledge, as reflected by paper-and-pencil tests, are associated with participation in this program (Whitman & Quinsey, 1981). Evaluations of any shifts in attitudes that may be produced by the course have yet to be conducted.

Modification of Inappropriate Arousal

Because of the relationship of inappropriate sexual arousal patterns to sexual offending (Marshall & Barbaree, 1984; Quinsey, 1984, 1986), nearly all behavioral programs contain an element that is directed to the modification of deviant arousal. At Oak Ridge, several forms of behaviorally oriented laboratory treatment procedures are offered in order to modify sexual arousal patterns, as manifested by changes in penile circumference to various stimuli. Basically, the aim is to lower patients' penile arousal to inappropriate stimuli. This section examines the criteria patients must meet in order to be accepted into a treatment program, briefly describes several of the treatment procedures, and outlines the evaluation of progress throughout treatment.

A patient must meet several criteria in order to be considered for the laboratory treatment procedures. First, the patient must display an inappropriate sexual arousal pattern on one of our standard assessments; that is, the patient must show relatively high sexual arousal to sexually inappropriate stimuli as compared with appropriate stimuli. The two basic assessments (visual assessment for age preference and auditory assessment for activity preference) were described earlier. An assessment must have occurred within the 6 months immediately preceding treatment, or the patient is reassessed. Second, the patient must understand and admit that he has a problem with his sexual arousal. Third, he must understand the nature of the therapy. Finally, the patient must be cooperative and consent to the treatment procedures. Patients are informed that treatment is voluntary and that they are free to withdraw from the program at any time, for whatever reason, without penalty.

Methods: Four basic treatment procedures are used: biofeedback, signaled punishment, olfactory aversion, and masturbatory satiation. All treatment occurs in the sexual behavior laboratory described previously.

Biofeedback is used with either auditory or visual stimuli (Quinsey, Chaplin, & Carrigan, 1980). It involves the illumination of lights inside the chamber that informs the patient of the state of his arousal. In this procedure, a patient either views slides or listens to audiotapes while his penile circumference is monitored. Plethysmograph output is sent to a Schmitt Trigger (an analog-to-digital converter) that illuminates lights when a certain preselected criterion is surpassed. The criterion is set by the therapist and is approximately half of the maximum response exhibited during the preceding session. Stimuli are constructed individually for each patient.

In the case of visual stimuli, several sets of slides are generated from our pool. Each set consists of 10 slides of adult females and 10 slides representing each of the patient's deviant categories

gories as determined by the assessment. Audio stimuli consist of six scenarios describing consenting heterosexual activity and six scenarios describing nonconsenting heterosexual activity (rape). Scenarios are either chosen from the pool of previously recorded tapes or are generated by the therapist with the aid of the patient to reflect the relevant inappropriate fantasies.

In a treatment session, a patient views slides and/or listens to tapes while his penile circumference is being monitored. If penile circumference surpasses the present criterion during presentation of an appropriate stimulus, a blue light is illuminated. Alternatively, if the criterion is exceeded during presentation of a deviant stimulus, a red light is presented. A patient would normally participate in a series of biofeedback sessions involving a different set of stimuli, presented in a different random order each day.

Signaled punishment uses the same stimuli and the red and blue lights as described above (Quinsey & Marshall, 1983; Quinsey, Chaplin, & Carrigan, 1980). A mildly painful (but harmless) electric shock, however, is associated with arousal to inappropriate stimuli. During the recording interval for a deviant stimulus, a brief shock is delivered via a probability generator at the end of 40% of the 5-second intervals in which the patient was above criterion (i.e., the red light was on). These shocks are delivered via an arm band that is attached to the upper part of the patient's left arm. Shock intensity is determined by the patient before each session.

Olfactory aversion is similar to signaled punishment but, rather than using a shock, an aversive odor is associated with arousal to deviant stimuli (Laws, Meyer, & Holmen, 1978; Kaletzky, 1980). We have experimented with several noxious odors including those obtained from rotting meat, valeric acid, and ammonia. During a session, the patient is instructed that when the red light is illuminated, indicating that his penile circumference has surpassed the preset criterion during the presentation of an inappropriate stimulus, he is to inhale deeply from a squeeze bottle containing the odoriferous substance. The therapist can monitor the patient's behavior via a one-way mirror to ensure compliance with the instructions.

Masturbatory satiation is the final method of modifying sexual arousal that is used in our laboratory (Marshall, 1979). Unlike the preceding treatments, penile circumference is not monitored throughout this procedure. A patient is taken into the assessment chamber and is seated on the reclining chair. The therapist sits outside the chamber where he can see the patient through the one-way mirror and hear him via the intercom. The patient is instructed to masturbate while verbalizing a consenting (and age-appropriate) heterosexual fantasy until ejaculation. At this point the patient continues to masturbate but now verbalizes his deviant fantasies. The patient masturbates and fantasizes throughout a long series of hour-long sessions. The goal of treatment is to satiate the patient with his inappropriate fantasies through their extensive rehearsal in a state of low sexual arousal (Marshall, 1979).

Evaluation of Progress: Each patient participates in a pretreatment assessment. In the case of an auditory session, the standard tape described before is used in the pretreatment assessment. In the case of visual sessions, a pretreatment set of slides (known as the individual diagnostic sequence) is constructed for a patient's particular deviant interest group. This set consists of 5 slides of adult females, 5 of sexually neutral scenes, and 10 slides selected from the patient's deviant category (ies).

A patient's course of treatment is determined by his progress throughout sessions. Normally, a patient would begin with a pre-intervention assessment followed by five sessions of biofeedback. A postintervention readministration of the original assessment would then follow. The assessments, though, do not use the slides or audiotaped scenarios used in treatment, thus making the tests a conservative estimate of the generality of treatment effects. If significant improvement has been made from the biofeedback sessions, treatment could end here. Otherwise, the patient would enter the signaled punishment phase of treatment. Normally, this would consist of 10 sessions followed by another assessment. If progress were slow but there appeared to be some trend and the patient were willing, another 10 sessions and assessments would follow. The criterion considering preferences to be changed is a statistically significant shift. Considering the number of test stimuli and the single-subject design, this is a very conservative criterion.

If significant changes were not achieved or if for some reason the patient were unwilling to receive the shocks, olfactory aversion would be employed. This would occur in blocks of 5 to 10 sessions, depending on the patient's apparent progress, with each block being followed by an assessment. Masturbatory satiation would be used only in those instances where significant changes could not be brought about with the previously mentioned programs and would be employed only in cases where the patient was sufficiently verbal and had well-formed deviant fantasies.

Evaluation: Quinsey, Chaplin, and Carrigan (1980) found that signaled punishment significantly decreased sexual arousal to children in 10 out of 14 child molesters treated with this technique. Signaled punishment was more effective than a biofeedback alone or a classical conditioning aversion technique. Physiological posttreatment measures of sexual preference for child as opposed to adult stimuli have been found to be significantly (although weakly) related to sexual recidivism over a follow-up period averaging 29 months (Quinsey, Chaplin, & Carrigan, 1980). Over longer periods (averaging 34 months), however, only pretreatment measures of relative sexual age preference were related to recidivism. These results suggest that treatment effects do not last indefinitely and, therefore, support Maletzky's (1980) strategy of employing quarterly "booster" sessions; child molesters treated in Maletzky's program have been found to have very low recidivism rates.

Problems

One of the difficulties in treating institutionalized men in any setting is that the results of treatment and/or assessment occasionally have a bearing on release decisions. Because of this, some patients decide on their own or, more frequently, are advised by their lawyers not to participate. This situation arises because patients or their lawyers sometimes believe that laboratory evidence of inappropriate sexual arousal would result in

375

longer confinements for their clients. This is particularly true of patients who have previously asserted that they are "cured." Another difficulty relates to the length of time some patients are kept in the institution. Some patients, for example, sex murderers, are kept for many years. Although we attempt to treat sex offenders at the time when they have some chance for release, the indeterminate nature of their committals makes this a difficult issue. One must avoid the situation where a patient is not considered for release because he has not been treated and is not treated because he is not considered releasable.

A number of problems in program implementation are associated with the types of patients whom we see. Most are very low in socioeconomic status and, although we attempt not to impose our values, this leads to concerns about the content of the material taught in the heterosocial skills and sex education programs, as the therapists (and literature) are middle class. A large minority of our patients are retarded, and some are low-functioning psychotics. These patients have difficulties in attending to the material and in retaining it. In our group programs, we form homogeneous groups based on verbal ability in order to be able to perform the repetition that is necessary for those who need it.

All of the difficulties associated with treatment in a maximum security institution affect the sex offender program; these problems include conflicts between security and treatment, difficulties in attracting and keeping treatment staff, few female staff, and the like. A more important problem, however, is the lack of aftercare. Patients released from Oak Ridge are scattered among institutions of disparate kinds located across all of Ontario. Developing a systematic and consistent program of clinical follow-through under these circumstances is simply impossible at present.

Turning to the issue of program evaluation, the sort of evaluations that are and are not feasible should be clear, given the nature of the present program. Pre- and posttreatment change studies are relatively easy to do, as are assessment validation studies that depend on the differentiation of known groups. Follow-up studies are difficult but can be done so that change in theoretically relevant variables associated with treatment can be related to subsequent recidivism. What is even more difficult is a follow-up comparison of randomly selected treated and untreated sex offenders. Although we assess more persons than we treat, the treated and untreated groups are not comparable. Persons who are treated by us must first be accepted by the institution, which means that they are "sicker," have more offenses, and are often less intelligent than the majority who are refused admission. They then must be accepted by us for treatment, which means that they have the types of problems we treat— inappropriate sexual arousal, poor social skills, and inadequate sexual knowledge. Most of the offenders who are accepted by the institution exhibit the sorts of difficulties that we treat. Our treatment cases, unlike our assessment cases, are a highly selected and unusual group of sex offenders.

Conclusions

Our experience, as well as others' (e.g., Kelly, 1982; Laws & Osborn, 1983; Marshall & Barbaree, 1984), has shown that a behaviorally oriented treatment program for sex offenders can be maintained within a maximum security institution. The Oak Ridge program results in improvement among theoretically relevant measures, such as sexual knowledge, heterosocial skills, and sexual arousal patterns. The program appears to lead to lessened recidivism in the short term.

In the future, more sophisticated follow-up studies are required. Although we and others have shown that short-term change in various target behaviors can be produced with behavioral programs, the relative contributions of the various treatment modalities to long-term outcome are unknown. Several research strategies are required to provide the answers to this and related questions: the comparison of comparable treated and untreated cases; the multivariate prediction of outcome from multiple measures of therapeutic change; and between-groups comparisons of different treatment interventions.

Acknowledgments

We wish to thank Grant Harris and Marnie Rice for their reviews of an earlier version of this chapter.

References

Abel, G.G., Becker, J.V., & Skinner, L.J. (1985). Behavioral approaches to treatment of the violent offender. In L.H. Roth (Ed.), *Clinical treatment of the violent person* (pp.100-123). (Crime and Delinquency Issues: A monograph series). Washington, D.C.: National Institute of Mental Health.

Abel, G.G., Blanchard, E.B., Barlow, D.H., & Guild, D. (1977). The components of rapists' sexual arousal. *Archives of General Psychiatry, 34,* 895-903.

Abel, G.G., Blanchard, E.B., & Becker, J.V. (1978). An integrated treatment program for rapists. In R.T. Rada (Ed.), *Clinical aspects of the rapist* (pp. 161-214). New York: Grune & Stratton.

Bem, S.L. (1974). The measurement of psychological androgyny. *Journal of Consulting and Clinical Psychology, 42,* 155-162.

Callner, D.A., & Ross, S.M. (1976). The reliability and validity of three measures of assertion in a drug addict population. *Behavior Therapy, 17,* 659-667.

Chaplin, T.C., & Quinsey, V.L. (1984). *Cognition Survey.* Unpublished questionnaire. Mental Health Centre, Penetanguishene, Ontario.

Davidson, P.R. (in preparation). B*ehavioral treatment for incarcerated sex offenders.* Psychology Department, Queen's University, Kingston, Ontario.

Feild, H.S. (1978). Attitudes towards rape: A comparative analysis of police, rapists, crisis counselors, and citizens. *Journal of Personality and Social Psychology, 36,* 156-179.

Feldman, M.P. (1966). Aversion therapy for sexual deviations: A critical review. *Psychological Bulletin, 65,* 65-79.

Freund, K. (1981). Assessment of pedophilia. In M. Cook & K Howell (Eds.), *Adult sexual interest in children* (pp. 139-179) London: Academic Press.

Groth, A.N., Longo, R.E., & McFadin, J.B. (1982). Undetected recidivism among rapists and child molesters. *Crime and Delinquency, 28,* 450-458.

Kelly, R.J. (1982). Behavioral reorientation of pedophiliacs: Can it be done? *Clinical Psychology Review, 2,* 387-408.

Langevin, R. (1983). *Sexual strands: Understanding and treating sexual anomalies in men*. Hillsdale, NJ: Lawrence Erlbaum.

Laws, D.R., & Osborn, C.A. (1983). How to build and operate a behavioral laboratory to evaluate and treat sexual deviance. In J.G. Greer & I.R. Stuart (Eds.), *The sexual aggressor: Current perspectives on treatment* (pp. 293-335). Toronto: Van Nostrand Reinhold.

Laws, D.R., Meyer, J., & Holmen, M.L. (1978). Reduction of sadistic arousal by olfactory aversion: A case study. *Behaviour Research and Therapy, 16,* 281-285.

Lawson, J.S., Marshall, W.L., & McGrath, P. (1979). The Social Self-Esteem Inventory. *Educational and Psychological Measurement, 39,* 308-311.

Maletsky, B.M. (1980). Self-referred vs. court-referred sexually deviant patients: Success with assisted covert sensitization. *Behavior Therapy, 11,* 306-314.

Marshall, W.L. (1979). Satiation therapy: A procedure for reducing deviant sexual arousal. *Journal of Applied Behavior Analysis, 12,* 10-22.

Marshall, W.L., & Barbaree, H.E. (1984). A behavioral view of rape. *International Journal of Law and Psychiatry, 7,* 51-77.

McGovern, K.B., Arkowitz, H., & Gilmore, S.K. (1975). Evaluation of social skill training programs for college dating inhibitions. *Journal of Counseling Psychology, 22,* 505-512.

Perri, M.G., Richards, C.S., & Goodrich, J.D. (1978). Heterosocial Adequacy Test (HAT): A behavioral role-playing test for the assessment of heterosocial skills in male college students. *Journal Supplement Abstract Service Catalog of Selected Documents in Psychology, 8,* 16 (ms. 1650).

Pithers, W.D., Marques, J.K., Gibat, C.C., & Marlatt, G.A. (1983). Relapse prevention with sexual aggressives: A self-control model of treatment and maintenance of change. In J.G. Greer & I.R. Stuart (Eds.), *The sexual aggressor: Current perspectives on treatment* (pp. 214-239). Toronto: Van Nostrand Reinhold.

Quinsey, V.L. (1973). Methodological issues in evaluating the effectiveness of aversion therapies for institutionalized child molesters. *Canadian Psychologist, 14,* 350-361.

Quinsey, V.L. (1977). The assessment and treatment of child molesters: A review. *Canadian Psychological Review, 18,* 204-220.

Quinsey, V.L. (1981). The long term management of the mentally disordered offender. In S.J. Hucker, C.D. Webster, & M. Ben-Aron (Eds.), *Mental disorder and criminal responsibility* (pp. 137-155). Toronto: Butterworths.

Quinsey, V.L. (1983). Prediction of recidivism and the evaluation of treatment programs for sex offenders. In S. Simon-Jones & A.A. Keltner (Eds.), *Sexual aggression and the law* (pp. 27-40). Burnaby, British Columbia: Criminology Research Centre, Simon Fraser University.

Quinsey, V.L. (1984). Sexual aggression: Studies of offenders against women. In D. Weisstub (Ed.), *Law and mental health: International perspectives* (Vol. 1, pp. 84-121). New York: Pergamon.

Quinsey, V.L. (1986). Men who have sex with children. In D. Weisstub (Ed.), *Law and mental health: International perspectives* (Vol. 2, pp. 140-172). New York: Pergamon.

Quinsey, V.L., & Bergersen, S.G. (1976). Instructional control of penile circumference. *Behavior Therapy, 7,* 489-493.

Quinsey, V.L., & Carrigan, W.F. (1978). Penile responses to visual stimuli: Instructional control with and without auditory sexual fantasy correlates. *Criminal Justice and Behavior, 5,* 333-342.

Quinsey, V.L., & Chaplin, T.C. (1982). Penile responses to nonsexual violence among rapists. *Criminal Justice and Behavior, 9,* 312-324.

Quinsey, V.L., & Chaplin, T.C. (1984). Stimulus control of rapists' and non-sex offenders' sexual arousal. *Behavioral Assessment, 6,* 169-176.

Quinsey, V.L., & Maguire, A.M. (1983). Offenders remanded for a psychiatric examination: Perceived treatability and disposition. *International Journal of Law and Psychiatry, 6,* 193-205.

Quinsey, V.L., & Marshall, W.L. (1983). Procedures for reducing inappropriate sexual arousal: An evaluation review. In J.G. Greer & I.R. Stuart (Eds.), *The sexual aggressor: Current perspectives on treatment* (pp. 267-289). New York: Van Nostrand Reinhold.

Quinsey, V.L., Steinman, C.M., Bergersen, S.G., & Holmes, T.F. (1975). Penile circumference, skin conductance, and ranking responses of child molesters and "normals" to sexual and non-sexual visual stimuli. *Behavior Therapy, 6,* 213-219.

Quinsey, V.L., Bergersen, S.G., & Steinman, C.M. (1976). Changes in physiological and verbal responses of child molesters during aversion therapy. *Canadian Journal of Behavioural Science, 8,* 202-212.

Quinsey, V.L., Chaplin, T.C., & Carrigan, W.F. (1979). Sexual preferences among incestuous and non-incestuous child molesters. *Behavior Therapy, 10,* 562-565.

Quinsey, V.L., Arnold, L.S., & Pruesse, M.G. (1980). MMPI profiles of men referred for pre-trial psychiatric assessment as a function of offense type. *Journal of Clinical Psychology, 36,* 410-417.

Quinsey, V.L., Chaplin, T.C., & Carrigan, W.F. (1980). Biofeedback and signaled punishment in the modification of inappropriate sexual age preferences. *Behavior Therapy, 11,* 567-576.

Quinsey, V.L., Chaplin, T.C., & Varney, G. (1981). A comparison of rapists' and non-sex offenders' sexual preferences for mutually consenting sex, rape, and physical abuse of women. *Behavioral Assessment, 3,* 127-135.

Quinsey, V.L., Chaplin, T.C., & Upfold, D. (1984). Sexual arousal to nonsexual violence and sadomasochistic themes among rapists and non-sex offenders. *Journal of Consulting and Clinical Psychology, 52,* 651-657.

Record, S.A. (1977). *Personality, sexual attitudes and behavior of sex offenders.* Unpublished PhD dissertation, Queen's University, Kingston, Ontario.

Rice, M.E., & Quinsey, V.L. (1980). Assessment and training of social competence in dangerous psychiatric patients. *International Journal of Law and Psychiatry, 3,* 371-390.

Spence, J.T., Helmreich, R., & Stapp, J. (1973). A short version of the Attitudes Towards Women Scale (ATW). *Bulletin of the Psychonomic Society, 48,* 587-589.

Stermac, L.E., & Quinsey, V.L. (1986). The social competence of incarcerated sexual assaulters. *Behavioral Assessment, 8,* 171-185.

Ulrich, R.E., Stachnik, T.J., & Stainton, N.R. (1963). Student acceptance of generalized personality descriptions. *Psychological Reports, 12,* 831-834.

Watson, D., & Friend, R. (1969). Measurement of social-evaluative anxiety. *Journal of Consulting and Clinical Psychology, 33,* 448-457.

Whitman, W.P., & Quinsey, V.L. (1981). Heterosocial skill training for institutionalized rapists and child molesters. *Canadian Journal of Behavioural Science, 13,* 105-114.

Wolpe, J. (1958). *Psychotherapy by reciprocal inhibition.* Stanford: Stanford University Press.

Yates, A.J. (1970). *Behavior therapy.* Toronto: Wiley.

Crown Counsel Policy Manuals

Province of British Columbia
Ministry of Attorney General
Criminal Justice Branch

File No: 55360-00
No.: Div 1
Reference: PMC 8-16-90
        Cons/Rev
        JRC #83-#85
Cross-Reference: CHI 1 NAT 1.1 SPO 1
Date: 1-1-91
Title: Policy
Subject: Diversion

For the purposes of this policy, diversion is defined as a pre-trial procedure whereby a Crown Counsel uses his or her discretion in a case by case basis not to prosecute an alleged offender. Instead, the alleged offender is referred to an individual or agency (with or without the intervention of a probation officer) with the intent of establishing an agreement by which the prospective divertee undertakes to accept, and is given the opportunity to demonstrate, personal responsibility for the alleged offence.

Participation in a diversion programme is voluntary and, if a diversion agreement is reached, the Crown relinquishes its right to prosecute the divertee for the offence which gave rise to the decision to divert, regardless of whether or not the conditions of the agreement are met.

The diversion program emphasizes the importance of providing an alleged offender with the opportunity to act in a responsible manner. The diversion agreement enables the divertee to assume responsibility for his or her behaviour by honouring the negotiated conditions. Those conditions may include making restitution to the victim or society for loss suffered as a result of the offence, undertaking to effect a reconciliation with the victim, voluntarily participating in various counselling programmes, or a combination of these.

It must be emphasized that the purpose of diversion is not retribution or, except in an incidental way, deterrence. Diversion should be viewed as a positive and humane alternative which, for some cases, has the potential to provide greater benefit to the offender, the victim and society than would be expected from further processing through the criminal justice system. Diversion programmes, as they operate in B.C., are not viewed as part of the criminal justice system, but are administered through the Corrections Branch of the Ministry of Solicitor General.

Guidelines

1. The Crown must be satisfied that there is sufficient evidence against the accused and, but for a diversion programme, the case would have proceeded to trial.

2. The Crown must be of the opinion that to divert the alleged offender would not endanger the community.

3. The offence must not have been of such a serious nature as to threaten the safety or tolerance of the community.

4. An accused who has a criminal record, has previously been diverted or has received a warning letter, should not be diverted except in extraordinary circumstances.
   Administrative Crown Counsel should consult with Deputy Regional Crown Counsel before diverting such an accused.

5. Persons alleged to have committed an offence under the drinking driving provisions of the *Criminal Code* should not be diverted.

6. Only in *exceptional* circumstances should an accused who commits an assault within the family or any sexual assault be diverted. Cases involving children as victims are subject to special considerations (see CHI 1, #6). If Administrative Crown Counsel believes *exceptional* circumstances warrant deviation from this rule, Regional or Deputy Regional Crown Counsel must be consulted.

7. The alleged offender should be advised:
   (a) Of the circumstances of the alleged offence;

(b) that he/she has the right to consult counsel of his/her choice;

(c) that he/she need not accept the diversion option;

(d) that he/she may have access to the Court if he/she wishes to dispute the charge; and

(e) that if he/she is convicted of a subsequent offence, the court may be informed of the fact that they had previously participated in a diversion programme.

7. [*Sic*] The offender must admit responsibility for the offence.

8. If the prospective divertee appears to be attempting to delay unnecessarily the making of a diversion agreement or, if such an agreement cannot be reached within a reasonable time, the Crown shall proceed to Court with the charge.

9. Conversations between the prospective divertee and Crown Counsel, probation officers or diversion agency personnel, with respect to the offence which gave rise to the offer of diversion shall not be used at trial should a diversion agreement not be concluded.

10. A person will be deemed to have been diverted when a diversion agreement has been finally approved by a Crown Counsel. A divertee shall not be charged with the offence(s) which gave rise to the diversion or to any other offence arising from the same circumstances nor shall proceedings be re-instituted in the event that the divertee fails to honour the terms of the diversion agreement [see *R. v. Jones* (1978) 40 CCC (2d) 173 B.C.S.C.]

11. The RCMP has agreed to maintain a record of diversion cases on the Police Information Retrieval System (PIRS). This service will be available throughout the province at those locations where the law enforcement agency uses PIRS. In order to keep the diversion files current it will be imperative that Crown offices advise police agencies of diversion decisions.

12. Diversion records should be used in assessing suitability of a prospective divertee in a subsequent case, as well as by the court in determining a suitable sentence should the individual be convicted of a subsequent offence.

3. Special considerations may apply to aboriginal people (see NAT 1.1).

Province of British Columbia
Ministry of Attorney General
Criminal Justice Branch

File No: 55100-00
No.: QUA 1.1
Reference: JRC #61, DPI #7
Cross-Reference: PRI 1 QUA 1
Date: 1-1-91
Title: Policy
Subject: Quality Control—Charge Approval—Police Appeal
Regarding Crown Decision

Inherent in the charge approval process is an invitation to the police to discuss reasons for rejection of a charge with Crown Counsel who rejected the charge. It is, therefore, the responsibility of the police to contact the Administrative Crown should they wish to discuss reasons for rejecting a charge. While protocols with the police may be developed at the local level, each Crown Counsel office should be the initial focus for police concerns.

A Chief Constable or Officer in Charge of a detachment who disagrees with a decision not to lay a charge and who disagrees with the attempts to resolve the matter at the local level, may ask Regional Crown Counsel for a review of the decision. Regiona Crown Counsel shall ensure that such a review occurs and advise the senior officer of his decision.

A Chief Constable or Officer in Charge of a detachment wh disagrees with that decision may ask the Assistant Deput Attorney General, to review the decision and if asked, th Assistant Deputy Attorney General will review the matter an advise the senior officer of his decision.

In addition to the foregoing, a Chief of Police or Depu Commissioner of the RCMP in the province may appeal charge approval decision directly to the Deputy Attorn General, but only if the situation is urgent or a matter of signi cant public interest or public policy.

The Criminal Justice Branch recognizes the responsibility the police to lay an Information where they have reason believe any part of the Crown's decision making process has been tainted by corruption or impropriety. It is expected this procedure would only be invoked upon exhaustion of the appeal process by a Commanding Officer. An Information, therefore, would be sworn by, or on behalf of, a Chief Constable or the Deputy Commissioner, RCMP.

It is expected that the Deputy Attorney General would always be notified in advance of the police intention to swear an Information in these cases.

Where an Information is sworn by the police on behalf of a Chief Constable or the Deputy Commissioner, RCMP, following exhaustion of the appeal process, both the Regional Crown Counsel and the Assistant Deputy Attorney General must be immediately advised.

In any other case where an Information has been sworn by the police contrary to a decision of Crown Counsel, the private prosecutions policy applies, see PRI 1.

Province of British Columbia
Ministry of Attorney General
Criminal Justice Branch

File No: 55340-00
No.: DIS 1
Reference: Cons/Rev
             JRC 69, PMC 8-8-90
Cross-Reference: POL 1 VIC 1 YOU 1.5
Date: 1-1-91
Title: Policy
Subject: Disclosure—Particulars

Criminal Justice Branch policy confirms the practice of full, fair and frank disclosure of the nature and circumstances of the Crown's case to defence counsel or the accused. Accordingly, to facilitate achieving the objective of full disclosure, the following steps should be followed:

A. Provide as a Matter of Course in all Cases
    After a Charge is Approved:

1. A narrative of the facts or circumstances (a copy of the Narrative pages [FORM PCR 201] of the Report to Crown Counsel) including the names of witnesses except where there is reason to believe that disclosing a witness' name could put their safety at risk. Crown Counsel should be particularly cautious about releasing names and statements of witnesses, whether civilian, institutional, or police, in cases involving offences occurring in penal institutions. Any questions should be referred to Regional Crown Counsel;

2. A copy of any statement given by the accused to a person in authority;

3. Statements made by the accused to others if those statements are to be used in evidence;

4. A copy of the criminal record of the accused;

5. A copy of any professionally prepared report or report by an expert on which the Crown intends to rely at trial and a copy of any contradictory professional or expert reports obtained by the Crown or police during the investigation;

6. Access to any exhibit in the possession of the Crown and where applicable, copies of such exhibits including books, papers, photographs and tape recordings;

7. Any authorizations upon which the Crown intends to rely for the purposes of seeking to admit intercepted private communications;

8. Particulars of similar fact or accomplice evidence where Crown Counsel intends to lead that evidence;

9. Information concerning any informal out-of-court identification of the accused;

10. A copy of any relevant witness statement providing its release will not compromise the safety of the witness. The witness should be advised the statement has been disclosed prior to testifying. Crown should use discretion in disclosing the witness' identity or location.

B. *Provide in Appropriate Cases*

A copy of the relevant criminal record of prospective Crown witnesses (see CRI 1). However, special considerations appl[y] to youth records (see YOU 1.5).

C. *Provide Upon Conviction*

1. Victim impact information intended to be submitted on sentence;
2. Psychological/psychiatric reports on accused or victim prepared for sentencing.

Defence counsel should be advised copies of search warrants and informations of belief are available from the court registry unless a sealing order is in place.

The list set out above is not intended to be exhaustive, and the release of either additional information or information at an earlier stage than set out above should be determined on a case by case basis. It is expected that Crown Counsel will keep defence counsel or the accused apprised of any new information gathered between the time of the initial disclosure and the time of the completion of the hearing or trial if such information is relevant to the case.

Crown Counsel should always be aware of their duty to act fairly and dispassionately in the course of any prosecution. This duty includes advising the defence in a timely manner of the existence of witnesses whose evidence may be adverse to the prosecution or supportive of the defence, notwithstanding Crown Counsel does not intend to lead such evidence as part of the Crown's case, see *Cunliffe and the Law Society of British Columbia* (1984) 13 CCC (3d) 560 (BCCA).

The police, and other investigative agencies, often provide Crown Counsel with confidential information and material which relate not only to the matter under investigation but also to investigative techniques, other individuals, names of informants and the like. Information of this nature should be included in the form designed for this purpose—Form PCR 220, and should not be disclosed without prior consultation with the police or other investigative agency.

Province of British Columbia
Ministry of Attorney General
Criminal Justice Branch

File No: 55340-00

389

No.: DIS 1.1
Reference: Cons/Rev; DPI, #8
          PMC 8-16-90
Cross-Reference:MED 1 PRO 3
               CHI 1 YOU 1.5
Date: 1-1-91
Title: Policy
Subject: Disclosure of Information to Parties Other than the
Accused

Criminal Justice Branch files are confidential.

Occasionally, investigative agencies, other organizations, or other parties both from within and outside Government, may request information from Crown Counsel files for their purposes. It is recognized that Crown Counsel have a professional responsibility to assist other organizations and agencies in appropriate cases.

The following are some exceptions to the general rule of confidentiality.

1. Where Crown Counsel is requested by counsel not involved in the criminal proceeding, or others, to provide information on a case, the request should be referred to the original investigative agency. It is usually the best able to provide such information. Only where the investigative agency rejects the request without a reasonable explanation should Administrative Crown Counsel consider the request. Following are guidelines to deal with such requests:
   (a) all requests should be in writing;
   (b) the written requests should state the purpose for the information;
   (c) the reason for the refusal of the investigative agency to supply the information should be stated;
   (d) where information is requested concerning an accused who is also the subject of civil litigation, actual or anticipated copies of medical, technical or scientific reports should only be released under a subpoena, or where the author, upon request of the applicant, has consented;
   (e) where the request is for the identity or location of

witnesses, it should first be determined if the witness requires or has requested protection of their identity or location. The investigator should be consulted in such cases. Where it is determined the witness' identity should not be released, the request should be referred to Deputy Regional or Regional Crown Counsel. In any event, the identity or statement of a witness should not be released without notifying the witness in question; and

(f) Deputy Regional Crown Counsel should be consulted where any doubt exists about the propriety of releasing any requested information on a case.

2. Crown Counsel has a responsibility to assist the appropriate agents or their counsel who are acting to protect children and other vulnerable persons. It is important to provide assistance where the effective protection of children and persons at risk is of paramount consideration. Requests for information in this category should be dealt with by specially designated Crown Counsel responsible for child abuse or Administrative Crown Counsel (see CHI 1).

3. Professional organizations and governing bodies have an interest in being apprised of cases where a member has been charged with a criminal offence. There is a specific policy with regard to providing this information in appropriate cases (see PRO 3).

4. The media are entitled to prompt answers to appropriate enquiries. For guidelines applicable to their requests see MED 1.

5. With respect to students, academic researchers or volunteer agencies interested in Criminal Justice Branch information, general information from our files such as topic papers, bibliographies, useful contact agencies or persons and other broadly based non-confidential information may be shared. However, such persons or agencies would not have open access to Crown Counsel files without approval of Regional or Deputy Regional Crown Counsel.

6. Special considerations apply to the public disclosure of information relating to cases where a decision is made not to prosecute. Adapting recommendation #8 of the Discretion to Prosecute Inquiry:

(a) Where a decision not to prosecute has been made, and the public is not aware of the police investigation, there should be no public disclosure relating to the case.

(b) Where a decision not to prosecute has been made, and the public, a victim or other significantly interested person is aware of the police investigation, it is in the public interest that the public, victim or other significantly interested person be given adequate reasons for the non-prosecution.

If the decision not to proceed further with an investigation or not to recommend charges to Crown Counsel was made by the police, then the police should explain their reasons. If the police recommended charges and Crown Counsel decided against a prosecution, Crown Counsel has the responsibility to provide the reasons for the decision not to prosecute. The responsibility for making the announcements in high profile cases will be determined by the Assistant Deputy Attorney General in consultation with Regional Crown Counsel.

(c) Police reports, and other sensitive investigative documents should not be made public where a decision not to prosecute has been made.

(d) Legal opinions should not generally be publicly disclosed. Regional Crown Counsel, in exceptional high profile or complex cases, may direct otherwise.

Province of British Columbia
Ministry of Attorney General
Criminal Justice Branch

File No: 55100-00
No.: QUA 1
Reference: Cons/Rev. DPI #5
            JRC #60, PMC
Cross-Reference:QUA 1.1 LEG 1
                QUA 1.2 DIS 1.1
Date: 1-1-91
Title: Policy
Subject: Quality Control—Charge Approval

Section 504 of the *Criminal Code* allows anyone to lay, and directs a justice to receive, an Information alleging a criminal offence. In British Columbia, it has long been the policy of the Ministry of Attorney General that Crown Counsel review all allegations of criminal conduct and apply a single, consistent charging standard before charges are approved and an Information laid. This system of charge approval has received the endorsement of the Justice Reform Commission and the Discretion to Prosecute Inquiry.

The charging standard and procedure to be followed are set out below. Any Informations that are laid without the prior approval of Crown Counsel should be dealt with under the private prosecutions policy, see PRI 1.

A. *Charge Standard*

Allegations must be examined to determine whether there is a substantial likelihood of conviction; and if so, whether the public interest requires a prosecution of the accused.

1. *Substantial Likelihood of Conviction*

In determining whether a charge should be laid, Counsel must first conclude that it is likely there will be a conviction after considering all relevant matters including the available evidence, the anticipated defence and the applicable law. A substantial likelihood of conviction is significantly more than a *prima facie* case, but considerably less than a virtual certainty of conviction.

During the charge approval process, Crown Counsel does not have the benefit of hearing the testimony of Crown witnesses, either in direct or cross-examination. Nor does Crown Counsel have the benefit of hearing the defence evidence, if any. During the course of a trial, the Crown's case may be materially stronger or weaker than counsel's initial assessment at the early charge approval stage. For this reason, Crown Counsel must be flexible in applying the substantial likelihood of conviction standard recognizing that the more serious the allegation, the greater the interests of justice in ensuring that provable charges are prosecuted.

2. *Public Interest*

Counsel must next determine whether the public interest

dictates a prosecution. There are a number of factors counsel should consider in assessing the public interest in a prosecution:

(a) the nature and seriousness of the allegations;

(b) the harm caused to the victim, if any;

(c) the personal circumstances of the accused, including his or her criminal record;

(d) the likelihood of achieving the desired result without a court proceeding, including an assessment of the available alternatives to prosecution; and

(e) the cost of a prosecution compared to the social benefit to be gained by it. This will include considerations such as the degree to which this offence (as opposed to this offender) represents a community problem which cannot be effectively dealt with otherwise.

In considering the public interest hard and fast rules cannot be imposed and flexibility in decision making at the local level is essential if the Ministry is to respond to the legitimate concerns of each community.

B. *Applying the Charge Standard*

If counsel is to accurately apply the charge standard, the Report to Crown Counsel (RTCC) must provide an accurate and detailed statement of the evidence available. The following are the basic requirements for every RTCC:

(a) A comprehensible description of the evidence supporting each element of the suggested charge(s);

(b) where the evidence of a civilian witness is necessary to prove an essential element of the charge (except for minor offences), a copy of that person's written statement;

(c) necessary evidence check sheets;

(d) copies of all documents required to prove the charge(s);

(e) a detailed summary or written copy of the accused's statement(s); and

(f) accused's criminal record (if any).

There may be cases where the RTCC will not comply with the quality control standards. The RTCC should then be returned to the investigator with a request for additional information before a charge is approved. If the accused is in custody,

Crown should not seek to detain the accused in custody without sufficient written material from the police to justify both the charge and the detention.

If the offence is serious and there is sufficient evidence to charge the detained accused but insufficient information to determine Crown's position on release, resort may be had to s. 516 to adjourn the show cause. This should be used only where it appears necessary to protect the public.

In applying the charge standard Crown Counsel's important obligations are to:

(i) make the decision in a timely manner;

(ii) record the reasons for the decision; and

(iii) where appropriate, communicate with those affected, including the police, so that they understand the reasons for the decision.

CLOSE PURSUIT
A Week in the Life
of an NYPD Homicide Cop

In this gripping exposé, Carsten Stroud takes readers into the life of a cop—we're with him during the chase, at the autopsy table, the visit to the victim's mother. We're in his head, sharing his dreams and his nightmares.

As Stroud follows Detective Kennedy through a week of investigations—the stabbing of an out-of-town college student, a brutal rape-murder—he explores the psychic landscape of police work: the low morale, the compulsive commitment to the job, the strange intimacy that binds cop and criminal.

Fast, gritty, suspenseful, *Close Pursuit* delivers all the drama of the best cop fiction—plus the power of a true story told in a unique and explosive style.

"A strong, clear and admirable picture of the working life of a homicide detective."
New York Times Book Review

"For a close and compassionate look at a unique police department in a unique city, *Close Pursuit* wins top marks... This book is surely required reading."
Hamilton Spectator

"A spellbinding view of a world like no other."
The Detroit News

"A riveting tale of a real cop's work in a fascinatingly brutal city. It is a superb piece of writing, perhaps the best cop story I have ever read."
Winnipeg Free Press

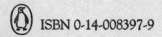 ISBN 0-14-008397-9

sniper's
moon

Detective Frank Keogh has a rare gift—for killing. He picked it up in the jungles of Vietnam and perfected it as an NYPD sniper in New York's mean streets. Yet on a steamy August night in the South Bronx, when a cop Frank has had a blow-up with is murdered, no one seriously believes him capable of the crime. Then the body of Frank's mistress is found, and the gruesome m.o. recalls a long-ago case that Frank must know about: it was solved by his father.

As homicide detectives scramble to arrest a cop gone bad, Frank Keogh escapes, fleeing cross-country, his only hope to make some very fast connections—to the father from whom he is estranged, and to a case whose long shadow could destroy him.

"Complex…powerful…heartfelt…
Stroud has made excellent use of his insider's knowledge
of police work."
Calgary Herald

"Crackling with narrative energy, punched-up prose, and
a deep-grained savvy about cop ways and mores:
Stroud's a thriller writer to watch."
Kirkus

"Don't miss *Sniper's Moon*. This Carsten Stroud is
downright wonderful."
Tony Hillerman

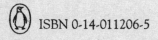 ISBN 0-14-011206-5